# A GARDEN *of* HER OWN

KATE PHELPS

 FriesenPress

One Printers Way
Altona, MB R0G 0B0
Canada

www.friesenpress.com

ISBN
978-1-03-918999-7 (Hardcover)
978-1-03-918998-0 (Paperback)
978-1-03-919000-9 (eBook)

*1. FICTION, LITERARY*

Distributed to the trade by The Ingram Book Company

S ri Lanka is not the place to fall in love. It's too hot.

She sweats, dashing from one class to another, camera and bookbag sticking to her skin. She sweats before the sun is high, choosing fruit at the market and hauling clay pots of buffalo curd back to her room. She sweats standing motionless beside buildings, waiting for the photograph that will preserve this face, that dog lying in the street. And she sweats long after the sun has quit, pages almost moist to the touch as she reads under often-flickering lights.

But she does. Fall in love.

At first, it's simply the freedom of being just nineteen, half a world from home. Unburdened by the bitter cold of a New England winter, the dull weight of a family Christmas, she navigates each moment as if airborne. Needing only the lightest of fabrics, the barest of sandals between herself and the bright, white air, she slides easily past shop fronts, along boardwalks, young and unencumbered.

Later, it's the small discoveries that touch her heart. In Batticaloa, she studies the towering pillar of a Hindu Temple, its deities in half relief, frozen in place for eternity. And in Dikwella town, at the Wewurukannala Vihara, dwarfed by a huge Buddha statue, she contemplates the cruel experiences of the underworlds.

She travels to Rekawa Beach, where in the glow of her red night light she watches a green turtle deliver its eggs in a soft-sided cavern of sand. For an hour or more, to the sounds of the scratch and scrape, the rhythmic thud of waves on the shoreline below, she stands transfixed while the mother turtle completes the ritual, finally lumbering back into the warm, dark crests of the Indian Ocean, leaving her eggs to chance.

From a train window, she shimmers in the reflection of the morning heat, which rises in streaks from the rice paddies where a buffalo stands, an egret perched on its back. All around, deep greenness of the equatorial landscape hovers, steamy and wet and sultry.

The thing she notices that day, navigating once again the streets of Colombo, is a tall westerner walking some lengths ahead. He's notable already for the unruly curls, his faded tee shirt, pale green sarong, loose leather sandals. The worn words "Free Nelson Mandela" are just legible on the back of his shirt. As tuk-tuk drivers slow to shout at her, insistent she climb aboard, and armed soldiers in khaki uniform patrol the main thoroughfare from the back of trucks, she finds the slogan brazen, heartening. The demand, "Free Nelson Mandela," bids her follow. She trips to keep pace, not wishing to lose the words, the shirt, the man, in the hot brown crowd.

What she doesn't reckon with, chasing along after him, impulsive and free, is just where following can lead.

# ONE

The day Amy turned fifty began simply enough. Graham had left early for work, as usual. Amy had an appointment on Cuttyhunk, expecting to be home by late afternoon, and for a change, her sister was joining them. They had a 7:00 p.m. table booked at Fathom's for Amy's annual hit of fresh oysters. It was a birthday routine that had evolved over the years, one that, this year, she could have done without.

With clear skies and easy air, the day was calm for mid-May. Armed with her notebook and tape recorder, Amy stood in a restless gathering behind the rope, waiting for the ferry to start boarding. She was looking forward to the hour-long crossing, planning to review her notes from a seat on the deck. Her cell phone buzzed inside her bag.

"Hey, kiddo." Amy's sister's voice came booming over the line.

"Hey, Alice."

The cluster of passengers jiggled into motion, smoothing into a single line heading up the ramp. She pulled the ticket from her back pocket.

"I'm really sorry to be pulling this . . ." Alice began.

Many steps reverberated on metal. Amy held the phone closer to her ear. "Say again?"

"I can't . . . haven't left D.C. . . . till four this morning!"

Amy handed the ticket to the man at the top of the ramp, scurrying to secure a seat inside, where it was quieter. "Let me sit down first . . . What were you saying?"

"I said I won't be able to join you tonight. I've been up for the last three nights in a row, and I'm just too wiped to make the trip. I'm really sorry."

Amy heard the familiar rev in her sister's excuse. "It's not a biggie, Alice. Are you okay?"

"Well, I'm thrilled how it worked out—one of my more elegant resolutions, but my schedule's all thrown off." Alice was an international arbitrator, a jet-setting lawyer whose schedule was always thrown off.

Amy was neither surprised nor particularly disappointed. "It's okay, really."

"So, it will just be you two this year. Too bad, for such a big one."

Amy brushed that aside. Hitting forty-five had felt weird. By now, the numbers had little meaning. If anything, they marked a new delight: disbelieving comments like "You're not forty-nine!" only made her feel young and sexy.

"I'm kind of relieved, anyway," Amy confided. "I've got a busy day. I'm happy to scrap dinner."

Her sister bubbled with protest so rapidly, with such vehemence, Amy walked it back. "Or not. We'll do a rain check."

One long blast of the horn followed by three short ones bellowed overhead, and the ferry lurched into motion. "I'll call you later," Amy said. "Take care, okay?"

"And you have a happy, happy birthday!!" The trill was forced, insistent.

"Will do."

It gave her an excuse, Amy thought happily, letting her and Graham both off the hook. Pulling off festivities wasn't her husband's strong suit, and like him, she had better things to do today. Quickly, she googled the restaurant, clicking on the phone icon. A recording announced Fathom's was still closed, so she left a message, articulating her name and number loudly over the rumble of the engines, just to be sure they canceled the right group. A man seated across the aisle shot her a look, as if party to some covert act of resistance. She glanced back at him, feeling sassy. Then she dialed her husband. She felt like she'd been sprung from a burden, sure that Graham would feel the same.

"What do you mean, cancel?!"

She was surprised by the heat. "Or postpone. Whatever."

The line went quiet. "Why?!"

"Because Alice can't make it. Because we don't have to. Because I don't need oysters."

"You don't like them?"

Graham sounded angry. Maybe he was simply irked to be interrupted at work, but the unreasonableness bothered her. Amy tried another tack. "I'd just as soon not go out tonight. It'll give me longer on the island. I thought you'd be pleased." She sounded almost apologetic, wanting to forgo her own celebration. The man across the aisle was listening in, his eyebrow arched with curiosity.

"Well, I'm not. It's set already. I don't want to have to cancel." Graham circled the problem, defensive. "Anyway, I want oysters. Tonight." It was her husband's command and control voice, and Amy shrank back into silence. "We'll talk later," he said, and hung up.

She put down the phone, pressing her face to the glass. Overhead, a gull carved an arc into the blue, unrestrained by family obligation. *Fifty*, she thought. If it meant anything, surely it was being free to say "No thank you" or even "Let me think about it." What she thought, stubbornly now, was that she wouldn't call Fathom's back.

It was really her current assignment that made her bold. Normally, she wasn't one to contradict Graham; it had always seemed easier not to. Now, though, with a new project of her own—one for which she'd already been paid an advance no less—Amy was fueled with a surprising shot of assertiveness.

"Sounds like he doesn't agree."

She turned, surprised. "Sorry?"

Her fellow passenger was watching her, a wide smile on his face. "Sounds like you'll have to rebook that table."

It struck Amy as a kind of challenge, maybe open flirtation, but she didn't want to play. "Well, it may sound that way, but, no, actually, I won't." She was about to announce that it was her birthday, that she was a professional woman, that no one pushed her around. But she didn't need to tell him all that, tell him her name, learn his. "No, he'll just have to suck it up." She shook her head, dismissing the man—and Graham—with one final flounce.

The irony of it all wasn't lost on her: this little bout of willfulness. Amy wasn't anything like a real professional. Her garden writing career, such as it was, was as accidental and haphazard as her life. Graham's mother scoffed at even calling what she did a career. Early on, Dina had had to acknowledge Amy's green thumb, because that was hard to miss. But when Amy had started to write too, Dina had referred to Amy's gardening column in the local paper as her "little columns". And when these were published in book form, she described the "book"— pronounced with some amusement—as an aberration of chance, maybe attributable to Graham's prominence as an architect. Amy half suspected that her mother-in-law might be right, wondered whether Graham didn't agree.

She pulled her bag closer and gazed across the water. The filmy outline of Cuttyhunk was solidifying on the horizon, gray against the brighter sky. Waves slapped against the ferry's hull, breaking into froth as they passed, and two white butterflies appeared, circling each other on their journey before fluttering off again. Unlikely, she mused, so far out. Still, here she was, maybe just as unlikely, under contract to write a second book. "Unique female gardeners and their stunning garden designs" is how she'd pitched it. Edith Roosevelt was her first subject.

Walking across the dock was already a pleasure. The sun was warm, nearly overhead, and a nice breeze hit her skin. Fellow passengers fanned out, cyclists and hikers striding and pedaling off in three directions. Others, being greeted, disappeared into golf carts. Her man from the ferry was one of these. Met by a wife-like woman, he bounced away too, leaving Amy on her own. She hoisted the bag on her shoulder and set off toward the southeastern side of the island.

A good mile from the harbor, the land rose steadily and buildings became sparse. Only rough yellow grasses and scrubby pine dotted the mostly open landscape; a small garden by a shuttered cottage lay overgrown with lily of the valley. As she cleared a rise, the road turned, and there, suddenly, was the Roosevelt property. What she'd thought from a distance was a pocket of brambles revealed itself to be a quite substantial hedge, dense with age. Peeping out from it was the ancient roof and wind-whipped façade of a large, two-story home, very simple, formerly white.

Edith herself was standing in the doorway, like she'd been watching for some time, impatient for the visitor's arrival. "Ferry late?"

"I don't think so," Amy said, reaching out her hand. She hadn't expected so tall a woman. The voice, when they'd spoken on the phone, had sounded elderly and worn, but Edith, for all the sagging skin and bulging knuckles, was an inch taller than Amy, easily five-foot-seven, with a posture that kept her looking down on all she surveyed. "Amy James," Amy said. "Thank you for seeing me today."

"Glad to have you." Edith did a cursory inventory, as if confirming this to be the woman who'd called a week earlier. "Shall we start in the garden first? Or do you need to sit?"

Amy wanted to unload her shoulder bag and dig out her recording equipment, but there was an implied preference to the question, so she nodded accordingly. "Let's start with the garden!"

She followed Edith down a broad walkway alongside the residence, deeply shrouded in leathery rhododendrons and tall holly bushes. Edith moved slowly enough that Amy could get a close look at the other plants as they went, wide patches of shiny ginger and speckled brunnera, some sizeable white and pink bleeding hearts. The old lady was mostly silent as they walked, her long, denim skirt sweeping the backs of her calves, her feet steady in wool socks and sneakers. The path ended at a wide half gate, under an archway of climbing rose, prickly with new growth. As they cleared the gate and Edith stepped to one side, Amy was ushered onto a stone terrace. Spread out beyond was the garden. Like an import from a European court, the garden was massive and formal, draped across the hillside. Cascading levels of geometric beds aproned out before them, interrupted at intervals in low privet shapes. A stone balustrade studded the perimeter below. Through it, the ocean glistened.

"It's early in the season," Edith said. "But you get the idea."

Amy did. At some point, there had been serious money here. Enough for major excavations, the building of shallow stone steps everywhere, four ornate marble urns, and a pair of copper peacocks strutting by a dry fountain in the far corner. But there had also been years of underinvestment, a lurking wildness, maybe simply old age. Amy struggled for the words.

Her phone rang, and happy for the interruption, she pulled it out. Edith eyed her, lips pressed.

"Amy James? This is Deb from Fathom's. You called to cancel a booking? For a party of three?"

Edith was backing away, censorious.

"Yes?"

"We don't seem to have a booking for a party of three for you tonight. Not under James."

That confused her. Still, she didn't have time for an argument. "Okay. Thanks anyway," Amy said.

She slid the phone back into her bag, giving her hostess an apologetic shrug. "Messed-up plans."

Edith sniffed and turned, leading them toward the first urn nestled in a low mound of emerging mint. Amy noticed an elderly man by the edge of a bed below, steadily trimming one of the privet balls. A rake and tarp lay by his feet, littered with green. The clippers looked heavy in his hands. "Joao," Edith said. "He helps."

Amy nodded, wondering how much. They spent over an hour that way, Edith guiding her around. Only a few flowers had blossomed, the violet alliums, like lollypop soldiers, some late tulips and vivid grape hyacinth, but Edith identified where the summer perennials would be emerging, what color the roses would be, come June and July. And Amy commented generously, where she could, falling in with the imagined glory of future months, and, she suspected, wishful memories of an earlier time. When they were by the hellebores, its petals face down beneath a large laurel, her phone rang again. She intended to only see who it was and ignore it, but it was Jason, never one to call without a reason.

"My son," she said, excusing herself. "Hey."

"Happy birthday!"

"Thanks."

"How's fifty treating you?"

"So far, so good." She clocked Edith, her back now turned. "But I'm busy right now, hon. I'm with someone who's showing me her garden, and I need to get off the phone."

"Don't hang up yet! I just wanted to make sure you don't stand Dad up tonight."

"What?"

"He called. He wants to celebrate with you. Don't stand him up, that's all." Jason waited. "Okay?"

She wanted to know more but let it go. "Don't worry. We'll celebrate. It's all good."

"So you're going home?"

"Of course. Yes." This seemed ridiculous. "Anyway. We'll talk later. Love you."

"More messy plans?" Edith asked.

Amy nodded, as confused as ever. "I'm so sorry about that."

Edith eyed her coolly. "Does he know you're at work?"

Amy couldn't help a dismissive shrug. "Yeah, no . . ." The thought of either Jason or Graham putting much stock in her professional priorities was almost laughable.

"You should train these people," Edith said.

They did eventually go indoors, where Edith served some lemonade and a piece of walnut banana bread and Amy started to record. She prompted at first, prodding with questions to be sure of the dates, the cast of characters. But as Edith settled into the narrative, Amy sat back, watching more than anything, the gleaming eyes and gnarled fingers, the sharp line of collarbone.

"Turn of the century." Edith cocked her thumb. "The one before. A handful of New York stockbrokers set up this exclusive men's fishing club on Cuttyhunk. Mostly wild, wealthy men escaping the heat of Manhattan. Men who loved the stink of fish and cigars. They abandoned their wives for the most part. Except my grandfather—he was one of these crazed rich fishermen—poor man, he had my grandmother, who was not keen on abandonment. She had him build a second home here on the island, after which she became bored and decided she needed a garden too, hiring a designer from England, importing marble from Italy, flying in the ceramic tile from Lisbon." Edith laughed. "It might have been that that pushed him to the edge, but when Wall Street crashed, my grandfather finally jumped, leaving my widowed grandmother somewhat disoriented."

"Jumped . . . ?" Amy wasn't sure she'd heard correctly.

Edith nodded, her eyes dancing in the telling. "As in, out a tenth floor window. Yes! He was one of those we all read about." Edith rolled her eyes dismissively. "Anyway, she sold their 8th Avenue home and retreated with her daughter, my mother, to Cuttyhunk full-time."

"Wow."

Edith was on a roll. "My grandmother's only activity, apparently, besides the nightly imbibing, was weeding and deadheading the garden out back, also done mostly after dark. My mother, meanwhile, was colorful and wild like her father and she loved the island. Grew up here, left for school and came back with a rich New Yorker of her own. My parents married out back, in a fairly riotous affair, so I'm told, surrounded by fat, blue delphiniums and Asiatic lilies.

"Soon after I was born, my father, too, took a running jump." Edith waved off Amy's shock. "Jumped ship, that is. But my mother and I stayed put. My mother was resourceful. Doing well out of the divorce, she started some investing herself. I went to the schoolhouse, up on Tower Hill, and off to college after."

"Had you planned to return here?" Amy asked.

"No, not particularly. I had no plans at all. I imagined I'd do what all young women do—have a career." She chuckled at the memory. "I wanted to be a reporter, even though no women that I knew of were reporters, so I can't think what got that in my head. Then I'd marry, I thought, own a car."

"Hah!" Amy chuckled at that.

"But when my grandmother died, it was like spring had arrived! It was just my mother and me, with this extravagant setting behind the house, so we began to make the most of it. We threw wedding after wedding. She had one more, my mother, and I did it three times." Edith looked out the window, a grin still fixed on her lips. "A girl could do worse," she said.

"Married? Three times?" Amy couldn't help herself.

"I did. Joao out there's hoping to be number four." Edith laughed. "Anyway, weddings just became a habit. Now I rent out the venue, charging the heck out of people for theirs. One thing to be said for marriage: it's lucrative, if you know how to play it." Edith poured herself another shot of lemonade, making clear she was done for the day.

Amy wondered what her agent would make of this lady, this tale. "I'd like to come back, with a photographer, and the woman who does our illustrations. If that would work?"

"Of course you can. In a couple of weeks, the iris beds and the poppies will be superb." Edith took her time standing up, but her laughter was youthful. "Might even catch a wedding!"

Amy thanked her, disappointed to be released so early. There was still more story to be unearthed, and it wasn't clear to Amy how the woman managed it all, including those three husbands. Shouldering her tape recorder and stepping back outside, she considered talking to some neighbors, checking out the old fishing club. But as she started down the hill, she caught sight of a familiar vessel entering the harbor, and the responsibilities toward her own, only husband pressed in on her. Amy picked up speed, surrendering her plans as she trotted toward the early ferry.

# TWO

Driving home, Amy tried out phrases that best captured the Roosevelt garden. It was thrilling to her, thinking like a writer again, and she itched to get her thoughts on paper. As she turned into their property, a near-perfect opening sentence landed, fully formed, in her brain.

She parked in front of their house and slipped quietly into the front foyer, shuddering at the sudden loss of warmth. By design, their expansive home was cool and serene. The entranceway was unencumbered but for a shallow rill of still water. A stainless-steel water panel cut through the foyer to the far side of their living room, where the shimmering surface appeared to penetrate glass into the garden beyond. Graham's architectural designs were rightfully heralded for their fluid, open style, but they sometimes struck Amy as *too* cool. The perfect opening sentence flittered from her mind.

Haps had been waiting, his back end twitching when Amy opened the kitchen door. "Hey, mister." She lowered her bag onto the counter and took his face in her hands, nuzzling the top of his head. "How're you?"

The golden mass shook with pleasure. "Let me pee first," she told him. Graham generally did the end-of-the-day walk while she tended to dinner, but as he wasn't yet back, and they were going out—*If not Fathom's*, she thought guiltily, *somewhere*—Amy figured this might be a nice gesture on her part.

Sitting on the toilet, the dog's nose cold against her knee, Amy felt the day shrinking back around her. As ever, a dog demanded attention; there were meals to prepare, and soon enough, a husband to placate. "The stuff of life," her mother had yawned once, as if only an idiot would expect otherwise. In Amy's case, she'd intimated, quite a privileged idiot. Amy flushed the toilet, watching the water circle down the drain. She prayed her memories of Edith Roosevelt wouldn't disappear as easily before she could get them in writing.

In the past few months everything *but* writing had claimed Amy's time and attention. It had been almost half a year since she'd signed the contract with her publisher. Her mother's declining health and sudden death had proved all-consuming. Alice was, as ever, too wrapped up in arbitrating other people's conflict to be of much use, and there was never a question of asking Graham to step up. So Amy had had to organize everything: her mother's move into assisted living, the preparation of her parents' home to put on the market. She'd even had to schedule the memorial service—an absurd three months into the future—around the clashing calendars of her busy family.

She could—had to—now begin to move forward on the book. Finally, she had time to realize the project she'd imagined since first presenting it to her agent, the vision that she'd nurtured during the long year in which Ella had shopped it from one publishing house to another. Amy felt liberated at last, anticipating with excitement the garden visits and interviews to come. Besides Edith Roosevelt in Cuttyhunk, there was Jada Reed in Tennessee, Gabriella Diaz in Marathon Key. These women and others, in Charleston and Chicago, Vermont, Texas, Colorado, New Mexico, and Seattle, were to Amy the gardeners who best exemplified the unique artistry women could demonstrate in stewarding Mother Earth. Her writing would celebrate them all.

Her phone rang. It was probably Graham, and Amy winced, recalling his irritation from earlier. He was probably checking on her whereabouts. She glanced at the device quickly, preparing an instinctive defense. But it was Sandy calling, the artist who had done the garden illustrations for Amy's first book. Eager to know about Amy's initial foray into their next project, Sandy had made Amy promise to call and fill her in as soon as she was off island. Amy let it go into voicemail, promising herself she'd call back right after walking the dog. Sandy always brought with her a degree of agitation, and Amy needed the exercise first.

She turned to her furry companion. "Come on, bud. Your turn."

In fact, Amy always enjoyed their trek once they started. Haps loped easily along, rarely straining at the leash, jaunty with his own handsomeness. Usually, a passerby would stop to pet him, often issuing a "lovely coat" or "pretty dog." The regulars, of course, knew Haps by name. And Amy, whatever the weather, found something to observe, the bits of seaweed on the sidewalk, the emergence of new grasses in the marsh, the movement of boats on and off the mooring field—all signs of shifting seasons by the harbor. Spring, by itself, created excitement. By summer, she'd be traveling the country, immersed in her new book.

Although not a best friend, Sandy Ionella was an excellent partner. Insistent where Amy was accommodating, fiery where Amy was calm, the artist had broken into Amy's life with a professional aggression that had taken the garden writer by surprise. It had been the first hot morning of the South Shore Open Garden weekend. Amy, locally popular for her weekly garden column, envied and admired for her bountiful garden, had been answering questions, surrounded by a group of fellow enthusiasts, earnest and inquisitive, same-y in their sturdy footwear and wide-brimmed hats. The tall stranger had stood behind the ladies, striking in her skimpy tee-shirt and short dungaree skirt. Back then, Sandy's hair was a brassy orange and she'd been on the arm of a stone wall builder from Vermont, just the first iteration of many styles and colors and lovers to follow.

"You could save yourself the effort," Sandy had said. Rudely, Amy had thought at the time. She'd been mid-sentence, identifying a blue bush form of clematis, and pencils had been scratching away at her every word.

"What you need is drawings of all the beds, with an identification of each plant." Sandy had pushed her way to the front, her Vermonter in tow, and handed Amy an example of one such illustration she'd done. "Then people can take the drawings home. Copy the bits they like." She'd waved dismissively at the notebooks and scribblers. "Let folks enjoy the tour. Smell the roses."

There had been something engaging about Sandy, besides her distracting figure and fluorescent hair. Amy had seen it in the expressions of her small audience. One or two had nodded in agreement, pouted their lips as they considered the suggestion, laughed at themselves and their own eager notetaking. But at the time, Amy had recoiled at the interruption, politely taking the artist's business card, leaving Sandy and her brawny partner by the miscanthus.

Only later, when Amy's newspaper editor first suggested the idea of collecting her best garden columns into a book, and Ella, the editor's niece, agreed to become Amy's agent, did Amy remember the artist. She'd sought Sandy out, reviewed her other sketches and impressed with the riveting watercolors and the clearly inked labels, she'd recommended Sandy to Ella.

They'd proved a good combination. Although, for Amy's taste, Sandy was still too rude.

As they came inside, Amy's cell phone was ringing from the kitchen. She hung up the leash and crept toward the noise.

It was Sandy again. Amy pretended she'd just arrived back. "Hey, Sandy."

"Hey you. So, how'd it go?"

"It went well! Interesting woman. You'll love the garden."

"Glad to hear it."

"Think Newport. Gatsby."

"Okay. Sounds good. You're home?"

"Uh huh."

"And getting pretty for dinner tonight?"

"Not especially." Amy hadn't remembered even telling Sandy about dinner.

"Well, do. And wear a skirt. It'll make you feel special." She sounded like a life coach. "If nothing else, it'll make Graham happy."

Sandy had never particularly liked Graham, wondering aloud sometimes why Amy'd married such a self-absorbed man, more than a decade older than herself. Amy had tried telling Sandy that she hadn't known Graham back then, back when he was fun and astonishing. But Amy had long since stopped trying. Single women are hard to convince. The furthest Sandy would go was to acknowledge Graham was easy on the eyes.

"We're going to Fathom's, not the Four Seasons." As she said it, Amy was reminded that it might not be true.

"Whatever, deck yourself out," Sandy insisted. "You deserve it."

*What I deserve*, Amy thought, *is to stop having people tell me what to do.* "Okay. But we have to plan our next trip to the Roosevelt place. The gardener, the layout—it's all very special."

Sandy cut her off. "We'll talk. Just wanted to make sure you'd made it back in one piece. Now, I gotta go. See you later."

Amy sighed a quiet acceptance. That was Sandy. "Brusque" was putting it mildly.

Amy tucked her notebook and tape recorder back on the shelves over her desk in the kitchen. She was particular about the alignment of everything in this, her designated writing spot, and she straight-ened the notebook with a last touch of her fingers, sweeping them lightly across the lid of her laptop. She wouldn't be opening it tonight but wanted everything ready for an early start in the morning. Now, however, she needed to switch gears, get her brain around an evening out.

Haps at her heel, she poured herself a glass of wine and headed through the dining room to the back patio. She shifted a lawn chair to face the sun and sank into it. Haps circled twice and settled by her feet. The last of the day's heat was still radiating off the bricks, giving maybe half an hour before the line of shadow swallowed them both. She inhaled the calm of the sheltered spot, the spicy vanilla of the viburnum across the lawn, and attempted to ease into her better self.

It had been wrong, trying to cancel dinner reservations. For all his recent tetchiness, his curious disaffection of late—with her, with everything—she wanted Graham to feel good for a change. His hov-ering mood, whatever it was, the look of frustration that crossed his face, left her constantly unsure whether it was something she'd done or said. Almost daily, she'd recognized his tendency to assign blame, however obliquely, for something he found amiss. What she needed, for a change, was for him to find pleasure in her company, his home. Of course, she would also like to rediscover that gratitude herself, for their life together, their familiar routines and pleasures. Because they were basically good, she told herself, tried and true. A squirrel perched overhead chuckled noisily.

Around her, her own garden was filling out, the old green sooth-ing and protective, the buds fat with promise. She closed her eyes to the myriad tasks everywhere, smelling in only the generosity of it all, nature's bounty. *A girl could do worse,* she thought, her mind sailing back over the trees, across the sound, to the old lady on the island.

Two hands warmed her shoulders as a kiss landed on her hair.

16

"Here you are." Her husband sounded pleased.

"Hey, hon." She tilted back.

"Have a productive day?" With him, nice didn't cut it; a day had to be productive.

"I did. You?" She patted the chair next to her, hoping he might settle.

"Yup. Have you showered already?"

"No. What time is it?"

"Time to move." He gave her his hand, pulling her up.

Graham was a hard person to ignore. Partly, he came to authority naturally—the first born, a man. Partly too, he was an easy person to embrace. Tall and toned, Graham made the perfect cushion for her face. She leaned into him, ready to be held.

"C'mon. Places to go."

Graham put on his lilac shirt, so she did wear a skirt. As she was coming downstairs, she heard him in his study. "Yeah, she's here. We won't be long."

Only then did it hit her. *Light dawns on marble head.* She could hear her father's humor, remembered his knuckle rapping her skull. By the time they'd driven into the Yacht Club parking lot, Graham insisting that this had been the plan all along, she was braced for the big surprise.

The rear dining room had been cordoned off, and yellow balloons and crepe paper festooned the ceiling and walls. A big "50" blazed in gold over the door. Yellow and white daisies graced the tables. That's what she noticed, before being encircled by beaming bodies, laughing, jittering in anticipation. Then she started realizing the individual faces: Jason, not in New Haven at all; Catherine, Graham's daughter, from a thousand miles away! Betsy and Kayed, their neighbors. The Whytes, more neighbors. Andy, Graham's sailing buddy, and his wife, Judith. Dana, Graham's partner, and his wife, Lois. Caroline and Lisa from her gardening club, Sam from the newspaper. And Sandy, who was supposed to be away somewhere. It occurred to Amy then, seeing the gleam in Sandy's eye, why she hadn't joined her in Cuttyhunk, that she'd engineered this whole event.

"You brat!" Amy said.

"You fucking moron!" Sandy laughed. Her spiky turquoise hair glistened in the light.

Even Ella, Amy's agent, had made it, minus the scholarly thick-rimmed glasses.

Amy had to pry her hand from her open mouth, unable to stop shaking her head.

"Well, that was close." Jason came up behind his parents, an arm around each waist. "Wasn't sure you two were going to make it tonight!" Laughing, he planted a kiss on his mother's cheek, pleased at his own contribution.

Her guests watched, partly curious, smiling nervously still, and Amy blushed. All this attention, all this collective nervous energy seemed to hang on her next word. It was as if, having thrown her into the deep end, her friends and family now waited for her to surface, signaling the party could begin.

"Well, you did it!" she announced grandly. "You got me!" And she let them all laugh again at her gullibility. Pointing at Sandy, she added in a stage whisper, "Now, I'm guessing, with her organizing this, there's probably a bar somewhere close . . ."

As folks started queuing up for their first drink and eased their way toward the buffet table, Amy took a deep breath. Decked around her were the individuals who defined much of who she was, and she was fascinated by the strange and loyal collection. While she'd been lounging obliviously with Edith, walking Haps, dozing on her patio, each of her guests had been making a special effort to get here. Digging deep into her reserve of energy, she began to do the rounds.

She saved her stepdaughter for last. Slim and dark-haired, Catherine was seated at a table toward the back corner, sharing a large plate of crudités with Amy's agent. A tall plastic cup of wine was in her hand. Amy swooped down on her from behind, cradling Catherine's head in a tight embrace.

"I can't believe you made it! This is the most amazing gift, seeing you like this." Amy held on, kissing Catherine's hair.

"If I could breathe, I'd say thank you," Catherine said laughing, rolling her eyes upward. "Watch my drink."

Amy looked at Ella, filling her in. "Did she tell you she came all the way from Chicago for this? Her stepmother's fiftieth birth-day?" Amy stood upright, patting the place over her heart. "I mean, that's something."

"It is," Ella agreed. "Maybe she loves you."

"Well, it's too far to come with dirty laundry." Catherine's humor was evenhanded, pleasant. "I figured if my brother and father could show up, I could handle a flight east. I mean, hell, Amy. You're turning into a grown-up!"

What Amy thought in that moment, with the delicious near-mother-daughter sense of possession and warmth, was that the once scrawny, needy child she'd wooed back into Graham's life all those years ago had herself grown up. That was the gift—that it had been so worth the trouble.

Amy finally slumped back into her seat. She'd been on her feet for hours, kissing, being kissed, letting each guest laugh anew at her failure to suspect. Dinner was a buffet, delicious, not one oyster in sight. And afterwards, the center of the room was cleared for some serious dancing. Amy was in fine form, her body fluid and assured. Graham too, got to his feet. He looked happy, Graham, back at it, and Amy was reminded of when her husband's directness, in the form of a firm grip on her back, a slight pressure of his hand, had sent her spinning with abandon.

It was getting time to go, but Graham clinked his glass, wanting a last word. Their friends stilled, giving him the floor.

"This lady is one difficult person to rein in," he began. "And I should know, after almost thirty years." People laughed. "But just so you know, I wasn't the one who started it. She stalked me from the beginning!"

Amy recognized the oft-repeated boast, tolerating it as ever, with a smile.

"So here's to that young lady!" Graham lifted his glass and others followed suit. "Here's to the woman who managed to put up with me all these years. To the woman who managed to raise my two impossible children. Here's to the woman who makes every patch of earth more gorgeous than even Mother Nature imagined." He took a breath, a theatrical pause.

"To the woman who writes, maybe?" From the audience, Catherine reminded her father.

"Hear, hear!" Amy's agent knuckled the table.

Graham nodded, thrown off his stride. He looked down at his wife. "Here's to . . ."

Amy thought she saw a flicker of fear in his eyes.

"Here's to . . ."

It shook her, watching him hesitate, and she prayed for the silence to end.

"To . . ." He tried again.

*Amy,* she wanted to whisper.

"To my wife! Happy Birthday!"

A chorus of them rang out.

# THREE

She dug a little hole with her finger, by the daylilies. The soil was warm already, like chocolate cake, and it felt good in there. With her clean hand she picked the teabag from the mug of tea by her knee and dropped the wet little sack deftly into the spot, then slid the soil back over. It was the ritualist in her, this morning routine, her "tour of the garden" giving her a sense of what was to come, the balance of things.

It had rained in the night and the ground was spongy. Nearby, the leaves of lady's mantle looked decked for a party, the captured beads of moisture like pearls on a gown. A dove swooped in, landing by the feeder, followed by its mate.

"Nice out here, isn't it?" Graham was crossing toward her, a steaming mug in his hand, his slippered feet damp from the grass.

"It's a perfect morning," she said, turning. She had slept well after their lovemaking and felt light, easy with happiness. Under the feeder, the two doves nodded into the scattered seed.

"Want some breakfast before you disappear?" she asked.

Graham was dressed for work, but for the shoes, and she had her own agenda to look forward to. After bagels, she would spend the morning writing up what she'd seen of the Roosevelt garden, maybe researching further into the family, all those weddings held on the site.

He stood close. "No rush. When you're ready."

She looked up. "Not in a hurry? That's nice."

Then she noticed the first of the bleeding heart blossoms, the tiny valentines unclenching their tight fists. "Oh, look." She indicated. "Here they come."

He crossed to the bush, crouched down to touch, following the arch of the stem with his finger. The blossoms dangled below, like charms from a bracelet. "I love these guys."

"Mmmm." She watched the curls on the back of his neck.

He inhaled deeply, pausing before standing back up. "I'm not going straight in this morning." He spoke as if to the plant, then looked at his wife. "There something I need to talk to you about."

He looked too serious. Not angry, not sad. Just serious. "Okay," she said. She was disappointed, sorry that he had chosen such a beautiful morning to talk. At least it was sunny.

"Let's go inside," he said.

The kitchen table was already set. A small plate, knife, and napkin on each placemat, the butter and marmalade between them. Graham stationed himself by the toaster, the white bag of bagels ready on the counter, so Amy took her seat. Even Haps seemed to sense the tone, removing himself to his bed in the corner.

"I wanted to tell you this before," Graham began, tearing apart an onion bagel with his long thumbs. He pressed the ragged halves into the toaster. "But it was your birthday."

Amy stiffened in the chair. "What?" was all she could manage.

He glanced quickly at the toaster before looking her square in the face. "I've noticed it for some time . . . You probably have as well."

*I've noticed a lot of things*, she thought, but kept her mouth shut.

"I've had a diagnosis you need to know about."

Amy stared.

"I got the results last week." He exhaled carefully. "I've been diagnosed with Alzheimer's," he said. His eyes bored into her like they were drilling for oil, daring her to erupt.

She didn't. She kept his eye, remembering to breathe.

He wasn't joking. That was her first thought. And this wasn't the kind of distress signal that she might use, a comment meant to earn sympathy, win points. He meant it. Alzheimer's. A death sentence.

Amy swam in his gaze, horrified. She watched the delicate lines framing his mouth, and a fleeting notion of dearness floated by. *That was kind of him*, she thought lightly, *letting me enjoy my birthday.* But then a second thought roared in, drowning the first. He'd waited to tell her. The betrayal of it choked. So it had been days since he got the news, weeks since whatever test he'd had, months probably that he'd been sitting with this. And he'd kept it from her all this time?

A thin line of smoke emerged from the toaster, and she pointed at it.

He reached for a knife, stabbing carefully into the contraption, freeing their breakfast. He was about to throw the smoky mess into the trash, so she stopped him. "I don't mind them burned," she said. She passed over her plate, accepting the blackened halves.

"How do they know?" she asked finally, feeling bold.

"They know." Graham grabbed another bagel from the bag, slicing this one with a sharp bread knife.

"From one test?" It seemed dangerous to ask, but she needed to know. "I mean, I thought they couldn't tell these things . . ."

"Amy." His voice stopped her. "I've been going for tests for eight months. They know."

She ducked her head, dizzy with the information. *Eight months!* she thought wildly. *When? Where?* Her brain raced backwards, searching.

"And if you'd stopped to think, babe, you probably knew it too."

What she knew, what she'd seen, all the moments she'd swallowed as petty grievances, flooded through her. The times she'd tolerated his odd outbursts and strange lapses, wondering what she'd done wrong, hoping to hide her growing disappointment in silence. This he'd seen as her culpability. Tears sprang to her eyes, filming her vision.

He turned away, watching his bagel, bright against the hot wires.

She was reminded of other times he had pivoted in just this way, turning his back to her, giving her time to absorb his news. Graham was no stranger to long-held secrets.

In that heady first year in Sri Lanka, when she'd believed herself his muse and he, her mentor, traipsing across the hot island together, the world in their wake, that first secret had felt like betrayal.

"What's this?" she'd asked innocuously, lifting a scrap of paper that had fallen from his bag. They were living in Colombo then, in his rented rooms on McCallum Road, and she had been putting away some supplies.

"What?" Graham was already slicing into a letter he'd collected from the post office down the road.

"This. Western Union," she said, holding up the yellow-rimmed page. "Ninety thousand Sri Lankan rupees. Wired to Ottville, Illinois."

He was smooth with his response, but swift. Taking it from her, he folded the paper calmly, tucking it into his shirt pocket. "It's a money transfer." Which answered nothing.

"What for?" she pressed, her curiosity growing.

"Five hundred dollars." He had tried going back to his letter, hoping she'd leave it at that.

"But what for? Who do you know in Ottville, Illinois?" she insisted, forehead scrunched in distaste. The name itself sounded odd, a backwater nowhere, and it annoyed her, somehow, that he would have such a connection.

He looked straight at her, and said, as if he were stating something she might already have guessed, should probably have known, even though it was really no business of hers *to* know, "Child support. I have a daughter. It's for her."

That was the first time he'd done it, turning his back, leaving Amy to make sense of exactly who she was dealing with. Giving her the chance to jet, too, if that's what she decided. But of course, in the days that followed, Amy had prodded, and Graham had shared, and the emerging reality—a college romance, an unwanted pregnancy, a reluctant marriage—became almost bearable to imagine. To accept. Especially when the wife, she'd been told, had become feverishly unhappy, unwilling to travel with his work, disinterested in his career or indeed her own, a burden of a wife who, in the end, wanted only her Midwestern town and molded Jell-O salad and parents and aunts two blocks away, who wanted him out of her life. The child support became a virtue, seen in that light.

Amy had become used to watching her husband's back at times like this and learned to love it maybe most of all, a powerful V, long and slender.

Graham took his time, spreading a second dab of marmalade on his last bite.

"What I'm doing now is putting my affairs in order. And that'll mean some changes."

"You're not . . ." she began. Again, wishing to object, slow the train.

"No, I'm not dying. But I need to readjust my life, so I can manage this thing."

She saw that, his exquisite need to manage.

"I'm letting Dana buy me out of the partnership, so I can be more independent."

"You're quitting work?" Amy's voice had shrunk almost to a whisper.

"Of course not!" It came out as a scoff. "But I'm refocusing. I'll just be doing design now, no more firm responsibilities, just my client work."

She nodded, as if with him.

"And I'll be working from home, giving me more privacy, fewer distractions."

"Oh." Amy glanced at her little writing corner across the kitchen, her laptop sitting there, exposed.

"And one other thing. I'm sorry, but you have a right to know."

Amy looked back at him, struck by the strangeness, his mentioning her rights.

"I've asked one of my Senior Associates to work alongside me," he said.

"Meaning?"

"To take on more responsibility, get to know my clients better."

Graham's demeanor was so sure, his posture as upright as ever.

"Would he be working here too?"

"She." Graham nodded.

Amy pushed her chair back, taking her mug to the coffee pot on the counter. As she poured the steaming brew, dark forms gathered behind her eyes. *Take your time*, she told herself, controlling her breath. *Take your time.* Turning, she saw him, back straight, face averted. "More coffee?" She held the pot up.

"No thanks."

She crossed to the bay window, looking out.

"The one thing I'm asking of you," he said, as if there were just one, "is that you keep this to yourself. I can't do this, can't keep my clients, if anyone were to know."

Amy's mind raced to the faces around them last night, the pressing affection. "But the kids, Graham. My sister, your parents."

"No. Please don't." His face had paled, the dark curls making him ghostly. "This will take a while, Amy. I have time yet. I'll tell them when I'm ready." His fingers had spread wide against the table's edge, as if holding him up. Then a decision, and he leaned back. "We can do this. I know we can."

Her phone broke the moment.

"I bet it's Alice," she said, needing permission to move. "I won't say anything."

Graham nodded, rising from the table. "I'll be off."

She put out her hand, to slow him down. "Honey. I'm sorry . . ." she said.

"Me too." He nodded, his small smile one of relief.

# FOUR

L ate in the afternoon, a soft rain started to fall. Hearing the patter against the windows, Amy looked up from her computer. She swiveled around in her chair and arched her back, arms stretched overhead. The sun was still emitting shafts of light into the room, and outside the air shimmered with a kind of maverick joy.

She had made it through the day without breaking. That alone was a miracle. That she had managed to write at all brought some much-needed relief. She'd captured the connection between gardener and garden. It was there in the details: the vivid blue of the grape hyacinth, the lighter hue of Edith's eyes, the pits and etching of the wind-torn stone, the weathered lines of Edith's face. There was more to do, more to research. Still, Amy had been lost for minutes at a time in the flow of it, recreating the broad garden beds into smooth, rolling sentences. It made her glow with quiet satisfaction, and what it told her was that work could be a balm. Sitting there in the glimmer of her peaceful home, she had grasped more profoundly than ever why Graham was so set on keeping at his. He would continue to work, Amy knew, whatever it took.

It hadn't been that difficult, not telling her sister. Earlier, when Graham had headed upstairs to change his shoes, and minutes later, walked solemnly to his car, leather satchel over his shoulder, his secret close to his chest, Amy had had a moment of needing to tell Alice everything: *He's sick, Alice. Graham's losing his mind.*

"It was a wonderful party!" she'd said instead. "We danced for hours!"

Her sister had worried about keeping the party a secret. As a person who preferred a level of control of her own life, Alice considered surprise parties about as much fun as *Candid Camera*: a chance to make fools of people caught off guard. Still, Alice had been happy for her younger sister, relieved that her own absence hadn't disrupted all that planning. And yes, Alice had assured Amy, she'd make it to New England sometime this summer and they'd celebrate together then.

Now, stiff from sitting, Amy wanted some air. Outside, the afternoon still gleamed, the light drizzle sparkling against the greenish sky. She turned to the retriever, sleeping peacefully in the corner.

"C'mon. I need the company."

But as they left the yard, crossing the road in the eerie light, Amy felt suddenly vulnerable. It was unnerving, leaving the house with her new knowledge, as if a neighbor might stop her suddenly, bursting out from behind a hedge, sticking a face from a car window. Even something as benign as a "how are you?" was a trap into which Amy must either fall with a full confession or dishonor with a lie. *Me? I'm married to a man diagnosed with Alzheimer's; have a guess!* she imagined blurting in the grocery aisle. Or, to an acquaintance from the gardening club: *Well, my husband's got dementia and he kept it from me for eight months.* Spoken airily, as if discussing the weather. Amy envisioned herself winging it, the next time she saw Dana, Graham's partner, or worse, Lois, Dana's wife. Would she explain to Lois, her friend of twenty years that Graham was no longer a safe bet, business-wise? *I'm fine, but Graham, he's a liability; how are you?* And what would her sister think? All these years, regarding Graham as such a bright catch? *I'm good, Alice. Graham's walking the streets in his boxers, but we're doing well.* Of course, the other, simpler option, the customary response, troubled her more: *I'm fine,* a lie which would later emerge—and be remembered—when Graham's condition became obvious. The hurt realizations, the distancing that that would cause, come the time.

They followed the shore road until the harbor came into view. Cormorants by the inner buoy were diving for fish, one emerging with the silver prey shimmering in its tightly clamped beak. Amy struggled to hold a thought as firmly in her brain, the practical implications of her husband's diagnosis evading her grasp before slipping out again. Notions of life with a future Graham were like the furred images of the buoys out in the channel, tangible and important but lost in the afternoon's haze.

Passing the curve where the road neared marshland, Amy imagined herself being pulled under in the swampy terrain. For a quick second, she considered calling Alice back with her news, but just as quickly rejected the idea. No, Alice would try to take charge. Never one to go limp in the face of Graham's sometimes extreme directives, often critical of Amy's willingness to do so, Alice would only cause more trouble. Amy exhaled wearily.

Then, as if from nowhere, an inspiration hit her. She should call Matt! She could! Graham's brother, her once-trusted confidant—at least during the short and repetitive periods of his bachelorhood— Matt would be the perfect person to talk to. Now a mature man at long last, temperate and self-effacing, Matt would help Amy make sense of what was on the horizon. But mostly, out of affection for her, Matt could keep a secret. The thought of talking to him brought Amy a moment of peace, a beat of longing.

She loped easily under some overhanging branches, the airy canopy like a mint doily against the darker blue above. But then the faces of Jason and Catherine interrupted her reverie. Tell Matt but not tell the children? That would only intensify the betrayal, even if they never found out. No, keeping her word with Graham was either keeping her word or it was not. Any duplicity on Amy's part, even in confiding in a wise and dear brother, would not be right. Amy choked down the burden, forcing more adrenaline through her system.

She picked up the pace, her dog trotting behind.

From the west, charcoal clouds moved overhead. The aluminum sheen of lingering sunlight disappeared, and the world darkened. Heavy drops, at first sporadic, eventually persistent, became serious. Amy and Haps broke into an awkward jog, splashing each other, becoming idiotic as they ran. Seeing her dog's expression of surprised abandon, his mouth open to the downpour, Amy laughed aloud, laughed uncontrollably until her face crumpled and hot tears streamed down her cheeks.

Back in the kitchen, Amy rubbed them both down with towels until his coat stopped dripping and her skin tingled. Haps munched happily on an early dinner and Amy warmed her hands on a mug of tea.

Ella's call interrupted her. "Great party last night! Sandy did a good job, don't you think?"

Amy struggled to shift gears. "I do. Yeah, that was fun," she managed.

"And I loved meeting your stepdaughter. What a nice woman."

"She is," Amy agreed. "I take complete credit for Catherine."

Ella laughed. "Of course you do. Now, tell me: were you *really* surprised?" Her agent was a cynical, direct kind of person, never letting wishful thinking interfere with reality.

"I was," Amy insisted. *Mostly,* she thought, but didn't say.

Ella let it slide. "Anyway. I didn't get a chance to tell you in all the celebration, but I've found us a photographer."

"Oh!" It was something Amy knew Ella'd been working on, but a detail she'd forgotten about completely.

"Name's Zach Markham." Ella chuckled her throaty laugh. "He's pretty full of himself, but with good reason. So, bring him when you take Sandy back over to the island. I'll send you his number."

"That's great." It was a humbling reminder. Amy had been planning her return to Cuttyhunk with Sandy without stopping to think who would be taking the photographs! A former photographer herself, the oversight was telling. "What is he charging?" she asked. "Can I even afford him?"

"Of course. He's on the same deal as Sandy: one thousand on signing, one at delivery and acceptance, the last grand on publication. I've paid him his first check already." Amy took a moment to swallow the irony of her financial arrangements. Her designer and photographer were each on a straight take from the publisher's ten grand advance. Ella'd worked wonders to get her that much. But of the ten thousand, her agent scooped 15 percent right off the top. So far, having received the first payment, Amy had theoretically earned just $833.33, which, at Ella's advice, she'd set aside toward marketing and publicizing the book. It was true that Amy alone—or she and Ella alone—would reap all the rewards of royalties. Sandy and the photographer weren't in on that. But as the publisher was planning a four-color hardback, an expensive proposition, Amy's percentage of sales was a miserable 8 percent. And no one, Ella hinted in her own ever-practical explanation, expected to out-earn the advance.

Ella continued, unfazed. "I assume the interview went well?" That was typical Ella, asking questions in a declarative sentence.

"It did," Amy assured her. "Yeah, Edith Roosevelt has an interesting story. And the garden is really . . ." She almost said "spectacular" but opted instead for "impressive." "For such a remote island . . . in all that wind? It's . . . I'll send you what I've written as soon as it's done."

"How soon is soon?"

"Umm . . . in the next week. I've got to go back with Sandy—and I'll bring this Zach guy with us—but then it shouldn't take long. I've started writing it already."

"That's good. Definitely send me what you've got." There was a pause and Amy heard Ella move something on her desk. "You know, it might be a good idea to have some intermediary deadlines over the next few months. What d'you think?"

Almost instinctively, Amy was offended. "The editor's given me a deadline already," she said, trying to sound reasonable.

"Oh, I know. September 30th."

"Right . . ."

"Right, but that's four months away, Amy, for all twelve chapters. "

"I know."

"And there's no give there—you fail to produce on the 30th, and the publisher cancels the contract. No second advance. No book!"

Amy's fingers tightened round her mug. "Yeah . . ."

Ella took a deep breath. Her voice was cool now. "Yeah, and frankly, Amy, I'm a bit worried. It's been nine months since we signed the contract, and in all that time, you've produced exactly nada."

"They didn't *send* the signing check for six months!" Amy's voice rose with a hint of injustice.

"As we expected."

"I know." Amy conceded, "But, *you* know—"

"I know. You've had some family . . . things." Ella paused. "But now you need get back at it. And I think you should use me as a kind of . . . timekeeper. Commit to passing in, say, three chapters— to me—at the end of June. Another three in July. You know, so that I can be sure that you're on track." Then Ella just said it: "Because *my* reputation's involved here, too, Amy. The stakes are high for me too. And for Sandy. And now Zach."

Amy curled in her chair. She *had* managed her deadlines. Every column she'd written for the paper had made it to the editor by Tuesday at 5:00 p.m. despite all the family distractions. And who was Ella, of all people, to scold her? Young, single . . .

Suddenly, a more chilling realization interrupted the bitter refrain. Ella was right to be worried. For nine months, as a result of her mother's illness, Amy had failed to produce anything. Now, with Graham's diagnosis threatening to upturn her daily life, what were Amy's chances of *ever* keeping up? Her chest tightened. This second book, Amy knew, was a much more ambitious project than penning some weekly reflections on her garden for the local paper. She was not a seasoned author. There was probably no way she could pull it off.

A planned retreat came quickly into Amy's mind. She should tell Ella the truth and give back the first advance, before she dragged Sandy anywhere, or bothered to even meet this Zach character. She'd just have to swallow the costs as well as the humiliation she guessed Graham's reaction would engender. It might even be easier. Before she began crisscrossing the country or getting in deeper with all those remarkable gardeners, before she wrote another word, she should get the whole pressing fantasy off her back. The long-held dream dissipated like frost in the morning sun.

It was strangely familiar, her despair. It came as if on cue, with an awful predictability, as if these episodes in Amy's life could end no other way but with her feeling hopeless and defeated. It always began with fear. She'd come to know that much, although fear of what, she didn't always see. And instantly, the fear became rage. A wild, blinding, delicious instinct to hit out and inflict pain, generally to whomever was close at hand. Generally Graham, Amy conceded, although now she could have happily whacked Ella with something heavy. Then the rage, too, morphed—even before it had had its day, done anything of any use—and Amy was swallowed by the cool, blue lights of shame and sadness that she was such a pathetic person, that her life was so lacking in resolve. That was her pattern. And here she was again, ready to give up.

Oddly, this time a deep stubbornness gripped at her gut. It wasn't a thoughtful consideration of her options, or a measured assessment of how long it would take to complete the writing. She didn't even stop to muse over the likely slow progression of a disease, one that could well take months and years to surface. Instead, a howling *FUCK YOU!* bubbled up from her gut. This book, these women and their gardens, her writing, was what gave Amy's life joy.

Steeling herself, Amy spoke calmly. "I think the deadlines make sense," she said. Then, just to seal her fate, she added, "Because I can do this."

Ella seemed relieved. "Okay then. A deal."

"A deal," Amy repeated. She thought she'd faint.

Graham was quiet when he returned that evening. He carried a large carton into his study, in it a couple of framed awards Amy hadn't seen in years, his mug with the firm logo. She guessed it had happened.

"How'd it go?" she asked when he reemerged. "Did you talk to Dana?"

Graham shrugged. "He'll be fine," he said, and went upstairs to change.

Amy carried on, preparing a fresh vinaigrette for dinner. She cut into a lime, squeezing half into a bowl. It couldn't have been easy. She imagined the two men ending their decades-long partnership. Distracted, she sucked at a finger, the sharp sour of the juice making her lips pucker.

"What's for dinner?" Graham was back, softer in sneakers. He headed for the leash, hanging by the door.

"Salmon." She paused. Then, "What did he say?"

"He knows he has to buy me out. We still need to agree on the health insurance." Graham patted his thigh. "C'mon, Haps."

So that was how he was going to do this, Amy realized bitterly. After dumping his worst nightmare on her lap, upending everything in both their lives, he was going to bottle it all back up, keeping his thoughts close, not asking for hers.

Amy almost told him that the dog had been out already, but let it go. Another walk would do him good.

# FIVE

One week later, Graham emerged scrubbed and fresh from the shower. "Today's the day!" he announced.

Amy was still in her nightgown, still snug under the covers after a night of interrupted sleep. "What day?" she yawned.

"It's on the calendar," he said, sing-song.

She thought through a blur. All that was on her calendar, after the dog and garden routine, was setting up the next two garden visits with Sandy and Zach. "Humor me."

Graham looked over, disapproving. "My Senior Associate moves in today."

Her eyes sprung wide. "You're kidding."

"It's on there."

"What time?"

"Generally we start work at eight-thirty. I wouldn't expect her later than nine."

Amy glanced at the bedside clock. Already, it was after seven. "Why didn't you say something?"

"I just did." He began doing up his shirt, taking care with each button. Even though he had begun working from home, Graham still dressed for the office.

"I mean last night! Yesterday sometime!" Amy threw back the covers, swinging her feet to the floor.

"You've got time. All she'll need is some space." He climbed into his khakis, unflustered.

Amy lunged for the bathroom. "Did we even talk about where she's going? I thought you were putting her in with you." Graham's study, as large as their living room, offered plenty of space.

"No. Not with me. I thought maybe the den, or the guest room." He stopped as she slammed the door between them. "I put it on the calendar, Amy," he said, voice raised. And then, pleased with himself, "Who's forgetting things now?"

At eight-thirty precisely, a yellow Jetta turned into their driveway, slowing to a stop behind Graham's battered Volvo. The driver turned off the ignition and sat for a moment, as if taking in the celebrated house and garden. Finally, she emerged from the car.

By any reckoning, Moira Richards was an attractive person. The reckless strawberry mane, the long neck and legs suggested something from a Victorian novel; only the jeans and fitted jersey landed her firmly in the here and now. As Amy appraised the young professional standing calmly on their property, Moira turned, noticing the face through the kitchen window. Amy raised a hand in greeting.

"She's here," Amy shouted.

At the front door, Moira's hand was cool and firm. "Hi. Mrs. James?"

"Amy. Yes. And I'm guessing you're Moira."

Moira strode to the middle of the foyer and stopped, hands on hips, the fiery mop turning slowly. "This is a stunning place," she said.

"We're lucky," Amy nodded. The dash of earlier, clearing the clutter from a hasty breakfast, oiling down the kitchen table to a simple shine, taking a fast sweep of the floor hadn't hurt. Even Haps was standing at attention, the early sun striking the gold of his coat.

"Welcome!" Graham emerged from his study.

"Hey, Graham." Moira beamed. "I made it! Eight-thirty, as promised." There was an open familiarity to her pleasure that gave Amy pause.

"Excellent," he smiled.

They all stood for a moment, the two women waiting for direction.

"So . . ." He turned to Amy. "Where did you decide to put our new roommate?"

Amy fixed her smile on Moira. "We thought the den might be best."

"Great." Moira shrugged. "I'm happy wherever you put me." Then she laughed. "And I actually know where your den is. I studied the plan of this house when I was at school."

It had been years since their house had been on the cover of architectural magazines, and it took Amy back, remembering how widely her privacy had been breached. Now, once again her home was to be subjected to an outsider's scrutiny. Amy cringed, wondering what else the eager young architect knew, or would come to learn about her and Graham's lives together.

Graham seemed pleased. "Let me help you with your things," he said. "Did you bring it all today?"

"Desk, computer, twin screens, printer, filing cabinet." Moira grinned at Amy. "I even brought my own tea bags."

"Ah," Amy said. "Just the thing."

It took some doing, setting up Moira's office. Pushing the settee to the far side of the room, they positioned her standing desk by the wide west-facing window, affording the young designer some "perfect light." Cords stretched across the floor to a thick power strip, accommodating her twin screens, her computer, printer, and speakers. Lamps were moved, and two side tables dispatched to the basement. By ten, Moira seemed settled, her equipment spread about her.

Alone in the kitchen, Amy vibrated with the new presence. It was odd enough, having her husband moving about in his study down the hall. Having him there, in the long hours when the house was normally hers, made it hard for her to settle, to concentrate, as if at any moment his figure would fill a doorway, issuing its demands. Having a stranger in the den was worse. The imposing desk now disturbed the openness and tranquility of the once perfectly balanced room. She imagined Moira, centered there on their Persian rug, alone with their art on the walls, their titles on the bookshelves, gazing out at the emerging peonies. Amy wondered what the woman was seeing, whether she was working at all.

A creeping burn of discomfort, like acid indigestion, coiled through her. Bookended between Graham and Moira, their professional energies dominating the atmosphere, Amy felt oddly insignificant, as if she were once more the little sister, completing her homework at the kitchen table while Alice, in seventh grade and heavy with assignments, retreated to her private sanctuary upstairs with its grown-up desk.

This kitchen, however, was Amy's favorite room in the house. This was exactly the layout she had lobbied for when, baby on hip, she'd imagined every possible answer to her needs. While Graham had focused on the arresting design features of the building, Amy had held out for her own more domestic dream space: uncluttered counters, wide sills of steel trays, filled with gravel and dotted with house plants and cuttings. Her kitchen had the deep cabinets and plentiful closet space, the double soap-stone sink and large round table, positioned comfortably within a graceful sweep of windows. She'd even planned for the small alcove and inbuilt desk, with its little dedicated shelf for unopened mail, under a corkboard for the annual calendar, next to hooks for everyone's keys. The alcove remained Amy's station, command central, and it was where she chose to write.

The clock on the kitchen wall clicked loudly as the two hands crossed, bringing Amy to. She needed to get back to work. Carefully, Amy reread her notes on Edith Roosevelt's garden, reminding herself what she knew of the woman who owned it, the islander's exacting personality.

Alex dialed Edith's number. Communicating effectively with her subjects and organizing schedules wasn't the creative part of writing a book, for sure, but it was part of her job now, one she had to get right. Alex tapped her fingers on the desk, waiting for Edith to pick up. The repeated rings sounded scratchy, as if the line to the island was frayed, deep under the ocean floor. Finally, Edith answered. It took some warming up, reestablishing their connection, but Amy repeated the request to return for a second visit, this time with the illustrator and photographer in tow. In spite of the spotty reception, they agreed on the time and date.

The call was just wrapping up when Moira appeared in the kitchen doorway. Amy held up her palm, shaking her head, giving the intruder fair warning.

"I'm looking forward to seeing you again," she continued into the phone.

Moira wiggled a box of mint tea, eyebrows raised.

Trying to ignore her, Amy tucked more closely into the receiver. "The weather looks promising for the next several days."

Behind her, Moira tiptoed toward the electric kettle, bringing it to the sink. The water came on with a noisy gush.

Amy strained to hear Edith's question.

"Nine-thirty?" came the faint voice on the other end.

"That's right," Amy confirmed, underlining the details on her calendar. "Tuesday, the 11th. Nine-thirty a.m."

With a clunk, Moira placed the full kettle back on its pedestal, flipping the switch with a loud click. A red light flashed.

"And three of you?" Edith's voice was almost lost in the din.

Amy raised her voice, finding it hard to concentrate. "Yes, three of us: one artist, one photographer, and me, the writer."

Moira nodded, grinning, as if part of the conversation.

"I think you'll be pleased," Amy managed, sounding upbeat, confident.

Moira gave Amy a thumbs up.

"Well, okay then," Edith said. "Meanwhile, take good care of yourself."

"I will. Thanks again. You too."

"Goodbye, then."

"Bye." It took all of Amy's strength not to slam down the receiver.

"You're good," Moira said. She'd been enjoying the show, appreciating the display of good customer relations.

Amy stared. "And you're noisy," she finally managed.

"Oh, I'm sorry." Moira was genuinely surprised. "I was trying to be quiet." Then, inspired by a stroke of manners, "Would you like a cup?"

Amy sighed. There was a time, she knew, when she had been just that oblivious. In fact, sitting there, taking in this pretty girl in her scoop-necked jersey, Amy was reminded of herself, when she was cute and ripe, when she just took what she wanted.

Graham hadn't been wrong when he'd bragged about how he and Amy had met. She *had* stalked him. That day, thirty years ago, when she'd first spied the man walking ahead through the streets of Colombo—her camera, as ever, slung round her neck—she'd thought, mainly, *What a great photograph.* He was a head taller than the pedestrians around him, a shade lighter, his hair a mop of curls instead of Sri Lankan black and straight. She followed him to his watering hole, the Chandrasiri Gallery. Built around an indoor garden, part bookstore and part exhibition space, the place bristled with activity: installations, concerts, lectures. It was there, in the café, she'd tracked him down, relaxed with his avant-garde cluster of contemporaries, bottles of Lion Lager piling up around them.

Over several weeks, Amy had insinuated herself into this crowd. She was an artist too, she told herself; she belonged. She had drunk Tiger, to get his attention. The evening of Geoffrey Bawa's talk, watching the venerated architect engage with his devotees, she'd overheard word of another party afterwards, to which Graham and his cohorts were planning to depart. Amy didn't ask whether she could join them; she hadn't been invited. Instead, she asked a woman at Graham's table if she had room in her car. Amy was wearing her silk halter top, her shoulders were lovely, and she felt brave and entitled.

"You parlayed that nicely," Graham told Amy that first morning as they lay naked together on top of the sheets.

"What do you mean?" she asked, feigning innocence.

"You see what you want and you go for it," Graham said. "I like that in a person."

Only later, months after she and Graham became an item, did she learn that the driver, the woman she had asked for a lift, had been Graham's lover.

Today, of course, Amy's brilliant young prize of an architect was no longer young, in fact, the very opposite of a prize. Graham James, sooner or later, would lose his mind. Amy was sure Moira had no notion of that.

The young woman plunked herself down at the kitchen table, and Amy couldn't think of a polite escape. Carefully directing the conversation away from Graham's life, she asked Moira about hers.

The young professional shook her back her hair, happy to share. "Well, I'm from New York. The city," she clarified. "I began studying psychology at Antioch and ended up studying architecture at RISD." She grinned. "So that tells you something! I never was in Graham's class there, but that's where I heard of him. And Faxon

& James were my first choice." She sipped on her tea. "There wasn't really a second. Other architectural firms paid more, but they weren't doing the kind of work I wanted to do. I really resonate with water-integrated design. That's what I like about Graham's practice. Even if their office was out in the boonies, and me a New Yorker! But when they made me the offer, I jumped at it." Moira pulled her heels to her crotch, her knees splaying effortlessly. "And both of them, Dana and Graham, but especially Graham, they're real mentors. I've learned a ton working with them. And this situation . . ." She raised her arms, palms out. "I couldn't believe it when I was invited to work here."

Amy smiled to herself. *Tell me about it*, she thought.

"It was like, are you kidding? Working exclusively with Graham James' clients? In a heartbeat!" Moira leaned back in her chair, casual and relaxed.

It struck Amy anew how truly clueless Moira was as to why she'd been chosen. But Amy recognized the hunger in the younger woman, her willingness to grab at opportunity, and she kept silent. It wasn't her job to put the girl right. It didn't even feel like a lie.

# SIX

The two-tone irises stood tall in their formal clusters, the vivid purple and white bold against the pale sky. Elsewhere, bands of orange poppies exploded in marked counterpoint, the whole a hillside of striking dissonance. Only the humble spikes of Sandy's turquoise hair provided a comic relief.

"What's she doing exactly?" Edith Roosevelt had been watching the artist move among the beds, pad and pencil in hand.

"She does the sketches of the borders. Diagrams, really, that show what plants are located where."

"And these go in your book?"

"That's right," Amy said. "Each chapter will have the story of the garden, a biography of the gardener. And alongside will be photographs, all color, of different views of the garden. And then one or two diagrams. Sandy does those. They're ink drawings, touched with watercolor. And labelled, so the plants are easy to identify. She does lovely work."

"So your readers can copy." Edith hadn't warmed to Sandy; she'd found her insistence on using the Latin terms for flowers excessive.

Amy laughed. "I'm not sure anyone will copy exactly. But it gives people good ideas for groupings, ways to use companion plants in certain settings." She sensed Edith's resistance to the idea. "You'll see." Amy's hands began shaping the air between them. "Think large photographs, blocks of text, maybe some half-pages of diagrams. I'll show you the galleys when we pull it all together." As she said it, the promise seemed presumptuous. Still, Amy was somewhat in awe of Edith, enjoyed being perched up here again with her, overlooking the Atlantic. Amy wanted to inspire confidence.

The older woman's finger then pointed to Zach, prone on his stomach by the lower balustrade. He seemed to be photographing the ocean through the ancient stone railing. "And what's he doing? It doesn't look like he's focusing much on the garden."

It didn't. But Amy was reluctant to call out, ask Zach what he was up to. Although affable looking, in the way that sandy-haired, nondescript thirty-somethings could appear, the photographer had a quiet resistance to him, as if upon the suggestion of criticism he'd simply turn away and stop listening. Ella had been wrong, Amy thought: the guy wasn't so much full of himself as maybe highly sensitive, assertive around his art.

"My hunch is that he has the shots he needs for the book. I'm guessing now he's just enjoying the view."

Edith sniffed. "And what about you? Is the written part done?"

"Not yet," Amy admitted. "I've been speaking to some of your neighbors—"

"I know," Edith said.

"And I've gotten some wonderful information, more about the early fishing club. The island's school that you attended."

Edith cut her off. "You spoke to Mort. He told me."

"Yes, well, everything I learn helps me understand the relationship between you and your garden."

"I'm sure you've got plenty," Edith said. It reminded Amy of her mother's tone when declining second helpings. *You've had a great sufficiency*, Julia used to say, as if Amy'd been contemplating an orgy. Amy had learned not to argue.

Below them, Sandy and Zach were standing together now, talking by the fountain. "They friends?" Edith asked.

"Just met today." But Amy noticed it too: the two heads were close.

"So, tell me about you," Edith continued, changing the subject. "Obviously married. Have at least a son. What else should I know?"

Amy paused, her own story in comparison feeling so much less dramatic. "One husband—an architect—married for thirty years. One stepdaughter, who lives in Chicago. A son, our son, in grad school down in New Haven."

"Oh, be brave!" Edith chided her. "If the kid's at Yale, just say so."

"He's at Yale."

"And you're a famous writer . . ."

"No!" Amy laughed. "Although, my husband's fairly famous. I'm just the writer of a weekly gardening column and the author of one small gardening book." She laughed, self-conscious. "He's the expert; I'm the jack of all trades, master of none."

Edith sobered suddenly. "I don't think that's funny. If writing's what you do, you should master it." The voice was stern, and Amy recoiled, stung. "And when you're writing about me," Edith continued, "you'd better get good."

From below, Zach and Sandy had begun to approach the terrace. Inspired suddenly, Zach started snapping again with his camera, framing Amy and Edith over and over. Being captured in that moment, still smarting from Edith's remark, Amy held up her hands, waving him off. It only made the cameraman more aggressive. Like a wasp, he moved closer, rotating the lens, closer still.

"My, you're assertive!" Edith said, staring into the shot. But she was posing too, more intrigued than anything.

"Perfect left ear," Zach said at last, easing the camera onto his chest. "When there's a shot that good, you can't let it go to waste." He reached underneath the table, carefully opening his camera bag, finding a cloth to wipe his lens.

"Are you done?" Amy asked, watching him.

"For now," he said. "I am anyway." He nodded at Sandy. "What about you? You get what you need?"

"Think so." Sandy patted her sketch pad. "I'm using the two central beds. They show the most imagination, the biggest variety." She'd meant it as a compliment, but Edith bristled.

"Tell you what I love." Zach said deftly. "The rim of lavenders—by the Portuguese tile? The different blues and violets are a wonderful touch." He squinted up at the bright afternoon sun. "Hard to catch on film, though, this time of day."

"Should have come earlier," Edith said tartly.

"You're right." Zach almost ribbed Edith with his elbow. "Next time I'll bring a sleeping bag."

It looked like flirting, and Amy was instantly riled, jealous of Zach's easy rapport with their hostess. Inside, Amy was still rumbling with Edith's admonishment of her being a jack of all trades. It was an expression, that was all. The kind of self-effacing comment that Amy associated with humility, not a bad thing, surely. Watching Zach get away with his easy familiarity, cocky with his own apparent talent, made her want to hit them both.

Fortunately, Joao arrived, bearing a stringed box of pastries, and they all moved indoors. Talk turned to the merits of pasteis de nata over querjadas de sintra. Sandy liked them both; Amy preferred the egg custard. Joao loved the white bean curd ones best of all, and Zach voted with him. The conversation flowed easily, their stories braiding together. Savoring her final pastry, Sandy was reminded of a happy fortnight hiking in the Azores, and Joao regaled them with talk of the agapanthus and blue hydrangea growing wild on his home island of Sao Miguel. Zach had been there too, it turned out, guest of Tall Ships America, photographing his way from Cape Town to Horta—in one instance, high up in the scaffolding of the great clipper as they crossed the equator.

Amy shared her own overseas story, telling them about her years in the hills of Sri Lanka, where Graham had built them a small home, and they grew pepper and cinnamon in the jungle outside. Only Edith kept her silence, stationary by choice on her own garden hillside, except to say that she, too, knew something of sailboats.

Before they left, Zach pulled out his camera again, snapping calmly at the vase of flowers, the lace tablecloth, Joao's rough hands. The camera caught Edith, mouth open in a laugh.

The last out the door, Amy turned for a final goodbye. "Thanks again," she told the old woman, "for letting us invade like this."

Edith's palm rested on Amy's forearm, dry and cool. "I'm glad you came. I don't know your friends yet, but you . . . I think you mean well."

Surprised, Amy almost melted in the warmth of it. She wanted to answer back, but Edith cut her off.

"I want you to do well, too. Make this a very good book." Edith's eyes were laser-like, bright within the softened face. "Because what you do is important. So, trust your instincts, sharpen your skills." Then the leathery hand tapped Amy gently, and Edith nodded, marking the end of the visit.

On the way back, the three found seats on the side deck, protected from the wind. They had exhausted conversation for the moment, and Sandy and Zach sat back, their eyes closed, faces tilted toward the late day sun. These two were here because of her, Amy thought watching them. Two artists, two more on this journey of hers. As the ferry whipped across the water, high and dry over the waves below, she felt an odd power, the power of being a good writer. That, and the familiar fear of being found out, that maybe she wasn't good enough.

"I'm going to catch a beer," Zach announced as they descended into the parking lot. "Any takers?"

"I'm in," Sandy said.

Amy considered the time, wishing she needn't. At home, Moira would be gone by now, Graham maybe out with Haps.

"Amy?" Zach asked, head cocked.

Amy paused. A late dinner wasn't a crime; it wasn't all that late. But she'd become more attuned recently to when Graham was at home on his own, as if the disease might suddenly descend unannounced while she was not there. Only two days earlier, she'd had to remind him to bring his keys with him when he was leaving the house. Clearly, he'd forgotten them, but his response had been calm. "Don't worry, babe," he'd said. "Forgetting your keys is just aging. Forgetting what your keys are for—that's Alzheimer's." He'd laughed, kissing her forehead. "That's when you can begin to hover." Still, Amy worried.

"I think I'll pass," she said now, regretting it.

Zach shrugged.

"Come on, Ame. One beer," Sandy nudged. Clearly, Sandy wanted this.

"Nah." Amy grimaced. "I'm good."

Sandy's eyebrows dipped. "The good wife," Sandy explained to Zach. "You'll learn, over time. This is what we're dealing with."

Zach glanced at Amy briefly, considering the disclosure. Then he smiled. "Whatever. It was a good day." He effected a one fingered salute. "See you next time."

And while Amy fumbled for her keys, the two headed off in the direction of Zach's car.

Graham was sitting at her desk in the kitchen, reading something. It startled her, seeing him there when she walked in, tucked into her alcove, and she let out an involuntary, "Oh!"

"Hey." He didn't look up from the page, just lifted a hand in greeting.

"What are you doing?" she asked, trying to keep the tone from her voice.

"Reading this passage you wrote."

"Why?"

"It's interesting," he said.

Amy emptied her bag on the table, noticing the sink filled with dishes. "I mean, why are you at my desk?"

Graham did look up then, amused. "Because it's where you keep your writing. Anyway," he added, "I'm sick of my study. Makes me claustrophobic. Good day?"

"Yeah. Very." She thought of her colleagues, relaxing now over a cool brew. "How about you two?"

"Making progress. Moira's pretty gung-ho. Talked the Bristol couple into adding a solarium to the new wing."

"Wow."

"Only the second time she's ever met the people. No, Moira's . . . something."

"Think you could encourage her to be as energetic with her dirty dishes?" Amy tried to make it light.

"Oh . . ." Graham remembered. "I told her I'd take care of those. That's not her fault. But!" He grinned widely. "I put dinner on already. So you don't have to think about feeding us."

Amy had planned on roast chicken for dinner, having left one to thaw on the counter. It was gone, but she couldn't smell anything cooking. She crossed to the oven door and opened it, expecting to see the naked bird, undressed. Inside, there was nothing, just 350 degrees of heat.

Her first instinct was to hide the fact.

"I even cut up garlic cloves and inserted slivers of them into the skin, like I used to do," Graham boasted. Still he seemed clueless. Amy moved to the refrigerator and checked inside. There on the middle shelf sat the cold bird, jagged with darts of white, sitting in a pan lined with tin foil. Squares of butter stuck heavily to the rubbery skin.

She pulled out the pan, doing her best, "This is going to be great," she said. "Thanks for getting it all ready." Then, before placing it in the oven, she removed the plastic package of organs still hiding inside, plopping it unceremoniously in the sink.

If Graham realized what he'd done, there was no sign. Instead, he handed Amy the printout of what she'd written, new red markings staining her words. "We can go through this now together if you'd like. Except for a few places, it flows fairly well."

Amy sat, willing herself to look at the page, his notes like cat scratches everywhere, and let his authoritative voice wash over her.

"Never start a sentence with 'Because.'"

There was a time when she had loved being coached by her husband.

She could see them, standing together on the polished cement floor of their new house in Kandy, cool in spite of the tropical heat, a fan paddling the air overhead. They were curled over the broad desk he'd built, the one that tilted like a drafting table, wide enough to accommodate two. Her negatives were laid out like jigsaw pieces; studiously, they picked one up, put one down, finding the best.

Graham had been planning a series of lectures at the University of Peradeniya on the use of Indigenous materials and the role of water. Her photographs of Wijewardene House, the Hilton Hotel, Seema Malaka, and the Sri Lankan Parliament showed fine examples of modern buildings tailored to a specific environment. Ignoring the advice of others, he had planned to use Amy's pictures in his lectures, championing their partnership.

It had been a plum assignment for him and a rare opportunity for her, to have her own work find some use in the greater world. They had made a project of it, preparing his lectures, trekking from site to site across the island, standing on trains, sleeping where they could, in cheap hotels that charged extra for the sheets. Graham had sketched and taken notes, while Amy captured the perfect vantage points through her lens, lingering under the tiled wooden roof of the temple on Beira Lake, soaking in the filtered light, the sound of water underneath the pontoons. They'd dashed back to their cinnamon hillside to oversee the cement foundation being poured and had returned again to watch the walls go up. For nine months, they traveled and built, traveled and prepared.

The campus of the university was the most beautiful in the world, seventy hectares of forest and sky, great, green trees, the Mahawali River, and the Hanthane mountain range. She had gone with him on that first lecture and had sat in the back of the fine hall, nervous and proud, her connection to the lecturer her own smug secret.

Later, a colleague had convinced Graham he was wrong not to go with a professional photographer. So Graham had commissioned another series of images and used them in his lectures instead of Amy's. "Because I need to put my reputation first, Ame—you get that." And she had, kind of.

She had skipped the following lectures, crushed with the shame of it. On her last visit to the campus, she had roamed the gardens alone, dwarfed by enormous flowering trees, stopping by crystalline streams, listening to the birds. She had sat atop the steep grassy bowl of the open-air theatre, the semicircles of seating spiraling down to the stage below and had thought, *Maybe not photography. Maybe not.*

When they finished reading through her work, Amy put away the printed pages and turned her attention to preparing the rest of their meal. She was tired of listening to Graham's opinion and hungered for some time alone. But while she set the table and mixed up a salad, he sat watching her every move.

"Do you think about it much?" he asked, breaking the silence.

She gave him a quizzical look, knowing exactly what he meant. "About what?"

"Dementia. Do you notice anything yet? See any change?"

Amy stopped what she was doing. Graham's superior tone was gone and now he seemed to be seeking reassurance. The shift made Amy squirm, but it also moved her, this rare sign of vulnerability. "I don't think so," she began carefully. "I mean, of course I notice . . . moments of forgetfulness, times when you seem out of sorts . . . But whether it's a change? Or even anything other than normal stuff? I'm not really sure. I don't think so."

"Honestly?"

"Honestly, hon."

"I wonder whether it's obvious, that's all."

"Oh, Gray, nothing is *obvious*," she assured him. "Anyway, you're bright enough to be the smartest guy in the room even using *half* your brain." She laughed. "And you've always been fairly unpredictable. Nothing's changed there." She rested her hand on his shoulder, feeling a surge of affection sweep over her.

"It'll get worse."

She paused. Everything in her wanted to steer clear of the drama, not indulge his foray into pending doom. "I know. Someday," she acknowledged. "But that doesn't seem to be where we're at now. Today, you're working, I'm working, we're doing fine. We'll both know when we're not."

They ate, finally, and after sitting quietly before the ten o'clock news, retired to the bedroom. She turned off her light first, eyes heavy. She was aware of his restlessness, listening as he closed his book, picked up another, finally leaving their bed to stalk the downstairs. The loneliness she felt was a peculiar one. It was sad, cleansing even, but without the freedom of being alone.

# SEVEN

*Of the four hundred individuals who make Cuttyhunk island their home, only ten live there year-round. For most, even the hardy souls who relish the simple summers, the winters are just too cruel. Ferocious winds and freezing gales wrench the very lungs from the chest. Yet here, atop one of the barren hillsides of this stony, distant islet, Edith Roosevelt lives and gardens . . .*

It was a bit florid, and Amy wasn't quite sure how to characterize Edith without turning her into some kind of Rock of Gibraltar, but Amy liked the idea of opening with the island. She carried on typing, the words flowing easily. At this rate, she'd have a full draft to Ella by the end of the day.

"'Lo!" The voice of Andy Jeffers, Graham's sailing buddy broke her concentration.

Before she could respond, he stepped into the kitchen, knocking on the way.

"Hey," he said. "Didn't see you out in the garden. I was looking for Graham." Andy was one of those committed sailors who, when the season arrived, grabbed every spare moment to get out on the water. Always dark from the sun, weathered and rough, Andy was about as tactful and finely tuned as his rubber Crocs. "He here?"

"In his study." Amy tipped her head in the general direction. "Were you guys going out?"

"Uh, huh." Andy squeaked his way across the floor, rapping loudly on the study door. "Ahab! You ready?"

Graham appeared, carrying a carton of siding samples. He looked dazed but rallied quickly, dumping the carton on the kitchen table and dashing for the stairs. "One second! I'll be right there!"

Haps had now moved in on the visitor, head and tail waving hospitably. Avoiding the cold nose headed for his crotch, Andy patted and pushed Haps away with rough affection, taking a seat by the table.

"Don't see you much at the club these days, Amy. Wanna join us today?" For years, Graham and Amy had spent long afternoons on Andy's boat with him and his wife. The invitation was merely Andy's way of being friendly. Now that his wife had given up sailing for golf, the last thing Andy really wanted was another woman on board. For Amy, all that testosterone on a thirty-foot Tartan was something she could pass on.

"Been busy lately," Amy said. "But thanks anyway."

He noticed the computer. "What, writing another column?"

"Writing a book."

"Ah." Andy's eyebrows lifted. It was beyond him, such a hobby. "About flowers?"

"That kind of thing."

"Okay!" Graham bounded back down the stairs. He'd found his favorite shorts and polo shirt in the hamper and was grabbing his shades from the top drawer. "Let's go." He patted the dog's head and managed to find Amy's ear with a kiss. "Don't wait dinner." Then, "Love you."

And the two were off.

Now, with Graham gone until dark and Moira off in Bristol with clients, Amy had all the space she needed to finish rewriting the Roosevelt piece. She could read her sentences aloud, stretch noisily, tap dance across the kitchen floor, whatever it took to give the elusive phrases room to assemble themselves. The luxury of it made her giddy, in that moment deciding to celebrate with some cinnamon toast before she began again.

Of course she'd noticed. Amy'd known instantly that Graham had forgotten the sailing date, and of course it gave her pause. Daily now, Amy was alert to each of her husband's actions, speculating whether he was being absentminded or increasingly forgetful, careless or failing. For all the years she'd known him, Graham had been that mercurial mixture of formidable energy and a remarkable memory for all things work and travel, but with a casualness, a forgetfulness about little things. That's who he was. Lately, though, Amy was watchful: lazy or crazy? The impact of both was the same, but only one required empathy.

The land line rumbled by her desk. Without thinking, she lifted the receiver. "Hello?"

"Hey, Amy. Gray there?"

It was Moira, friendly and assertive as usual.

"No. Just went out. Why?" Moira didn't need to know that Graham was off on a sail.

"I'm here with the owners, and we're waiting to go through some samples. What time did he leave?"

"Um." Amy looked at the clock, as if it would help. "Are you at the site?" She was simply buying seconds. "How long will you be there?"

"Only until he gets here with the samples. We're at the house, and the Clarksons are flying back out after lunch."

"Okay. I'll make sure Graham is on his way. Don't panic," Amy added calmly, as much for herself as anyone. "I know he's got them."

"Good." Moira hung up.

Amy closed her eyes to think. It was just possible the men hadn't reached the club, or if they had, hadn't yet left the mooring, so she dialed her husband's cell, toes dancing in place. *This could work*, she thought. It just could. But a muffled bell sounded from the kitchen table, in time with the ringing against her ear. She followed the noise to the carton of samples and found Graham's phone glowing inside.

Amy had been to the site in Bristol only once before, years ago, the first time Graham had been hired for the house. Graham and Dana had just formed their partnership, and Faxon & James had been printed on the sign outside.

A monument to the late 19th century, the mansion was set on a thirty-two-acre estate overlooking Narragansett Bay. It crouched like a relaxed stone lion, paws out, facing the water. A wraparound porch, heavy with white columns, afforded views on three sides, all resplendent with sloping lawns and deep, rectangular borders. The place reasserted itself freshly in her memory as she drove through the gate.

Back then, the owners were progressive Yankees, the kind that prided themselves in befriending the help. Upon learning the architect's young wife had an interest in gardens, they'd invited her for a guided tour. Amy recalled sitting in the front seat of Graham's new Volvo, her linen shift high on her thighs. The car's leather had been hot beneath her, and she had worried about the wrinkles settling into the back of her dress. Graham's jacket and tie were lying across the back seat, and the windows were open wide. She had splayed her fingers against her hair, to keep it from whipping at her face.

Graham had prepped his wife nervously. "It was Mrs. Sprague's *mother* who created the borders, not Mrs. Sprague herself. So don't go praising her too much, she'll just correct you." Graham had been surprised at the invitation. He'd mentioned his wife's hobby at an early meeting only as a way to make conversation, and now this.

Amy had understood the moment, appreciating the broad leap this assignment represented in her husband's career. She'd spent the prior six years just trying to keep up, following him through his adventurous stage, when he was just a quiet explorer seeking inspiration in the Far East. When they'd pulled up roots and moved to Baltimore, it had taken her months to see how effectively he'd transitioned his style to the coastal possibilities of the U.S. Still the outlier, with his pagoda-like, water-centric bids, Graham James had never been the first choice then, not the name that sprang to mind when fine homes, public structures were put out to tender. But increasingly, with his confident style, his piercing immediacy, Graham James had become the surprising dark horse, whose occasional offbeat success made the client joyous, proud to have taken the chance.

"Do you think she'll know all the plants by name?" Amy was nervous that her own knowledge might prove too thin to see her through.

"It's not a test, Ame." But he laughed. "It's supposed to be fun, as a kindness to me."

She twisted her wedding band, tight on her heat-swollen finger.

But Mrs. Sprague wasn't even there. The gardener, an elderly man named Prescott, gave them the tour instead.

"Guess we didn't need to dress," is what Graham said after, driving home.

Now, Faxon & James were back, having designed a second extension for the place. The old mansion was in new hands, and the gardens, once the jewel in the property's crown, were lost in the mess of extensive renovations. Amy slowed the car, taking in the scene. Tarps lay scattered around the porch and single boards lay atop them, giving wheelbarrows a narrow path on which to transport the stones for restructured walls. The foundation of the new wing occupied what was once a formal parterre, and piles of lumber lay raw and blonde around its perimeter. Where years of leaf mulch had enriched beds of perennials, builders' footprints left their mark, erasing the once sharp delineation between grass and garden. The damage made Amy feel faint.

She pulled in behind the portable toilet, another affront to the breathtaking view, and stepped out of the car. Moira and Mrs. Clarkson were just circling the porch, pointing up at a tree, now closer to the spreading construction site.

"If it has to go, so be it," she heard the owner say.

Lifting the carton from the back seat, Amy headed for them, trying to avoid the pockets of mud. "Moira!"

Moira turned, not exactly pleased to see who it was. "Hey, Amy." Said as if Amy were part of the plan, a welcome arrival. "Good timing." She took the box, shifting it onto her hip as she perused the contents. Moira was the consummate professional; no way would she interrogate Amy as to her husband's absence—not in front of the client. "Just what we needed. Thanks."

Amy fell into line. "I was coming to Bristol anyway. Thought I'd like to see the progress here." She turned to the homeowner, surprised anew at how such a young person could be so wealthy. "It's coming along, isn't it?" she tried, giving the woman an encouraging grin. "You getting excited?"

Mrs. Clarkson gave Amy a bored look. "There's a lot still to do." Then, distracted by the siding samples, she turned to Moira. "Are those the colors?"

Amy nodded briefly. "Well, I best get going. Enjoy." She moved back across the porch, trying hard not to run.

Creeping along 24, finally crossing the Mount Hope bridge, she was still simmering. The traffic was thick and slow, giving her too much time to stew in her own juices, too much time to play it over in her mind—Graham's careless planning, Moira's bullish directives, that young owner's rude tone and carefully trimmed eyebrows. *They aren't my clients*, Amy fumed to herself, hating the subordinate role she'd had to play in this dance, at a site where she'd once been a guest. But she knew, deep down, that Graham's work, the Clarksons' satisfaction, paid her bills. And it worried her, deep down, the fragility of it all.

It took time to let it go, shake off the irritation. Midafternoon, Amy returned to her desk, struggling to find the flow. Each new sentence, as if carved from a flawed rock, stood uneven and coarse. She backspaced and deleted, scrolled through entire paragraphs and started again, losing sight of each detail as quickly as it came to mind. Edith's laugh: gone. Edith's skirt: gone. The wooden house: way past gone.

At seven o'clock, she deleted the last anemic sentences from the screen, blaming all the interruptions, hating her life. By eight she'd inhaled a bowl of cereal and was dozing on the couch over a rerun of *Law and Order*, Haps puttering in his sleep by her side.

"You awake?" Graham was whispering, tiptoeing sock-foot across the wooden floor, hoping she wasn't.

"Yup." She opened her eyes.

"I'm home."

"I see that."

Haps sniffed loudly, sensing the salty presence in the room, and ambled to his feet.

"Hey, bud."

She watched as Graham stroked the dog's ears.

"There was a carton. . ." he said.

"I delivered it."

"Wow." He tried for an element of surprised cheer. "You didn't have to do that. Thanks," he added lamely.

She sat up, rubbing her eyes. "Turns out I did."

"Well . . . thanks."

She took her empty bowl to the kitchen, leaving it in the sink. "Night."

"The sail was terrific," he told her back.

"Terrific."

"Perfect wind." Then, when she didn't respond, "You going to bed?"

She left him to figure that one out as she climbed the stairs. "Haps needs to go out."

"Amy!"

The command held her there.

"I'm sorry!" he said. "Is that what you're waiting for?" He stood there, hands hanging loose by his side, his sunburned face gleaming in the light of the television.

She pondered the question. "Yes. I guess I was. Because that probably means you won't pull that shit on me again."

"Wow. You are pissed. She is pissed," he informed the dog.

What he resembled just then, what she saw, was an adolescent, not a man with dementia, and she felt heavy with the job of adult, angry at his artful irresponsibility. "Graham, if this is you being thoughtless, leaving your little errands for me to run while you duck out to play, then fuck you. I've got work of my own."

He looked blankly at her.

Cruelty shot up from the soles of her feet. "And if it's you being forgetful? If this is what it's going to look like? I gotta tell you, it's not cute."

A tremor of recognition tightened his face. Before he could respond, she turned, leaving him in the half light.

Upstairs in the bathroom, she locked herself in, still shaking with fury. The face in the mirror was pink with anger, and the eyes staring back venomously dark.

Amy recalled a *Nature* program she'd seen on television some years earlier. It had been about rats and how they survived, living on the edges of the human environment, scuttling about, often unseen, eking out their own needs from the excesses of the dominant culture. But when they were cornered—Amy remembered viscerally the video of this, just how vicious they looked—rats would leap out, teeth and claws bared, flying straight for the jugular.

She cupped some cool water into her palms, trying to rinse the heat from her cheeks.

It wouldn't get easier. She knew that. And reacting in astonished outrage wasn't going to change a thing. Her once useful marital tool kit, stocked with a variety of handy responses to her many small, wifely grievances now seemed entirely inadequate. She'd perfected indignance, self-pity, escapes to the garden, and forays into her writing, but even these would not suffice now. No, in the face of Graham's pending madness she'd have to find a sturdier, more appropriate set of reflexes.

She dabbed her face with a towel and stood for a moment, blowing out a smooth, protracted sigh. But as she struggled for composure, worries sharp as tacks penetrated her thoughts. *I'm only fifty,* she realized in panic. *What will I do for health insurance? How much is there in his retirement account? How will we manage?* Then all the other little mysteries that Graham had kept so decidedly within his domain—the boiler, their internet provider, the power switch for the water wall, the deed for the house in Sri Lanka, the maintenance schedule of their cars, those details Amy had happily left to him to manage—assembled on the horizon as an invading hoard.

She'd need to take on all this, too, she realized solemnly. And in the course of all that, she'd need to try to love him.

# EIGHT

Almost every day lately, she did or said something she regretted. Jumpy when someone entered the room, stony-faced when someone smiled, Amy watched herself becoming critical, often impatient, not the person she wanted to be at all. The writing was slow going, each word harder to locate, the assembled sentences clunky, like a pile of broken chalk. Some mornings she woke very early, hoping the still of the house would permit her the freedom to flow with creativity. But most times, the electric silence of predawn only rang in her ears, and she'd find herself out in the garden instead, seeking accomplishment in deadheading flowers and pulling weeds. Her weekly newspaper column took days to produce, the last one dangerously close to a pretentious study of the color blue.

Physical exertion became a welcome distraction. She spent an afternoon upturning a perfectly active compost heap and replanting a large azalea, happy with the resulting ache in her back. She went alone on a lengthy hike along Sconticut Neck out to the West Island Town Beach. Many mornings she took Haps on the longer route at a quicker pace.

Maybe it was the Vitamin D, maybe the regenerative power of sleep, but one morning, not seemingly different than the others, Amy awoke refreshed. As she sat at her laptop, a voice came to her in a narrative style similar to Edith's, declarative, immediate, unembroidered, and she was able to complete the piece on Edith Roosevelt. She sent it to Ella, fairly sure. Finally, the short chapter seemed almost flawless, but in the way a new baby is, at terrific cost, leaving her doubting she'd ever manage another.

Most of the time Amy knew it wasn't anyone's fault, certainly not Graham's, or even Moira's, but she wished they would both go away, wished even more that she could.

It came as a strange relief, then, when Alice phoned.

Weeks earlier, her sister had scheduled a walk-though of their parents' home in Providence with a local antiques dealer, convinced there was some cash to be made from the many pieces no one in the family wanted. It hadn't been a priority for Amy. Graham had refused to allow any of her parents' "brown old tat" into their home and both of her children had shown a firm, if polite, disinterest. Amy had begged off this particular task, weary by then of all the moves and distractions of the previous six months. But Alice had been determined, horrified at the thought of leaving ready money on the table. "Inefficient" was the term she'd used. So Alice had taken it on herself to accompany the dealer on the walk-though and negotiate the optimal selling price. Except, now, of course, too busy to make the trip, Alice needed Amy to go instead.

"What time will you be back?" Graham asked when she informed him of her plans. Already he'd wanted to know why she was going *that* day (couldn't it be *another* day?), and for the second time he remarked on Alice's tendency to make commitments she rarely kept, as if her sister's unreliability were some fault of Amy's. As she gathered her bag and keys, he peppered her every move with questions: What? When? Where? How?

The only question he didn't ask was Why?" Graham understood without asking why Amy should be saddled with the antiques venture. His wife had long been the person in the family to handle these invisible, unpaid jobs, something her accepted status as the unemployed one had always earned her, with scant regard for the time they took. What he may not have fully understood, although Amy knew keenly, was that she'd often welcomed such tasks; however resentful she felt, she also secretly prided herself on being the thoughtful one, the one who kept everyone else's show on the road.

"This shouldn't take long. I should be back by midafternoon." She said it lightly, trying to conceal the impatience she felt, her eagerness to be off.

"Well, I hope it's worth it," he said.

"Me too!" She smiled and slipped quickly from the house.

Growing up, Amy had only ever known one family home. Her parents, through prudence, hard work, and the invisible flow of generational, middle-class good fortune, had moved into the four-bedroom colonial before she was born. Her childhood had been entirely encased by the house, set in the leafy enclave of Providence's East End with its brick sidewalks and steep inclines, the interlocking campuses and youthful, student vibe. Even in the last year, since moving her mother from the building, and after emptying it of every personal artifact but what Alice insisted were valuable antiques, Amy still felt a warmth for the place, as if walking in the back door, she'd find her mother correcting eighth grade math quizzes on the kitchen table, the ceramic cookie jar on the counter with a handful of Fig Newtons inside. Now, the property on Arnold Street was about to be the home of another young family—hopefully, anyway. Amy's thoughts flashed forward to the scheduled closing date after Labor Day. But Amy still had a proprietary fondness for the place. Still the house spoke to her, gutted, lonely, but waiting with love.

Driving up the street, Amy saw who she assumed was the dealer, already standing out front. The woman was tall and middle-aged, wearing a tight, navy skirt and unfortunately high heels. It gave Amy a rush of empathy.

"I'm early," the woman insisted as Amy hastened toward her. "Don't mind me." She flashed a hand, clunky with jewelry.

Amy didn't. As she opened the front door and let them both inside, her focus was on the stuffiness of the house. Traces of her mother's scent still permeated the downstairs, and dust motes flickered around them on the still air. She opened some windows as they walked from room to room, impressed again at the stock of elegant pieces her parents had inherited, loved with lemon oil over the years. Every room contained something of beauty, each item resonating with story. Amy's heart lifted at being back in their presence. *And*, she quietly acknowledged to herself, *Alice was savvy to insist on getting it all appraised.*

But the large woman, having oohed and ahhhed with appropriate regard, was interested in only a small selection of what was there. "I'll take the four-poster, the twin brass beds, and the dining table set." It sounded more like an assertion than an offer. "And I like the inlaid desk—that's nice," she added, almost as an afterthought. "Say, two thousand?" Her eyes glimmered like shiny agates.

Amy guessed she was being lowballed. Hearing Alice's outrage complaining inside her head, she tried to haggle. "That's it?" she managed, but haggling wasn't her strong suit.

"I think so, yes." The dealer smiled benevolently, as if regretful she couldn't do more.

Feeling cornered, all Amy could think about was having to come back, to meet the movers. "Will you take them off the premises today?"

"Would that be a deal, then?" the eager dealer shot back too quickly.

*Ahh, she's negotiating!* "If you can be out of here before two," Amy asserted. It was a silly condition, one that did little to improve her small winnings, but when the woman nodded and made a hasty phone call to arrange the move, Amy added another. "Would you take it all?" She was thinking now about the furniture that was left, the remaining antiques, like unchosen orphans, standing bereft in each room, yet another trip to offload these items, an extra job she didn't need.

The woman stared back as if she were dealing with an idiot.

"For two thousand," Amy clarified. "Everything."

With hardly a wobble, even in those spikey shoes, the woman considered the offer. "Bring the large truck," she told the person on the phone.

The van was loaded, and the woman left, her heels clicking like a hammer gun down the sidewalk. Amy tucked the check into her pocket and retreated inside.

Her mother's writing desk and her father's rocking chair beamed back at her from the front hall. Amy glowed, giddy with the results of her negotiations. At the last moment, she'd decided to keep these two pieces for herself, and the antiques dealer had acquiesced with barely a shrug, smug in her own shrewd dealmaking. Here were the rewards of showing up, Amy realized, of being clear about what she wanted. She'd take the pieces home with her when she came back on closing day, knowing that task, too, would be hers alone. Then, Amy imagined happily, she'd put the desk and chair into her new study, no business of anyone's but hers.

Relaxed at last, Amy carried the ladder-back rocking chair into the back yard and sank into its rickety embrace. In their youth, her father had railed against the girls rocking in it. "It's a Queen Ann," he'd explained solemnly, something that had held little meaning then or later. When they'd become old enough to sit in it "more responsibly," Amy had discovered the chair was, in fact, rather uncomfortable, the broken strands of its rush seat often sticking into the soft underside of her thighs, but it was perfectly sturdy. Defiantly now, Amy pushed back in the chair, feeling it creak in protest. She pushed harder, setting up a regular rhythm, back and forth, digging a groove into the lawn.

It was a relief, being there on her own. Even with the occasional sound of cars passing out front, the shrill whir of a siren piercing the city below, Amy felt hidden from the world, like a hermit in a shrouded corner of a wide wood, far from the bustle of civilization. Mostly, she knew, it was a particular escape she was feeling—free from the daily frustration of Graham's uneasy moods. Amy lifted her chin, pressing her head back against the wooden slats. Oh, if she could just leave it all behind, return to this place where she was the child, with little responsibility but to finish her homework, complete her few weekly chores.

A robin swept down from the neighbor's tree, stepping toward her across the small lawn.

"Hello, fatso," she told him. "You live here now?"

The robin stared back, undisturbed by the human voice. Then he carried on, poking gingerly into the grass.

A year ago in spring, Amy's mother had sat just in this place, on a similarly warm and peaceful day. Although diminished by poor health, Julia had been able to sit outside and direct Amy, rather bossily, as Amy recalled, as to where she wanted the annuals to go. Bright orange begonia and Cambridge Blue lobelia were Julia's flowers of choice, and Amy had dutifully obliged, hopping from one place to the next, digging each little hole in sets of three and five, sprinkling in a shake of Osmacote before filling each hole with water, then plopping in the plants and pushing the earth back firmly in around their roots. There'd been a robin in attendance that day, too, Amy remembered, hopping after her, waiting to see what the softened earth would produce.

The joy of that bright afternoon almost stung. Amy loved pleasing her mother, almost as much as she loved the smell of the soil, the delight the new circle of color had brought them both. Now, she crumpled with the pain of it. She squeezed her eyes and mouth tight, fearing the cold surge of sadness welling up inside. A deep frown creased her forehead, and her lips began to tremble. The tears spilled out and for some lost minutes, Amy sobbed.

*You're going to be fine,* she heard eventually. *You got your work, you'll be fine.* It was Julia's formula, as if the Protestant work ethic were the cure for everything, and the voice was as vivid as if her mother had been there with her. Scolded and reassured, wrapped in a remembered tenderness, Amy wiped her face and rose to go.

The drive home was a long one. Cars competed angrily for vanishing openings, desperate to make good time. Amy held the middle lane, sticking slavishly to the speed limit. She was obstinate with sadness, in no hurry to get home.

Just as Amy collapsed onto the couch in the living room, her phone went, as if on cue.

"So, how did it go?" Alice. Not even a hello.

"They took the lot," Amy told her.

"Wow! And . . . ?"

"That's it," Amy said. "Everything's gone." She didn't expand.

"And how much did we *get*?" Amy could hear her sister already congratulating herself on her shrewd insistence to sell.

"Two thousand," Amy replied.

The silence was huge.

"Ahh." Alice said. "For *everything*?"

Amy toyed with a sarcastic response but refrained. "The house is finally empty," she said instead. "We are done, Alice."

"We're back!"

Amy heard the door slam in the kitchen. Haps wagged into the room, pouncing onto the couch next to her. "Graham and Haps are here."

"Well, okay, then," Alice said, clearly reluctant to let the matter rest. "Sounds like you'd better look after that husband of yours." Then, as if she couldn't resist, she added, "I suppose you did your best."

The comment hit Amy with a slap, and she clenched her jaw in silence.

"So . . . that's it, then," Alice said. "Good job, I guess. I'll let you go. Bye bye for now." The cadence was lilting, carefree.

"Bye, Alice." Amy nestled her face into Haps's soft fur.

"That's a pretty scene." Graham stood in the living room door, his height filling the frame. "Looks like you made it through the day." He sat next to them, patting the dog's rump. "My friend here decided it was time for a walk and took us a way we never go. I let Haps lead the way. Which was delightful." Graham's hand found Amy's in the fur. "And I walk in, and here on the couch in the living room is my lovely wife, waiting for me."

She wanted to weep, his good cheer, his obliviousness to her mood, and she wondered, as she was beginning to do more frequently lately, whether his oblivion was just typical man or the creeping sign of his disease. She forced a smile, returning the gentle squeeze of his hand. Maybe the trick, what she would have to learn in this marriage of hers, was compassion. At times of disappointment, rebelling inwardly at having to produce a semblance of love, maybe compassion would do. She could work on that.

Later that night, when Graham's hand slid across her waist and his penis prodded at her thigh, Amy had her chance. Initially, momentarily, she'd considered feigning sleep. The day'd been too full, had lasted too long. But lying there, his breath hot on her back, her conscience rattled in objection. She couldn't do it, couldn't reject him. Graham was losing so much already, and she wanted to please him, knew he needed to please her.

"Mmmm," she murmured tentatively. His thumb grazed a breast, and she shifted to face him. Pressing her lips to his neck she ran a finger along his collarbone. "You're awake," she said lightly.

"I am." She could hear his grin. "How did you know?"

"Just a notion . . ."

His arms wrapped around her, tightening her body to his, and she felt his knee nudging its way between hers. They were in this now, and Amy prayed he'd take it slowly, giving her time to warm up.

In thirty years, their lovemaking had explored every variety on the spectrum—from hot and stupid to cold and calculating, bored and efficient to practiced and elegant. They'd been outrageous and indulgent, emotional and lighthearted, in the course of which Amy had even learned to give orders when warranted: *Wait. Go down on me. Hurry up. Make it last.*

Tonight, though, she couldn't tell him, didn't want to instruct. She wanted to be known. She wanted to be brought to the edge, wordlessly, to have him unlock all that had bottled up within her as he'd once done so effortlessly. She widened her legs, opening herself, hoping for the magic to begin.

Consciousness was what intervened. Despite the enticing film of sweat pooling between them, and the deep earthy smell of their embrace, in spite of his knowing touch and the hiccups of desire that bumped along her clitoris and nipples, she couldn't sustain any momentum. She was thinking too hard.

In the end, just as his rhythm signaled the final lap, the mental effort of caring for this man intruded, and she fell behind. It was a choice, between going along or not, between faking orgasm or speaking up for her needs, and the former just seemed kinder.

# NINE

*ow you're cooking!* Ella's email was short and to the point. She'd obviously read chapter one and seen the photographs and designs from Cuttyhunk. *Looks like the three of you are going to be a team! Keep up the good work!*

Amy smiled as she put away her phone. She and Zach had been waiting in the car for Sandy to emerge, and finally their partner was climbing into the front seat.

"Christ! What kind of a person begins the day with an 8:30 a.m. appointment?!" Balancing her travel mug between her knees, Sandy swung to attach her seat belt.

"Morning, sunshine." From the back seat, Zach's voice was sunny, teasing.

Sandy shot him a dark look. "Oh God—another morning person." She dropped her bag at her feet. "Already I'm outnumbered."

"You are," he said amiably.

"So, you all set?" Amy glanced over at her passenger, making sure. Everything about Sandy jittered with haste and dash, the loose jersey still sloped off a shoulder, a bra strap grinning at the world. Only two cool, clear ribbons of eyeliner were polished and in place.

"Notebook, pencils. Caffeine. All good." Sandy took a swig of coffee and settled back. "So, where to today, Jeeves?"

Amy checked the rearview mirror before pulling out. "Providence, Rhode Island. Home of one Mariann Kingsley."

"Remind us," Zach prompted, leaning forward in his seat.

"Dr. Mariann Kingsley," Amy added. "Lives on the East Side, near RISD, in a pretty upscale neighborhood, in an otherwise plain-looking Georgian. But in the back yard—well, you'll see. The garden's really an extraordinary design, well hidden from the road, with an unusual approach. You literally walk down into it." Even speaking to the air, her focus on the road, Amy felt her enthusiasm rise.

"Sounds fun." Zach maintained his cheery tone. "Eh, San?"

"And what's she like?" Sandy asked, not stifling a yawn.

"Friendly, accommodating. We didn't speak much over the phone. I just told her about the project, said we'd like to include her garden in the book." Amy took the ramp onto the highway, waited to merge into the ribbons of vehicles.

"I thought you knew her." Sandy was still grouchy.

"My mother did," Amy corrected. "They were neighbors. I went on a garden tour there once. Years ago. As I recall, Dr. Kingsley was pleasant, soft spoken." Amy laughed, realizing. "Well, she's a thera-pist. I guess she would have to be."

"Sounds very boring." Sandy leaned her head back, closing her eyes.

"Except she built this bizarre garden," Amy said, persisting. A detail caught in her memory. "And wore very expensive shoes."

Sandy grunted. "Well, the shoes—now there's a real hook!"

"How does she qualify as unique, then?" Zach zeroed in on their mission. "Unique enough for the book, I mean."

It was a good question, the kind she'd come to expect from Zach, now hovering by her right shoulder. She wanted to give him a convincing answer. But in truth, Amy wasn't sure, Superficially, Mariann was like many professional women of a certain age, innocu-ous enough with their low voices, pale apparel, and careful calendars.

Still, underneath that middling appearance, Dr. Kingsley hinted of someone worth investigating, too ordinary to be the designer of such a zany garden for there not to be more to the story. Amy caught Zach's eyes in the mirror, his brows arched as he awaited her reply. "You'll see," she said, hoping she was right.

Sandy snorted. "Unique in the sense that she's different from Edith Roosevelt?" It was the first sign of good humor from her, and the atmosphere in the car lit up with it.

"Well, that's not hard!" Zach agreed, laughing.

Amy nodded. "Edith's pretty unique."

"Yeah—you sure can pick 'em," Sandy ribbed. "Anyway," she added, "It's your gas money."

Amy wasn't put off by the teasing. As tensed as she'd been preparing for their visit, she was excited to be on the road again. The day was shirtsleeve-warm, the air fresh and clean after an overnight driving rain. At least for the next several hours, it would remain quietly overcast, the optimal conditions for an outdoor interview and the perfect sky for sharp, colorful photographs. Zach—the one Ella had first described as being so difficult—was proving just the opposite. Amy found herself looking forward to being in his company; that morning she'd been mildly more aware of her appearance as she dressed for their outing. And Sandy, although high maintenance, frequently needling with pointed questions or cynical comments, could be counted on, ultimately, to show up and produce.

"Team Amy" is what Graham had jokingly called them earlier that morning. When he'd turned over in bed, still soft and warm, his hair unruly, watching as she dressed, he'd questioned the early departure.

"We've got an eight-thirty appointment," she'd whispered, unraveling his fingers from her blouse. "Eight-thirty a.m. sharp."

"Oooo. Sharp." He grinned. "Very impressive." His hand reached for a standing leg, not wanting to let go. "And is 'Team Amy' ready for the world today?"

It was playful, and she liked it. Almost as much as she liked having a day's work ahead, another chapter to wrap her thoughts around.

"We are." She held his head in her palms and kissed him on the forehead, backing away from the bed. "And I'll be back before lunch."

"Indeed," he said, twitching an eyebrow.

"And will you be here when I get back?" It was a throwaway line, just a way of saying she cared.

He chuckled. "Where would I go? I work here, you know."

Amy heard just the tinge of something, self-pity maybe, but let it go. "I know," she said. "So, good. I'll see you in a few hours."

And she was off, the car full of gas, her expectations high.

Dr. Kingsley answered the front door some unhurried moments after the bell. Quietly attractive, with her blonde, Boston bob and defined jawline, Mariann Kingsley was much as Amy remembered. In linen trousers and a crisp, lilac shirt, a lilac cotton sweater tied around her shoulders, she looked the kind of fit, measured woman who'd picked up jogging in her forties and never stopped. Amy held out her hand.

"Hi," she said. "Amy James," she added, stupidly.

"Hello. Of course." Warm smile, eyes taking in Zach and Sandy.

"And these are my colleagues, Sandy Ionella and Zach Markham." Amy stepped aside, to allow for handshakes all round. In the transfer, she noticed Sandy's eyes instinctively checking the shoes, and couldn't help but look herself: snakeskin Jimmie Choo ballerina flats. Bingo.

"You're right on time, which is perfect," Mariann said.

"We were warned," Sandy only half-joked, pulling her eyes from the footwear.

Mariann's eyebrow danced. "Ahh . . ."

Zach corrected smoothly. "Mornings are good." He gave the doctor an appreciative handshake. "This is such a great background," he added, appraising the classical doorframe behind her, the elegant fanlight over it. "Would you mind if I did just a head-and-shoulder shot before we go to the garden?" He held his hands up, thumbs at right angles to his fingers.

Mariann squared her shoulders slightly, standing taller. "I'd rather you not," she said pleasantly, pulling the door shut behind her. And then, just as smoothly, "Let's go around the side way, shall we?"

Amy shot a look inside before turning to follow. She'd been distracted by a partial view of the interior, with its spacious, high-ceilinged area, stamped with a large, pale blue Persian rug, a curved stairway at the rear, tall windows behind. It would have been nice to have a peek into the inner sanctum, but Amy nodded obligingly. "We're following you."

Their hostess slipped gracefully down the front steps ahead of them, turning as she spoke. "I'm glad to see you all, you know. I just hope I've planned enough time to give you what you want this morning."

Zach was cute, not cowed by her first refusal. "We're pretty good at getting what we need. Just point us in the right direction and we can take it from there." He pulled his camera out of its case as they walked, checking the sky once as they rounded the corner of the building. Sandy tromped closely behind Dr. Kingsley, and Amy pulled up the rear, trying to remember this walkway from her visit years ago.

A large smoke bush had filled out with bright purple leaves. Swirls of new hosta and tendrils of lacy fern prickled up around the slate walkway. Their route was crowded with vegetation, and the scent of honeysuckle perfumed the air.

"Just watch your step here," Mariann held back some branches of forsythia overreaching the path. "I haven't done the pruning I should." She let Sandy and Zach pass by, stepping in next to Amy. It was a deft maneuver, and Amy sensed she was being zeroed in on.

"Actually, I've been thinking a lot about this meeting since we spoke on the phone," Mariann confessed. "Even took a look at your first book,' she admitted, a sly grin hovering on her upper lip. "Which was really a joy, by the way." She sounded almost surprised, something that Amy heard and tucked away. "How did you happen upon this latest project?"

Clearly, Dr. Kingsley was trying to set the narrative for this interview, keeping the focus on Amy and off herself. Like shutting the door to the house, the doctor was obviously adept at concealing her own story while plumbing the lives of others. Maybe therapists just did that automatically, Amy reasoned generously. They had their warming-up lines ready, knew all the icebreakers by heart. However firm and gentle Mariann Kingsley's manner, though, Amy cautioned herself, it was up to her to find a way in.

She smiled, lifting a palm with a shrug. "It just came to me," she said, obligingly. "Partly I've done enough writing about my own garden—I still do that for the paper. And I wanted to take on something . . . deeper. Something involving the people who do gardens." She laughed, self-conscious. "If you can call garden writing 'deep.'"

Mariann's gaze was steady, enigmatic. "I guess that's what you'll find out," she said.

Amy caught the tone. There was a challenge to it, superior, and Amy struggled with her own familiar insecurities. Amy returned the look. "I'm a writer," she said to the doctor, more assertive than she felt. "It's all about finding out."

They had emerged out of the barrier of bushes, onto the edge of a wide, perfect lawn. It stretched green and flat behind the whole of the house, to the stockade fence way at the far perimeter. At first pass, it looked like there was nothing at all to see. But on closer look, right at the center of the broad, verdant stretch, lay a low, flat stripe of bright color—dark reds and deep purples—like LEGO bricks laid end to end. And as they approached, the stripe widened into a rectangle, a deep shoe-box of color, spilling inward like an inverted pyramid. They had arrived at Mariann's garden.

It was set entirely below ground, with stairs carved into the four corners of the large hole taking the visitor down to a central point, a postage stamp of grass some eight feet lower. Carefully, they walked single-file down the earthen steps and stood back-to-back on the small lawn. Quadrangles of blossom loomed up around them: giant hyssop, blue mountain mint, jewels of geum and Sweet William. Clumps of emerging day lilies, Black Mondo Grass, green mounds of phlox, not yet flowered but strong-stemmed and bulky, rose up on all sides, magically not keeling over from their precarious foundation on the graduated terrace. On the uppermost tier, flaming red poppies and dark purple delphiniums stood guard. It was as if Mother Nature had opened her womb.

"Wow," Sandy managed. "Talk about being in over your head."

"Yeah. This is incredible," Zach agreed.

"It's even better than I remembered," Amy said to no one in particular.

Mariann smiled graciously. "So . . . I guess you can take it from here?" She dipped her head at Zach, her eyes bright with delight.

"We can," he confirmed.

Sandy and Zach peeled off, onto their respective assignments. Sandy pulled out her notebook and pencils and walked to the bank on their left. With alternatively rapid strokes and precise, careful lines, she began sketching the first of four sides, lost in inventory. Zach crossed to a far set of steps, and laying himself on his back, his camera fixed to his face, let the blossoms spill over him. Left on their own, Mariann led Amy to the small gardening bench at the vortex of the space and took a seat. She watched her guests with a satisfied interest.

Amy positioned herself at the other end of the bench, reaching into her bag for her recording equipment. Mariann placed a hand to stop her.

"I know you mentioned taping this, but I'd rather you didn't." Again with the inscrutable smile and gentle touch. "I have a story to tell you, but it really needs to be in my own time, my own way,"

Amy was surprised, not a little irked. "You needn't be worried by this," she said, indicating the small device. "I just want to make sure I don't misrepresent what you say, that I don't forget some telling details."

Mariann dismissed her with a small shake of the head. "No. I really prefer you don't."

Amy took a moment, finally deciding to let it go. It felt like a concession, a big one, and Amy struggled to present a gracious smile. "Okay," she agreed. "I'll try to pay close attention."

"Good," Mariann replied, almost hmmphing in victory. "Hopefully I'll be clear and you'll be able to retain the gist of things."

Amy wanted to remind the counselor that writers brought their own perspective to the process, that she wasn't here simply to take dictation, but she refrained from doing so. False humility, she told herself, would get her further. She settled back against the bench and started with her first prompt. "Maybe you could begin by telling me how you chose this . . . style of garden—"

But Mariann interrupted. "Anyway, if you get it wrong, or forget what I say, then I'll tell you. Presumably, I get to review the thing before you head to the printer."

The comment threw her, and unease bubbled deep in Amy's gut. No way would Amy's editor agree to this, and Mariann Kingsley knew it. Amy'd already told her how the process would go, tape recorder, lack of draft review and all. She stared at the woman's lavender bodice, Zach and Sandy poring ecstatically over the tiers of blossoms behind her. The emergence of conflict at this stage felt like a power play, some kind of deliberate bait and switch.

Trying for the same measured voice, Amy responded slowly. "In fact, no. That's not how I work." She looked back at the other woman, holding her gaze.

Mariann kept her cool. After what felt like forever, she finally spoke. "Well, we can just sit here, if you prefer," she said evenly.

What the hell was going on? Alarm shuddered inside Amy. Suddenly, she disliked everything about Mariann Kingsley. Hated the muted clothing, the unoriginal haircut. She recoiled at the trim waist and tailored fingernails, the effortlessly upright posture. Mostly, what Amy resented was the regal self-assuredness, the woman who made a life's work wallowing in the secrets of others. She was tempted to stand up and bolt.

Just then, Sandy looked up from her notebook, flashing Amy a satisfied thumbs-up.

Amy inhaled deeply, trying to slow the hammering in her chest. "Why did you agree to be in the book?" she asked finally, surprising herself with the question.

Mariann's eyes sparkled, wary of being played.

"I mean, it's a book about women who garden," Amy continued. "What of this is so troubling?" The comment hung in the air, as simple as the fragrance of peony blossoms.

Mariann licked at her bottom lip and closed her mouth. She looked down at her hands, stroking an index finger with her thumb.

Amy could see the thoughts piling up in the woman's mind and tried again. "I've come to think that people—women, mostly— garden for a whole range of reasons. And they're interesting reasons, that say something about who these people are, what they value." Amy cleared her throat, giving time for a response. When she got none, she continued. "Sometimes, it's simply for show, not really worth investigating. But some gardens are extraordinary, really worth writing a book about."

Mariann remained still, but her eyes were engaged now.

Amy kept talking, offering Mariann something of herself. "My garden at home is almost that special. People like coming there. Not just to see me or my husband. Not even just to see his spell-binding design of a house." Amy fluttered her fingers, like a deaf person's applause. "He's an architect," Amy added, almost rolling her eyes. "Quite a well-known one. But I know—in the last few years, anyway—folks come for the garden. There's something about it that welcomes people. Makes them feel good."

Mariann was watching her closely now, waiting for the punchline.

"I think it's for a lot of reasons. Color, texture, enough repetition. Always it's changing, each new week a different plant or combination of plants ready to take center stage. Viewers trust there'll be some-thing beautiful to see, that they won't be confronted with a fading patch of . . . I don't know . . . wasted hyacinths or the papery stems of dying tulips. There's always something else emerging to focus on, promise in the passing of seasons. You know?"

Mariann nodded. "Of course I do."

"Of course you do." Amy paused, thinking about her borders back home. "But . . . and I've been thinking about this a lot . . . I think what people see in my garden is something, frankly, I don't see anywhere else in my life, and that's boldness. My garden is unapolo-getically bountiful. Indulgent. Daring, sometimes. Love a plant? I put it everywhere. Fancy an off note? in it goes, however discordant. And because I'm brave with it, things just sizzle. And viewers sense this. They're entertained. Willing to suspend their disbelief, like an audience at the theatre."

Amy could see Mariann the professional analyzing everything she'd just said. So she summed up, getting back on point. "I've written about my own garden, though, and I'm not interested in writing about myself." She caught the corner of a smile at the edge of Mariann's lips, and thought she sensed a veil lifting. "But . . ." Amy shrugged, leaning in toward the other woman. "I do want to explore what it is that's so seductive about *other* gardens. Extraordinary ones. Like yours. I want to show the power that owning land gives certain women. Women like you."

Having steered the conversation back in Mariann's direction, Amy waited to see what would happen. Slowly, almost imperceptibly, the doctor pressed her shoulders against the bench, as if her whole body were trying to pull away. Maybe unconsciously, she drew in her fingers, now two tight fists in her lap. It was no good. Something was keeping her silent, and Amy was at a loss to know how to proceed.

She looked to see where Zach and Sandy were positioned now, how much of their work they'd completed. It would be embarrassing, Amy thought, if she were the only one of the three to have failed in her task. Back in the car, she'd have to have to admit how badly she'd misjudged this interview.

"Over the past year," Mariann began quietly, "strangers started sneaking into this garden."

Amy held her breath.

"We're not open to the public, as you know." Mariann only glanced in Amy's direction, before looking back at her hand. "But individuals find their way here, often early in the morning, sometimes at dusk, to walk down the steps, sit on the bench."

Amy watched her, waiting.

"Because a kind of community has evolved. Here. Because of the garden. And I've come to understand how necessary this place can be. To people like them. Like me."

Amy didn't want to break the spell but needed to understand. "Other gardeners?" she asked softly.

"No," Mariann shook her head. "Other parents." This time her expression was shadowed, as if beseeching Amy to catch up.

But it was a curveball that Amy couldn't field. Her face crinkled with confusion.

Mariann wiped some imagined pollen from her lap, craning her head back for a moment. When she spoke again, her voice was more robust. "For the past year, I've been thinking of finally acknowledging what was happening around me, what was emerging here in this garden." She shuddered with a surprised laugh. "And then I get a phone call from you, out of the blue, saying you're writing a book about women and their gardens, and it seemed . . . " She wove her fingers together making a basket. "Synchronistic. It seemed time." She tutted to herself, shaking her head again. "But I can't trust just anyone. I don't want my story to be simply a garish frill in a collection of unimportant or self-indulgent reflections. Showy ladies who care about status or some such . . ."

Amy smiled. "So far, that's not the plan."

Mariann straightened her shoulders again, apparently believing what she'd heard. "I'm guessing you know what happened."

Amy's mind spun. She didn't. She shook her head.

"You don't know about the garden?" Mariann repeated.

Again, Amy shook her head.

"Oh." Now Mariann was surprised. "I thought that might be why you asked me. Because you already knew."

Amy did her best to show her honesty. "Really, I don't know anything. Except I'd been here once before." Then she added, for total transparency, "Oh, and that you were my mother's neighbor." The thought occurred to her: maybe this was what was behind the doctor's reticence. But the look on Mariann's face suggested something else, something worse. "What is it you thought I knew?"

Mariann sighed, a thin line of resignation and determination sealing her mouth. Delicate wrinkles emerged from her puckered lips. Finally, though, she relaxed, as if somewhere a spigot had opened, and liquid relief was coursing through her arteries. "When we first moved here," she started to explain, "myself and my husband and three children, there was an inground pool here." She unclasped her hands, spreading them out from her lap.

Amy followed the hands, to the plants looming nearby. *Of course.*

"I had just started my practice; my husband worked at a law firm downtown. We had just moved in four days earlier." She shook her head, as if still surprised.

Mariann described cartons of unpacked china, clothes still not hung in the closets. "Four days," she repeated. "It was early September. My two older children had just started at their new schools. The baby was . . ." Here she trailed off. "A baby. I'd hired a local woman to look after him during the day, be there for the kids when school got out." She paused, the look of late summer distant in her eyes. Then she went on.

She'd been at home that afternoon. The kids were all in their suits. The sitter was out there. And she was about to join them. She'd noticed Jonas on the diving board, but just then the phone rang in the kitchen. It was a client of hers, really anxious. She'd lit a cigarette, trying to get him off the phone—all that agitation when the sky was so blue.

Mariann's eyes foreshadowed what was coming, and Amy steeled herself, not wanting to hear the rest.

"So, there was an accident." A muscle twitched by Mariann's lower lip.

She fired the sitter. Closed up the pool, keeping it off limits, even in those hot weeks of September. And when her husband walked the children to school in the morning, she was still in bed, and she couldn't get out. She couldn't get out of her nightdress all day long. She stopped bathing. She couldn't leave the house. And she couldn't, of course, see anyone.

By now, Mariann was no longer looking at Amy. She was back in her recollections, lost to the world.

It took maybe eighteen months for her husband to depart, torn up by the silences and loneliness and fury, and another several before he sued for custody. And she couldn't believe the woman she was now, mooning about the house in a worn muumuu, eating bowls of Kraft Dinner late into the night, silently accepting a world in which her mother had to move in and take charge, the woman being petrified that she'd lose her grandchildren. Mariann just watched as her mother commandeered the kitchen, inserting green back into the family diet, reestablishing the line between homework and television, and she wondered at all that energy.

Then one day, a former colleague came by. Someone must have let her in—Mariann wouldn't have. She saw her standing in the foyer, eyeing the porch off the living room, and she went to speak with her. By the time the colleague had left, Mariann had agreed to let her build an office for two—two therapists. "In the house, in that porch." Mariann pointed toward the lilac side of the house. "And I'd committed to go back to work."

A faint flush graced Mariann's cheeks as she rejoined Amy in the present. "And that, really, is where the story of the garden begins. Or begins again. I got healthy, and I built a garden, where the pool used to be."

Amy held the doctor's gaze, letting the silence say it all. Finally, eyes burning, she shook herself free, and managed a response. "No. I didn't know," she said. She was contemplating the phrase "I'm sorry for your loss," worried that it was a little late, maybe odd, considering she was here because of a child's death, when Mariann cut her off.

"So, is that deep enough for you?"

# TEN

Back at her writing desk, the narrative flew across the screen. Tiers of flowers blossomed on the page, and the quiet, commanding voice of Mariann Kingsley permeated every line. Amy had googled to learn more about the precipitating event, discovering which child had died and how. But weaving through the story, much as Mariann had done, Amy managed to avoid the details, capturing simply the resonance of a child's death embodied in the explosion of living stems and leaves and petals. And, carefully, she evoked the odd club to which Dr. Kingsley had found herself a member, describing the visitor they'd seen when they were leaving Mariann's yard, another mourning parent, a pleasant gentleman in a plaid, short-sleeved shirt, his eyes averted as if to protect their anonymity as much as his own.

Amy regarded a memorial garden as almost heartbreaking, onerous. It made her feel selfish and callous to admit it, but she had a visceral aversion to the notion of endless remembering. But she didn't weigh the piece down with her judgment, fearing it could do Mariann a disservice. Instead, she kept to the miracle of the deep garden and celebrated the surprising creativity that had emerged from one tragic event in this woman's life.

As she completed her first draft, Amy experienced a growing confidence in herself as a writer. She was pleased with chapter two.

"Break time!" Moira unloaded a grocery bag behind her. Cheese, salami, sweet pickles, and thick rolls cluttered the long counter, and deli smells filled the air. Carefully, Amy saved the file and closed her laptop, turning to face the commotion. Graham pulled mayonnaise, mustard and lettuce from the refrigerator, setting out plates, knives, and napkins. A funfair of food. Amy wanted in, ravenous suddenly.

"I'll join you," she said.

"Do!" Moira was surprised, stepping to one side to make room. "I got plenty."

Amy stood, helping herself to a stiff roll, slicing it down the middle and flattening it open. "What's the occasion?"

"We've got another contract!" Moira's whole body radiated.

"Excellent," Amy said, taking a plate.

"But this one will need some careful handling," Moira continued. "Some question about propriety." She sounded so sophisticated, a player now in firm management.

Graham grumbled softly. "I don't think so."

"Why?" Amy reached across for some lettuce. It was the first time in days she'd joined them for a meal, the first time she'd ever seen the least hint of a disagreement. It intrigued her.

"I just don't think it'll be a problem," he said. "They haven't been clients for years now."

Moira eyed him, knifing into the mayonnaise.

"Who?" Amy asked.

"Jamestown Library," he said.

"They're building a new children's wing," Moira added.

"Oh."

Amy layered some pepperoni into the fold, more than was healthy, piecing together the information. "And the propriety? Does this have to do with Dana?" Just asking it pumped dread into Amy's gut. Dana and Lois were friends of theirs, and Dana Faxon, on a pure business front, could also be a formidable foe. "I hope you're not doing some kind of an end run around one of Dana's clients."

"The library was our client, not his. A dozen years ago. And it's me they wanted, not Dana." Graham pulled a beer from the fridge and sat at the table, taking the sub in his fists.

Moira asserted herself, claiming some credit. "I know a person on the board," she told Amy, "their children's librarian, and I suggested to her that theirs was a project we'd like to design: Graham and me. I wasn't thinking about the legality of the thing."

"I don't think it'll be an issue." He pushed a sliver of pickle back into his sub. "Anyway, it's up to the client who they choose, not us, not Dana." He darted a look at Moira, signaling her to end the discussion.

Amy couldn't let it go. "Don't you and Dana have an agreement about that kind of thing?"

"We do, and we're fine." Graham took a large bite.

"Anyway," Moira said. "The non-solicitation doesn't really involve me." She shrugged, her slender shoulders, light with victory. "Still, I feel bad, you know. For Dana."

Amy guessed the girl had missed the point. "It's not just his *feelings*," she said.

Moira ceded, "And money, sure . . ."

Amy stared at her husband, worried. "Is this risky, Gray?"

"I don't think it is!" His words muffled in food.

"'Cause this is no time to get into any legal problems, not now."

*Now* had a meaning, and he shot back, slamming the glass mug back on the table. "Can we talk about something else?!"

Amy froze, watching the spilt beer tremble in little puddles by Graham's fist. She guessed that he was in trouble, caught between his old partner and his new, and that maybe for the first time in his life, Graham was out of his depth. She directed her gaze onto her own plate, poking the curl of lettuce that had managed to escape the roll.

Moira ignored the little outburst. "Anyway, that's why we're celebrating. I signed the Clarksons for a new solarium, and the Jamestown for a new wing of the library. That's two!" She looked at Amy, beaming. "We're on a roll!"

"You are on a roll!" Ella said the next day. "The Roosevelt chapter and now the Providence one?" Ella's enthusiasm barreled down the phone, almost knocking Amy over. "I'm really impressed."

It was only nine in the morning and her agent was already revving.

Amy held the phone, grinning. Hearing Ella's feedback was like a hit of heroin; instantly, intense pleasure flooded her veins.

"So, you loved it? The swimming pool story?"

"It's painful," Ella acknowledged. "And the garden sounds bizarre. But you made it work."

Amy wanted to shout with relief. "And did you like what Sandy and Zach sent in?"

"Everything! Really, we're getting there. Now . . ." The good news delivered, her agent plowed on. "I want you three to get yourselves to Delaware as soon as you can. Mostly, I want to see what you can do with someone a bit more normal for the next chapter."

"Normal?" The word was offensive on many counts.

"Well, traditional, then. The Copeland woman is at least more what one expects of a gardening book, more Abby Rockefeller. Big-moneyed estate. I'm just saying: she's a good counterbalance to the first two ladies. So, get her garden in the can soon. Make it a hat trick."

It all seemed very real suddenly, and for a happy ten minutes, Amy sat at her desk in the kitchen, soaking in the praise and possibilities. The notion of life as a real writer filled her imagination. *Writer*, she thought, dazzled. *I write.*

Much of her life, Amy had grabbed at diversions, dabbling in photography, hunting mushrooms, sewing Halloween costumes, as Graham's triumphs propelled them from one home to the next. Gardening was just the latest hobby, the one that stuck. Then the gardening column happened. Then the collection of them. All of it, she acknowledged, had been supported by his success. Her casual attitude toward earning money, too, was the dubious luxury of his accomplishments.

Writing was the quiet prayer she'd always practiced privately, her way of centering herself against the sudden shifts of family and Graham's career. Now this preparation, done over years with no expectation of fame or fortune, now this was surfacing as an actual way of being. An identity all her own. From what had been just garden journaling at first, pottering about with phrases to best record her changing perennial beds, she'd found herself employed, as if by accident, first as a weekly garden columnist, then the author of a book, a compilation of her most popular columns.

But this latest project, this book felt different, more authentic, deeper. This book gave her voice. Selecting the unique gardens, meeting and understanding other women, realizing her own angle on it all, Alex was creating new meaning in the world. She was a writer.

Pushing back her chair, closing her eyes to the familiarity of the cupboards and counters around her, Amy rolled the images over in her mind. She imagined herself traveling the country on trains, buying coffee at airports, reading to groups of strangers in independent bookstores. Alone in hotel rooms, ordering room service, eating pizza in bed; she saw her future self attending book fairs and conferences, meeting other writers, talking about writing. Writing more. Amy imagined the next book, and the next. Maybe biography, maybe fiction. Never bored. Honing her talents, getting good. At last, getting really good.

Next door, Graham's voice rose from nowhere, staccato and angry. He sounded like he was mid-argument, not giving an inch, and the distraction rattled her mood. Tension and hostility swept through the room, scattering her thoughts like pollen. For a second, she found herself poised forward, trying to listen in. She feared it was Dana on the phone, threatening Graham over some broken agreement, and Amy wanted to rush into Graham's study, get him off the phone before he made more trouble for himself. But it could also be Moira, Amy realized, there in the study with him, speaking so softly Amy couldn't hear.

She stood up, tiptoeing carefully toward the study door. Amy knew she couldn't simply barge in; Graham's study was his sanctuary and his business, professional or otherwise had always been off limits. With Moira's influence tipping the scales, however, Amy wondered whether her husband needed her to intervene. She was trying to think of some excuse for knocking when the study door opened suddenly, and Graham's body nearly crashed into hers.

"Jesus!" he said.

"I was just . . . about to knock," she managed, stepping back.

He gave her a dark look. "Why?"

She hadn't figured that one out. "I was . . . I was just about to put the kettle on," she finished weakly.

Graham sniffed. "The door was closed."

"Yeah." She caught the inference: *You know the rules.*

"So what do you want?" he asked tersely. "Come on." His circling hand indicated he was in a rush. "I've got to speak to Moira about something." He was still agitated, and Amy was frightened she'd make it worse..

It was an opening, though, so she steeled herself. Indicating his office, she said, "Could I talk to you for just a sec?"

Graham cast a quick look in the direction of Moira's end of the house and sighed. "One minute." He stepped back into his study, holding the door as Amy followed him in. He crossed his arms, almost checking his watch and sighed. "What?"

92

"I was thinking . . ." she began unsteadily, "for this new work arrangement to . . . work, that maybe I should take some of the pressure off you . . ."

"What are you talking about?" His confusion was genuine.

"Just . . . I think I should know more about, you know, how the house works, what our finances look like. When bills need paying."

He gave her a blank look.

"There's a lot at stake," she continued quickly, "with your health . . . changing . . . and there's no reason I shouldn't step up a bit. Take over at least some of the *worrying*." She smiled, as if making a joke. It sounded stupid as she said it, and Amy was frustrated at her inability to be clear. *What I want,* she thought frantically, *is to know what's going to happen to me!*

Graham's eyes remained hooded, as if he were casting about for the reason his wife had turned that instant from a tulip to a cactus. Then his gaze cleared, and a cynical smile spread across his face. "Oh, God, that's all I need!" He even laughed. "Now you want me to train *you* to look after *us*?"

Amy recoiled.

"Hey," he shrugged, letting it pass. This time he did look at his watch. "Go for gold. Everything you want to know is pretty much on one flash drive." He pointed to his desk. "Top drawer on the left." Then, leaving the study, he chuckled over his shoulder. "Knock yourself out."

Amy waited, hurt by the sarcasm. But alone in his study, in a rare moment of decisiveness, she walked to his desk and opened the drawer. There were three flash drives there, the labels indecipherable. After a moment's hesitation, she took them all.

Back at her writing desk, Amy struggled to return to her work. This morning she wanted to set up the Delaware garden trip, review the research she'd done on Bess Copeland, keep the happy momentum of her book moving forward. She'd stood the flash drives like dominos at the edge of her desk, not out of sight, but just out of reach. They tugged at her curiosity, but she would save them for later. Anyway, she'd need some real privacy in which to study what was filed inside. Now was neither the time nor place.

It took real effort to clear her mind of all the anxiety. It would be easier, she knew, if she could stop caring about Graham's business. But that wasn't likely, or practical. What she'd really need—what other writers must have in their lives, she guessed—were some better boundaries. A clear commitment to write, and better boundaries.

From Moira's den, the sound of raised voices once more filtered out to the kitchen. Then it came to her. She was also going to have to move. This perfect alcove, the perch she'd claimed for herself, everything else radiating from it, was not the place Amy would learn to concentrate on her own success.

Abruptly, without a second thought, she packed up her desk and left the kitchen.

Upstairs, the guest room looked as if it had been waiting; even the dust motes were suspended in anticipation. Usually abandoned, a placeholder for folks who didn't come anymore, the room sat at the rear of their home, down a long hall from the other bedrooms, with a bathroom of its own. The north-facing eaves kept it cool and dark, and she entered as one would a chapel.

There was a lace runner on the table by the window, spread under a small vase of dried flowers. Setting her supplies on the bed, Amy pulled the side chair up to the table and sat down, trying it out for size. For all the years they'd owned the chair, its seat cushion rich in floral needlepoint—something Graham's grandmother had stitched in the early years of her marriage— Amy doubted she'd ever actually sat in it. Maybe no one had. But it was comfortable, fitting her nicely up to the table's edge. Inspired, she moved the vase to the dresser and folded up the runner, wiping her arm across the surface of the table, removing a faint sheen of dust.

She plugged her laptop into the wall by the table. She would need a desk lamp here, eventually. Maybe even a small throw rug to place below the chair. But as she turned on the computer and it glistened to life, she wakened to the possibilities before her. And the quiet! Looking out the window, she could see the angle of the one streetlight by the edge of their yard, sprouting through tree branches and the top of an ancient rhododendron. No one, save for the possible passing skunk, would see her up here, facing the window, even at night, with her face lit by the screen.

It had been here all along, Amy reflected soberly. Nothing had prevented her from staking claim to this perfect writing space years earlier, nothing but her own lack of confidence. At last, however, with a room of her own, she felt like a professional.

When she descended for lunch, Amy had the house to herself. Moira's and Graham's cars were both gone and Haps had been left on his long leash in the back yard, dozing in a dog-sized dent under a lilac. Indulgently, Amy helped herself to a large salad, crumbling in some feta and taking the time to toast a handful of walnuts in a frying pan. All morning she'd spent successfully negotiating her trip to Delaware with Bess Copeland, Sandy, and Zach, and was luxuriating in the prospect of another outing, another completed chapter, more positive feedback from Ella. The project was turning into exactly the challenge she'd hoped for: eager subjects, enthusiastic colleagues, and an increasingly impressed agent. Most of all, Amy was becoming the person she'd always wanted to be.

By the time she'd consumed her salad, Amy was impatient to spend some time on the flash drives. Bringing an iced coffee upstairs to her new desk, she eagerly inserted the first drive into her laptop.

It was filled exclusively with architectural proposals. Project overviews and site plans, vision statements and community impact assessments. There were floor plans and main evaluations, and more arcane slides too, identifying shadow studies, precedent materiality breakdowns, contextual massing diagrams. They were projects of decades earlier, some of his best work.

Though nothing of informational value—there were no record of current bills or bank accounts—the files gave Amy pause, and she savored afresh her husband's wonderful designs. Who else thought to bring waterfalls into people's living rooms, introduce the sky and its elements into the middle of their bathrooms? Probably the Romans, Amy conceded, certainly there were others. But Graham had managed to merge modern expectations with ancient, natural delights in a way that made his work rare. It certainly made her remember just how special he was, why she'd loved him from the start. Her mind drifted back.

It had been just after they'd moved back to America, a rare few days he'd taken off from his Baltimore assignment, and they'd spent the week camping in the woods on the Delmarva peninsula, close to a site where Graham was bidding on another project. The smell and feel of greenness had saturated her sensibilities. "I'd like to live in a treehouse," she'd opined that day.

"Why not a small forest, growing straight up through each room?" he'd suggested. And that evening, he had designed just such a home. Built of logs, canvas and glass, the little construct was a necklace of cubes within cubes, each hosting an inner courtyard of mid-sized saplings. Like a daisy chain bristling with radiating petals, the swoops of canvas allowed the natural elements to flow inside and out. Every space reverberated with both the movement and stillness of a living glen. Even the front walk, a pimply ribbon of small, smooth stones embedded in concrete, was reminiscent of the river rocks Amy had collected during their hikes. "Thank you, my love," he'd announced, handing her the sketch. "You never cease to inspire." Then, "Keep thinking wild, Amy, it's the only way to go."

She'd been grappling at the time with her own lack of direction. Having followed him from Sri Lanka to Baltimore, she'd still not competed her college degree and felt under pressure from her academic parents to re-enroll. Graham was the one person in her life who seemed unfazed by his young partner's lack of academic accomplishment. "You're a creative talent," he assured her. "Just look what you realize every time you take a photograph or stick your hands in the earth! Anyway, Amy, people like us can't worry so much what other people think."

It was the *people like us* that had comforted her, made her feel special, sanctioned her uncredentialed wavering. Only years later did she realize that Graham had in fact cared desperately what other people thought. After all, he'd managed to build an enviable reputation around his own creative talent, assuming, probably, that it was enough for them both.

Wistfully, Amy removed the first flash drive and inserted the second. This one was closer to the mark, containing dozens of financial files and spreadsheets. There was a rough monthly budget for three and four years earlier, a multi-page Excel file comparing projected social security income if retiring at sixty-two, sixty-six, and seventy. She located only one Visa credit card and one personal bank account, although she knew there should be more. But one small file contained all his account names and passwords, sixty-three different entries from Graham's American Airlines Frequent Flyer program to their auto and home insurance provider account. It was overwhelming, the array, and she decided to copy the file, rather than pursue each account in one sitting. At the end, as the list was organized alphabetically, she found his Vanguard retirement information. Feeling like a trespasser, she navigated her way into this account. What she saw brought instant relief. For all his wild impulses, myriad projects, and radical detours, her husband had saved, after all.

Zip drive three was all pdf's: multi-page mortgage refinancing documents, old insurance claims, an ancient will of his, from before their marriage. There was a record of the Sri Lanka property, and a copy of the deed to their land in Padanaram. By then, she was weary of looking, the fuzzy gray type of the legalese making her dizzy. Promising herself she'd return to the job another time, Amy replaced all three drives in Graham's desk drawer. She wasn't entirely clear on every detail under her husband's purview, but she knew enough to know where to find things. Most importantly, she thought, they wouldn't starve.

Graham waited until that evening before mentioning the empty alcove. "Moving out on me?"

They were seated in the living room, looking for a program to watch. His face was serious over the remote.

"Not yet," she chuckled, trying to keep it light.

Amy hadn't yet told him about how well the book was going, how pleased her agent had been, for some reason wary of overloading him with her success. And although she'd wondered what he would say about moving her computer—and had all kinds of earnest appeals ready to spin if needed—she hadn't found a way to discuss that either.

"I'm right upstairs," she cocked her chin, "in the guest room."

"Where will we put the guests?"

It wasn't a question he'd ever asked, not a concern he'd ever had, and Amy almost said as much. Instead, she shrugged. "Jason's room? Catherine's?"

Graham frowned. "Those are theirs."

He was right: they were, Jason's still half alive with his presence, shelves sagging with college textbooks, some fleeces and shirts hanging in the closet. Liverpool's Fernando Torres still flew across one wall, his solid red kit like a lipstick smear. The room reeked of success and athleticism, a decidedly male quality that kept it so very Jason.

Catherine's room was lighter, softer, with its pale peach walls and off-white trim. Translucent curtains hung in the three windows, floral print tiebacks of light orange and pink creating a lilting swag effect around the perimeter. The room was used only rarely, on Catherine's infrequent trips back east, but it was still hers, and Amy maintained the original décor to keep it that way. The feminine touch was a placeholder of sorts, for the stepdaughter Amy had worked so hard to bring into the fold. Catherine's room was a real option for guests, had been for years.

Amy tried appeasing her husband. "Me working upstairs will mean you and Moira can use the kitchen whenever," she said, pulling her feet up under her on the couch, "Without me disturbing you."

"You don't disturb me." Graham chose a travel program and put down the remote. He sat back and rested his palm on her head, messing with her hair. "Anyway, I like having you around."

"I'm around, hon. I'm always around."

The episode was a tour of Spain, a place she'd never been. She ducked under his arm, shedding the hand, and sat that way, feeling his shoulder against her ear. The guide's voice had an urgency to it, encouraging them in.

"Is it getting to you?" Graham's words drifted warm across her forehead.

"What?" She looked up.

"You know." His fingers drew a circle by his forehead. "Living with this?"

The grayish pink of the Alhambra filled the screen, Moorish and permanent. "Is it getting to *you*?" she asked.

Graham tossed his head back with a humph. "I wake up every morning now, feeling stupider. Every morning." She saw the tremor of his mouth as he spoke. "And sometimes I think the whole world, everyone I speak to, can see it. That Moira suspects something. That the clients wonder where I went."

Too quickly, Amy flicked her hand, dismissing his fears.

But Graham kept speaking. "I think you see me failing, too, and I worry that you won't even miss me, the old me. That you'll just watch as I slip off the rails. That you'll get sick of how I am, who I've become."

Amy's conscience lurched.

"I'm sorry if it's driving you away. I don't want that, Amy."

"Graham, I'm not going anywhere. Really."

Loud cheering exploded from the television: the running of the bulls in Pamplona, and throngs of men in white racing through the narrow streets, the beasts closing in on them from behind. Amy shifted on the couch, wishing one of them, at least, could speak of love. She put her palm on his knee.

"You seemed pretty agitated the other day, at lunch," he reminded her. "Are you angry about the library job?"

"Not at you." She chose her words, thinking back to the overheard phone call. "I don't want there to be any problems, that's all. With Dana. He's an old friend."

"Not so much a friend, these last few years." Graham found her head again, stroking her hair. "But it'll be okay. Just let me work it through with him."

"But Moira's in this now, pushing you . . ."

"I need her right now!" Graham's voice rose and fell. "She'll be fine," he said.

Amy tried to let it go. On the screen, two stately flamenco dancers strutted and lurched in tandem. Amy watched the flowing trail of ruffles on the woman's skirt, wondering at the weight of it, how the woman managed. What Amy wanted was for someone else, beside her, beside Graham, to help them navigate this disease. Someone who understood them both. "Could you tell Dana the truth?"

"Sometime. I promise." Graham laughed a miserable laugh. "Then he'll thank me for leaving."

They stayed together on the couch, touring Seville, Granada, and Barcelona, and Graham relaxed, his wife within reach.

Later, though, when he slept, Amy lay with her eyes open, her mind swimming in discomfort. *He needs me,* she told herself, feeling a revulsion climbing her windpipe. *But what about me? What about what I need?* He snuffled in his sleep, curling like an infant in her direction, and a creeping self-pity tugged at her skin. Every position she tried, first on her left side, then on her right, became too uncomfortable to bear. Finally, she snuck from their bed, crept down the hall and sat at the little desk, the door closed behind her.

Out of habit, she opened her computer and clicked on Google Maps. Their tiny home deep in the bushes and trees of Sri Lanka was only a shiny rectangle of flat roof, but the grainy shot provided a hit of instant escape just the same. The familiar search took her back down the Kandy-Kirimatiya Road, past the edge of their patch of land in Sri Lanka. She moved from view to view, her screen filling with dusty tarmac and aggressive vegetation. Just partially visible in the mist, an occasional concrete dwelling and tea shop appeared in the shots, hanging off the shoulder of road over the steep incline below. Amy shuddered with longing and regret, wary of the emotional dark tunnel she was about to enter.

A sudden blip disrupted the quiet journey. Quickly, guiltily, Amy left the screen and closed her laptop. She reached for her phone and opened her messages, curious to see who it was at this hour. A text from Sandy; the one-liner just read, *Hey, famous writer, fancy a night out this Saturday?* Then a smiley face.

Amy grinned reflexively, relieved by the interruption. It felt like a rare little blast from the past, the kind of note she used to receive from friends over the years, meaning "We should celebrate!" or "Time to bitch!" or sometimes simply "My life's boring me to distraction, what's happening with yours?"

That Sandy would send such a text surprised her. Sandy wasn't that kind of a friend. She and Amy rarely did things together. Still, Amy thought, rereading the message, Sandy *had* organized her surprise party. That's something. And now they'd be traveling together! Maybe they were about to be better friends. Or—the cynical idea crept in there too—maybe Sandy just needed a new drinking buddy.

Whatever! Amy admitted to herself that she could use a laugh. *Sure*, she texted back. *Why not?*

# ELEVEN

Over the years, there had been times of regret. Times that sent her spiraling back to her cinnamon hillside in Kandy, wondering what life might have been like had she stayed. But those weren't all the time, for sure; there were whole months and years when Amy didn't think back at all, preoccupied instead with the responsibilities and routine of her daily existence, inspired with the little hopes and projects right in front of her. And there were special moments too: precious flashes in time when she had been struck with the awareness that maybe this particular instance made it worth the loss, made up for leaving her fertile patch of earth with its exquisite light and rich, red soil, where she'd been so completely, so confidently, happy.

The hour after she'd finally married Graham was one such moment. Hearing his expansive laugh across the Wilsons' wide back lawn and feeling connected to it, vibrating with it, as if through a taught telegraph wire—that had been a blissful interval. And when she brought Jason home for the first time—after his days in the incubator, too tiny and fragile to be trusted into her care—that was another. And maybe a third was the evening Catherine let Amy read her to sleep, the night her stepdaughter had really hugged her for the first time.

Of course, those times were contingent, Amy thought now, and they relied on the presence of others. Those times were less about her own utter joy and more about her relief at having a husband, a son, a stepdaughter. Anyway, Amy mused, gazing at herself in the mirror, she could have had Graham and Jason, even Catherine, to the extent she did, if they'd stayed in Sri Lanka.

She shook her head in disapproval, trying to smooth the lines by her mouth with a genuine smile. She knew that a dash of resentment surfaced every time she felt regret at having surrendered her little tropical farm in exchange for this mature existence in stony New England. She also knew that wallowing in self-pity wasn't healthy. It wasn't pretty either, she recognized, ruffling her fingers through her hair, giving it some bounce.

From now on, Amy told herself, she would try to avoid those little excursions into disappointment and pay more attention to what was going well. Amy forced another smile. It required a mind shift, for sure, keeping herself to the present. She'd have to steer clear of past regrets and change the channel on any fearful projections into the future. Narrowing the focus in that way, her life today could look really quite good. Now, with the writing, with the second chapter done and dusted, she was finally pursuing something of her own, something that mattered, with a kind of purpose and assuredness she hadn't felt in years. She could wallow in a little gratitude for a change.

Amy removed the small, gold hoops from her ears and placed them in her jewelry box, rooting around for the silver danglers instead. The silver ones she rarely wore, too outrageous for her routine comings and goings in simple suburbia. Tonight, she and Sandy were meeting up at Fathom's on Pope's Island for an early dinner. In that company, Amy knew she could be extravagant and still not detract from the garish artwork that hung everywhere from her friend's frame: the shards of metal circling the neck, the plasticine objects ringing the fingers, the feathers floating from the ears. Amy slipped the hooks of each little chandelier through the holes in her earlobes and admired the dance of them by her jaw. The woman in the mirror looked more like the young woman she'd been in the tropics—self-confident and hopeful, decorative and ripe.

"Will you be late?" Graham stood at the back door, watching as she headed for the car.

"What's late?" she teased, kicking back her heel is if frolicking from a stage.

"Forget it." He turned to go back inside.

"No, stop!" she added, laughing, hurrying back to give him another hug. "It's just I rarely make it past ten before falling asleep. So, no . . . I don't expect I'll be late."

"Whatever." He shrugged, kissing her head. "You need your girls' night out."

"Two girls," she reminded him, holding her fingers in a V. "Not exactly a bachelorette party."

"No male strippers then?" He let up a bit, grinning at the thought.

"In New Bedford? God, I hope not."

"Well, have fun." He directed Haps into the back entry.

"I'll try," she said.

She was stopped at the traffic light on Route 6, feeling pretty and frolicsome and her mind did a quick review of her existence. It really *wasn't* a bad life. It was a Saturday evening, and on the pavement to her right a family of four was making its way from Buttonwood Park. The mother was navigating a stroller, appeasing its overtired occupant with some small reward, what looked like an animal cracker, while the toddler arched in defiant complaint. The father carried the older sibling on his shoulders, the girl's pink sneakers cupped in his large, dark hands. Alone in the car, with only herself to consider, Amy sighed in relief.

To be fair, whatever horrors the future might bring, right now she shouldn't complain. For one thing, however grumpy at times, distant at others, Graham had really never stopped her from doing whatever she wanted. Like going out with Sandy on a weekend night or starting the book. He hadn't said no. In fact, he'd expected Amy to follow her passions—just as he'd always done. Now, she acknowledged, even when he might be feeling anxious about his health, maybe nervous at being alone in the house, Graham was as he'd always been. If not actively supportive, he was open-armed, easy.

She drove along Kempton heading toward the harbor, past the small homes, the dregs of a driveway yard sale, a brightly painted housing project. On this soft evening, wearing her special silver earrings, even that pivotal decision to leave Sri Lanka she remembered generously. Graham had made a point of letting Amy decide for herself what to do, whether to go.

"I know you love it here," he said. They'd been climbing the steep path behind their home, to the lot by the road where they kept their car. On either side were her newly planted cinnamon bushes, and Amy had been bending over them, admiring the fresh growth. Every minute or so they'd stop walking, and she or Graham would reach down to a foot or ankle, to pick off a shiny black dollop before it became long and snakelike. "Leeches and all, you've been happy here," he acknowledged. "So, I'd never tell you to leave. You'll have to make up your own mind on that one."

"But you're leaving," she said, wishing she'd dared ask whether he truly loved her, wanting his answer to mean he'd stay put because of it.

"I've got to go, Ame. The offer in Baltimore is special, one of a kind." And when she remained silent, he added, "And I'm not learning here anymore. Not like I was."

They made it to the car, a vehicle so decrepit you had to access the driver's seat from the passenger-side door. And before climbing in, he took her chin in his hand and told her, "I want you to decide what works for you, Amy—because I love you." Then he clambered over the stick shift, swearing that one day he'd make himself infertile driving such a car.

She couldn't resent Graham. She'd made her own choice.

Sandy's car was parked outside the restaurant when Amy drove in. She hurried to the front desk, irked she was the one to arrive late. A receptionist directed her to the deck out back. Sandy was already settled at a table there, sipping on a short lime drink. Another sat across from her.

"Hey!" Sandy smiled, lifting her glass. "Tom Collins with lime. I took a chance and ordered you one. That good?"

"Great," Amy agreed, a bit thrown. She sat down, putting her bag in her lap. "Been here long?"

"Nope. A while." Sandy grinned. "I like the view."

"Yeah. This is nice," Amy said, looking about at the harbor activity. The last of the fishing boats were winding up their nets, and she let her gaze rest on the preoccupied men while the petty agitation left her system. "Cheers!"

"Absolutely," Sandy said. "To the stink of the sea!"

The smell wasn't obnoxious, despite the heat pushing offshore from the city, and Amy eased into her drink.

"So. Is this a two-chapters-down-and-ten-to-go celebration, or just a happy-to-be-alive celebration?" she asked. It seemed a downer, the moment she asked it.

Sandy beamed. "All of the above."

Amy nodded, still unclear. "Okay."

"Plus, we never do this. You never leave your home and garden. And I've been way too preoccupied . . ." It looked as if Sandy was about to say something else but changed her mind. "Anyway, we're about to travel the country together, so we need the practice!"

"I'm for that," Amy agreed.

"And I think we should begin to up our game a bit, you and me."

"We have a game?"

"Of course we do! We're published! We should behave like it. This is our second book, you know. You're a professional garden writer. I'm not a half-bad garden illustrator and pretty decent fucking artist."

Amy laughed, her colleague's insistence contagious. "We've even got a very cool photographer on the team. You're right!"

"Damn right, I'm right. Although tonight's about *us* stepping up. And starting tonight, Amy James, *you've* got to get used to living large!"

Instinctively, Amy detected an underlying criticism, wondering what she'd done to deserve it. The encouragement felt more like cajoling. "And how should we do that?" she asked, playing along with an easy grin. She thought suddenly of the publisher's paltry advance, one that would barely cover all the travel the three had ahead of them.

"Well, one thing, besides this—" Sandy raised her glass again "—is we should be thinking large. Like the *next* book. And we should start planning it now. We should go even bigger."

"Oh, wow," Amy managed.

"But next time, it should be gardens of people who are really famous," Sandy scolded suddenly. "Superstars that readers would buy the book for, just to see where these people hang out."

Amy sipped at her drink, already wanting another. "You mean like royalty and rock stars?" The thought made her gag.

"At least." Sandy almost brayed, her laugh was so big. "And think worldwide. Why shouldn't we hit Vienna and Beijing, Fez and Dubai? I've always wanted to see Copenhagen and Lima. Why not?"

Sandy was off on her own, and Amy felt awash in her wake. She tried to keep them on the same planet.

"Well, first we gotta finish the book we're on right now." She said it with a smile, but it came out like a reprimand.

"Lord, Amy . . ."

Hurriedly, Amy tried to undo the damage. "No, I just mean, of course we should think big. I agree with you. Meanwhile, though, we've got some cool stuff to do this summer! Like, this Bess Copeland? The next stop we're doing in Delaware?" Amy's voice attempted enthusiasm. "She doesn't look bad. She's not famous, but she's old money. Someone Ella really likes the looks of."

"Not exactly Meghan Markle," Sandy quipped. "Now if *she* gardened, that'd be cool." Sandy's eyes danced. "We could meet Prince Harry."

They both chuckled. The waiter came and they ordered their dinner.

"Edith and Mariann are good finds, though, don't you think?" Amy looked to Sandy for agreement. "If the others are as interesting as them, I won't complain."

"If we sell a lot of books, none of us will."

Of the three of them—Amy, Sandy, and Zach—Sandy always spoke less about the reason for the book, more about the money. Her goal was to get her name out there and attract more paying customers for her art. Although both she and Zach were financially insecure, Sandy had a harder time selling her work. Zach's photographs had a commercial breadth of appeal that Sandy's illustrations just didn't. He lived exclusively off his photography; Sandy often found herself having to teach an Adult Ed class, or waitress the odd banquet. It made her crasser about their project than Amy was comfortable with.

Sandy raised her hand at a waiter, pointing two fingers down at their glasses followed by a thumbs up. She sucked a small ice cube into her mouth.

"You know, Edith called Zach," Sandy announced slyly.

It took Amy a moment. "Edith Roosevelt?"

"Uh huh. Asked him to her wedding. In August."

Amy's teeth crunched into the ice. "I didn't even know she was getting married!"

Sandy was snide. "Why? She's always getting married."

"But, you mean, Edith asked Zach? Not you or me?" The hurt of it embarrassed her.

"Oh, not as a guest! No: Edith wants Zach to photograph the event. She and Joao were pretty taken with his shots from our visit there."

That calmed Amy down some, but only just.

"And," Sandy added, "she said Zach could bring a friend, just for making the effort." There was heat to this bit of news, and Amy paused, taking it in.

Registering, Amy asked quietly, "Did he ask *you*?"

Sandy was dismissive. "I said no. I think it's a bit early for that."

Their waiter arrived with the second round, followed quickly by two plates of oysters, two bowls of salad, a basket of fries, another of bread. Suddenly the table was active with goodies.

"We should get together more often." Amy tried to sound jocular. "Seems like a whole lot I've been missing." She picked at a fry, greasy and hot, and bit off the end.

Sandy lifted a rough shell to her mouth, tipping it back in a noisy slurp. Wiping her lips with a napkin, she said, "Zach's nine years younger than me and a very weird guy. We're just having fun."

It was a cavalier remark and struck Amy as unkind. "Well, watch yourself. Graham's ten years my senior. We were just having fun too."

"And how's that working out?" Sandy couldn't stop the smile that crossed her face.

Amy forced a laugh. She reached for an oyster, also knocking it back, and felt the slick mollusk slip by the lump in her throat.

Now would have been a good time to open up, sitting with a friend, the alcohol singing in her veins. In an ideal world, now would have meant a chance to unload about everything: Graham's illness, the many changes at home. It would have been a relief to talk about his faltering professional judgment, about Moira and her relentless ambition, the rockiness of their new venture. There was a weight of worry Amy longed to tip from her shoulders, drop right there on the rear deck of the quiet bar.

What Amy managed, well into her second drink, was a description of her new writing desk in the guest room, the relief she felt having some space of her own.

"And I've had my own studio since I left college." Sandy dredged the last of her drink,

"Some of us just take longer," Amy said.

"Some of us may never arrive." Sandy's fingers went up again. Two more.

The comment hurt, however carelessly made, and Amy's throat tightened. A real friend, one who understood her, would never have said such a thing. It's what Amy longed for now, her cheeks hot against the cool evening air.

Now, her eyesight felt fuzzy as haloes of glow erupted around harsh floodlights near the harbor, doubled in the greasy skin of the water. Sandy's face across the table became harder to read, the sockets under her eyebrows, the hollows below her cheek bones shadowed in darkness. Amy'd had too much to drink. She worried how she'd drive herself home, how she'd manage the walk to her car.

The next two glasses arrived.

"Not for me," Amy said. Even shaking her head made her dizzy.

"I thought it was girls' night out."

"It was. It is." Amy selected a thick slice of bread. "My tolerance just isn't what it used to be."

The house was lit up like a fairground when she got home, the door and windows open wide and every room ablaze. It was as if a wild party of celebrants had roared through the place and Amy's mind jumped to from confusion to concern: uninvited guests? A break-in? But as she tiptoed through the downstairs, turning off lights as she went, the place was empty and deadly silent. Her heart racing, Amy sprinted for the stairs, terrified at what she might find at the top. Halfway up, her feet, leaden from drink, betrayed her. She crashed onto the wooden treads, her shin screaming with pain. Hobbling at last into their bedroom, she found Graham asleep in bed, his mouth open, hand curled under his chin.

She stood at the foot of the bed, provoked beyond reason by his unbothered repose. The thought of crawling in next to him reviled her on every level. She was still a bit drunk, she knew, and jittery from the fall, the drive, and the useless onrush of panic.

She took herself into the bathroom, closing the door before turning on the light. She didn't notice the pile of mail until she'd squeezed out the toothpaste. The letters sat in a small puddle of water, to the right of Graham's sink. She reached with her free hand, lifting them, the bottom one soaked through. Shaking them off, she balanced them precariously on the corner of the towel rack. She could only guess what had happened. He must have had the letters in his hand, only to be reminded of them when he'd needed that hand again, upstairs in the bathroom. It made a kind of sense, but the fact of it addled her.

Amy caught her own face in the mirror, eyebrows knitted, lines etched across her forehead. *God*, she thought. *What will I look like after a year of this? Two?*

She rinsed and spat, taking care not to back into the letters, spooked by them balanced there.

It was too late to open each item, bills, mostly, a credit card offering. But one, once she leafed through them, made her glad she'd looked. Sitting on the toilet, Amy ripped open the small envelope, thick and creamy white. It was a short note, in handwriting almost too tight and crooked to comprehend. But the message from Edith Roosevelt sang through. She wanted Amy at their wedding. Only a small affair, just for a few friends. Zach was coming, to take photographs. Maybe Amy could come with him. Maybe it would help her with the story.

It was something, an act of friendship, and Amy smiled.

# TWELVE

**M**oira stood patiently in the middle of the kitchen, letting Amy finish.

"And there should be enough here to last Haps until I get back, but Petco carries this brand if you run out. It's on Route 6."

"I know it," Moira nodded. "It's only for two nights."

"Three days." Amy swirled, scanning the place for last reminders.

Moira smiled. "I think we'll manage."

Amy nodded. Much like they'd managed already. Managed to upend the household with their joint venture, taking over not just the den now, but the kitchen too. Managed to railroad Dana into relinquishing two of his best former clients while having to meet the steep buy-out agreement. Between them, Graham and Moira had managed to become quite a ferocious pair. And if Moira was the mastermind behind this evolution, as Amy presumed, the least the girl could manage was to keep her eye on the dog, the dishes, the garbage.

It felt like setting out over a deep abyss on a swinging bridge, but having decided to risk it, she buried her anxiety beneath calm directives and forward motion. They were expected in Delaware for garden number three the following day, and it was time to depart.

Zach had offered his car for the trip. "Because I felt like it," he explained, dropping Amy's suitcase through the sunroof into the back seat.

When she'd added in her laptop, her raincoat, some packed food remembered at the last minute, she knocked on Graham's study door. He'd been cocooned there since dawn, leaving Moira in the middle of Amy's fluttering.

"They're here, hon," she announced through the door, alerting him to the time.

When she opened the door, Graham was seated at his desk, his profile to her.

"Can I have a goodbye kiss?" she asked.

"Sure," he said, turning his head. He reached out an arm.

She walked to him, gracing the top of his head with her lips. His hair hadn't been washed in some days, and it made her recoil.

"Be good," she said finally, patting his shoulder.

"If it's the only option."

He wasn't going to budge. Still annoyed that she was actually going, this was as generous as he was going to get. She turned to leave.

Just as she reached the door, he asked, "Where are you staying tonight?"

Amy sighed. She'd typed out her hotel's address and phone number. Moira had a copy; his was laying on his desk.

"Philadelphia." She pointed.

Graham followed her finger, saw the page.

"I'll call when we get there."

"Okay," he said. "But you don't have to if you're having fun."

The possibility danced in front of her, but she managed a friendly retort. "I want to. Want to make sure you don't forget me while I'm gone!"

It had been meant as cheerful banter, a joke. Under the circumstances, she realized, a poor choice.

"Okay," he said. "If *you* don't forget *me*."

It was so pathetic, she thought, him sitting there, bathed in hurt and self-pity.

"Love you," she claimed, and made for the car.

Despite the underlying hum of disquiet she felt, leaving him there without her for three days, the relief of actually driving away was enormous. The further they got from familiar scenery, the lighter Amy became. Sitting in the back seat, stuffed in with the bags and coats, she felt like the child. Up front, Sandy and Zach were the attractive parents, their hair short and wild in the wind, Sandy slipping CDs into the Kia's sound system, crooning along. On occasion, one would turn to the other, an arm around a shoulder, a shared smile. There were happy, windblown comments between them that Amy couldn't make out. Zach owned the driving. "Only if you insist," he'd said to Amy's promise to relieve him somewhere on the Connecticut Turnpike. "I like it behind the wheel." Sandy was the point person, checking her GPS for the road conditions ahead, shouting route variants for the shorter way. Sandy found them *pizza nearest to me* as they crossed into New York, a gas station off Exit 7. Relaxing her head against the headrest she let her colleagues steer her away.

Sandy was faintly apologetic when they headed for their bedrooms, the lovers to theirs, Amy to hers. But as she closed the door after her, Amy didn't think twice about the other two falling onto the same bed, cared less about the romantic exclusiveness. She was pleased to be alone. That first night, she ran a bath, soaking for an hour. Later, thick in her towel, centering herself on the queen-sized bed, all four pillows propped behind her, she surfed the channels, committing to none. At ten, she phoned Graham and wished him sweet dreams. It was terse, his response, but he seemed to be surviving her absence and was clearly in one piece. Relieved, cuddling down under the crisp sheets, she opened a book.

They began their research the next day at the extravagant grounds of Deloures just outside of Wilmington. Handing them publicity literature from the Information Desk, Bess Copeland was receptive and gracious, classy in the understated way that certain wealthy people are. Educating them as they walked, she took them past the regal handwrought gates, tall and black, studded with golden scrolled leaves. They paraded down the grand allées, past the endless statuary and elegant fountains, through the boxwood garden. There were miles of neatly shorn grass, whole yards of fragrant roses, great urns of matching geraniums, and complex garden borders, rich with design and variety. The woman's knowledge of the botany was substantial and her familiarity with everything about her ancestor, E.I. Copeland, went on forever: gun powder manufacturer, industrialist, philanthropist. Zach changed digital memory cards twice, and Sandy filled an entire notebook with garden schemes. But Amy struggled to find the personality, the hook she needed.

They were seated now at a small table behind the visitor center, set apart from the rest of the patio. "Were you the only one of your generation that stayed put?" she asked, fingering her straw.

Bess cocked her head, as if finding the question a curious one. "Two of my siblings and three cousins are all on the board," she replied.

"Do they still work full-time at Deloures?"

"Not really." Bess smiled her pleasant smile.

"Are they as involved in the gardens as you are?" Amy was hoping there might be an expression of devotion, at least, something to explain Bess remaining within the same several acres for an entire lifetime.

"We're all committed to keeping the Estate flourishing," Bess said.

Amy sipped at her drink, trying to find a better way in. She was tempted to be direct, asking Bess what it was that kept her there, whether she'd ever experienced some misfortune, some life incident that maybe her garden had helped to heal. But taking in the polished exterior, the woman's noble façade, Amy tried forcing a chuckle instead. "Do you ever just want to do something different, get away somewhere?"

"Oh, yes!" Bess brightened. This was easy. "I travel every January, take off for ten days and see the world."

*Only ten?* Amy thought, remembering to close her mouth.

"And then I come back here," Bess continued. "We do our best planning in the winter months, when we have time to breathe."

"And do you have many changes in the pipeline, in your planning?"

"Not a one," Bess said, in all seriousness. "I'm a heritage keeper. And E.I.'s heritage is a significant one."

It would have seemed rude to argue. Amy scanned her list of questions, wondering how best to probe without being disrespectful. But Bess Copeland was smooth, refusing all entreaties to expand on her own story, as if compared to the exquisite setting, personal truths might come off as bad taste.

Amy worried aloud about it, back at the hotel.

"So she's on the Board of the Deloures Foundation and runs the internship program. Hardly a potboiler."

"You want maybe a hidden murder in their somewhere? An illegitimate child?" Sandy was tired from the walking, ready to relax.

"I imagine you could figure out what she's worth," Zach said. "Money always spices things up. Maybe they all fought over it." He pulled the bowl toward him and filled his fist with peanuts.

"Maybe she's a creepy cat lady, gets whacky when she's home in her jammies," Sandy said.

Amy watched them both, thinking. "I don't know how she can stand it. I mean, they've not come up with a new garden design in over fifty years! How can you be a gardener and not want to try something of your own?!"

"Well, it's really a museum," Sandy said, "A place for tourists."

"Doesn't follow," Zach said. "Read up on the Isabella Stewart Gardner Museum. Those folks *struggle* with having to keep everything as it was; they bridle under the restrictions and look for temporary ways to get around them, just to add variety. No, this lady is happy with restrictions."

Amy took some peanuts from the bowl. "Well, I don't get her. And it's not like I didn't try."

"What did you ask?" Zach asked.

Amy laughed ruefully, remembering. "I even tried being cute, you know, asking whether she'd ever wanted to run away."

"From all that wealth?" Sandy hooted.

"You asked her that?" Zach spoke through the nuts.

"Kind of. She said she travels all over the world—ten measly days a year!"

"And you let her get away with that?" Zach was sitting forward now, his brow creased with impatience.

"I guess I did."

"And did you ever talk about the irony?" he was pressing her now, and Amy squirmed.

"Which one?"

"The irony of all that fortune built on war materials, gun powder and explosives? The irony that rapacious wealth is what's behind the comfortable power of beneficence? The gap between dirty money and gorgeous gardens? Did you happen to ask Bess Copeland about that?"

"It's not a political book," Sandy countered.

But Amy shook her head, understanding what Zach was getting at.

"No," she admitted. "I didn't."

"You're going to need to toughen up, Amy, ask harder questions," he said. "Else all we've got is another overpriced gardening book." His voice was dismissive. "Beautiful photographs, sure, lovely sketches, but not much human insight."

Back in her room, Amy sat with her notes, bristly with discomfort. Zach was annoying, but he was right. If the book was going to work, she was going to have to get to the heart of what in their gardens was so central to these women. Like Edith in hers, and Mariann, hers.

It forced Amy to think harder about her subjects and her relationship with her own garden. She already knew what it was that she found so intoxicating about sticking her hands in soil. There was the simple labor of it for starters. Moving rocks, digging holes, hauling barrows of compost. Not man *against* nature, but woman *in* it. In the quiet early mornings, in the relief when the rains came. She'd come to understand all the adapting gardeners had to do—to the weather, the pests, the changing climate. It struck her as almost female, that capacity to adapt. Most of all, Amy thought, scribbling madly in her notebook, just to get it down there in black and white, there was an almost spiritual trust, a faith in a vision of what was going to be, next season, next year, after twenty. Edith had that. Mariann did. So did she, Amy knew: the willingness to keep at it because of that vision, that little glimmer of hope. Nurturing a garden, nurturing oneself. Amy wrote another short list in the margins: pregnancy, childbirth, raising a family, keeping the faith. It looked old fashioned, until Amy thought of the other ingredient, something else she recognized in women like Edith and Mariann. Gardening was an act of resistance. Where was that in Bess Copeland? Unless that cultivated museum of hers was Copeland's own act of resistance.

Zach had been prodding Amy, she knew. And it had felt healthy, felt as if he'd expected her to do better. She would rise to the occasion, she decided. It was her book to write, her experience to explore, and she owed herself that much.

Around ten, Amy reluctantly changed gears and phoned home. Simply thinking about her husband again unearthed all the darting possibilities of her absence—the stove being left on, Haps going unfed, Graham losing his keys, or his temper! However, the voice that came across the line sounded placid and unruffled. His monologue about his day, though both tiresome and repetitive, not once asking about hers, was its own reassurance. When finally he started to wind up, he had just the one question: "Miss me?"

"I do," she said. But as she climbed into bed, the real truth was troubling. She savored being alone. That was the real truth.

It was late afternoon by the time Zach dropped her back at the house. Moira had left for the day and Graham was off somewhere. Haps, at least, was happy to see her. And, for all her intermittent worry, at least the place hadn't burned down.

There was, however, mess everywhere. Stoically, she poured herself a cold glass of wine and took a sip, waiting for her pulse to slow. It felt like payback, all this mayhem—the dirty countertops, full sink, spilled yogurt on the floor. Punishment for having been gone. *Two nights!* she thought angrily and took another sip. Then she hauled her suitcase upstairs, leaving it on the unmade bed, and came down again, spending a long hour cleaning up.

Graham was guarded when he returned. "Have you started dinner?" he asked, making a point of looking over all she'd cleaned up. His tone was unfriendly, as if he'd been stewing on a minor hurt since her departure days earlier, and in the ensuing hours the pot had bubbled to a thick mix.

Amy bit back a clever reply. "Not yet," she said. "Why, is there something special you're hungry for?"

"Nope," he replied. "I'm not that hungry." Without another word, he turned and walked to his study.

"Nice to see you too," she said quietly to his back.

There was nothing for it, she realized. Her clearing up had apparently insulted some remote place in his heart; not to do so would have driven her crazy, and eventually he would have resented that as well. Seeing no option, Amy chose to ignore his sulkiness. She prepared a quick sandwich, headed upstairs and went back to her work.

Thirty minutes later, she phoned Bess Copeland. "I realized there's a question I didn't ask," Amy began.

"Of course," Bess replied, "although I thought we'd covered everything." Still so formal, so pleasant.

Amy glanced at her notes. "I keep thinking about the peaceful environment you've created there at Deloures. That, and the enormous fortune your family amassed by selling war materials." Deliberately, she gave that a moment to sink in. "Do you feel any personal disconnect between the two: the violent greed and the generous beauty?" And then she waited, letting the woman try again.

The response emerged slowly, lilting with a near musical quality. "Hmm," Bess intoned, seemingly more bemused than offended. "Personal disconnect?" She paused again, as if considering the notion. "No," she said at last, offering nothing more.

Amy sat there, pained with the silence. *Wait*, she cautioned herself. *Wait.* She began counting to one hundred in her head, refusing to fill the gap.

"You know," Bess said, eventually, "A beautiful garden isn't the least impressed with the beliefs of our visitors." It was said in a kindly voice, but the mild rebuke was clear. "That's what's so transcendent about nature, what I appreciate about being in it: the natural world really doesn't care what people think."

Amy smiled to herself. *Keep talking. I'm listening.*

Bess took her time, but once she warmed to the topic, her motive became clear. "My mission is to provide beauty and joy. In doing so, I create joy in my own life. That's what matters," she asserted calmly. "In my opinion, joy is central—and essential. Whether you wish to characterize my family's wealth as indictable—building a business from producing black powder, exploiting workers in what was truly a very risky industry, or working alongside the men, as my great-grandfather did, sharing the risk. He was every kind of person: an opportunist, if you choose to look at it like that, a profiteer, a brilliant inventor, late in his life a generous philanthropist. It's not up to me to judge, nor am I impressed with the judgment of others." Bess's voice never lost its sweetness, but Amy could hear the forceful current that ran beneath it. It reminded her of a spring stream heading down from the mountains, carrying on its surface fragile boats of twigs and leaves. "What you experience when you visit his garden beds and fountains, the calming views and clean, open walkways, is basically healthy plants. The estate was his desperate gift to a loved one who never did love him back." Bess stopped as if heightening the drama. "But even that little piece of family folklore doesn't particularly impress me, one way or the other. I focus on the flowers. And frankly, I'm quite like the flowers we grow." Bess chuckled deep in her chest. "I'm not into shame. I do joy."

Writing the Deloures chapter was like the best moments of running. Sinuous and swift, oily and hot, her words sped just ahead of her thoughts, filling the screen.

Amy had all kinds of lingering judgments about the Deloures Estate, its vestiges of great wealth, power and indulgence. But what she resonated with, what became the focus of the chapter on Bess Copeland was the enviable mission of its mistress: the woman's ability to elevate joy above all else. *Imagine,* Amy realized wistfully as she crafted the sentences, *not caring what others think! Insisting on the importance of creating beauty and joy in one's life.* It was simultaneously outrageous and tantalizing.

With a day to spare, Amy emailed the draft to Ella. It was only June 29th, and the promised three chapters were done and delivered! Proud of what Team Amy had produced, she felt pumped for July. Tennessee, Marathon Key, Key West, and Charleston. The way she'd planned it, they could cover all four of these gardens over the next thirty days. They might even add in Chicago. This would leave her room to breathe and even revise, if necessary, the last three chapters over August and September.

This was not going to be a sprint; she knew that now. The next few months were going to be more of the same: daily burying the barbed worries and the hurtful moods at home in order to maintain a routine of consistent craft, made up of research, reflection, and writing. But Amy trusted herself. By engaging with the lives of these women gardeners, she'd found a confidence and source of strength that had long been missing from her life. These creative, accomplished ladies were the hot air balloons that would sweep Amy above any rough terrain of her own life, delivering her to the finish line of Book Number Two.

The truly difficult challenges would be when she *wasn't* working.

# THIRTEEN

The fourth of July began hot and heavy, the air still saturated with the week's rain, as if another downpour was due before the reprieve. Amy woke when the light was only a noncommittal smudge. She dressed in the gloom and tiptoed downstairs. Haps was curled on his bed in the kitchen, and she stroked him heavily, bringing him to life. There was a full day ahead, thick with people and events, and she needed the walk behind her before the clatter began.

They followed Cove Road toward the harbor, the wet sand from the pavement sticking to their feet. A speckled patch of white on the water, a flock of seagulls, bobbed like litter. Out beyond, in the mooring field, two men were on the deck of the thirty-three-foot Alerion, their shapes dark against the brightening sky. This was the one, its sleek red hull, gleaming teak deck, that Graham and Andy spoke of in hushed words. On race day, when its metallic mesh sails fanned out from the mast and the yacht tipped deeply into the wind, this was the one they dreamed to beat.

She and Haps walked as far as the bridge, stopping for him to claim his spots along the way. He was becoming like an old man, peeing every other minute, but Amy indulged him, taking the moments to absorb the peace. Stopping by the bridge railing, she scanned the docks and yacht club for emerging activity. On the lawn, tables had been set out already, the heavy black grills wheeled into place. There was a system to celebrating Independence Day at the club, honed by generations of yachters and their families. She and Graham, Jason and Catherine had woven it into their own lives, nervous and excited in the first years as newcomers, when membership was as much family fun as professional strategy. Now it was tradition, bullying in the way cultural ritual can be, a summer placeholder, but they kept to it. At one point, even Amy's mother had bowed to the regime, and every person the children had ever dated learned to keep the day free. There was the race and then the cookout and then the precious awards under a setting sun. Too much food and way too much alcohol, but mostly weather and wind and the pressing hours of group anxiety, with everyone hoping to win.

Navigating the long day with a household of family ran as a full symphony under her thoughts. Earlier the prior evening Jason had arrived with a new girlfriend in tow, collecting Catherine at the airport on the way. Catering to the needs of each was demanding enough. Doing so under the shadow of Graham's diagnosis, still his closely guarded secret, only upped the ante. More than once, she'd tried to muster the courage to bring it up with him, thinking of different ways to word the request: "I think it's time, Gray" or "Wouldn't you feel better? I would feel better!" And each time, she'd lost the courage, too kind to say out loud that *someone might notice*. Instead, she'd promised herself to keep it light, praying that Graham's behaviors would let her.

A young woman, a bright fleck of white shirt over pale khaki shorts, descended the ramp leading to the club's launch. It was nearly six: time to get back.

Catherine had risen ahead of the others, ready with a full pot of coffee. She was wandering the garden with a mug of coffee when Amy returned. "I'd forgotten how many flowers there are in the world," she smiled. "It's still a paradise, Amy. Not sure how you keep it all up."

"Don't look too close. It hasn't had the attention it needs this year." Amy unhooked Haps's leash, herding him indoors. "Wait there, I'll join you. Just need my caffeine."

She put the kettle back on to boil, dropping a tea bag into her mug. Already the family invasion was visible: dirty wine glasses standing on the counter, a half bag of Doritos clipped and left beside them. Jason's baseball cap lay upside down on the alcove desk, his backpack hung over a kitchen chair. Amy poured in some milk and walked back outdoors.

Her stepdaughter had lost weight since her visit over Amy's birthday, noticeable now as she stood by the tall hedge, outlined in foliage. It was probably the cost of her recent breakup, maybe the pressure of her new job. But it pleased Amy having Catherine back, however diminished she looked with her pale skin and thin, dark hair, only a memory of softness about her.

"I love that you tour the garden," Amy said. "No one does that anymore." Amy joined Catherine, dipping the tea bag up and down, making the water dark.

"And I love that you keep it up," Catherine replied. "Not sure whether I'd make the effort to return if it weren't for your flowers. What's this guy?" She pointed down to a singular green plant, its branches like fingers, splayed wide, ungainly and plain.

"Verbena bonariensis. That one's a volunteer, from over there." Amy indicated a swath of them in an adjacent bed, many more splayed fingers, still flowerless. "Late in July, the flowers begin. They're teeny." She made a tight circle of finger and thumb. "But the stems get tall, like wires, and the blossoms float over, like butterflies." Amy smiled. "Come in August some time." She bobbed her bag for the last time, dug a little hole in the soil and buried it.

"I may be moving next month. Need a cheaper place now that Moneybags has left." Catherine chuckled.

"How's that going?" Amy was careful, inquiring into her step-daughter's life. Although theirs was a stronger bond, after the many years of visits and correspondence, the relationship was built on a shaky footing. Catherine was the same little girl who'd been abandoned by her freewheeling father for six years, and Amy was still the rat bastard's new, young wife. It had taken Amy's diligent insistence to make the visits happen, hours of undivided attention, weeks filled with beach trips and baking goodies, gluing seashell families and painting their nails together before Catherine had thawed. Even after all that time, even as an adult, she had her edges.

"I'm good! Learning to relax again. Not waiting up every night, worrying when or whether he's coming home." Catherine shook her head. "It was just stupid. I don't know why I didn't see that coming." She splashed the dregs of her coffee onto the lawn, before remembering. "Oh, sorry."

Amy brushed it off. "Acid is good for it."

"And how are you guys making out? Graham still ruling the world?" Catherine had never forgiven him, not really.

Amy grinned. "Still trying." Then she corrected herself. "Actually, life has slowed down a bit. Your dad's left the partnership. He's been working from home."

"Yeah, I noticed the den. That must suck, having two architects underfoot all day."

"I've moved my desk up to the guest room. It's working out."

Catherine waved her off. "Don't. Now I'm free again, I can't stand the smell of sacrifice."

"Morning!" Jason stood at the kitchen window, waving them hello.

"Just tell me you're writing," Catherine said before waving back.

"I'm writing," Amy assured her. Then to her son: "Hey, hon. We were just coming in."

Jason and Nina had helped themselves to pastries and coffee and were seated together at the table when Amy and Catherine walked in. Graham hung back, contemplating them all.

"Dad, how long does the race normally take?" Jason was thinking ahead.

Graham was leaning against the counter, nursing his coffee. "Four, maybe five hours?"

He seemed off this morning, apart from the rest of them, and Amy's heart tugged as she watched him.

"So, you can hang around the club, stay here, read if you want." Jason was laying out options for his guest, bending tradition. "Dad and I are crewing on this guy's - Andy's -boat. But we won't be forever."

Nina smiled. "I know." For assurance, she added, "My uncle was a sailor."

"Really?" Everything about her son's girlfriend interested Amy.

Nina obliged. "He crewed for the Newport to Bermuda race for years. So, I'm familiar with the waiting."

"Well, hopefully you won't be waiting for five days," Graham said.

As it turned out, the wait was unbearable. The winning boat, a J24, swept in in record time. They could see it coming for miles, its acid-green spinnaker visibly advanced from the rest. Trying in vain to catch up was the Alerian, and much further back the bright baubles of sail—bunched like beads on a necklace—trailed behind. Fresh cans of beer popped open and raw burgers were added to the grill, the sailors joining their friends and family on the lawn, tired, burned, spent.

Only two families kept their eyes to the horizon, seeking out Andy's Tartan, hunting for the familiar red and white stripes. Amy cooked the chicken; they were hungry, it would taste as good cold. And they listened as the awards were handed out, enduring the roars of applause, the guffaws and wisecracks of the sailing fraternity. Tolerating, too, the occasional look of concern and pity that fellow members shot their way, an unspoken contempt for failure at sea. Andy's wife had a last beer and left for home, bored or irked, Amy couldn't tell. But Amy waited, keeping her concerns close to her chest. Nina rejected both wifely options, dialing Jason directly.

"They don't generally pick up mid-race," Amy said.

"Just wanted to make sure they aren't dead." Nina listened through another few rings before slipping the phone back in her pocket. "Anyway," she added, "someone should tell them the race is over."

Catherine had returned to the house, leaving Amy and Nina still overlooking the harbor, uneaten food packed in hampers at their feet. The sun had set, only a memory of crimson light washing the horizon, when the last boat finally grunted toward shore, chugging under power. By then, the sails were down, the spinnaker long ago bagged, stored back in the V berth. Andy was at the helm, Jason standing on the bow, holding onto the roller furling, as if on watch.

"I only see two." Nina said.

Amy strained to see through the furry darkness. "Me too," she said, alarm leaking into her system.

"Hope no one's hurt." Nina's voice was steady. She fingered her phone but thought better of it.

The women stood together on the lawn, minutes crawling by, watching the boat circle the mooring. Jason reached over to pole in the pennants, kneeling as he secured them to the cleats on the bow. Silently, the women followed the launch as it puttered out to the mooring, sidled up to the Tartan's deck and let the men aboard. There were three. Of course, there were.

Andy walked off first, stormed up the ramp and left the club in a huff, passing Amy and Nina without a word.

"Whoa," Nina whistled, impressed. "Something's gone down."

Jason came next, diving first for the hamper, grabbing a can, popping open the tab, drinking deeply. He shook his head at his mother, a tight grimace glistening on his lips. "Talk about bloody," he said. "Don't even ask."

Nina produced a drumstick and he took it, throwing an arm around the girl's neck as he bit in. She kissed his greasy cheek while he chewed.

Amy watched them, envious of their easy rapport. Then she turned to her husband, coming up slowly from behind. Graham seemed sunken, as if he'd lost inches out there, so she was surprised when her chin found its familiar home by his collarbone. He hung on her, not quite in an embrace, more like he was resting.

"Rough afternoon?" Amy held him against her chest.

"Not fun," he said. "Fine on the way out, lost our edge turning back." He pulled away, looking distractedly at the open basket.

"There's food," she said.

He shook his head. "The wind changed," he told Amy. "That happens. And suddenly, we're miles behind. Then Andy starts yelling nonstop, like the world's at an end."

Amy noticed Jason's frown as he listened.

"Okay. And I fumbled the spinnaker," Graham continued. "Somehow. I couldn't get . . . I don't know. Sometimes it happens in a race . . . You know. But Andy goes off. And I say, 'Fuck it.' There's more to life."

Graham looked at his wife, needing confirmation.

At almost any other time, Amy might have agreed. There was so much more to life than the obsessive-compulsive need to come

131

in first in a boat. But today, this avid preoccupation—like all else with Graham's world—was drifting out from under them, and nothing in the world would have made her happier than to have her husband and son bring in Andy's Tartan lengths ahead of the J, the red Alerion.

Swallowing her disappointment, she nodded. "There is more to life," she said. "Shall we go home?"

The evening was mercifully forgiving. Catherine did more than her share of cleaning up, happy to distance herself in the kitchen. And although twice Amy sensed Jason watching her and Graham intently, as if waiting for some revelation to be acknowledged, they all managed to navigate past it. Nina zeroed in on some architectural books in the living room, engaging with the photographs of Graham's many projects dotted across the world. She and Jason ended up thigh to thigh on the couch, books open on their laps, as Graham found his voice, answering the young woman's questions, remembering earlier triumphs.

It filled her heart, seeing Graham like this again, and for some time Amy listened in, nodding with recognition. She remembered the day Graham had been nominated for the Progressive Architect's Award. The afternoon he phoned from the office, the sound of a popping cork in the background.

"Get a sitter," he'd told her. "And wear something sexy."

There'd been laughter behind him, and she could tell Dana was somewhere near, egging Graham on. The four of them—Lois had been very pregnant then, bigger than a beach ball—had been cloistered at a small table at an Indian restaurant on Route 6, their faces glowing orangey-red under the lights. They'd been passing *Architectural Magazine* back and forth between them, the pages greasy from the onion bhaji.

The nomination had been for their design of a wooden boat museum in Bristol, Connecticut. Two pages of photographs documented the museum's angled glass frontage, the internal slate wall glistening with a steady sluice of falling water, the fountain feature that had become a signature of Graham's. On page thirty-six, there was a quarter page picture of Dana and Graham, on the lawn outside their office in Mattapoisett, the wooden sign before them boasting Faxon & James, carved in goldleaf. "You're ruining it!" Dana said. But they'd bought several copies, one for the office reception room, one each for their parents, their homes. Being nominated was not the same as winning, not yet. But they were on their way.

The men bought a bottle, splashing second helpings for each other. As she wasn't drinking, Lois kept sipping at Dana's wine. Amy was drunk enough, mostly from the news, the energy radiating from the two men. Under the table she had her palm on Graham's thigh, sliding her hand up to graze the edge of his balls. The nomination had gone to Faxon & James, but it was Graham's design. Amy knew this; she assured him silently, pressing into his leg.

The next week, the firm won the bid for the new Cavendish Library at the University of Chicago. Everything had been building, Amy remembered: the success and the sex, and Graham James, almost too hot to touch.

It was past eleven, now, and Amy was exhausted. She left them there, Graham and Jason, and Jason's eager girlfriend, all three shining in the victories of the past.

Catherine stopped her in the hall upstairs. "Dad seems off. Is he okay?"

Amy hesitated, still soaking in the happy conversation below, not knowing which part of "off" to address. "He clearly had a bad day on the boat," she said.

"But he's just so . . ." Catherine sought the word in Amy's eyes, willing a response. "Kind of out of it one moment, then as arrogant as ever the next."

"I don't know," Amy began. She shrugged. "He can't be arrogant all the time." It was meant as a joke, a sign of alliance.

Catherine stared. "You can tell me, Amy. You can tell *me*."

But Amy was too slow to respond, unprepared for this appeal.

"Fine. Goodnight," Catherine said simply, went back into her room and closed the door.

Amy lingered there, in the darkened hallway, processing what had just happened. The day had been so fraught, verging over the cliff of Graham's oddness, but there had been family and sharing, too—the kind of day Amy had always longed for. She and Catherine, best of all, had been close and easy throughout. It shouldn't end this way. She couldn't just turn on her heel, leave Catherine hurting on the other side of the door. What Amy wanted was to try again, take Catherine by her elbows and, forehead to forehead, tell her exactly what was going on. She wanted to hold the young woman and rock her in her arms, ready the girl for what was to come. She owed Catherine this, she thought.

Amy raised her hand to the door, knuckles ready to rap lightly, then stopped herself. Echoes of witty banter drifted up from the living room. Downstairs, her husband was reveling in the glow of his talent and accomplishments, maybe one of the few last times he would be doing this. If Amy were to tell Catherine tonight, Jason would learn the truth by breakfast, and he, too, would be stripped of these last prideful, delightful moments. Ones he'd need as well, to see him through the coming months of loss.

The children would be gone in two days, Amy told herself, but Graham, her first priority, would still be here, needing her loyalty, her help. She'd have him to face every morning, after they'd gone. She'd be answerable to him.

# FOURTEEN

It was Jason who found her the next morning, out by the shed. He was alone, half-clad in some jersey shorts, tan line showing. His tousled hair reminded Amy of a boy.

"Hey," she said, wanting to touch.

"Hey, Mom." He stood there, his arms crossed in front of his naked chest.

"I was just coming in. You guys ready for breakfast?"

"Not yet. I needed to have a word, before." He shifted in his bare feet, pawing gently at the grass with his toes. "What's going on?"

Amy attempted a look of confusion, offered a wilted smile. "As in . . . ?"

"Dad." He stared at her, waiting for a response. When he got none, he plowed on. "All yesterday . . . then again last night. Something weird happened. After you went to bed."

Amy raised an eyebrow. "Here?"

"With Dad. Yeah."

Amy felt herself, inhaling slowly. "Well, what?"

"We were looking at his books, you know. And Dad was talking about the different jobs, places he'd been. And he starts telling Nina all kinds of, like . . . lies . . . " Jason's face colored with the word.

Amy kept her voice low, hoping he'd do the same. "What kind . . . ?"

"He started bragging about all these awards he'd won—some Aga Kahn Special Chairman's Award for Architecture and a, a . . . Progressive Architect's Award." Jason stopped. "It was creepy, Mom. Cause I'm sitting there. You know, and at first I'm thinking maybe I just didn't know about these. Maybe he did win these." Jason's eyes were big now, round in the telling. "But I googled it last night. And no way. No way did Graham James win the Aga Kahn!"

"Oh, Jason . . ." Amy didn't know whether to commiserate or vomit.

"So we might . . . leave earlier," he said.

"What?!"

"I can't sit through that again. Not with Nina, soaking it all in, encouraging him. I'll either end up telling him he's whacked, or I'll tell her he's full of shit, and . . . well, that's not why I came home."

She reached for his arm, part comfort, part restraint. "Honey . . . "

Jason pulled back. "What's up? He loses it in the race, he loses it last night. Has something happened?"

Once again, she felt the screen come down, the spin begin. "I wasn't there . . . I mean, I wasn't on the boat."

"He lost the spinnaker, Mom! Let the sail drop into the water, and then instead of just reeling it in, he starts unreeling the lines." Jason's fists clenched and unclenched, rotating one over the other in demonstration. "The whole sail got sucked under us. And if Andy hadn't grabbed the lines, it could have gotten jammed in the rudder. But Dad just stood there, like he didn't have a clue."

Amy envisioned the scene, sorry to have heard the details. She struggled to bring them back to land. "I heard you talking last night," she said. "It all seemed pretty normal, at least before I left."

Jason's fists were at his hips now, reminding her once again of a boy wanting his way.

"One thing I can tell you," Amy said, affecting transparency, "Dad's been under a lot of pressure recently. Starting again, working from home. It's taken some toll. So, I know what you mean: sometimes he's a bit cranky, a bit spacey." This was such bullshit, and she saw her deceit reflecting back at her. "And, to be fair, he was *nominated* for the Progressive Architect's Award. He was. Are you sure you didn't misunderstand him?" Amy was on a roll. "And Graham's mentor Geoffrey Bawa did get the Aga Khan Chairman's award."

"Can you hear yourself?"

It was contempt she saw now, but she couldn't stop. "He might have misspoken, or you might have misunderstood." Amy shrugged, frustrated. "I wasn't there!"

Jason waved her away, as he might a fly. "Yeah, well, we're taking off." And he stormed back into the house, his back beautiful, like his father's.

It was more than she could manage, to follow him indoors. She turned to her garden, simpler in its needs.

The scent of her roses came to her, and she inhaled deeply. Amy loved the faint, clean fragrance as much as she loved their soft, buttery yellow, especially alongside the heady display of balloon flowers. It was gratifying, those deep blue blossoms prominent in the early July display. Already though, some of the spent flowers had gone limp, now papery and white, resembling so many bits of used Kleenex. She bent over, snipping the dead ones two at a time with her fingers and thumbs, the milky sap sticky on her skin.

Jason and Catherine could have their anger, she thought sadly. And they could focus it on her if that helped. Amy moved slowly, letting her hands engage with the stems and blossoms while her mind rumbled in discomfort. She shifted on to the patch of bright daylilies and began deadheading those as well. The injustice of it struck her: neither child had been prepared to confront Graham himself. They'd only come quietly to her, wanting some truth, some version that they could handle. Like their father, unwilling, or maybe unable to be honest about what was happening, each of them—Jason, Graham, even Catherine—were expecting her to carry the emotional burden of the now-heavy relationships.

As if evidence of the pain she was feeling, deep red stains from the severed flowers, dark like India ink, appeared on her fingertips. She sighed, rubbing her hands together then wiping them on her shorts. Soon enough, there'd be clarity, ugly and permanent. In the interim, she decided, finally, she'd let the confusion reign, permitting Graham to bask in the reputation he'd built, in the world when their father really was as wonderful as he imagined.

She had worked herself all the way round by the front of the house when Catherine appeared in the driveway, Jason and Nina not far behind. All three were carrying their bags.

"There you are!" Catherine approached Amy tentatively, a tight smile quivering on her lips. "I should have guessed you'd be out here." She glanced along the garden bed, as if appreciating what Amy'd done. "Lookin' good . . ."

Amy straightened up, seeing in a glance what was transpiring, the changed plans, the early departure. She tried to make it easier. "You all off, then?" She held out her arms, hoping for at least an embrace.

"Jason offered a lift to the airport. It's on his way," Catherine said, her voice apologetic. "Didn't want to drag you out for no reason." She gave Amy a one-armed hug, holding tight to her bag.

"No, that's thoughtful of him," Amy offered, accepting Catherine's shallow embrace.

"Anyway," Catherine said, "you've already outdone yourself—as ever." Her stepdaughter made a lazy circle with her head, indicating Amy's universe in general, not wishing to say more.

*Meaning what?* Amy wondered viciously—the garden, the meals, the clean bedding? "It's always a joy," she lied.

Catherine turned toward the car, and Amy followed. She stopped short when she saw Jason and Nina, already seated in the front seats, clearly impatient to be off. Then, through the kitchen window, she noticed Graham watching the children's departure. His isolation seemed to radiate out from where he stood, shadowed as he was by the angle of the morning sun. Her heart bled for him. Crisply, Amy blew her son a kiss. "Drive carefully," she intoned, pretending all was well. Then, repeating their grandmother's favorite line of farewell, she added, "Precious packages!" The false notes in her voice trilled like shards of thin glass.

"Thanks a lot, Mrs. James," Nina said gamely, her elbow out the open window, and Jason muttered a "Thanks, Mom" as the car crunched past her down the drive.

Puffs of white, like chalk dust from the crushed shells, settled slowly back into place. She felt the vacuum of their absence and stood there, locked in a moment of hopeless emptiness, not knowing where she could go, or how.

"They didn't stay long, did they?" Graham appeared by her side, his words less question than comment. "Something happen?"

Part of her wanted to scream, "What do you think?!" But the greater, gentler part of her knew that he was experiencing the same sting of abandonment. Amy swallowed the pain and tried for a happy distraction. "Do you feel like going for a swim?" she asked suddenly, eagerly, hoping he'd agree. Although weary with sadness, the notion of a bracing dip in the ocean seemed a joyous option.

His face registered surprise, a spark of *maybe*. "Where?"

"West Island? Horseneck Beach? Right here at the harbor? I don't care," she said, trying to keep the tone light. "We don't even have to swim swim; let's just get wet somewhere." She grinned stupidly. "It's been a while, eh?"

"Get wet together?" he repeated, giddy with innuendo. He smiled broadly, seemingly alight with all the times they'd swum together: the Indian Ocean, Chesapeake Bay, jumping into the Atlantic off Andy's boat.

It seemed the ploy had worked, and they headed toward the kitchen, the radical notion of locating their bathing suits foremost in her mind.

Indoors, though, he paused, interrupting himself with a remembered thought. "But we need to talk first."

She turned, not ready to be let down. "*Now?*"

"Sit down, please." Graham directed. Then he waited until she'd plunked herself into a kitchen chair. "It's not good news," he said. "But you've been busy and we've had guests . . . I couldn't tell you with all the distractions . . ."

Amy sat upright, waiting as Graham squared his shoulders and found a comfortable stance.

"I've been diagnosed with Alzheimer's," he said finally.

Her breath caught in her throat. A frown deepened across her forehead.

"What?" he asked, watching her closely.

"I . . . Is that it?"

"I've been diagnosed with Alzheimer's," he repeated, as if she were slow.

It took her several beats to respond. "I know," she said finally.

Graham blinked, confused.

Then she admitted. "You told me this already, hon."

"Oh," he said. He looked disappointed, as if he'd been hoping for some bigger reaction, maybe some compassion. "I guess I forgot." He turned from her, trying suddenly to locate something on the counter, a mug, a bagel, before giving up, his hands hanging by his side.

They drove out to Round Hill Town Beach.

Family groups, lively with children and bristling with plastic gear, were filling up the area closest to the snack bar and toilets. Amy found parking at the far end of the long lot, where few cars had yet settled. She had packed some cold chicken, a large clump of red grapes, and half a bag of potato chips and bottled waters, left over from the day before, and filled another canvas bag with two large beach towels. At the last minute, Graham had thrown in a magazine to peruse, and Amy'd grabbed the novel by her nightstand, some sunscreen, an old hat. It was a beach day, something they hadn't done in years.

Their chosen stretch, protected by a small hillock of beachgrass, was blessedly free of seaweed, and the sand for yards around was smooth and fine. Silently, Amy and Graham each spread out their towel and lay down, he on his stomach, she on her back, and eventually they surrendered to the sound of the incoming waves, the aroma of wild roses and salt air.

It was a relief, lying there, her skin tingling with the sun's heat, refreshed by the faint riffling of the ocean breeze. As ridiculous as she sometimes felt, baring so much of herself in public, Amy loved the sensation of wearing a bikini, the near nakedness that left her thighs and belly exposed to the elements. Her feet drooped in opposite directions, and she felt the cool air sneak into the crotch of her suit.

Just inches away, Graham's body lay soundlessly, similarly exposed, and she breathed in through her nose, seeking his scent. It impressed her how they had done this, the two of them, operating instinctively around each other for so many years with such easy expertise. Whatever was going on in their respective minds, Amy mused—and *that* she could hardly fathom lately—their *bodies* knew how to navigate together, how to find peace.

She turned her head just an inch, glancing down at the curve of his bum, the long legs downy with dark curls. Her husband's form had always struck Amy as elegant in its design. Like the buildings he created, Graham's look was at once simple and unassuming and stunning in the way he was put together. Durable and graceful, reassuring. She reached over, placing a hand on his leg.

"Ooh," he shuddered. "Cold hands."

"They're not," she insisted.

"Mmm. Don't."

*I was being affectionate*, she thought defensively, but she retreated, stunned into silence by the sudden depth of her hurt.

It was the confoundedness of her situation that struck Amy, as much as anything. What she understood, what she'd managed all these years with this partner, was how to accommodate herself to him. Even when not thrilled with the direction of their lives, she'd learned to find small, real pleasures in the white space of his ever-colorful life. It was an accommodation that they both accepted, a way to navigate together, but it was based on the confidence that his choices, his clarity, was sufficient for them both. Now, though, that was something neither could trust.

Amy's thoughts drifted upward, seeking solace from the cloudless blue.

"I'm going to go in," she announced finally. "Wanna join me?"

He lifted his head from the towel, considering the water. "Actually swim?"

"Mmmhm. Come on." She stood over him, putting his torso in shadow.

He hesitated, shielding his eyes to look at her. "Naw. You go ahead."

So she did. The sand was hot underfoot and she fell into a trot, eager and reluctant at the same time. When she reached the water, she didn't pause. The shock of cold slapping at each sensitive zone in her body, her thighs, then crotch, her stomach, then breasts, she plowed on, finally diving in headfirst to get over the hardest part. She kept moving, pulling herself through the waves while her body accustomed itself to the cold. It was energizing and wondrous, empowering and liberating, as if her body had learned to fly.

Her lungs expanded as her muscles warmed up and she fell into a steady pace, increasing the distance between herself and the beach.

Like a tiny alarm somewhere far away, Graham's voice entered her consciousness. "Amy!" She treated the sound like a dream and carried on, ducking through an oncoming wave.

"Amy!" The full awareness of him caught up with her. Reluctantly, she slowed, let her legs drop beneath her, and turned on her back to look.

Graham was tiptoeing into the surf, the water just at his knees. He was taking his time, uncharacteristic of the man she knew. Generally the one who charged in, egging her to keep up with him, Graham now appeared hesitant, as if needing support. He waved. "Wait up."

Amy paused, treading water with her arms and feet. But the pull of the shoreline, like a powerful undertow, drew her in, and she began a slow breaststroke back.

# FIFTEEN

The next morning, Ella called just before nine. Graham had already retreated to his study and Moira was in the den, working quietly. Amy was lingering over her tea, the dense fog of the family weekend still heavy on her mind. Lollygagging, as her mother used to say.

"Three chapters down, nine to go," Ella reminded Amy. "It's the 7th already! Twenty-four days left in July. Your next trip should begin immediately."

It was her agent's not-so-subtle version of encouragement, and it worked. Shelving the new nagging worries, as if on automatic, Amy ditched her cooling tea, brewed some fresh coffee, and headed upstairs to begin the planning. After some time on Expedia checking flights and hotels, however, it became obvious that Amy's share of the advance wasn't nearly enough to fly them all to every garden on their list. It made more sense to save her small stash for the August swoop, when they'd be heading further west. The trip along the East Coast, Amy figured, could be done by car.

She phoned Sandy to suggest as much. Her colleague's voice was lively. "You mean you want to *drive* to the Keys?!"

"It'll be fun," Amy answered. "Anyway, it makes it do-able: cheap hotels, couple of sights along the way. Think of it as a road trip."

"Thelma and Louise?" Sandy chuckled. "Think how *that* ended."

"And Brad Pitt," Amy reminded her. "Think about *that*, while you're at it." She chuckled to herself. "How's it going, by the way? You and Zach seem pretty compatible."

"We're just playing, Amy," Sandy warned. "Don't get weird on me."

Amy backed off. "Anyway, I figured we can see all four gardens and make it back in under two weeks. Tennessee, Marathon Key, Key West. Maybe spend a couple of nights there, and then hit Charleston on the way back."

"Couple of nights in Key West, you say?" Sandy's voice warmed.

"Mai Tais at Bahama Mama's? My treat," Amy coaxed.

It was that simple.

Zach, too, was agreeable. He texted his reply: *up 4 2 wks. Cn take the Kia again.*

Then a second text: *yippee.*

Amy spent the next hour checking Google Maps before phoning the four gardeners on her list.

Nancy Forrester in Key West was the first one she got through to, and to Amy's relief, she assured her they'd be welcome any time. "Just phone when you get here. You can poke around as long as you like." Amy reminded Nancy that she'd want to speak with her, do an interview. "Yeah, that's fine. I'll be around somewhere. It's just me and the birds," the gardener said calmly, "and we're not going anywhere." Amy thanked her, scribbling a happy checkmark next to Nancy's name.

Kika Trainer in Charleston was more exacting. The Trainer garden was a quintessential Southern Eden of moss-strung trees and flowering bushes, camelias, azaleas, and rhododendrons. It boasted an outdoor art gallery featuring exhibits of small and mid-sized art. Amy's team would need to arrive before July 26th, when the current exhibit would be closing. And they could come only on a Thursday,

Friday, or Saturday between noon and five. Amy noted the details and promised to call back with a specific time and date. She rang off, already soured on the place.

But she spoke at length to Jada Reed, the Black Tennessean with the family market garden, and Gabriella Diaz, the Dominican ex-pat with the organic cooperative in Marathon Key. Amy was secretly proud of herself to have included these women in her collection. True, they looked like crass touches of diversity for the book; Sandy had already dismissed them as mere tokens. But at least the book wasn't all comprised of White, affluent types that typically dominated the pages of *English Gardens,* an orientation Ella and her publisher didn't seem terribly driven to correct. Their notion of unique women was more geographical, artistic; race and wealth hadn't been a particular consideration. More importantly, however, Amy'd given herself a chance to explore worlds she wouldn't otherwise have access to. With Jada and Gabriella, she could learn and grow.

Booking the motels proved fiddly and time consuming, but by the time weariness overtook her, Amy had located some entertaining places to stop on the way, to break up the driving. She typed the itinerary and emailed it to Zach and Sandy. She was ready to go; they had a plan.

That night, though, Amy's sleep was troubled. After hours of tossing, she sank into a worried dream.

She and Graham were on a shoreline, sitting at a small patio table. Tourists—Brits and Germans mostly—were scattered about under umbrellas, women in pricey swim tops and men in coral-colored Bermuda shorts and vividly printed shirts. Children were playing in a swimming pool nearby and she wanted to join them, but she couldn't, not having worn a suit. It was already so hot when a great boom sounded from somewhere. The children hadn't heard it - they were making such a clatter - and some dove into the pool, part of a game she couldn't follow. She wondered if she shouldn't go warn them, but she was grounded there, unable to move. Further out, the shoreline looked darker, became closer suddenly, and the ocean lifted, as if waking, shrugging its shoulders, and the salt water advanced. Spilling into the pool, the water rose onto the patio, swirling around their ankles. Then it retreated again and finally everyone stood to watch, the children and their parents, all these stunned vacationers. Graham was pointing to a dog racing away from the beach and over their heads birds exploded from the branches of trees. He grabbed her hand and they ran together, through a long hotel corridor and into the road beyond, running and shouting to others as they passed. *Run, run!!* The waves returned, nearly the size of buildings and the water overtook them, sweeping them high off the earth. She felt Graham's body heaved aside, jolted by some floating weight, a tree, maybe, or a car, and the fingers of Graham's hand slipped from hers. Then she was carried, swept like a cork, bobbing and dipping, brushing against objects, not buried, not broken either, but swirling in the rush of the water.

Amy came to, gasping for air. Stumbling into the bathroom, she washed herself awake with a warm washcloth, letting her face drip over the sink. Seeking the solidity of the floor with her heels, her thighs against the solid, stationary porcelain, she waited until she felt safe and awake. But the enormity of what she'd committed to in real life hit her like a brick. She'd planned to leave Graham alone for two weeks. It was a reckless, selfish decision, and she knew it. A cold dread climbed through her body, and she avoided her reflection in the mirror. Turning off the light, she tiptoed down the stairs.

The time on the clock read 6:13 a.m. Late enough, she reasoned quickly. Alice would be up.

"Good morning!" Her sister sounded like she'd downed her first coffee.

"Hey," Amy replied. "Have a minute? I gotta run something by you."

"About four. I'm just heading out. What's up?"

Amy couldn't think that fast and wasn't ready to be concise. "Well . . ." her voice faltered, not knowing how to proceed. "I, um . . ."

"Well, you're either pregnant, having an affair, getting a divorce, or D, none of the above."

Amy tried to smile. "D."

"Or you're calling to admit that they really paid you *four* grand for all those antiques. Not just two. Right?"

"Sorry."

"Oh-kay." Alice's tone softened. "Well, you're not allowed to be sick or dying, Ame. We've had altogether too much of that this year."

"I'm not." Amy paused, then added quickly. "It's Graham, Alice. *He's* sick."

Alice sounded relieved. "Oh, hon, I'm sorry," she said. "What's wrong?"

Amy looked over at Haps, wondering if he was listening. The words stuck in her throat.

Alice tried to guess. "Not canc—"

Amy cut her off. "He's been diagnosed with Alzheimer's." There, she'd said it.

"Oh *shit,* Amy."

"Yeah." The silence on the line ricocheted between them, and Amy could practically hear Alice's brain computing the next few plays. Amy hurried to get in first. "It's not terrible yet. Graham still seems . . . pretty normal most of the time. I mean, he can manage. You know. But I've got a lot of travel coming up—for my book— and I think it would be risky to leave him too long on his own. I mean, he'd probably be fine. I've left him for a couple of nights, and except for the pile of dirty dishes when I got back, there wasn't a problem." Amy struggled to explain it all, so that Alice would understand. "But he's getting worse, getting flustered." She got to the tricky part. "He doesn't want anyone to know, though. That's the problem. He's working from home now, and he has an assistant here working with him who doesn't know a thing about his condition. She's young—very ambitious. But meanwhile, he's trying to keep all his clients happy. I promised I wouldn't tell a soul, Alice, and—"

"Whoa! Whoa! Stop!" Alice said. "Take a breath!"

Amy stopped, trying to do just that.

Alice seemed to be collecting her thoughts. "Well, you can't leave him on his own," she said. "That's the first thing."

The shock of the simplistic response came like a blow, rendering Amy speechless.

"Of course you can't, Amy," Alice said, more sternly this time. "You know that."

"I know, "Amy said, "but what about my *work*?

"Well—"

"I've got nine places to see in two months, Alice. I have to travel. I can't make up what the gardens look like, pretending like I've interviewed these gardeners . . . I'm under contract—"

"Okay—"

"—and if I don't go, I'll lose everything—the book contract, everything!"

"Hey!" Alice barked. "Calm down." Then she almost chuckled, slowing the pace. "Who do you think you're talking to? This is me. I'm not suggesting you quit your job. Not at all. You simply do what other working women do—you hire someone to look after things while you're gone. You delegate!"

Amy inhaled. "And what do I tell people?" The horror of what was being asked made her sick inside.

"You tell them the truth."

"But Graham doesn't want—"

"I know. You said that." Alice hesitated, timing the next comment with care. "But things have changed. Now it's gotta be *you* who takes charge, Amy. If you want to work, you've got to work it out."

It was like being punched in the gut.

"Do you have home health care services around you?" Her sister's rational manner continued. "I'm sure you must."

*Oh, fuck you!* Amy thought. It was the preaching tone as much as anything, the sure, holier-than-thou earnestness that made Amy's stomach curl. She wished she hadn't called in the first place and deeply regretted having shared Graham's secret. She couldn't tell people the truth! Graham's career—their financial security depended on it. Had Alice even been listening? But, as ever, Alice had done it again, ignoring everything that Amy'd said. That was the problem with her sister, Amy thought angrily to herself. Always sure that Alice's way was the only way. She'd been doing it her whole life, and this morning was no different. Miserable with frustration, Amy struggled to find an exit line. "Yup. I'm sure we do," she said. "I'll check it out."

"Or visiting nurses. I bet Graham's own doctor would have some suggestions. I know there are caretaker support groups—"

Every word Alice spoke made Amy angrier. Sizzling with resentment now, she needed to end the call before she started to scream. "Yeah, probably. Anyway. I know you gotta go," she said. "But Alice, please don't tell the kids. Promise me you won't."

"Amy, honey—"

"Just promise!"

"I'm not going . . ."

"Thanks. Now, I need to get off the phone. But thanks." And she put the receiver down, as quickly and quietly as she could manage.

Amy, Sandy, and Zach were scheduled to depart the day after tomorrow. Gone for fourteen days. Thirteen nights. Two weekends and ten weekdays. Amy's brain ran the timeline, calculating the risk. Moira would be in the house most of that time, Amy figured. She'd probably take care of lunch every workday. So, just evenings and nights, breakfasts and dinners. If Amy left the refrigerator and freezer filled . . . If a neighbor dropped in a couple of times. If Andy took Graham out sailing once. Maybe Khayed and Betsy would invite Graham over one Saturday night for dinner. Amy churned through the options. What were the odds, anyway, of something awful happening? Like Graham getting locked out. Like Haps wandering off. Like a fire. Her emotions ran the circuit, finding herself back at the starting point each time, her head revolving with worry, trouble, and guilt.

After breakfast, she dressed carefully, wondering which outfit would help her the most. Her linen trousers were more appropriate for the tony little club, but the tee-shirt dress better exuded the aura of an artistic friend in need. She went with the dress. For a final touch, she added in her sea-glass earrings, the pale blue drops highlighting the shade of her eyes. Who knew? It might help. What she really required was balls and humility, but at least getting the costume right couldn't hurt.

Amy left the house and started the long, pleasant walk down Smith Neck Road toward the Round Hill Community Golf Club. The day was still and warm with great puffs of overhead clouds that brought interludes of shady coolness as she walked along the coastline. Andy had told her that his wife had an early tee time and would probably be finishing up by ten, so Amy took her time. She needed it anyway, needed the time to think.

Their last exchange had been a bit odd, following the disastrous race, when Judith had left the yacht club in an exhausted retreat. And at Amy's birthday party, though they were friendly enough, she and Judith hadn't shared a particularly personal or lengthy conversation. But the women had a reliable history together. Sailing buddies for years. That counted for something.

Amy talked her way into the club's bar, an informal indoor/outdoor space overlooking the last hole. She knew many of the members, and the bartender was an old classmate of Jason's. Small world, really, although today Amy felt like an imposter, here on a mission of utter deceit. She picked up a forgotten copy of the *New York Times* and tried to bury herself in the unfinished crossword.

When Judith Jeffers entered the bar, she and her companions were still crowing over a delightful round. Someone had come in four under par, and the recriminations of the other three were noisy. Amy put down her paper and raised her hand. "Hello, Judith!"

Judith looked over to where Amy was seated, surprised. "Well, hi."

Amy rushed to explain her presence. "Andy told me you'd be here." She glanced meaningfully at Judith's friends. "Do you have a moment?"

Judith adjusted quickly, although clearly confused. "Sure, sure!" she said. She turned to the other women and muttered something to excuse herself. They nodded and pulled away, looking back at Amy with curiosity. "Let me just grab a drink. Would you like something?"

"Club soda?" Amy said. If she was going to be rude, she didn't need to die of thirst in the process.

Judith nodded, turned to the bartender, and placed an order. In Amy's estimation, Judith had it all together. Ever-pretty in a ponytail, her skin color a perfect summery almond, her arms and legs compared favorably to those of the Bionic Woman. The woman's slenderness reflected hours and years of tempered outdoor pursuits, tennis and swimming, sailing, now golf, all the while managing a busy house-cleaning service. Judith supervised a team of four, working herself as clients' needs demanded. Despite the inevitable hours of vacuuming and scrubbing toilet bowls, Judith rarely missed showing up for a doubles match or day sail, appearing at all times like the consummate lady of leisure. Hers was the ballast that had kept her family's financial world afloat, even as Andy's own ups and downs as a salesman had made tight times a regular occurrence. Amy was ever in awe of the discipline and calm.

Judith lowered her long frame into the seat across from her.

Amy forced a cheerful smile. "I didn't want to catch you at home with Andy hovering around," she began. "This is a bit of a weird request."

"Well, here I am," Judith said. "You've caught me." She fingered the sweating glass and took a long pull of her drink.

"You know I'm writing a new book," Amy started. "Well, maybe you didn't know that. But I am, and it's going to require that I travel quite a bit over the next few weeks." She noticed a yellow reflection in Judith's hazel eyes. "Anyway, Graham meanwhile has started working from home, so he's in the house all the time, lately. And he has a new assistant working there with him. Neither are particularly careful with cleaning up after themselves . . ."

Judith smiled knowingly. "Lord. One man at home is bad enough. Two would be—"

"Oh, it's a woman," Amy interrupted. "But she's no better. She's young, trying hard to impress the world with her professionalism, not eager to be branded as his housecleaner."

This factoid seemed to intrigue Judith, who waited for more.

"So, partly, I'm wanting to hire you. Your housecleaning service," Amy said at last. "But you specifically."

"Only partly?" The eyes narrowed slightly.

"No. Really *hire* you, but what I'd really like is if you could come by the house, like, every evening, you know, around five or six o'clock? For just an hour or two—two hours. You know, and tidy up the kitchen, maybe put something in the oven for Graham's dinner? I'll leave his meals in the freezer."

Judith looked perplexed before an inspired guess smoothed her brow. "Is this so the 'young assistant' doesn't stay into the evening?"

Judith seemed so knowing, so understanding, that Amy simply nodded. That excuse would do nicely.

"Weekends too?" Judith asked.

Amy shrugged. "I thought maybe Andy would invite him sailing one of the days. If he isn't still too pissed off from the race." Then she caught herself. "But only if he wants to." She sought a response in Judith's face, suddenly desperate to be done. "The whole thing sounds a little odd, I know."

Judith shook her head, her expression glowing with compassion. "It's not odd, trying to keep a family together, Amy. We've all done it." She seemed to be reappraising her old friend, intrigued by this new revelation about Graham and Amy's marriage. "And Graham knows I'll be coming by every day?"

"Not yet. But he'll be fine. I'll just tell him I don't want to find the house a mess when I get back. That I don't expect him or Moira to have to deal with all the kitchen clutter while I'm gone."

"Moira? Is that her name?"

"Yeah." Amy demurred. "She's . . . okay, really. But this would . . . you know, just keep things in order while I'm away."

Judith nodded, accepting her friend's reluctance to say more. "So, two hours. Every weekday?"

"For two weeks. And I'll pay your going rate."

Judith smiled. "I trust you. Anyway," she added, as if sharing a confidence of an intimate nature, "I know what it's like."

Relieved, Amy took her time walking home. Telling Graham about this new arrangement wasn't going to be easy. She knew he'd object. In all the years they'd lived together, he'd always vetoed the presence of a housecleaner. *Have a stranger touching everything I own? Whacking the walls and table legs with her vacuum cleaner while I'm trying to think? No thank you!* However, telling him the real reason she needed Judith dusting through his life every day was worse.

*What—you think I'm too mentally unhinged to manage on my own? Worried I'll stack the dishwasher wrong?* Amy's heart shrunk as she anticipated his defensive, sarcastic response. Slowing with every step, she practiced a string of excuses. As she neared the house, not one seemed good enough.

Graham and Moira were together in the kitchen, remnants of a midmorning coffee break scattered about. They were working over a finished drawing splayed across the kitchen table. Laughing and scribbling, they appeared energized by some design concept they'd hit upon for the children's library, clearly pleased with that morning's collaboration.

"Hey, Amy! Come see!" Moira turned the sheet in her direction. "Waterfalls, fish tanks, and dry books, all in one space!"

"Perfected acoustics and stress relief—even with kids," Graham gloated.

Amy walked over to have a look. She could see the signature water features shrunk to child-sized proportions. Blocks of liquid half walls and tall tanks shimmering with colorful fish defined a wide, peaceful arena of short shelving and lower seats. Arranged around the page were large color swatches: shades of teal and pale apricot, wisps of navy and blobs of buttery yellow made the design leap. "I like it!" Amy agreed.

"We're gonna win prizes!" Moira beamed, flinging her arms wide to include Graham in the pose. But as she did so, she sent the coffee press and platter of pastries crashing from the table. Dark brown liquid, crumbs and shards of broken pottery flew across the floor, bringing the celebration to a messy end.

"Shit," Moira said, leaping to avoid the spill.

"Damn," Graham echoed, his surprise edged with judgment.

"No problem," Amy assured them both, moving instinctively for the paper towels. Carefully, she dried the tabletop and mopped up the chair and floor beneath. "And when I'm away," she added, suddenly aware of the perfect opening, "I've got someone coming by every day to do this. So you two don't have to worry about keeping the kitchen pristine, you can focus on your work instead." She pointed again to the drawing. "'Cause it's so, so good!"

It was a cheap shot. Opportunistic of her to drop the news at such a moment, avoiding a tense one-on-one with her husband. But it worked. Neither Graham nor Moira pursued the issue in the moment, and Amy left them there, in their dry, clean work environment, and scuttled upstairs, one step closer to her own, precarious escape.

Only later that night did Graham return to the subject. They were in bed, ready to settle into their nighttime reading, and Amy was relieved to have made it through the day, all of her biggest concerns so neatly resolved.

"Course, if you didn't insist on all this travel," he said, as if they'd just been discussing it, "you wouldn't need to bring in someone to clean the house for you."

Amy sighed inside. She ignored the sexist implication. She could hear the warning shots of a looming row and had to choose which hill to die for. "That's true," she said, "But I am going to be away, and you don't do your best work in an untidy space." She tried returning to the page in her lap.

"You know I don't want strangers in the house."

"I know." Saying it out loud made her braver. "But it's not just our house anymore; it's an office now. And it's not just your home, it's mine too. And I want it kept clean."

She could sense his surprise, heard him change gears. "So who've you found to do this? Some bunch of losers with no work papers?"

Amy let that pass too, keeping her finger on the paragraph. "No, in fact. I've asked Judith."

"Who?" Graham's anger was audible now.

She looked over to him. "Judith Jeffers. Andy's wife."

It took him a moment to register. "Why her?"

"It's what she does," Amy replied, trying to be calm. "She's happy to do it."

Graham's face darkened, his frustration palpable. "When did you set this up? When's she coming?"

"I spoke with her this morning. We agreed on every weekday evening. I thought she might put in your dinner too, make sure Haps is fed."

"Christ, Amy! You're kidding!"

"I'm not."

"She'll expect to be paid, you know."

"I know."

She felt him stiffen with indignation. "Well, I'm not paying someone to do your job. That'll have to come out of your money."

Amy glanced at her book, the words in front of her now a haze of black figures. She reflected on the tiny advance from her publisher and felt the power of Graham's financial noose tightening. "If you insist."

"I do." And with that, Graham opened his book.

Amy sat, her mind reeling with what she'd done. She wished suddenly she'd taken the time to really study their finances when she'd first gotten access to Graham's files. She'd meant to. For weeks, the knowledge that she'd need to come to grips with how their bills got paid, how her husband managed their assets, had hovered in the back of her mind. But his resistance to taking stock with her, the few times she'd brought it up, had made raising the subject unbearable. Now, because it didn't suit him, because she'd incurred expenses he hadn't approved, he was going to close down the hatches, retreat further behind his wall of privileged information. Amy wasn't sure about any more than the two plus grand she'd last noticed in their checking account, but she couldn't remember when she'd last checked it. She was staring down two weeks on the road, meals, gas, and hotel costs for three. Paying Judith Jeffers. The unplanned numbers, dancing now, anarchic in the fog of figures, frightened her. Yes, she had her income from the paper. The small cash advance in her savings account. Oh, and the money from the antiques. But that was mere crumbs. Then Amy remembered she hadn't yet sent Alice the check for her share, and her heart tightened in shame. She was just so unreliable and impractical, Amy admitted to herself, lost in her own future world of hopes and landscapes. How would she ever manage caring for the two of them in the real world of the here and now? A remembered realization flooded her with relief. Of course! They still owned the house in Kandy, and her parents' home would be closing in just over a month. She'd forgotten that. She'd be coming into real money of her own soon. *That* was the soft landing that had kept her from taking responsibility; it wasn't simply that she was an economic basket case. That had been there all along, while she'd been crooning with self-doubt. Amy felt reassured. Of course she could be responsible. She would. But later. Not tonight. Tonight, she'd stick to her plan. And get some sleep.

But when her heart rate had finally slowed and her mind had made it back into the safe fantasy of her novel, he started over, his tone like acid. "So, I guess you expect to make money from all this?"

She didn't, not really. "Hope so," she said airily.

Graham huffed to himself, as if searching for her weak spot. "You think you're really that good, Amy?" His voice was earnest, concerned, patronizing.

Maybe it was his meanness. Maybe it was just her anger and exhaustion speaking, but she turned to him with a cold confidence. "I am, you know."

At the first sign of dawn, Amy slipped into the garden, a steaming mug of tea cupped in her hands. The bushes and trees were still outlined dark against a pale gray sky, and only the faint tint of lemon washed the strip of horizon where the sun would soon appear. The grass was cool underfoot and she sipped at her drink to warm herself.

She'd woken with a full list of last-minute errands marching across her consciousness, ones that had interrupted her sleep during the night. Pack her bags, her laptop, her phone charger, and notebook. Get to the grocery store and cook up at least some first few dinners to stock in the freezer. Write up some instructions for Judith. The lawn needed a last mowing and she wanted to chop back the Michaelmas daisies, the asters and phlox, reducing the stems by a third to ensure bushier plants and larger blooms in mid-August. Waiting until her return was too late in the month for this annual routine. And if she had time, she would also check their checking account. Remind herself precisely where that stood.

First, though, she needed the calm of her garden. And some inspiration. Amy had to produce two more garden columns for the paper before taking off, and her mind on that score was blank. She'd been thinking for weeks to tell Sam that this time, what with the new book and added travel, she wouldn't be able to come up with anything. That maybe her stint with the column was finally over. But Graham's reference to "her own money" had made her pause. The weekly income from the paper was hers, a small retainer in a storm of doubt. It was something she could count on.

She dug a hole in the soil under the asters and plunked in her tea bag. The plants were getting leggy already, nearly shouting for their Chelsea Chop. As she patted the earth back over, it came to her, the subject of one column, anyway. Half of gardening was planting and sowing. The other, though, was pruning, cutting back, deadheading. It was making space for what was coming. What better time to focus on the benefits of that?

# SIXTEEN

As they drove off, the last view she had of Graham unnerved her. He had ducked his head in turning away, as if not daring to shout a final goodbye, and Amy felt a wave of terror, leaving him alone with his ineptitude.

They made it past Philly in good time and treated themselves to a cheap dinner and an early night. The next morning, Zach and Sandy joined her at the motel café in a harried swoop, to grab some fruit and muffins and fill up their flasks with caffeine.

"Want to get on the road, see if we can avoid the snake pit around D.C.," Zach said, tucking the supplies into his bag.

"We're going to hit rush hour whatever we do," Sandy insisted. "I told you that."

"Got all your things?" he asked Amy, checking at her feet. "Of course you do. Good!" He resettled his bags on his shoulders and charged off for the parking lot.

Sandy's eyes narrowed. "He can be so unbearable," she whispered to Amy, as they scooted to keep up.

Zach, in fact, was anything but. Although the traffic was heavy, he opted to remain behind the wheel, adding sardonic commentary to a serious news station as they barreled south.

They were headed for Tennessee, a trip into the relative unknown, and Amy was glad to keep moving. The cowering image of Graham was still fixed in her mind, but she pushed it aside, searching for what was new outside the car windows. For several hours, the landscape changed little. Tarmac gave way to green and then back again, sprawl and box stores, jukebox diners, and Hardee's. Somewhere by Harrisburg, they indulged in cheap ribs at Dickey's Barbeque Pit, getting all red and sticky, destroying a thick pile of napkins as they ate. Sandy's lips shone with joy. "Sweet grease!" She beamed. "This is the life."

Back on the road, they played a silly road game of Amy's childhood, counting the number of license plates from different states, finding few. Until Zach suggested they count confederate flags instead. The number was sobering.

"It says this is a perfect honeymoon motel," Sandy laughed, scanning her phone.

They were nearing their night's destination, a nowhere town along Route 81, halfway to the former pig farm in western Tennessee.

"That's why you chose it, isn't it?" Zach laughed, his eyes grinning at Amy in the rear-view mirror.

"My only thought," she said.

"The pool is open through Labor Day and there's a view of the mountains from some of the rooms," Sandy read aloud.

"Oooo, I hope I get one," he chuckled.

"I chose it for the caverns nearby," Amy confessed. "I figured we should see the sights, while we're here."

Sandy and Zach looked at each other and laughed.

"We should," Sandy nodded. "Right after we try out that pool."

By the time they checked in, they were a team again. Skipping dinner, they changed into their suits and met at the pool. Amy tiptoed about in the tepid water, just barely swimming, letting the stiffness from the back seat drain from her limbs. Zach butterflied off on his own, and Sandy dove into the far side, coming up for air into a strong crawl. Then Amy spied the hot tub, steaming by the back corner of the pool. A young couple—a very thin woman and a hugely overweight man—were seated in one side of it, armpit deep in the swirling water.

"May I join you?" Amy tended toward politeness, especially when almost naked.

"Of course," the woman said, bobbing closer to her partner. "More the merrier!" She patted the surface of the water. The woman's small breasts only half filled the foam cups of her bikini, and Amy could see the thinness of her legs through the water. But the woman was big with friendliness, and Amy sank happily into the pool. Then the woman's large eyes shifted, her sights on Zach, stepping in behind Amy.

Amy too had noticed. Without his work shirt and jeans, Zach's body was noteworthy, his scantily clad figure suddenly radiating with suggestion. Amy had to work to keep her eyes off of Zach's perfect torso on her left, the husband's trembling flesh to her right.

"This is nice," she said to the couple. "Have you stayed here before?"

"Oh, lots," the wife said. "We love it."

"It's our first time," Zach grinned, sliding closer to Amy. Amy guessed he was playing with her.

"Well, you'll love it," the husband said. "Be sure to do the caves. Course, I guess that's why you're here."

"That's why," Zach nodded. "We're doing the caves tomorrow."

"Where you all from?" the wife asked.

Zach and Amy said "New York" and "Massachusetts" at the same time.

"Uh huh," the wife nodded, letting it pass. Then she glanced at Sandy, still doing her laps in the pool, and back to Amy's wedding ring, for the second time.

"Northerners, then." The husband stated, as if it needed confirmation.

"That's right," Zach said. "Nothing for it."

They simmered together in silence. A couple of times the husband shifted, directing a jet of water to hit him right in the back, and then slid back, the displaced water rising up their chests.

Amy was getting hot but didn't budge. She was wholly content, her shoulders and head exposed to the evening air, the water pummeling her below, the nice couple across from her, the beautiful body nearby.

Sandy left the pool and stood by the tub. "Hi, y'all," she said. "This looks cozy." Her turquoise spikes were glistening like the wetted back of a colorful male duck, and pearls of water dripped off her. Her own full bosoms jounced pitilessly as she settled next to the other woman.

"I'm Tracy, and this is Dean," the wife announced, as if now was finally the right time to tell them.

"Hello, Tracy-and-Dean," Sandy said. "And we're Amy-Sandy-and-Zach." It sounded like mockery.

"What brings you back this time, Dean?" Amy asked, determined to keep it friendly.

"We're celebrating our anniversary," the husband told them, his deep drawl syrupy and sweet.

"Us too!" Sandy said. "Isn't that a coincidence?!"

The couple exchanged a strained look. Then Tracy announced that it was time to go, too much heat not being good for a body.

"That was mean," Zach said, watching the pair drip off toward the lobby.

"Christ!" Sandy scoffed, stretching her legs, placing her toes where the couple had sat. "It'll give them something to talk about."

Amy stayed quiet and found a reason to leave shortly after: there was some writing to do, more research to catch up on back at the room. It was hard, seeing the unkindness. She didn't want to think of Sandy in such a way, as a mean girl, and it made Amy wonder how it happened that she'd ended up with such a colleague, such a friend. Settling down before her laptop, she made a quiet promise to herself, vowing not to allow any of Sandy's negativity or cynicism seep into the project, one that was becoming, for Amy, a journey of real delight, hope, even.

The rain arrived during the night, turning the sky grim and flat. The next leg of their journey, a straight shot to Nashville, would be eight hours, all highway, so they gave themselves a quick tour of Grand Caverns before heading off. The deep limestone cave was both crass and exciting, some of the spaces lit bright in multicolor, others tall and wretched, as if a great wedding cake was dripping its layers of frosting down from above. Some stone facades bragged tourists' names, the dates of their visits, other narrow paths required headlamps to make it through.

"I'd never been in a cave before," Amy announced when they finished. "Thanks for indulging me."

"Me neither," Zach agreed. "I'm claustrophobic, and I didn't die."

"Not bad at all," Sandy added. "Except for the smell."

This time, Zach was happy to hand over the wheel, not eager to drive in the rain, so Amy obliged. Sandy crawled into the back seat with her sketch pad, and Zach leaned against his window and closed his eyes.

Two different radio stations took them through southern Virginia into Tennessee. Even from the highway, they could sense the changing world, heavier with plant life, the sky saturated with moisture. This, Amy had read, was where kudzu was king, where it scrambled over the countryside, one foot a day. What she didn't know about the topography of the state was so much more than what she'd studied, and as they got closer, the gap in her knowledge began to worry her.

At lunch, she said as much. "I can't even remember whether the western part of Tennessee is where there's lots of clay or lots of sand. Just that it's good for cotton."

Sandy was dabbling on her phone. "Google it. Anyway, I'm sure Farmer Reed will tell you all that."

"Jada." Amy said. "Her name's Jada." It worried Amy that Sandy's rudeness and general lack of tact might surface during this visit, especially because of Jada's race. "Please don't call her 'Farmer Reed.'"

Sandy looked up from her screen. "Okay."

"I think all the information you really need is a sense of the history of this area," Zach said. "And keep your eye on the money: how the family managed to purchase the land, how they've managed to hold onto it."

Amy acknowledged she didn't know. The Reed family, descendants of formerly enslaved ancestors, according to Jada, had managed something of a miracle, with all their many acres. For the next four hours, sitting in the back seat again while Zach drove, she worried about how to ask. That night, she combed the internet, reading up on slave holdings in Tennessee, The Homestead Act, the Freedman's Bureau. It got late and she was too tired, too distracted to phone home.

A two-hour drive from Nashville, Reed Farm was some way from the main drag, a large wooden sign pointing them down a long, rutted road. Either side of the car, rows of vegetation hugged the land. Dust puffed by the windows as they bumped along, caking the view in reddish brown.

"Jeez, it really is a farm!" Sandy grumbled. "You sure there's a garden here at all?"

Amy scanned the fields nervously. "From what I've read. The pictures I saw showed both—crops and flowers combined."

"Long fucking way to come if you're wrong," Sandy muttered.

"Don't worry about it." Zach gave Amy a reassuring look. "You want each chapter to be different. Anyway, it's a nice change from New England and Delaware, whatever they grow."

Amy saw the garden building first, in a fenced-off area where some other cars and trucks were parked. A trio of fat limelight hydrangeas edged one side of the building and on the right stood a crepe myrtle tree, ablaze with purple blossoms. Under the wide, open structure, beneath a sloped wooden roof, deep crates of earthy produce were what caught her eye. It reminded Amy of the vegetable stands in Sri Lanka, with their bounty of fruits and vegetables, dirty and fresh. Over a dozen people were filling paper bags with items, weighing produce in hanging scales. Not a White person among them.

Even without Sandy's mood, Amy felt a growing wariness. The dust alone was distracting. Coating the bottom of everything—the fence posts, the bushes as they drove up, her ankles as she stepped out from the car—it was thick, like a second skin. And it weighed on her suddenly, reminding her that she was in unfamiliar territory, worried she was under-prepared for the interview she'd planned. The hours of cramming the night before seemed to melt away, the fading concepts not readying her for the walk across the powdery yard. Suddenly, Amy was nervous for the idiocy of her mission, the reach of her journey, and now, the color of her skin. Anxiously, she fluffed at her bangs.

As they lingered by the Kia, a woman approached from behind the wooden structure, her dark face darker in the shadow of a long-billed cap. Muscular and full-bodied, maybe five-foot-six and of indeterminate age, the woman wore her blue jeans cinched at the waist with a worn leather belt. Her long-sleeved plaid cotton shirt was rolled to her elbows. "Amy James?"

"Hi. Yes!" Amy said, smiling brightly. "A bit earlier than expected, I'm afraid."

"Early's no crime," the woman replied. "I'm Jada. Jada Reed. Welcome to Reed Farm." Her handshake was strong, her eyes welcoming. Noticing Zach, strapping on his camera equipment, she smiled. "You brought the film crew, I see."

Amy nodded, introducing her colleagues. Jada shook their hands, first Zach's, then Sandy's. "Traffic cause you any problems?"

"None," Amy replied. "Not once we cleared the city."

"Of course, we left pretty early." Sandy's complaint was audible.

"Didn't want to miss a thing, us," Zach added quickly.

Jada looked from one to another, part curious, part bemused at the trio before her. "So, some eager beavers, then! That's good to know."

"It's beautiful country out here," Amy said finally, her arms lifting. "So much open space."

"Uh huh." Jada beamed an appraising glance across the far field. "We're blessed all right."

"Is this all yours?" Sandy's question held the WASPish taint of surprise.

"Depends who you ask," Jada answer was curt and vague. But then she grinned, folding her arms over her chest. "Some folks are trying their damnedest to prove otherwise, but, yeah . . . it's all ours. For a hundred and some odd years anyway."

"Well, we're really eager to see the place," Amy said.

"We are," Zach echoed.

"Good then." Jada sniffed, giving Sandy a last look. "I'm not sure what will interest you, exactly, so thought I'd just show you the lot. Up for some walking?"

"Absolutely." Amy nodded.

"Let's go then." Jada turned on her heel, and with her long, easy stride, led them across the parking lot and into the first field.

Amy was feeling slightly off balance, as if already they'd proved themselves unworthy visitors. She returned her cumbersome tape

167

recorder to the car. Scurrying to keep up, she told herself to focus on the plants, pay attention to all that was new, and be ready to ask intelligent questions.

The farm was beautifully laid out. Great wide stripes of vegetation morphed from one shade of green to another: emerald to chartreuse, olive to khaki. First collards, then asparagus, turnips, then spinach. But as they made their way deeper into the field, Amy noticed more subtle dashes of artistry. Set into the verdant landscape were light splashes of blue and lavender, garish dabs of yellow, pink and magenta. Interspersed between the vegetables, flowers had been planted. At one spot, a narrow swath of low, wild columbine grew by butter beans, clumps of thigh-high bee balm by kale at another. Sprays of lantana interrupted thick lines of lemon mint. At the end of one row, another brilliant crepe myrtle tree emerged, feet taller than a tent of string beans climbing up converging lines of twine.

Amy glanced at her hostess. "You're an artist as well, aren't you? Not just a farmer."

Jada nodded. "I've been told," she said.

And Amy noticed for the first time some short plaits under the hat, ending in brightly colored beads. "It's good of you to give us the time," Amy said. "This time of year, I expect you're pretty busy."

"Always," Jada smiled. "But yeah, we've got some bumper crop now for sure." She stopped for a moment, watching Zach some rows back, frozen behind the lens. "You want shots of okra?"

"Everything," Zach said. "I want everything!"

Behind him, Sandy was sketching in her notebook, capturing the trim of yellow clover skirting several types of lettuce.

"That's for nitrogen, not so much art." Jada said. "Anyway." She waved, "Take your time. We'll keep walking."

She and Amy crossed through some tall stalks of corn, leaving the other two in their wake. Traipsing down the rich, earthy tunnels with this generous stranger, Amy began to relax.

"Eighty-eight acres all together. "Bout half non-forest, of which thirty-six are farmable." Jada pointed in the direction of the entrance. "We have a couple of farmhouses down that way. Another one set back in the woods. Where my brother and his family live."

"Where do you live?" Amy asked.

"The original farmhouse. With my niece and her kids. That was the family place, back when. I moved back in after grad school." She corrected herself. "Well, after working in the city about ten years."

That interested Amy. "What did you do—in the city?"

"Chief risk officer." Jada chuckled. "Corporate finance." She made a show of looking down at herself, the plaid shirt and jeans. "So long, pin-striped suit!"

Amy laughed. This is a story, she thought, almost writing it in her mind. The hot August sun, the red earth underfoot, the CRO-turned-farmer with her baseball cap and beaded hair.

At one point, they saw the top of Sandy's head through a wall of deep green, and they heard Zach futzing with his lens cap further along. But mostly, the two women moved alone together, Jada pointing out the newest crops, the trial rows, the fallow ones, busy with low, bright leguminous plants, peas, ground nuts, more clover. Some of the rows were raised, sitting atop lengths of old tree branches, last year's garden cuttings. Soil was packed onto the mounds, the vegetation hungrily feeding off it, bountiful. Reaching the far side of that field, they arrived at a hillock, overseeing a creek far below.

"Built this three years ago," Jada explained, pointing to the long bump of earth. "The rains here can be devastating. Nearly wiped out everything in 2010. Came up as far as the middle there." She pointed, eyes squinting south. She sucked her teeth, remembering. "But this has held up since."

They turned then, in the direction of the woods. "You like hogs?" Jada asked, an eyebrow raised.

"I've met one once." Amy admitted. "At a farm show. Why, do you still keep them?" She cringed inwardly at the thought of the slaughter.

"Heh. Well, yeah. It used to be all we did. Before extending the farm, making the gardens commercial; early on, the crops were just to feed livestock and family. What we did was raise hogs." They approached some wire fencing that disappeared into the trees. "This is the pen. Kind of. The hogs wander about in here." She indicated the tree-filled acres, going on, it seemed, forever.

"They must love it!" Amy said, happy again for the animals.

"Love it enough to reward us with the manure we need." As they stepped through the fence into the wooded enclosure, Jada added, "Don't be scared. They only bite when you try to trap them and drag them somewhere they don't want to go."

"I'm with them," Amy laughed.

"You and me both!"

It was cooler under the trees, and Amy was tempted to luxuriate in the peacefulness of the moment. But she knew there was more to ask, information she needed to probe. Admitting her stupidity, however, made starting difficult. "You mentioned earlier that some people were challenging your ownership of this farm. Can I ask how they can do that? Legally, I mean?"

Jada slowed to a stop, hand on hip. "Legally?" she snorted.

"Was that a dumb question?"

"How many Black farmers do you know?"

Amy felt uncomfortable. "I don't know that many *farmers*."

Jada suppressed a sigh. "How many Black *people*?"

"Some," Amy answered defensively. Then, she corrected herself. "Not well."

"Well, then it's not a dumb question: how would you know if you don't ask?" Jada's expression suggested a practiced tolerance.

"I did some research before coming here," Amy managed. "I mean, I know there've been acres of land taken from African Americans over the last century."

"Stolen, not taken. But you're right—hundreds of thousands of acres."

"So was it . . . the lack of clear wills and land titles . . . ?" It made her uncomfortable, sounding as if she thought Jada's family might have been too poor, too uneducated, to deal with the courts, so Amy changed tack. "I mean, weren't there the legal resources? Is that the . . . problem here?" She could feel heat rising in her cheeks but remembered Zach admonishing her: Ask the hard questions.

Jada lifted her chin, as if seeking strength from above. When she looked back at Amy, her forehead was creased. "Do you really want to understand this? I mean, are you going to make this part of your book?"

Amy brightened, an opening. "Yes!"

"Because you need to understand that I've lived with this all my life, all my family's life. Black Americans all have. You can't feel about this business of land the way we do. You get that, don't you?"

Amy nodded. "I get it," she almost whispered.

"Good!" Jada searched for the words, some way to make it simple. "Do you own property?" she asked.

"Me?" The reversal surprised her. "You mean, as in a house? Garden?"

"Uh huh."

Amy had to think. "Well, we own our home. My husband and I."

"And how do you know it's yours?"

Amy paused, thinking. "There's a deed. With his name on it."

Jada smiled at the detail. "Not yours?"

This seemed a bit personal. In fact, Amy's name had never been put on the deed, and the truth of it still embarrassed her, but she answered the question. "Well, he bought the land before we were married. He built the house. He's an architect. But I've never been worried that I didn't have a right to live there." She tried to steer back to her original question. "So, do you not have a deed, then?"

Jada frowned. "Oh, we've got the deed. That's been handed down in the same file for over a hundred years. Deed's not the problem."

"So . . . ?"

"And for all that time, the land passed from one generation to the next, children inherited the land from their parents, and handed it down to their children when they died. The land became what was known as heirs' property, a perfectly legal form of ownership."

"Okay." Amy hadn't known that term. "Then what's not legal?"

Jada smiled at her insistence on the term. "Do your parents own a house?"

Amy nodded. "They did. They're both dead now."

"Okay. And did you inherit their house?"

"My sister and I did, yeah." Amy grinned almost guilty with the fact.

"How do you know? Are your names on the deed?"

Amy raised an eyebrow. "No . . . I'm pretty sure it was in my mother's will. We're named there."

Jada raised an index finger. "And that's what we don't have."

"No will."

"You got it. Lot of Black folk didn't make wills. And it was common during Reconstruction, because most folk didn't have access to the legal system. And it continued during Jim Crow, because Blacks didn't trust the Southern White courts."

Amy let it sink in. The stark difference between her reality and that of Jada's kept Amy quiet. She glanced around her, at the beautiful landscape, the decades of cultivation and labor the place represented. She imagined quickly what she would feel if her own garden—any piece of it, hers for only twenty plus years—were to be stolen out from under.

172

Another question surfaced. "But why now? Your family's had this farm for years."

"Because now the land is worth something. Because now developers have learned about heirs' property. And because there are lots of us heirs. Lots of ancestors all over the country, all who can claim their right to Reed Farm. All it takes is one tenth-generation-of-a-second-cousin-once-removed, some long lost relative out in California or South Dakota to get collared by some moneyed developer or speculator, who goes to court, demanding their right to sell their sliver of it, and tries to swindle the place out from under us. There are laws and loopholes out there to keep a lawyer busy for a lifetime."

Amy let out a long breath. "Lord."

"Yeah. Lord." Jada laughed ruefully. "So now you know. Heirs' property: the worst problem you never heard of." She pointed at Amy. "Put that in your book, would you?"

By midafternoon, the visitors were tired, sunburned, and spent. Jada's niece's son brought out some sandwiches and iced tea, which they consumed noiselessly on the porch. After the last of them made use of the farmhouse toilet, Jada stood to pose for one last picture.

"Here's the deal," she said. "We need all the publicity we can get. The garden store can take care of itself. We do well on that. And the hogs've covered their own upkeep for decades. But this current court case is killing us. And even if we win this time, we know there'll be another. So, whatever you can do—with your pictures, your drawings, articles you can write—please do it. We're happy to be in your book. Meanwhile, we also need the publicity, and we need the cash."

She held out her hand, the end of it. "Come back anytime."

# SEVENTEEN

They were quiet at the table that night. It had been a mistake, planning a four-hour drive to Chattanooga after a day in the bright sun, and the travelers spoke little while they waited to be noticed by the wait staff.

"Rooms aren't bad," Amy said finally, hating the silence.

"Nope," Zach agreed.

The waitress sloped over, lazily placing their water glasses on the table.

Zach drank thirstily. "So, what's the plan for tomorrow?"

She dipped her head, defensive now for the itinerary she'd planned. "It's not bad. Three hours to Macon, Georgia. Quick stop at the Tubman Museum, grab us some peach pie—that's the highlight. Then another three to Lake City, Florida: Gateway to Florida!"

Sandy had her elbows on the table, chin on her fists. "I'm not going to a fucking museum, Amy."

Amy blinked. "It's Harriet Tubman . . . I figured, all this driving. We might as well see what's down here."

Sandy grimaced, reaching for her water. "What's this, then—the Amy James tour of the Deep South?"

Amy stared, startled by the dig. "No."

"'Cause I don't do guilt." Sandy lifted her glass, emptying half.

"We're driving right by it," Amy reasoned. "It's American history!"

"Well, I gotta tell you. All Americans aren't as taken by Harriet Tubman as you seem to be. Just like not a lot of the Americans who are going to buy our book are wowed by some Tennessee pig farm, just because it's owned by a Black woman. They're really not." Sandy's gaze bored into Amy. Not even a blink. "You're trying too hard here, Amy. And it's taking the book way off course."

"What are you talking about?!" Amy shot back. "It's one of the chapters our publisher agreed to." Involuntarily, Amy's eyes sought out Zach, checking his reaction.

It was slow in coming. "Reed Farm is a garden," he said at last. "There's design, intentionality, real artistry. It's a garden. It's in the book. It belongs in the book."

Sandy hmphed, shaking her head.

In the silence, her heart still racing, Amy calculated the shifting alliances. "No one has to go to the museum. We'll be stopping anyway; I thought I'd like to see it."

"I'll go with you," Zach said, ignoring Sandy's glare.

It was after ten when Amy phoned home. Getting into her nightgown, she realized how much she needed to hear Graham's familiar voice. His sane, comforting one. But there was no answer. Not at ten-fifteen, not at ten-thirty. At eleven, she stopped trying.

The night's noises never let up. In her wakefulness, it felt like she heard the whole of Chattanooga humming through the walls, the traffic outside, the duck boats and zoo, the falls in Ruby Cave. Next door, she heard, all too well, Zach and Sandy making up, and later an occasional siren. By dawn, she was stoned with the noise, and when it came time to set out again, she took her seat silently in the back.

They drove straight through Macon, Georgia, giving Harriet Tubman a miss, and made Lake City, Florida well before dusk. She was quietly resentful about missing the museum, about the wall of opposition that had built up around it, but she decided that one stop wasn't worth a battle. Once back in her room, a dismal second floor box overlooking a Wendy's, Amy wrote up the whole of her Reed Farm account, typing until her wrists hurt.

There was no having to search for the story here. The challenge was introducing new concepts without turning the chapter into a Social Studies lesson. But as Amy struggled over what to cut, there was no question of what to keep. The story was the dynamic between this woman and her property. It wasn't an individual thing, Amy realized as she wrote. Jada's whole family, the culture of struggle that defined her people going back generations, had informed this ferocious attachment to the land. But this individual woman, Jada Reed, perfectly symbolized the passion that Amy had been seeking for her book, and there was no way she would leave it out. Land was, after all, the whole point.

As she closed her laptop, a notion dawned. Owning property hadn't been something Amy'd ever considered particularly significant in planning the project. It was the stewardship of the land, the use gardeners made of it, that had always intrigued her. But as she ruminated on Jada's story, on Edith's, and Mariann's, Amy came to a newer appreciation. Land ownership, besides being significant, might even be the essential underpinning to creative agency, the agency Amy so sought in her own life.

It was late when she phoned home, and once again Graham didn't pick up. Too tired to indulge in worry, Amy satisfied herself with a calming thought. Judith Jeffers hadn't called, so Amy assumed that the daily visits were working as planned. No news was good news.

The early five hours' hop from Lake City to Miami gave them all time to breathe. Somewhere by Kissimmee, a local religious station came on the car radio. The high, tinny voice of the preacher was invoking his listeners to "put a little Gawwd in yo' lahf!"

Sandy's hand moved for the dial. "Don't change it," Zach said, "I love this shit!"

*As you heap that sugar into your first coffee of the day, don't forget to put a little Gawwd in yo' lahhf. And when you go to put a dab of cologne behind your ear, put a little Gawwd in yo' lahhf! And as you tuck your baby chile's stuffed teddy bear into bed next to her, be sure to put a little Gawwd in there too!!*

Sandy was the first to add one of her own. "And when you stick that reefer in between your lips, suck a little Gawwd into yo' lahhf!"

"And when you go to pork your wives . . ." Zach picked up the action.

". . . .put a little Gawwd in your life."

"Stick a little Gawwd in your wife." Sandy and Amy finished over each other.

For several miles, they found Gawwd in just about every crevice and place you could stick something, and like magic the three companions began to enjoy themselves again. They hit Little Havana on the last Friday of the month, when the area hosted its Viernes Culturales, and Amy pretended she'd planned the itinerary just for that. Much later, they trekked through Wynwood Walls, taking in the graffiti, the astonishing contemporary murals.

"It's what I should be doing," Sandy drooled, agog at the artwork.

"Nothing's stopping you," Zach reminded her.

"Except a lifetime of bad choices," Sandy countered, referring not so subtly to the purpose of the trip.

"There's always time to make new ones," Zach said. "A lifetime, in fact."

The next day, Amy was back behind the wheel. She'd done her research into the next subject, Gabriella Diaz, and lectured loudly as they left Key Largo. The top was down on the Kia, and her two companions leaned in to hear. "Her two brothers are some of the most powerful sugar barons in the Caribbean, Amy explained. "Diaz Corporation: think Domino Sugar, Florida Crystals. Benni Diaz and Alvi Diaz. They're from Cuba and they now own this vast sugar and real estate conglomerate in the U.S. and the D.R. Worth about nine billion."

In spite of the wide sweep of the bridges, the pale green water beneath their wheels, Zach and Sandy listened, attentive.

"B? As in billion?" Sandy's eyes widened.

"Makes you think, eh?" Amy enjoyed being the know-it-all, and she felt smug, having chosen Gabriella.

"And where does the sister fit into this conglomerate?" Zach asked.

"She doesn't. Gabriella took herself to Marathon Key and bought some land of her own," Amy answered. "Twenty or so years ago she built a cooperative organic garden. Tropical flowers, food, and fellowship. That's what I know."

"And what's her angle?" Sandy was suspicious, after Jada.

"That's what we'll find out," Zach grinned.

Amy held her palm up. "I just asked her whether we could visit, and she said yes."

"So she knows what we're doing . . . and she wants to be in the book?" Sandy's eyebrows knitted doubt with mistrust.

"Yes!" Amy was irked.

"Okay. Okay . . ." Sandy sat back in her seat, letting it go.

"She's looking forward to it," Amy said.

The three left it at that.

By now, they had the routine down. Zach and Sandy dawdled over their photographs and sketches, and Amy and Gabriella walked ahead, Amy floating her open-ended questions, listening for the hook. Gabriella Diaz didn't need to be prompted. A steely, dark-eyed beauty, stunning still at sixty, Gabriella spoke with a sharp Cuban accent.

"Sugar is killing the world," she said. "Look anywhere. At the fast-food industry. The people so large they need to wheel themselves through the supermarkets. Children who can't run. Knee surgery now common. Sick, fat people. Everywhere." She didn't wait for argument, but simply kept on. "So, if you have money, if you have a brain, you have to do it different." She stopped, pulling a dead leaf from a Palmyra Palm, crushing it in her hand, wiping the particles to the ground.

"And you had both . . ." Amy wanted her to say more.

"I did. But I wanted Diaz money to go in a different direction. So I bought this piece of the Keys." Gabriella's eyes moved across the wide, sandy plot, as if scrutinizing anew her choice of location. "We're out in the middle of nowhere, nothing but ocean for miles every way. Yet thousands of people pass through and they see what can be done." On the far perimeter, a stand of palm trees waved as if in response. "Then they go home with a new idea."

Amy took another look at the sturdy windbreakers of flowering bush, the carefully arranged bowers and beds, the exotic individual statements of rare tropical plants studded throughout. "And did you build it all from nothing?" She guesstimated to herself the investment and time it had taken, the replenishment the soil had required.

Gabriella nodded deeply. "Less than nothing." She nudged a crystal-flecked hair comb back into place. "It took a lot."

Amy struggled to imagine her hostess in those early days. For a gardener, the woman was notably clean. She wore clothing of pure whites and yellows, trim capris, jeweled sandals. As they traversed the paths, Gabriella was careful where she walked.

"I stepped back from sole ownership following Hurricane Andrew in the early '90s. The garden was devastated, and dozens of neighbors had to help me rebuild it. It took us nearly three years. Collaboration became a necessity, then a principle. And the move to organic evolved quickly after that. The garden is owned and managed collectively now. My role is more of a fundraising, marketing one."

They approached a small pond, edged with bromeliad and horsetail reed and crossed a short bridge to the other side. Open water lilies floated like fragile tea cups across its surface.

"Now we've introduced as many healthy foods in our gardens as landscaping plants," she clarified, "but I still hold out for color, structure, style. If it's not as elegant as an oleander, I vote against." She reached to cradle a crimson blossom the size of her hand. "Of course, I don't always win. When I started the garden, it was called 'Red Sister,' the common name for the Cordyline terminalis. It was either going to be that or 'The Dragon Tongue,' which is the Hemigraphis repanda." Gabriella's accent made the words sound even lovelier, and she smiled as she spoke. "But when we went cooperative, the group preferred 'Salud'. I don't always win."

"Wasn't that hard—relinquishing control?" Amy asked. "In my garden at home, I like deciding what goes where. I'm not sure I'd appreciate getting voted down if others had a say."

"Yes," Gabriella said. "It was, at first." Then she laughed, catching herself. "It still is, sometimes. But I get to share the worries too, and the work. And when I run out of ideas, there's always someone in the group who has one. Or a dozen." She smiled, lifting her eyebrows in Amy's direction. "Are you more of a solo player?" She indicated Sandy and Zach, engaged in their work. "You seem to work as a team, no?"

Amy chuckled to herself. "Sometimes. But it's not easy. Not for me."

"You have to work at it?"

"I don't always win," Amy admitted.

"Well, sure." Gabriella patted Amy on the arm. "We don't."

They entered the shade of the tall palms, and Zach joined up with them, listening in as he snapped away.

180

"Salud's mission is not just to model organic farming and introduce healthy food options for people," she explained. "Like this ambutan—rich in vitamin C, a potent antioxidant, without being too sweet." She touched a bushy clump of small global fruit hanging shoulder height from a tree. Pink with pale green thistles, the balls resembled explosions, almost cartoonish in their design. "We are not here just to educate. We work to make such health beautiful, desirable." She looked and sounded like a seductress, suddenly, and Amy noticed Zach feeling the same vibe. He captured Gabriella's profile, her dark, luminous hair held back by two elegant combs.

Sandy approached, pocketing her notes. "I've got what I need." It was her typically rude signal she was ready to leave.

Gabriella smiled graciously. "Alright, then. And you?" She turned to Amy and Zach. "Do you have any more you'd like to see—or know?"

"Do you think this garden of yours makes that much of a difference?" Coming out from behind his camera, Zach's earnest voice surprised them. "Your family, the Diaz Corporation, is hugely powerful, still flooding the world with sugar. You really think this is an effective antidote to all that?"

"Christ, Zach, enough," Sandy said under her breath.

Gabriella's eyes glimmered, the shadow of a smile on her lips. "Do you believe there is climate change?"

Zach replied instantly. "Of course."

"And what do you do about that?" Her white teeth shone.

Zach shrugged. "I recycle." He paused. "I vote."

"Yes," she said. "That's good, no?"

"I think so. Yes . . ."

"Do you think it's 'an effective antidote,' as you say?" Her fingers were woven together now, resting primly against her legs.

Zach took a moment. "I do what I can. But I don't come from wealth."

"And I did. And did what I could with mine." She laughed. "Now, it's spent. And now, I have a garden. We do what we can."

Sandy nudged her partner. "Happy now?"

But Amy was still curious. "Do your brothers support what you're doing here? The sugar barons?"

Gabriella gave Amy a quick look. "They're still who they are. Of course."

Amy persisted. "Do you get along with your brothers?"

"Of course. Our mother is still alive, and we gather every Christmas and Easter. In Santiago."

"But no arguments?"

"None. We don't talk."

"I guess that helps," Amy said.

Zach chuckled.

"We don't talk politics," Gabriella clarified.

"Amen to that." Sandy shifted in place, sensing things were finally wrapping up.

But Gabriella continued, her voice becoming solemn. Her index fingers made a tent by her chest. "I don't need to fight with anyone. I have my garden. We grow health here, beauty and health. Where would anger be, resentment, in such a place?" She indicated their surroundings with a graceful turn of the head.

Amy followed the woman's eyes, soaking in the deep greens, shocking blossoms.

"A woman with a garden," Gabriella continued, "that woman doesn't need to bring down a government or crush a competitor. She only needs to plant and nourish and grow." She pointed her careful nails at Amy's microphone. "There's the story. I've just written you your chapter."

The interview over, Sandy beelined for the car. Zach grabbed some final photographs as Amy thanked their hostess repeatedly for her time. Then they tumbled happily back into the Kia for the next leg of the trip.

Key West had been Amy's prize to them all, two nights in Hemingway territory before turning back for home. As they sped across the final bridges, she felt as free as the ocean. The gifts she'd plucked from the interviews were piling up, and Amy resonated with insight and gratitude.

At the bar, chickens pecked for food by their feet. The bartender, a pretty college drop-out from New Jersey, talked idly about the town's highlights. What they shouldn't miss, he told them, tucking his blonde dreads behind an ear as he dried some glasses, was the sunset at Southernmost Point. Tourists come for miles for that.

"What about the Ernest Hemingway House?"

"If you like cats." The kid nodded. "And keep an eye out for a urinal from his favorite drinking hole."

The breeze was just enough to blow the heat off the day. They'd downed an adequate, if inauthentic, Bahamian dish at Bahama Mama's, and wandered into this outdoor retreat, ten stools and a single bar, sitting in the dust under a string of lights. Sandy was already sloppy from the booze, and Zach and Amy watched as she downed another Rum Runner.

Amy asked their bartender about a Secret Garden in the town, a sanctuary for rescued birds next on their list.

"Yup. That too," the kid said. "That's Nancy Forrester's place, an environmental activist. Takes in unwanted and abandoned parrots. Has CDs hanging from the trees, like Christmas ornaments. It's nice, you know, if you like gardens."

"I've had enough gardens for a fucking lifetime," Sandy said. "Next book should be about bars."

Zach cast her a tired look. "Think bird sanctuary, Sandy. You'll do fine."

"I'm thinking another zealot." Sandy growled, running her finger around the rim of her glass. "We should be focusing on impressive women, not more whacky ones."

"I dunno," Zach said. "There's enough Downton Abbeys in the world already. I think the book is finally getting interesting."

"You're writing a book?" the kid said.

She was. Sitting in front of her keyboard back in her hotel room, the last refrains of a Jimmy Buffet song lingering on the night air, Amy felt at one with the world. Somehow, she'd managed to pull together the strands of a discombobulated life—her love of gardening, of travel, of writing—into something that finally resembled a career. Whatever the constraints back home, she concluded—only briefly acknowledging Graham's looming illness, his criticisms and growing negativity—she could do this. She was confident in a way she hadn't felt in years.

Over a leisurely breakfast the following morning, they heard talk of a tropical depression dumping heavy rains on parts of Puerto Rico and the Dominican Republic. They weighed whether to change their plans and decided against. But walking through Nancy Forrester's Hidden Garden just hours later, other agitated tourists were openly talking of an early exodus from the Keys. The depression had been upgraded to a tropical storm. By early afternoon, they climbed into the Kia for the drive home. Maybe it was a good thing, trying to outrace the approaching weather, Amy thought, taking her turn at the wheel. Maybe what she needed was urgency, a reason to drive straight through, missing Charleston, switching off for their cat naps, grabbing coffee, stopping for a pee, zooming north again. Given an alternative, she might have dawdled down there, on the edge of the country, for the rest of her life.

# EIGHTEEN

B ack in her own bed, she woke in waves, the soundlessness of the day coming close and retreating again. Her limbs lay heavy on the mattress, her elbows, knees, and feet like lead. Amy slid a hand over, finding Graham's side empty, and opened her eyes. The curtains billowed in, round against a slight breeze. Ten o'clock and already the sunlight was bright outside her window.

She'd made it safely back a few hours earlier. Hardly whispering goodbye and thank you to her companions, too tired to turn and wave as the car crunched back down the driveway, she'd stumbled gratefully into the house, where he'd left a light on over the back door. When she'd crawled into bed, Graham had rolled away from her, and she'd fallen dead asleep.

Amy walked into the bathroom, turned on the shower, and let the water rinse her to life. A short list emerged as she squeezed out the shampoo. Mostly, before anything, she wanted to review all she'd written, write up the Secret Garden in Key West, and refine her other two chapters before sending them off. Ella wouldn't expect them so soon, but Amy was eager for the feedback, greedy for support. And she wanted to meet with Sam, at the newspaper.

She set the shower to hotter, letting the water thrum against her back. The weekly deadline was becoming just more than she could handle anymore. Being held responsible for the tiresome word count, obliged to find anecdotes and lessons in her one small acre, finding for her readers tidbits of new advice after all this time, had left her drained. She'd rushed off two columns for Sam to use during the road trip, but the writing, squeezed into fractious hours, her mind elsewhere, had been tiresome, not the pleasurable romp of earlier articles. Amy turned, lifting her head back, placing her chest under the hot water. It wasn't a small decision. For years now, she'd been happy as the garden column lady, content with the small recognition she got from that. She had loved working with Sam too, appreciated the steady collegiality, careful editing and his ability to encourage the best from her. Besides being a good friend, Sam had been the one to find Amy her agent, brought Amy up in the world.

But now it was time. She hadn't expected the book to create such impatience, hadn't expected her gardeners to raise her sights in such a way, but they had. Edith invited celebration and ceremony into her garden. Mariann found redemption, made an amends in digging hers, and Bess held out for joy. Jada was a warrior, planting resistance and pride in every row, and Gabriella found peace in her mission, her plants the source of health and beauty. Even Nancy, Amy realized, from the brief hours they'd spent in her walled cube of lushness, with the harping caw of parrots intruding on the silence, Nancy, too had created more than simply a garden; she'd built a sanctuary. Amy hadn't found that added element of purpose in her backyard, not in her life either. It was travel and research that had awakened her to how much more she could accomplish, how much more she could learn out there, and she didn't want to be constrained by Sam's modest, repetitive expectations any longer. By anyone's.

Only then, as she stepped from the shower stall, did Amy remember the dog.

Haps hadn't greeted her when she'd snuck through the kitchen last night, and he wasn't on his bed when she entered this morning.

His leash hung from its hook. She knocked on Graham's study door, curious.

"What?" Flat, rude.

"Hey," she said, leaning in with a smile. "Good morning."

He barely acknowledged her, holding his place in the book he'd been reading.

"You're awake."

"Finally, yeah." She stepped into the room, just then noticing the piles of paperwork, opened books, ancient scrolls of renderings dotting the floor. "Sorry. You're busy."

"Uh huh." In the days of being away, this wasn't the greeting she'd anticipated. She shrugged lightly. "I just wanted to say hi. I'm back."

"I know. I heard you come in. Saw you this morning."

"Okay." Amy shrunk back. Obviously not a good moment. "Where's Haps?" She tried to mix the question with a forgiving smile.

"Outside. Turns out he likes that, being out there." Graham tossed his hands in the air. "All those walks, all those years. Turns out, he'd rather be on his own."

She stopped in her tracks, an argument forming quickly, but he cut her off. "Anyway, would you close the door? I can't think for the noise."

Amy pulled back, heading quickly for the back door. Out in the yard, there was no sign of the dog. She called quietly, so as not to be heard from the house, and walked toward the road, worry rising in her throat.

"Haps!" She repeated, more loudly, looking first in one direction, then the other.

Nada. Not a trace. Amy's pulse was moving now, and she fretted with a choice: take off down the road after him, and if so, which way—or check the back of the house, the patio, out by the far trees. Keeping her stride steady, she marched past the cars again, Moira's Jetta parked behind Graham's Volvo. *She's here,* Amy thought. *Where the hell was she when Graham let Haps out on his own?* Half racing now, Amy sped by the living room windows toward the patio.

"Haps!" she called again. This time shouting, trying to disturb the architects inside. "Haps!" The yard was quiet, and the fulsome plantings muffled the world outside. Wildly, she looked across the gardens, barely taking note of the clematis now cloaking the back trees with blossom, the perfume of the lilies. Her heart clenched with fear and fury made her thinking ragged. *Why had those two let him out? When had he gone?* She considered heading back to the road, searching there, before it was too late.

But when she got to the hedge, she caught sight of his silky tail, waving her way. "Come here, babe!" she called, half-order, half-plea. She crunched to her knees, arms open wide, as Haps bundled toward her, smiling and innocent.

"What are you doing out here, eh?"

He didn't answer, just wriggled his rump, happy to see her back.

She stroked his head, pulling his ears back with her fingers. "Don't do that again. Okay?" she said. His eyes, at least, responded with warmth.

Moira was carrying a carton toward her car when Amy circled back to the drive.

"Hi," Amy said, trying to conceal her rage.

"Welcome home," Moira said, not stopping to talk. Balancing the carton on her knee, she opened the hatch back door, setting the bundle into the car.

"Going somewhere?" Amy said.

Moira gave her a look, scorn tilting her eyebrow. "He didn't tell you?"

Amy shook her head.

Moira held up her palm, not wasting the time. "Ask Graham," she said, turning back into the house.

Amy stood there for a moment, holding tight to Haps's collar. Intrigued and angry, she returned to the kitchen to sit it out and wait. What she didn't do was interrupt the redhead's dramatic escape.

When the last load was marched through the kitchen, Moira slammed a set of keys on the counter. "Dana was right," she said, an unpleasant twist to her mouth. "You two deserve each other."

Amy's heart leapt, blood rushing to her face. "What?!"

"And if you think Graham James is going to survive on his own . . ." Moira ran out of steam, her words not keeping pace with her anger. "Pathetic." She shook her head. "You're pathetic." The young woman flicked her beautiful mane and stomped from the room.

Outside the kitchen window, a startled blue jay sped across the side yard, landing on a tall pine branch. Underneath, a flash of yellow appeared and disappeared as the Jetta pulled away.

A delayed reaction urged her to run after the woman, shouting curses of her own, enraged at being so defiled. But another voice held Amy there. If Graham had crossed the young woman in some way, and Amy guessed that he had—if he'd hurt the girl's vanity, denied her some fantasy, broken some unstated promise—then Amy had been somehow complicit. Because she knew her husband from years of watching him, and she understood him today. Amy hadn't warned the girl: even before his diagnosis, Graham could break hearts.

She envisioned her husband in the next room, listening to the sounds of his failed hopes, of Moira slamming out the door. She guessed he wouldn't emerge, not until he had another plan, another way to rationalize what had happened here.

Meanwhile, the senselessness of the scene hung in the air. What had happened in her absence? And where had Judith been in all this? There was a pile of unopened mail on the desk in the alcove, Graham's sweater slung across it, a sleeve hanging to the floor. A mug left on the table, the paper tag and string from the teabag stuck to its side. A scorched potholder lay by the sink, and the stovetop glistened with splattered grease, each shouting to be put right. It was all back on her, Amy knew. And then there would be more to fix, more damage to repair. The prospect of it all shot lead through her bones. One thing she would do. She rose from the chair and crossed to the cabinet. Inside, she found the box of mint tea that Moira had brought and threw it in the trash.

"Is she gone?" Graham came out, once he thought it safe.

Amy was in the den, removing the power strip from the middle of the room. She'd retrieved both of the end tables from the basement and pushed the settee back in place. Already the space looked almost normal again, familiar.

"What are you doing?" he asked, as if blind.

"Clearing up," she said, keeping her voice low, too irate to state the obvious. She pointed at a small pile of used pages. "Work related, looks like. You might want to go through them before I recycle."

He glanced at the pile of paper. "If it's work, don't toss it," he said. It was a simple directive, but it was the spark.

"Then take it!" She lifted the pile, heaving it at him. Pages flew everywhere, fluttering lazily, too gently onto the coffee table, sliding to the floor. Exasperated, Amy grabbed at the sheets, tossing them again, kicking at the pages underfoot. What she craved was violence, to cause real bodily pain. But they were the only two in the room, and there was enough pain here already. Amy sank into the settee, her arm over her face.

Graham stood motionless, waiting, as the final piece of paper settled in place. Then he sat too, in the armchair by the window, his long fingers splayed against the faded upholstery. Outside, two squirrels circled each other around the trunk of a large maple.

"Moira left because I told her she'd never be my partner," he said at last. "I told her she wasn't that good yet, and that there wasn't time for her to get that good."

Amy looked out from her arm, wary. Graham was going to tell her, now, his version of events, clear in his mind.

"What brought that up?" she asked finally.

Graham swallowed a chuckle. "She asked for a raise. Said she wanted to make partner within the year." He shook his head, bewildered.

Amy pictured the redhead, standing in the kitchen, hands on hips. "She wasn't here a year . . ."

"Not even half." Graham nodded.

A thought crossed Amy's mind. "Was that the agreement?"

Graham sighed and looked out the window, following the squirrels.

"Was it?" Amy repeated.

"No," he said. "But she probably thought it was."

Amy stared across the room at him. He sat like a king on his throne, the sunshine outside backlighting his head, detailing every curl. It struck her how unaware he seemed, deaf to the cries of enemies at the gate. Her heartbeat pedaled faster; her worries leapt ahead.

"What will this do to the practice?" Even as she asked, Amy was prepared not to be answered. Graham appeared lost in his illusions, further afield in his own crop of disappointment. "Are the contracts still yours?"

He gazed back, as if scanning her face for the first time. "What do you think, Amy? What do you think has happened?" It was as if he were testing her, screening her for loyalty.

She hated to think. His income wasn't something she'd ever bothered about, not in years. She hadn't needed to; Graham hadn't welcomed it. His shifts and leaps, his professional instincts and capacity to perform, had always proven remarkably prescient. Purchasing the land in Sri Lanka, racing across the Atlantic to Baltimore, of all places, borrowing the deposit to secure this property in Padanaram, leaving homes and designing new ones, taking wild chances and pulling them off. This had been his terrain.

She met his look. "I think you kept the contracts," she said.

He nodded. "I did."

"And Moira?" Amy needed to know this much.

"Has gone back with Dana. He took her back."

Graham shifted in the chair, crossing his legs. "I would guess that by now, she's told Dana about my diagnosis. By now, I imagine, most everyone knows."

"You told her?!"

"I had to."

It might have made a good ending for a film, Amy thought. An effective closing shot: the handsome man, the noted architect, seated calmly, legs relaxed. And then the camera pans back from the chair to the room, to the house, the beautifully crafted house. From the roof to the tops of the trees, the edge of the harbor, the ocean.

*If only it were just a film*, she mused, coming back to reality. Now there was the two of them, him: crazed and in charge, her: ready to bolt, a book in her heart.

"Tell you what!" he announced brightly, pushing himself from the chair. "How about you and I take Haps out to West Island? Get some air."

She mangled a reply. "That's pretty far . . ."

"Fort Tabor, then!" he said, reaching for her hand.

She couldn't remember the last time they'd been to Fort Tabor, not together. For a workday, there were plenty of others at the park, walking their dogs, riding bikes, pushing children in strollers. Most were elderly, some not. A toned twenty-something in a bright blue headband sped by, and a heavyset woman, jiggling with flesh, ran past them too. It was as if a national day of sun-worship had been announced, and they all had been the ones to respond.

Graham seemed enlivened by everything. He engaged in dog-owner chat, admiring homely mutts as generously as the truly lovely animals, once stooping to compliment a tiny hairless pug being pushed in a baby's pram.

They went to the end of the pier and watched, engrossed, as a grizzled Cape Verdean hauled in a black sea bass, holding the struggling body with the sole of his shoe, prying the hook from its mouth. Then they crossed around the fort to the path overlooking Buzzards Bay. There was a strong breeze out on the point, filling the air with the smell of wild roses. The huge flag on the fort flagpole snapped overhead, and the Elizabethan Islands appeared as minor gray lumps, a string of distant whales resting on the edge of ocean. Amy squinted, gazing toward Cuttyhunk, and she thought of Edith and the garden out there, another world.

Haps tugged at his leash, eager to go on. Graham took her empty hand in his.

"Things are moving faster than I'd hoped," he said, his eyes squinting from the light.

Amy kept her gaze on the horizon, an antidote to seasickness.

"But I've made provisions for you, for both of us," he continued. He leaned closer. "You've trusted my instincts for thirty years, Amy, and things have worked out. I just need you to trust me now. I know what I'm doing."

His voice was beseeching in a way that forced her to face him. But as she caught his eye, she recognized the expression as one of waning strength: Graham was too eager, too anxious. She squeezed his hand. "I'm not worried," she lied, angry that he'd spoiled the mood.

"Good," he said, gripping back. "Because I've sold the house."

# NINETEEN

S he wasn't sure she'd heard him correctly. "You what?"

"Last week. I called Charlie Morris and asked him if he was still interested in buying it."

A vague memory of Graham's former client wafted through Amy's consciousness, but Graham's words didn't compute. She clutched at Haps's leash, yanking him close. "You're kidding, right?"

Graham stood there, a patient glaze to his eyes. He seemed far from apologetic. Amy almost bit her lip, rushing to spit out the words. "Well, you can call him back, Graham. 'Cause we're not selling our house. I'm not going anywhere. It's my home. I live there!" The more she spoke, the angrier she got. Now she was white with it. "Why, for God's sake?!" She watched his face turn toward the ocean, his whole body shifting to tune her out. Amy grabbed his shoulder to pull him back around. "Listen to me! You can't do that!"

Graham stood motionless, neither resisting nor complying. His whole posture sighed, as if he were on a slow count to ten. "Amy . . ."

"I'll call him up!" she exploded. "I'll tell Charlie what's-his-name that you're crazy. That you're losing your fucking marbles, Graham! But no way . . ." Amy sucked in her breath, afraid to keep talking.

An older couple were making their way along the path toward them. They were walking hand in hand as if by ancient habit, apparently unaware of each other but for that physical join. Amy shrank at the sight of them. Embarrassed, she stooped to stroke Haps's back, and the dog seemed to pick up the cue. He smiled over at the approaching couple, his tail wagging.

The old man nodded hello; his wife shot Amy a censorious glance. But when they passed by, out of earshot again, Amy started in. This time, her voice was low and steely. "You're mad, you know. It's completely irrational. Why would you do that?"

"Because I had to. Because right now, while I still have my faculties, before I can no longer handle such a large property, while the market is good for us, I needed to set us up for a future that I don't think you can even imagine. We need to cut our costs, Amy, and God knows you can't see it, traipsing around the country like some debutant on an artistic jag. I needed to get us settled into a small, manageable place, simplify our lives—my life—so that I don't deteriorate any faster than necessary. So that when I'm . . ." She heard him hesitate, momentarily stuck with the words. "When I'm making no sense at all, when I'm really losing my fucking marbles, you'll be safe and financially settled." He waited, she guessed hoping he'd brought her round. "So don't interfere, please, Amy. Don't try and hold me back when I'm still bright enough and decisive enough to take care of things."

It was like watching a Jekyll and Hyde—the desperate, confused man in the shape of her proud, authoritarian partner. Amy hardly knew which one to address. "Well, you're not doing what you always do, Graham. Not this time."

He seemed intrigued, ready. "What's that?"

"Making your unilateral decisions. You've always done that."

She'd broken the rule of marital argument, using the word "always," and this time Graham turned on his heel and headed off toward the parking lot. He wasn't running or fleeing, but his long stride took him quickly from her. Amy shouted, but to no avail. "Stop!" she tried again, but when he didn't so much as hesitate, she had no choice. Pulling her keys from her bag, Amy raced to the car past him, ushering Haps into the back, and diving behind the wheel. Her heart was pounding.

Graham eased into the passenger seat and turned to face her. "Now maybe—" he held his palm to her "—before you start the car—you'll let me talk for a minute?"

It took everything she had to keep silent.

"Lots of things," he began slowly. "But let's start with what I always do. That seems to be your main complaint."

Amy hated his rational voice, but kept herself still, willing herself to listen.

"Apparently, I always make unilateral decisions. Is that your word?"

She barely nodded, simmering.

"And I think you're right." He almost smiled to himself, but his tone was deadly serious. "I've always been a fairly decisive person. Not impulsive. Not reckless or thoughtless, but . . . ready to act. Which I think has worked out well, frankly. And as far as I know, it didn't hurt anyone. Not you, not the kids, my colleagues. If anything, my success—or good luck, or whatever it's been—has been largely shared with the people in my life."

Amy felt her chest constricting, as if his logic were sucking the air from the car's interior.

"But you obviously bridle at the unilateral part. That I haven't talked to everyone about everything. That I'm not taking a poll every time I make a move."

"I bridle at you not talking to me." The hurt of having to say this out loud nearly crushed her.

"Okay. But it's not like I don't know what you think. What you'd like to see happen." He paused, his whole demeanor softening. "I know you didn't want to leave Sri Lanka." It shook her, that he'd remembered so far back, and she felt a flush of sentimentality,

196

remembering their life there together. "But I wasn't going to stay there." He spread his hands wide. "I just wasn't. So there wasn't a lot of point in arguing. In getting your hopes up that I might change my mind or be convinced." He sighed. "I know what I need and what I need to do."

"And what about what we need?" Amy's injury felt righteous to her. Score!

"I've taken care of our needs. For thirty years, Amy." He said it as if there were some debt she owed.

"And my needs?' Her voice was ragged now.

Graham looked at her with a kind of pity. "We're each responsible for those, Amy. I really believe that."

In the back seat, Haps shifted softly. Amy glanced into the rearview mirror and watched him for a moment, suddenly sad with exhaustion. When she spoke next, tears leaked into her eyes. "I need my home, Graham, a place to write. I need my garden. I'm guessing you and Charlie Whatsy never discussed that."

"No, we didn't."

A sob rose in her chest. The calmness with which he spoke.

He placed a hand on her shoulder, its warmth burning through her. "And I know you need a home and a garden. You'll have that again." He chuckled. "When have you ever not had a garden, Amy? You'll have one." He withdrew his hand.

It was like arguing with a wall. She tried not to blubber, wiping her cheek with the heel of her hand. "I don't want to move."

"And I don't want to lose my mind."

"Well, I'm not selling," she insisted stubbornly.

"Well, it's not yours *to* sell."

It was humiliating, as much as anything. Worse than not being asked, worse than being not heard. She'd driven back almost blind with it, barely noticing the red lights, the traffic around her. When they pulled into the drive, she led Haps into the house and retreated into the back yard, her head spinning with Graham's plaintive "And I don't want to lose my mind," his calculated "It's not yours to sell." What stung was the fact that she really had no power in the matter. A fifty-year-old woman in 2014, and she had no say because the house wasn't hers. Once again, she found herself with little choice but to follow along.

Amy pulled at some grass that had wormed its way into the peony bed, watching her fingernails fill up with dirt. She wondered idly whether this was grounds for divorce. Whether it rose to this level. But of course, she and Graham had other considerations now, higher problems than arguments over real estate.

Amy remembered her sister's comment, thirty years back when Alice had stayed with them in Baltimore, the afternoon in the sculpture plaza by the art museum where they'd gone to talk.

"You know what you're getting," Alice had said. "Graham's impulsive and daring and smart as a whip, and he's going to go his own way. You're not going to change that."

"I don't want to change him!" Amy insisted, all twenty-three years of her shaking with indignation. There was a line of fourth graders snaking their way through the outdoor exhibit, laughing at some ebony protrusions that looked like penises. She held her words as the school children giggled off.

"It's just such a bad time!" Amy was in a state then, for the first time her life with Graham feeling unsatisfactory, and she wanted Alice to take her side. "In two more semesters I'll have my degree. One more year!" She raised an index finger as if it were the holy grail.

"And he's got an offer he can't refuse." Alice's eyes had looked teal-colored that day, much like the tint of the Patapsco River reflecting the overcast day.

"Won't, more like."

"Distinction without a difference." Alice's gaze had been steady, not unloving, but there'd been no give. "The thing to remember is that you've got a choice. And thank God for that."

Amy hadn't thanked God. Everything else had been going so well. It was less than a month after the ribbon cutting at the Pratt Street Power Plant, the centerpiece of the Inner Harbor strategy. Graham and his fellow architects had been honored for their inspired renovations and Alice and Amy had rewarded him later that night with champagne on their roof deck. Amy had received an "A" in her creative writing class, her short story chosen for a campus publication, and Alice had been accepted into three law programs, to begin the following autumn. What Amy had wanted was for things to stay as they were, for her paw paw tree to bear its first fruit.

"One thing I've been told about early love," Alice had said. "It doesn't get better."

Amy gathered the small pile of pulled grass and crumpled it into her fist, carrying it to the compost pile at the back of the property.

The truth was it had gotten better. Seven white birches stood elegantly there, like a scene from a ballet, the tall pines behind them a painted backdrop, the stage floor thick with moss. Things had gotten better. Graham had taken the teaching gig at RISD and decided to move to New England, to find land to buy again. And Amy had decided to follow.

The first months were bumpy, Amy remembered. They were definitely bumpy. Amy agreed to at least look at some properties with him—in Rhode Island somewhere, he'd said, near your mother, as if that should silence her. Amy was ambushed by everyone's enthusiasm. That Thanksgiving, they'd all echoed Graham's logic around the plates of pumpkin pie: *Buying land and building your own place makes sense. Especially for an architect. Land here is relatively cheap, compared to Boston, and Providence is on the way up . . .*

"You've got parents within a stone's throw," Alice said, and Alice's husband chuckled at that. "Dubious benefit," he'd quipped, winking at Graham.

"You can transfer your credits, go to a decent college," was her father's advice; he said it without a blush, almost making Amy decide to stay in Baltimore on her own. But then Graham spent a weekend with a colleague sailing out of Padanaram Harbor, and he'd switched gears again, finding the perfect property in Massachusetts, one they'd both adore. And he bought it. Without so much as a conversation, he took a loan, signed for the land and began planning his home. Their home.

Amy walked onto the spongey ground under the birches. It was now solid moss, as far back as the pine trees and ring of ferns, moss you could walk on and lie on, as firm and clean as a carpet. It had taken several years before the squirrels had given up the fight. At first, when she'd established the soil, laying out patches of moss stripped from stone walls further down the road, the squirrels had tossed the patches to one side every morning, digging at the soft soil underneath, and at the residue of buttermilk and yogurt she'd used to feed her nascent plugs. And every day she'd replaced the patches, keeping the area damp, shaded from direct sun, threatening the squirrels with stern sermons as if they understood.

Today, it was one of her favorite spots on the whole property, a place she could come, be alone, and think. Had he factored this into the selling price?

What was amazing was that it had worked out as it had. Bitter as she had been then, Amy did love the plot. She'd seen the possibilities of Graham's dream home, and she'd treasured the generous yard, its protective trees and rambunctious flowering bushes, a hidden half mile from the harbor. It had been more than Graham wanted to spend, so he'd borrowed to get it. And instead of renting a cheap apartment in North Providence, he'd sacrificed: commuting to the city twice a week and buying the Airstream for them to live in until their home was up.

There hadn't been time for Amy to transfer for winter term; only enough time to find out she was pregnant, spending the early cold months of that new year circling the tiny metal space, weak with morning sickness. But then spring came, and with it a new job for Graham, at a firm in Bristol, on top of the teaching. And though he was busy or away more than he was there with her, she had good days, working part-time at the local bookstore, the rest of her hours perusing the site as the foundation went in, tying strips of tape where trees and bushes had to be spared the wreckage of construction crews, watching how long the sun rested where, what time of the day, from March through September.

Alice had been wrong. It had gotten better.

There were moments. Of course. Graham had accepted an even more demanding teaching gig, spending two nights a week in Cambridge now both autumn and winter terms. How do you argue with that, with Harvard, for God's sake? He hadn't.

And then after Jason was born, when she'd miscarried for a second time, being told not to keep trying, Graham had said it sounded like wise advice. It had been like a tractor driving through a sweet field of daisies.

But there had been other, better moments. Graham had started a new business partnership, closer to their house and had learned to love those evenings he could spend at home, appreciate his baby son, and later, summer weeks with his daughter, once lost to him. Catherine's mother had finally allowed the little girl to visit annually, and Amy had become the wife and mother Alice could only wonder at. Money began to flow in, and Amy transformed the old Airstream into a playhouse for Jason and his friends, built a green roof on the shed by the drive. Graham's design for their home won awards, and around it her garden had grown in size and reputation, until she was invited to join the local gardening club and speak at club events. She was begged to open her place as a stop on the summer garden tour, which had led to the gardening column and her first little book. It had gotten better.

In 1998, a Nor'easter dumped so much snow in thirteen hours, two great limbs from a tall pine tore free and crushed the Airstream like the tin can it was. They had it towed. Jason went off to boarding school, no longer interested in his playhouse, and Amy built the birch grove in its place, planted the saplings, the moss and ferns. She'd adapted.

Amy gazed across the lawn, where Graham had just walked onto the patio, Haps at his heel. Her husband raised a tentative hand: Peace, it said. Come back inside.

She nodded in reply. But she didn't know whether she could stand it, this next change. Whether she wanted to adapt.

# TWENTY

Amy was swept under in the flood of Graham's plans. Not only had he sold the house, he'd agreed to move out of the place by Labor Day. Almost in a rush of relief, Graham had also phoned the kids, his parents and brother Matt, telling everyone he knew, every neighbor he saw, of his diagnosis. He flung his news like candy from a passing float in a Fourth of July parade. It drove Amy mad.

Still, there was some relief in having Matt now in on the family secret.

She'd always liked Matt, through every iteration. Closer to his age than Graham's, she'd had an affinity with the younger brother from the get-go, defending him when he was young and wild, envying his storied romances. For three decades, she'd appreciated Matt's endless teasing and unplanned visits, warmed to his ready laugh. Now, her brother-in-law was in the responsible stage of life. He knew grown-up things and wore an expensive suit. A sophisticated financial strategist, Matt viewed everything to do with trusts and healthcare, tax write-offs and estate planning, as a delightful puzzle to be solved. He had offered his assistance, and to Amy's utter amazement Graham had accepted. So, Matt was coming for the weekend, to talk about the future.

Two days later, Graham decided to invite Jason and Catherine too. That's when Amy finally spoke up.

"It's looking like a convention!" she said. "What are we deciding here? Whose decisions are they?!" They were in Graham's study where he'd spent a crazed two days, emptying and reorganizing his filing cabinets in preparation for the move. Precise piles of Redwell folders leaned precariously about the space, creating narrow paths between desk and door, door and windows. Books were now piled on their sides along the half-empty shelving, organized by size and thickness.

Graham seemed irritated at being interrupted mid-flow. "It's an emotional time," he said. "But we can't afford to take emotional decisions. There are financial considerations . . ."

"You think I can't handle financial considerations?" she asked.

"I'm sure you can. It's just not something you have a lot of experience in, that's all." His voice was professorial, as if explaining why he'd given her just a C+ on her final. "When was the last time you looked at our insurance policies, calculated the value of the property, estimated the replacement cost of a boiler?" Have you ever?" Scorn crept into his voice, and he paused, trying to regain composure. "This is Matt's area of expertise, Hon. People pay serious money for his advice. I'd be crazy not to hear what he has to say."

Amy liked Matt. That wasn't her objection. "But the kids? And a mediator?" Graham had insisted on that, too, to facilitate the conversation. "What's that in aid of?"

"All of us are going to have our emotions, our opinions. It would be helpful to have someone here just to keep us on track. I have some very specific concerns about my quality of life going forward. Jason and Catherine probably have issues of their own that they'll need to deal with." He paused, then added, "I know *you* do." The last was said as if there were blame attached, and Amy flinched.

She saw herself, suddenly, at the end of a lengthy list of suppli-cants, not a partner at all. Humiliated and raw, she left him there in his study and retreated to hers.

When Graham rounded up Andy to tell him about the Alzheimer's, talking excitedly about the sailboat race, explaining his performance in light of the illness, Amy was forced to make some admissions of her own. Warily, she checked back with Judith and apologized for the earlier ruse. "I didn't know how to tell you," she told her friend. "Graham wanted to keep it to himself."

Judith wasn't fazed. She'd seen early on that the evening visits were mostly unnecessary, having sussed during the first week that Moira was no romantic predator. Once she learned the truth, however, about the actual diagnosis, Judith backed off from any future commitments. "That's more than I want responsibility for, Amy. It really is."

What Amy wasn't able to do was tell Ella or Sandy about Graham, and as a result couldn't mention his condition to Zach or Sam either. When she resigned from the paper and Sam was dismayed, almost too accommodating, she felt bad that she couldn't confide in him, her professional friend and champion for so long. It would come out. They'd all learn soon enough, but she just wasn't ready now.

Remorseful and resentful, Amy was still traumatized by what Graham had done. She couldn't find the right tone to discuss with anyone the worrying, tragic future facing her husband, too agitated with her pile of new responsibilities, the pending loss of her garden and home, to even pretend at the acceptance expected of a loving wife. Somehow she had to empty the house she'd lived in for almost thirty years. She had to organize movers and go with Graham to look at three condos he'd located, as if she cared one whit what cozy new dwelling she was being forced into with this controlling man. She hated it all. Secretly, she worried that she hated him the most.

Instead, she sequestered herself in her study, planning the upcoming month's itinerary. She booked flights this time, financing be damned, and she tucked the next three gardens into the first half of August: Chicago, Texas and Charleston. That left her more than two weeks to empty the house. Then in early September, after the move, they'd fit in Montana, Colorado and San Francisco, with a week or more to complete rewrites. Already, her mind dominated with work, Amy dreamt of giving most of their belongings away. *Toss it all*, she thought angrily. *And if I need a new sofa when the time comes, I'll buy one. Screw it. I'll buy two!*

But as the heat wore off, Amy was left with a sick, disgusted feeling. On her own in a soup of self-pity, she longed for the warmth of earlier times, when family and friends fit pleasantly into her life, when she was embraced as Graham's understanding partner, the younger wife and mother who did everything with a smile.

At least, she consoled herself, she had Edith's wedding to look forward to. That would be a bright spot in an otherwise relentless hamster wheel of duty and work. But as she tied up the August itinerary, she noticed the awful flaw in the wild planning that had become her life. This coming Saturday, the one the family had chosen for their mediation, was the day of Edith's wedding.

Friday arrived as if dropped from the sky. She'd decided against telling Edith in advance that she wouldn't be attending. It would seem more plausible if she called at the last minute, struck suddenly with a surprising bout of flu. It saddened her, infuriated her, in fact, but the stress of trying to jam in both the morning mediation and racing for an early afternoon ferry was more than she could handle. Anyway, Amy warned herself, what message would that be sending to the family?

Zach's text made it more difficult. *Should I pick you up?* he'd written, early Friday morning. (*Kinda like a date?*)

The fun of it made her smile, but with him, too, she kept her plans secret. *No. Thanks. Easier if I meet you at the ferry. 1:30, right?*

Amy didn't like the deception; she'd been looking forward to going with him—without Sandy, for a change—and she'd looked forward to enjoying themselves back on Cuttyhunk. She'd even pulled out her blue dress, holding it up against her chest, checking her reflection in the mirror. The color brought out the glint of her eyes, and the skirt swirled lightly, showing her knees. It would have been a treat to dress up. Maybe the jade earrings and her Mexican sandals.

Stuffing down her disappointment, Amy prepared for the family mediation. Somehow, in the few hours she had, Amy remade all the beds and filled up the kitchen with her favorite groceries. Vases of fresh flowers graced the dining and living rooms, and she assembled a special arrangement for Catherine's bedroom, the lavender and sweet peas her stepdaughter so loved. She even built a tempting lasagna for dinner, Jason's favorite dish.

The flowers had been the turning point. Adding that touch, Amy was readier now for her guests' arrival, almost hopeful for the support that being together might bring. Even in the face of the children's earlier anger, she expected that Jason and Catherine would be tempered by the reality of seeing Graham again, knowing what he was suffering. And Matt! As ever, Matt would be a gift.

Amy thought back to one of his best visits, like his others, spontaneous and timely. She, Graham and the baby had just moved from the trailer. Their new house was gorgeous and spacious, empty of all but the most basic of furniture. It was just after Jason had been born. They'd survived the long, worried days of hovering at the window of the nursery, looking in at the mewling bundles lined up in their plastic buckets, wriggling under the dimmed lights, fighting to stay alive. Graham, buried in projects, his designs finally attracting some attention, had been spending more hours than ever at the drafting table. Amy had been the one in charge now, fragile and alone, sure that she was doing it all wrong. She'd known her husband was distracted, having to cope with a weenie newborn and a zombie of a wife, so she'd tried not to ask too much. She stationed the crib in the middle of the living room, too terrified to put Jason out of sight, as if he might slip away and get lost under a cushion or strewn sweater. But when Graham did stop in, he sat there on the couch, staring woodenly at his new son, amazed and overwhelmed.

She was grateful when Matt came to visit. From the moment he met baby Jason, their little handful of a preemie, so precious and bewildering, Matt lavished on him a kind of confident adoration. The grandparents, Dina and Charles, their next-door neighbors, even Amy's own parents, had all peeked timidly into the crib on their first visits, seemingly revolted by such a minute human. But Matt had been boisterous with enthusiasm. "He's a corker," he'd said, arm over Amy's shoulders. "Looks just like me." Then he'd brazened the obvious: "Only smaller."

Matt had never managed to have kids of his own, a fact he'd pretended to be relieved about at every divorce. But Amy was reassured by his company, never worried when Matt tossed the baby overhead or sent Jason airborne on the soles of his feet, whooping with delight, as Jason's little fists clung to his uncle's fingers, his mouth wide with wonder.

Matt was coming, and all would be well.

Friday evening, however, did not go as planned. Matt's plane was delayed; Catherine flew in even later. Jason drove up, stopping by a friend's for dinner. So Graham and Amy made do with leftovers and saved the lasagna for the following day. Late in the evening, the most the relatives managed was to acknowledge each other briefly before hitting their respective bedrooms for the night.

Early Saturday, over the breakfast table, things warmed up somewhat. Matt probed Jason's academic choices, chiding him for a joint major in history and business. "MBA's a waste of time," he laughed. "Only less useful than a degree in history." He grinned with affection. "And I thought you were the bright one of the family." Then he teased Catherine over her first divorce. "I'm leading with three!" he bragged jovially. "You've got some serious catching up to do." Keeping to tradition, Matt also praised Amy's garden and wondered for the millionth time how Graham had been lucky enough to land her. What he didn't do was ask Amy why she'd married this nut—which was something Matt did every time they were together. He didn't go there.

After breakfast, they split up, preparing themselves for what was to come. The mediator was scheduled to arrive at ten. Jason was combing through his bedroom, probably trying to decide what of his possessions he wanted to keep, Amy guessed, now that storing them would soon be on him. Graham was still cocooned downstairs in his study, where he'd been since he woke. Matt was reacquainting himself with the books and photographs on display in the living room, intrigued at all he'd forgotten of his brother's home and sanctuary. And Catherine had made herself indispensable in the kitchen, tidying up the remains of breakfast, preparing a plate of fruit and cookies, tall pitchers of iced coffee and tea for the midmorning meeting. Amy descended the stairs, joining her.

"You're good to do this," Amy said, glad for a moment alone together.

"It's easier, keeping busy." Catherine wiped her hands on a towel. She glanced over at her stepmother, her face guarded. "I find this whole scene a little strange, to be honest."

"I don't blame you," Amy said. "It is."

"Was this get-together your idea?"

Amy shook her head. "No. Your dad's." Then, not wanting to seem critical, she added, "I think he just wants us all on the same page."

"Finally." The word dipped with meaning. Catherine moved two of the cookies on the plate, adjusting the layout.

It was an opening, and Amy took it. "I'm sorry," she said, "not to have told you when you asked."

"It was a pretty straightforward question," Catherine reminded her. "All you needed to do was confirm what I saw."

Amy frowned, eager to explain. "He wanted to keep it quiet as long as possible, and I promised I would."

"No longer possible, I guess." Catherine looked up, her eyes dark.

"Nope."

"So, what's changed?"

Amy grappled with the last many weeks, trying to think. "His assistant has left him, for one. I think he's in trouble with his work. He's losing confidence mostly. And that's making him . . . need us."

Amy crossed the kitchen to put a comforting arm around Catherine's shoulder, but Catherine held back.

"You're going to have to stop making promises, Amy. Start thinking for yourself."

It was a familiar charge of Catherine's, and Amy recoiled from it. Too many times in the past Amy had vowed to provide one thing or another to the kids, to Catherine in particular—the fated trip to Disney, a college tour on the West Coast, visiting the schools to which Catherine had applied, sometimes just a simple plan, like a drive to the mall. But Graham had often intervened. "Now isn't a good time," he'd said more than once, as if there were a preordained calendar somewhere visible only to him. And more than once, Amy had complied. Catherine was right. It had always just been easier.

Now Amy recognized the heightened challenge in her stepdaughter's eyes. Now, with the awareness of Graham's illness, Catherine was expecting Amy to finally step up for a change, stand up to the man.

The doorbell sounded in the hallway, breaking the spell. Amy jumped, more anxious than she knew. She tried for a smile. "That'll be her. You ready?"

Catherine shrugged. "Probably not."

A boxy, blazer-clad figure was on the front steps, staring across at the side garden when Amy opened the door. "I'm Lisa Saxe," the woman said, turning, offering her hand.

Amy took it, surprised at the iron grip. "Amy James." There was something familiar about the woman, and it caught Amy off guard. "You're our mediator, right?"

"I am." Lisa Saxe paused. "I'm also a former soccer mom," she said. An elfish smile crossed her face. "And now I know where I've seen you, heard the name."

Amy struggled with the connection.

"Our boys played on the under-fourteen team together, years ago."

Startled, Amy looked at her more closely, trying to square the white hair with the redhead of a decade past. "Oh, my goodness!" she said, catching on. "Of course."

"Yes. Well!" Lisa held up her palm, taking stock. "I think it's still ethical. Though we're supposed to be true neutrals, not friends with our clients . . ."

It took Amy a second before she answered. "Well, we're not," she said, smiling. "Just women stuck on the same sideline. Come on in." That little connection helped, however distant. Maybe now, Amy thought as she led the woman into the dining room, the mediator would go easy on her.

"Jason!" she shouted on the way. "Graham!"

Lisa Saxe walked to the far end of the room, taking the head of the table, and opened her briefcase.

Matt joined them first. A younger and shorter version of his brother, Matt presented as the professional he was. Tidier, without

Graham's curls, he looked prepared for a meeting at the office in his pressed, button-down shirt, his own yellow pad and fountain pen to the ready. He eyed the chairs. "Where do you want me?" he asked.

Amy shrugged. "Anywhere."

Lisa nodded authoritatively. "There aren't opposing parties to this conversation," she explained, "so yes—anywhere."

Catherine arrived next, carefully placing the tray of glasses in the center of the table. She left without a word, returning with the pitchers of drink. On her third round, she brought the plate of food, a soft handful of napkins. "Hi," she said to Lisa Saxe. "I'm Catherine. Graham's daughter."

Lisa's face brightened. "I didn't know Jason had a sister," she said.

"Half-sister," Catherine clarified, taking a seat across from her uncle. "A summer sister, more like."

The mediator glanced at Amy, then pulled out her paperwork. Navigating like they were strangers was going to prove challenging.

Jason and Graham entered the room together. They looked like a matched set, both tall and dark, both ready to solve problems, get something done. Graham took the end opposite Lisa, Jason by his side. Amy finally settled herself next to Matt, effecting a feeble introduction. "Jason, do you remember Mrs. Saxe? Her son was on your soccer team—eighth grade?"

Jason looked across the table.

"Bill. Billy Saxe?" Lisa said. Then, self-consciously, she fingered her hair. "Think red."

Slowly, Jason nodded. "Okay. Yeah," he said. "So, you're our facilitator?"

"I am. Lisa Saxe," she said again, looking around the table. "And besides being a former soccer parent, I'm also a Certified Family Mediator." She took a longer moment to check in with Graham, ensuring he was ready.

Amy felt herself relax. This lady knew her stuff and as Graham had promised, she was taking the helm.

"A mediator's job—my job—is to help families discuss how to ensure safety, care, and quality of life when a family member is no longer able to do that himself."

It was that simple and that awful. They had begun.

Lisa began by getting buy-in on ground rules: no interruptions, no personal attacks, an understanding that anyone could request a break and that, together, they would decide when to end the session. She explained her own role, not to force any decisions, but to create conditions for participants to air their concerns, their hopes, their suggestions on what the family could do to support their father, husband, brother, to support Graham.

It startled Amy, put like this. Of course, she realized. Of course this is why they'd been brought together, but hearing it worded so felt ominous suddenly, even more foreboding than the disease itself. They weren't here to support *her* at all.

Graham opened with his own concerns.

"I'm not yet getting lost in the neighborhood," he assured them.

Instantly, Amy wanted to object, thinking of the day Haps had taken Graham on a new route. Had he forgotten that? But she kept mute as he continued.

"I'm not using the remote to make a phone call. It's not that bad. Lost words, feeling less able to articulate a thought. That's happening, and it's troubling." Graham pressed his palms together, dipping his bottom lip to his fingers. "I also don't know how much longer I'll be able to do a creditable job of my design work. That's new." He reached for a cookie, setting it on a napkin in front of him.

Amy watched her children's faces, Jason still with a loyalty and adoration he wore like a badge. Catherine's brow creased, likely finding it strange to hear such vulnerability from a father who'd only ever been assertive and sure.

"I want to be certain that at all costs I won't be put into a facility," Graham said. "That's why I've sold the house. That's why I want to get a smaller, less expensive, more manageable place to live, for us both to live." He glanced at his wife, acknowledging Amy for the first time. "That's why I want the funds established to pay for aging in place, so I won't get stashed away somewhere, living with strangers." He kept his eyes on his wife.

His audience remained motionless, taking it in, looking everywhere but at her.

Graham turned, speaking directly to Lisa Saxe. "That's what I want from this meeting. To figure out how to protect myself from that."

Amy felt faint. In all of the scenarios that had flitted through her brain—moving from their home, living in a condo, existing somewhere without a garden, with a man who already left clutter in his wake, forgot to shower—nowhere had there been a notion of having to make such a lifelong guarantee. That never, ever, would he be put into care. The possible timeline stretched before her. Too dazed to speak, she was grateful when Matt began.

In his businesslike cadence, Matt was reassuring. Almost immediately he calmed the vague financial insecurities that had been building in Amy's mind since she'd first heard of the diagnosis. Matt spoke of the staggering sum Graham had coming from the sale of the house, the money still owed him from his share of the partnership, the expected return on investments from a considerable retirement account. Matt walked them through the preferable options of home purchases, the considerations associated with condo fees, the provisions covered through their long-term care policy. When Matt mentioned the sale value of the hillside property in Sri Lanka, though, it gave Amy a jolt. She'd never considered her little farm as an item on a balance sheet, nor had she imagined that it was a place

Graham would ever sell. She thought of the little cement house, her pepper bushes, the cinnamon trees alive with birdsong as a loved location, a place in her mind, a place to which she might someday return. But as Matt spoke, listing the assets, describing the liabilities and costs, Amy came to understand how much more Matt knew of their financial status than she did. Worse, Amy saw why Matt was here in the first place. It wasn't to discuss options as much as present them. His was a financial plan already in motion.

She looked up, the table silent again, and Amy saw Lisa looking expectantly her way.

Amy considered reaching for a glass of iced tea, to postpone the moment. But, out of nowhere, she found her voice. "We probably should talk about getting some help," Amy said. "The cost of that." She was looking at Lisa Saxe but saw her husband out of the corner of her eye. Graham shifted in his chair, breaking his cookie in half.

"Of course," Matt said calmly. "You'll want some assistance at some point. Visiting nurse, maybe someone to help with the housekeeping."

"A small place won't take much to keep clean," Graham said.

"But you'll want some relief staff at some point," Catherine said.

Graham gave his daughter an odd look, surprised at her interruption. "I accept that."

Matt spoke. "You're looking at between thirty-five, forty thousand a year for a full-time caregiver."

"We're not talking full-time," Graham countered.

"No, but using that as a reference point." Matt wasn't going to let his brother get flustered, didn't have a dog in this race.

Jason, however, did. He looked across the table at his mother, distrust lacing his voice. "Aren't you going to be there?" It was such a bald question, Amy blushed.

"Of course she is," Graham answered. "We're just talking about the odd day, visiting her sister . . ."

"'Cause it's crazy," Jason interrupted, "if you're thinking you can take off for two weeks again."

"She's not, Jason. Are you." Graham turned to his wife.

The voices felt deafening, and Amy struggled to respond. "I . . ." she began.

"It's just not safe!" Jason said.

"I could come up," Catherine cut in. "Every couple of months. And you're not that far," she told Jason. "How about *you* manage a weekend once in a while?"

"I've just started a job hunt!" Jason hissed back. "And you live in Chicago! Get real."

"This is nonsense!" Graham exploded. "Your mother will be here. What are we all talking about?"

Very quietly, Lisa Saxe raised her hand. "It might be a good time to pass the refreshments," she said.

"I like that idea." Matt reached for a glass. "Tea or coffee?" he asked the mediator, slowing the scene to a crawl.

That was Matt, Amy remembered, watching her brother-in-law. That's what he did in her life, he smoothed the waters. There'd been another time too, this one, many years earlier. Amy had lost the baby. Jason was three. She'd already miscarried once, a year earlier. But this second miscarriage, this second loss, had felt unbearable to her. It had signaled that they shouldn't keep trying, that one was their limit. Amy remembered phoning Graham in Cambridge, the days when he spent two nights a week there, absorbed with his teaching. She had put Jason to bed and was trying to comfort herself with a good meal and a video. But she kept crying, couldn't swallow the food, couldn't stand being alone. It was late when he finally picked up—out somewhere, he said. And when Amy asked him, begged him please to drive home, it was just over an hour, please don't spend this night away from her, he told her then, "Now is not a good time." But Matt,

Matt responded. He spent an hour or more on the phone with her, letting her cry, just listening. Then he called her back, an hour later, from a highway stop in lower Connecticut. And again, somewhere in central Mass. By then, Amy had eaten something, was almost feeling sane when the doorbell rang. And it was Matt, there at their front door. He didn't say much of anything. He scrambled himself an egg, made some toast, and the two of them sat in the kitchen, the world dark outside, until she was tired enough to go to bed. Then he held her until she slept.

Now, Amy felt her heart drumming in her ears. There were so many agendas operating here, so many interests flashing about her, she found it hard to focus on her own, to even know what they were. As the plate of food passed from one person to the next, Amy thought of her pretty dress upstairs, the wedding she'd sacrificed, and was impressed again with the depth of the hostility she held inside. Then she felt Graham's hand on hers, and she looked over to him, remembering he was there.

His eyes were boring into her, filled with an intimacy that only she could know. It was her history that she saw there: lover, wife, and mother. The gifted caretaker, the girl who'd made home home. She felt herself sinking into it, barely managing to stay afloat.

"Amy?"

Matt was holding up a pitcher. "Tea?"

"Yes please," she said, pulling her hand out from under Graham's. She reached for the icy glass, grateful for the distraction. Drinking slowly, she thought about what it was she had to say, with the family gathered together like this. The children, at least, needed to hear from her.

"Good cookies," Jason acknowledged, scarfing his second. Then, turning to the mediator, he asked, "Are we allowed to speak now?"

Lisa Saxe wasn't thrown by the sarcasm. She looked around the circle of faces, checking in. "If everyone's ready?"

Catherine and Matt nodded, and Amy and Graham followed suit.

"Because I have a few things to say." Jason took himself so seriously, Amy noticed, and worried at what was coming. "Obviously, you guys have to make some changes," he said, jutting his chin at his parents. "But it doesn't mean everything's got to change. I mean, Dad, you seem to be managing really well now."

Graham acknowledged that, dipping his head. "I managed to sell the house."

"Yeah. And eventually, you'll retire, live in a smaller place. Lots of older people downsize. So, life can go on pretty much as normal for a bit."

Amy wondered what planet Jason had found for himself.

"What I mean is . . . I mean, no one had to know about Ronald Reagan. He finished his term, and no one had a clue."

A look of horror spread across Catherine's face, one she shared with Amy. "I'm not sure that matters," she said to her brother, her mouth curled with distaste. "I'm really not."

"Graham James is a name lots of people know," Jason insisted. "That's all I'm saying."

"That's thoughtful of you, Jason. We know what you mean." Graham reached for his son's hand this time, finding allies where he could.

The silence was dull and drawn out, and finally Amy filled the void.

"I'm writing a book right now." She said it as if telling Lisa Saxe, as if everyone else had known, maybe just forgotten. "It's on a deadline with a publisher. So there will be some travel coming up. In the next few weeks." Her relatives squirmed uncomfortably. Even Catherine didn't appear ready to accommodate this, not at such short notice. "So we should probably find a person sooner rather than later, to cover." She closed her mouth before she took it back.

Graham was quick to disagree. "Well, I'm not okay with hiring some stranger now. I meant later, when it's necessary. I'm fine right now."

"Dad . . ." Jason was off again. "That's my point! Mom can't just go off . . ."

"She can if she has to," said Catherine.

"I don't need a sitter!" Graham insisted. "Look at me!"

"I'm not saying that!" Jason was angry. "If Mom is here . . ."

"She's got work!" Catherine's voice was climbing.

"I'm not about to burn the house down!" Graham insisted, furious now.

"But anything could happen." Jason's eyes sparkled, visualizing the worst.

"Enough!" Graham slapped his hand on the tabletop, making the glasses shudder.

Amy shrank in her seat and Jason froze in place. Matt lowered his head, fingering his watch. Only Catherine, regal and reserved, pushed back from the table. "Excuse me," she said, and left the room.

Lisa Saxe let the rest of them sit with it, waiting as the vibrations smoothed to nothing.

"Do you want to go on?" she asked, looking from face to face.

Matt was the one who led them through it. Speaking without notes, his voice careful, tentative, he offered what Amy guessed had been written on his lined pad from the beginning, the items he'd already discussed with Graham. She listened with growing detachment as the proposal spun out before them, like a roll of toilet paper dropped down a stair. It was fairly basic. Amy and Graham would buy the new two-bedroom they'd found in Providence. All of their financial resources would be invested in such a way as to ensure Graham's ability to remain at home, leaving Matt to manage everything, as Graham's new power of attorney. If and when Amy needed to travel, she would first contact Jason and Catherine, to see if they could "keep an eye out." No one dared define what that meant, exactly. And if Jason and Catherine weren't available, then Amy should locate a local person, someone who could pop in, "do a bit of housekeeping." But Amy should make every effort to limit the travel to one or two nights if possible.

By the end, the men at the table seemed relieved. Jason's arms were no longer crossed tightly. He sat back in his chair, loose and relaxed. Graham nodded his way to a standstill, just fiddling with the napkin he'd folded and refolded, now an accordion by his plate. Matt, still crisp and composed, jotted the last of his notes, the blue ink elegant on his yellow pad. And Lisa Saxe sat quietly, a neutral observer.

Catherine rejoined the group at the table in time for her uncle's summary. "Is that what you want, Amy?" she asked at the end, almost too gently to hear.

But Amy heard her and the question served as a lifeline, a last chance to rescue something for herself. Bravely, Amy shook her head. "I don't want to sell the house in Sri Lanka." It surprised even her when she said it, upsetting the calm flow of negotiations. Jason sat forward. Matt placed his fountain pen onto the table with a sharp click.

"Why?" Graham sighed. "We never go there."

"We might," was all she could say. "We might."

Matt turned to her, as if measuring the resistance. He glanced at his numbers again, shrugging. "It's not worth an argument," he advised his brother.

And then they were finished. A future wrapped up in less than two hours.

After putting the lasagna to heat in the oven, Amy escaped to the garden, grabbing her gloves and shovel from the shed. She went to a favorite bush, a small caryopteris by the patio, and dug it out of the bed, wedging it carefully into a five-gallon pot.

# TWENTY-ONE

She scrambled toward the queue of passengers filing up the ramp. Zach was leaning against the barrier watching her steadily, his hands raised in surprise. "I thought you were sick!"

Amy waved it him off, too frazzled to argue. "Didn't want to miss it. And I feel much better, I promise."

He reached out for the potted bush she'd been carrying, taking it from her. "Want a hand there?"

"Thanks." Amy passed the plant over, sighing with relief. "Sorry about that," she said. "I left a houseful back there. Just ran out of time."

"No problem." Zach appraised the dress, noticing the earrings. "You made it." Then he chuckled, indicating the plant. "Obviously enough time to dig up your garden."

Amy grinned. "I couldn't resist. I thought Joao would like this, to go near the fountain."

Zach nodded. "Good thinking: perfect blue."

They fell into line together, handed over their tickets, and took two seats inside on the upper deck.

It felt odd, being alone with him. The day had begun muggy and overcast, and she'd almost opted for her linen trousers and silk top. But when the sun had broken and the air cleared, she'd gone for frivolous, the prettier choice. Now she felt self-conscious, dressed up like a girl on a date. Amy pulled her skirt over her knees.

"This is for you." Zach plopped a magazine on her lap. *AARP*. "It's my father's."

Amy reddened, reminded so rudely of their gap in age. "You thought maybe I was old enough now?"

Zach ignored the reference. "No. Section on second careers. Page sixty-six. Check it out."

Amy opened the polished pages, flipping forward until she found the one. There, filling the bottom third of the page, was a photograph of an ample, grinning woman, a straw hat over her round, red face. Her hands were draped over cartons of green peas, a plastic tub of beets, and another of large, white onions. "Candy Adams Ellerson, sixty-three, the founder of Green Light Farms in Washington County, MN" the caption read.

Amy gave Zach a quick look. "You're into farmers now?"

He shrugged. "My father gave it to me. He thought you'd be interested."

"Do I know your father?" Amy teased.

"No. I told him about our project, about the last three women we visited. He thought this one might fit the mold." Zach pointed to the glossy nail polish, bright orange against the peas. "You gotta love her style. Anyway, we don't have a Midwest chapter; it's someplace different. And this lady is an activist. She knew her community was food insecure, nearest grocery stores over ten miles away? So she buys a sixty-eight-acre farm after leaving corporate America. They do community-supported agriculture. Something like seven pounds of fresh fruit and vegetables for twelve dollars a week. Or people can lease a quarter-acre for a dollar, or earn a plot through sweat equity."

Amy warmed, hearing his enthusiasm.

"Girls and gardens," he reminded her. "Girls and gardens with goals. Very cool," he said, holding up a thumb. "Oh!" he remembered, fishing into an inside pocket. "I also have this for you."

Amy waited, delighted at the second surprise.

He pulled out a manila envelope and handed it over. "Jada Reed mentioned wanting an article, something she could use now for publicity." She opened the envelope, pulling out three photographs. There was the farmer's face, burnished in the sun, long rows of vegetables, heavy and green against the dark earth, and a shot of the garden store. Deep in the countryside, it looked as if from another planet. "Those are the pictures for it. All we need now are the words." He grinned. "That should keep you honest." Then he turned, face to the ocean.

The heeled sandals were hard going on the rough road, and Amy wished she'd not been so vain. By the time they arrived at the Roosevelt place, she had a ripe blister on the edge of her little toe and the bodice of her dress was damp with sweat. She left Zach indoors, securing his camera case inside a closet and fitting the lenses into pockets of his jacket, preparing for the shoot, and she limped onto the stone veranda, eyeing a place where she could set the bush to one side, away from human traffic.

Standing on her own, Amy scanned the scene, looking for a familiar face. Joao was in a cluster of folks, down by the peacocks. They looked like Joao's people: short and dark, all touching and ignoring each other, the way that families do. A few small children scampered around and between the adults, some teenagers hung to one side. Scatterings of other guests were dappled about too: some elderly couples, several older women on their own, a seated row of conventional Yankees, men in their green blazers, women in pearls. Neither of the two neighbors Amy had interviewed earlier that spring were in evidence. She pulled at the front of her dress, billowing in some air, and climbed down to claim a seat.

It took some time for the ceremony to begin, and Amy sat back absorbing the view. The colors of the garden had changed again. They were more muted now, softer green and mauve, the pink blush of after-white. The ocean was dark, thickly striped with swathes of navy and teal, as if shavings of iron moved underneath the surface. A lone yacht crawled across the horizon, heading away. A heavy-set man carrying a violin brushed past her, and Amy watched him descend toward the central patio, where he removed his instrument from its case. An angular brunette stationed herself near him, black book in hand. Zach was everywhere, scrunching by the hydrangeas one minute, standing on a chair another. Edith emerged from the house, helping a wee figure with a cane navigate its way to a seat. Then Edith, too, headed down to the front, to stand next to Joao. Just as the violin music began, a man took the seat next to Amy. It was Mort, Edith's second husband. He grinned and she smiled back, not so lonely anymore.

The service was like a blessing. The musical notes floated above them just as a whisper of breeze pushed across the hillside. The minister began the reading, her voice fluid and deep. Even the seagulls swung quietly overhead, and the autumn blossoms swayed knowingly in place. Amy was lost in it all, happy with the fellowship around her. Marriage could do that, she mused, in awe of the power of the thing, how it brought people together, created so much joy.

The notion stuck in her windpipe.

Until it didn't. She remembered Graham's anger, his bitterness as she'd left the house hours earlier. "What are you doing?" he'd asked, "I thought we had an agreement!" Jason's arms were tight across his chest again, looming behind his father in the driveway, while Matt looked on sadly from the kitchen window. Only Catherine had stayed apart, taking the dish from the oven, setting out the garlic bread and salad Amy'd prepared for their lunch. Graham's voice echoed in her head, the rusty saw of it scraping with hurt and fury. "You're such a selfish bitch."

She swallowed, trying to keep her throat from closing up, tears from forming. Below her, Edith and Joao were promising their lives to each other, all the years they had left to give, but all Amy felt was a hardness, envious of their easy generosity. She hated the thought of her years ahead, resented the very notion of having to give them away to a dying man. Hated Graham for expecting she should.

She turned the ring on her finger and sniffed back a tear, ashamed of her own hostility.

Just then a hand appeared, a cotton handkerchief in its fingers.

"I know," Mort whispered. "It gets to you, doesn't it?"

Two glasses of champagne lightened the mood.

Joao's son-in-law pulled out his boom box, and the upper terrace became a dance floor. Kids and adults fell into line, doing the "Electric Slide," not missing a step. Amy set her sandals to one side and joined in too, clapping and stomping. Across the space, she saw Zach, one hand pressing his camera to his chest, the rest of him lost to the rhythm, and she beamed when he looked her way. Mort gave her a twirl after, as did Zach, making Amy feel young again. She even let Zach take a picture of her—"Perfect for the back cover!" he grinned before moving on to the other guests. And a granddaughter of Joao's chose Amy as her favorite partner. The little girl seemed taken, for some reason, with the lady in blue.

It was getting dark when she finally escaped indoors. Edith was seated on her own in the dining room, looking through some cards. Amy was relieved and surprised to have her to herself.

"Hello," Edith said looking up. "Winding down out there?"

"Almost," Amy said, "You'll be done with us soon."

Edith patted the chair next to her. "I like the caryopteris," she said. "Even though we said no gifts. What's the variety?"

"Lil Miss Sunshine," Amy grinned, taking her seat.

"Like you!" Edith's eyes twinkled. "You looked happy out there."

Amy deflected that. "It's a really nice party. I'm glad I came."

"Good." Edith's look lingered on Amy, noticing some reticence.

"I dug it from my own garden," Amy said, trying to move the conversation on.

"Oh my! Hopefully it didn't leave too much of a hole."

"Nope," Amy said. She flashed Edith a confident smile. "Anyway, I wanted you to have it." She considered her small act of defiance, the empty space she'd left behind by the rose bush, how ragged it had looked, how defiled. In a month, she thought ruefully, none of it would matter. She let her lids close briefly, the smile still fixed in place.

When she lifted them again, Edith was staring at her. "Don't tell me the book's not going well."

It surprised her, and Amy rushed to make good. "Oh, no. No, the book's going really well. We've got some wonderful women. Some more wonderful women," Amy corrected herself.

"Good." Edith's intonation ended on the up, demanding more.

Amy shrugged, wanting to unload, too scared to start. "The home life could be better. Not a great time back there right now."

"The famous architect? The clever son at Yale?" Edith tipped her head, as if to say, "How hard can it be?"

Amy swallowed, swiping some hair from her face. She thought of a cute response but decided against. "My husband's been diagnosed with Alzheimer's," she said.

Edith's face barely moved, only two thin lines deepening on her brow.

"Hmm," she said finally. Nothing more.

"We've known for a while," Amy continued. "Now, it's becoming . . . more obvious."

A swell in the music outside was followed by some youthful shouts. Edith put down the card she'd been holding. "How's your husband taking it?" she asked.

Amy rubbed her face with both hands, pondering how to explain. Thinking about how to describe Graham, a man Edith had never met, made Amy thoughtful for a moment, more filled with empathy. "He's in a rush, I think. Trying to control the world, to hang on, push it all off." She shortened it, realizing. "He's angry."

Edith watched her, listening. "You know the vows you take when you get married?" Edith asked finally. "Did you two take vows?"

Amy nodded, trying to remember.

"It says you'll love and cherish, have and hold . . . all that."

"In sickness and in health," Amy added heavily.

"Mmmhmm. Till death do you part." Edith raised an eyebrow. "Whatever. All that."

Amy flinched, sensing a sermon coming.

"But it doesn't say I promise to get hostile when he gets hostile. Get angry when he does. You're not breaking those vows if you don't suffer along with him."

Amy reflected. "I know that."

Edith sniffed. "Is he losing his mind?"

Amy objected to Edith's boldness. "Yes."

"Are you?"

Amy's hand fluttered. "That's not the point."

"Are you?"

"No."

"No." Edith shrugged. "And that's a good thing." She tried a reassuring posture. "We're all individuals. We've each got to find our own lonely way, in our lives, to our goals. That's it."

Amy felt a tide of resistance filling up inside. She wanted Edith to listen to her, understand her reality, not talk in homilies. It was hard to spit it out. "My husband's only sixty, Edith. He'll need care. Years of it."

"No doubt," Edith said, unfazed. "And you'll need to find happiness. Years of it."

A jolt of rage sprung to her eyes and Amy blinked it away. It felt punitive, burdensome of Edith to remind her of what she already knew. Amy pointed at the notes and scrawls, the cards Edith was reading. "This was nice," she said, in her calmest voice. "But it's getting late." She stood from the chair.

Edith nodded. "It is." Then, before Amy wheeled off, she added, "Thank you for coming. It made me happy."

Amy ducked her head. "Me too," she admitted.

Amy's former dance partner, Joao's granddaughter, had attached herself to Zach now, the small feet planted firmly on his larger ones. They were the last of the dancers. Her little body leaned back, arms outstretched, her face transported with delight. A handful of figures still stood about, watching the odd couple, the girl's puffed yellow skirt, the man's plain navy shirt, waiting for the dance to be over. When the song finally came to an end, the girl's father pressed down the button on his boom box and scooped the little girl in his arms.

"Time to go," he announced, whipping her up and over his shoulder.

"Aww," she whined, but flopped compliantly down her father's back.

"Happy day, Dad," the father said, patting Joao on the back. "Thanks again for the do."

Joao nodded wearily, waving his crew off.

Zach turned, noticing Amy. He wiped his face with the inside of his elbow and blew out heavily. "Carry me home too?" He smiled. "I'm exhausted."

"Wouldn't that be sweet," she said. "Got your equipment?" Amy was in no mood to hang about.

He nodded, heading inside. "Did you say goodbye to Edith?"

"Uh huh," she said. "I'll wait right here."

There was something familiar about this, she thought, standing in the shadows, watching Joao potter his way across the garden, fetching one last thing before he turned in. There was something so deadly about waiting for others, standing by as other people took care of their business, as if she had no timetable of her own. Sad, that it was happening now with Zach, that that's how things seemed to play out.

She nudged the folded tissue inside her sandal to prepare her blister for the walk to the ferry. And she thought of Graham waiting for her back at home. There was that to walk through as well.

# TWENTY-TWO

Ella's new office in Boston was Amy's idea of a stage set. Stained purple floorboards, pale gray fabric walls. She imagined the fun the designer had, putting together the motif. One chrome surface ran horizontally across the far wall, chest-high, as if presenting on a long metal tray the pristine books on display. There was chrome everywhere, in the tubular red canvas chairs, the spotlights high up in the corners, the framework of Ella's glass-topped desk. A lot of polishing required, Amy thought, but it sparkled.

Her agent had suggested an in-person meeting for a change, and Amy had been only too happy to comply. It was a nice break from the few days of penitence she'd had to wade through back home, while she and Graham adjusted to their post-mediation lull. He was still simmering at her insistence on attending Edith's wedding; she still burned that he'd sold the house. She'd taken the early bus up to Boston, dressed like a professional.

Ella had spent some minutes fixing their respective coffees, comparing the benefits of Keurig over French Press, and now they'd finally gotten down to discussing the book. Ella sat coolly in the chair across from her, fondling a pen.

"I've shared the chapters so far with the publisher," Ella announced. "Just to get their take while we're at the halfway point."

It was an inauspicious opening, and immediately Amy was on the defensive.

"Is that normal?" Amy asked carefully.

"Not really," Ella replied. "But I had certain questions, and the editor was willing."

"Do you *know* the editor?" Amy gripped her bag in her lap.

"Randall Pierce. Yes. One of their top guys."

That sounded encouraging. "But, questions… what questions?"

"I wanted to check in with them, that's all." Ella was stalling.

"Okay, and…?"

"It's all good," Ella rushed to assure her. "He trusts the voice," she said. "That's the main thing. He said it works well for this collection: smooth, natural. Almost conversational." Ella was reading from her notes. "He also said that you manage to include an extraordinary amount of information and detail. That it's quite sophisticated for a garden book."

Amy wasn't sure whether to thank him for that. She tried to sit more upright in the low-slung chair, the canvas seat giving her little purchase.

"He said that it's an interesting selection of subjects."

"Well, it should be," Amy said. "I mean, they already approved the selection." She tried to smooth the pitch of indignation in her eyebrows.

Ella nodded. "Yeah, he said it's an interesting group. Eclectic. That you've got a good eye." She waited for Amy to brighten up. "Randall Pierce is a brilliant editor, Amy, a man with a string of beautifully produced publications, and he's known for his sharp eye and often sharper criticism, so this is very good!"

"Good," Amy said, wondering what was coming.

Ella clicked on her mouse and brought up a screen on her laptop, hidden from Amy's view.

"Do you know Shelburne Farms, up in Vermont?"

She did. A rolling property along Lake Champlain. She remembered the buildings mostly, an enormous barn, the large mansion, rooms that, even back then, rented for over three hundred dollars a night. She wondered where Ella was going with this one. "Yes, I've been there," she said. "On a day trip from Burlington. We took our son there one day, to see the cheesemaking. Why?" she asked.

"That might be another garden to include."

"Of course," Amy said, bobbing dutifully. She hadn't remembered a garden, couldn't even think that there was one there, but she kept her mouth shut.

"He thinks we're looking at a fairly unique coffee table centerpiece." Ella smiled fully for the first time. "One that may require more printings than originally planned."

Amy's heart did a little dance. Something was happening here, and she waited nervously, not wanting to break the spell.

"He does have one suggestion, though." Ella began rolling her pen again, and Amy followed the long fingers, sliding up and back against each other. "He wants you to have another look at the subjects themselves. The women."

"The gardeners?" Amy wasn't correcting Ella, just seeking clarification.

"Yes," Ella said, drawing out the word.

"You mean, rewrite those sections?" Amy looked for her agent to elucidate. "What do you mean 'have another look'?"

"Shorten. Re-orient the focus. You have a tendency to get caught up in the . . ." Ella held out both palms, fingers curled upwards. ". . . in the . . . what Randall called the 'human mess' of these ladies, as if you're writing a personal interest story. He thinks it's a little distracting." Ella peered over at Amy, her glasses shiny under the lights.

Amy was speechless. She didn't know whether to feel stricken or outraged, both emotions tumbling heavily through her body. She licked her lips, tasting the reminder of lipstick she'd put on earlier. She could feel color rising up her face.

"Don't be offended," Ella said jovially, leaning back in her chair. "Randall thinks you can fix it. And I know you can. I wouldn't be meeting with you if I didn't. Here's some suggestions, though." Ella raised her pen, pointing it at her. "You tidy up those parts of the chapters, streamline those sections. And add in a trip to Shelburne Farms. Randall's a fan of the place."

Amy nodded, forcing a smile.

"And think positive! This is good, good news, Amy. And you're almost halfway there!"

Amy hid her confusion entering the elevator. Young, sharp-looking professionals bustled in and out again, lost in their own silent reveries, and she bit the inside of her cheeks to keep from talking out loud. When she emerged onto the street, hit the fresh breeze blowing up from Fort Port Channel, Amy's feet nearly tripped on the sidewalk.

Traversing the streets of Boston's Seaport District, bustling with new construction and wine bars, all the trappings of up-and-coming dot-com establishments, independent contractors and glistening condo towers, Amy felt part of the stream of success flourishing around her, but also strangely out of sync. It was as if she'd boarded a rollercoaster, hungry for the rush, but was now hurtling down a deep dip, shocked by her lack of control.

She shrugged her bag higher on her shoulder. It was the smart one, the one Sandy had insisted she buy the day their first book had been signed. An acid-green leather thing, shiny and deep, the bag wasn't something Amy ever had occasion to wear. Now, the oversized bag was simply a burden. She strode down Northern Avenue as far as the water, stopping to watch a small lobster boat tied up behind the Barking Crab. Men were unloading crates from the deck, heaving them into short columns by the bar's side entrance. If it were later, she'd have loved to go down there, book a table, order a drink to celebrate. She'd forgotten the fun of being in the city, the instant gratification at every corner, and wished that she could stay there and indulge.

She considered the condo they'd decided to buy in Providence, that short afternoon with Graham and the realtor. She registered why it had been such an easy, careless decision. City living had its attractions. Even under present circumstances, downsizing might offer other benefits, different ways of doing life. She thought of the walks they could take, the lit pathways by the river, gallery visits, nights out at the theater. Graham tall and knowledgeable at her side. Then she thought of the actual Graham, the one he was becoming. More soberly, Amy projected gardening in two pots on a balcony, and writing, her laptop crammed into the alcove off the hall.

A noisy family approached, two of the children arguing over the Happy Meal trolls found in their McDonald's bags. Amy turned from them and headed toward Summer Street, dodging the relentless commuters streaming from South Station.

Taking the bus from New Bedford had given her time to mentally prepare. Now, seated high up at the front, looking out the wide window ahead, Amy had time to reflect. Randall Pierce 'trusted the voice.' It was book speak, a way of saying he liked her writing. She was sure of that. Had he called it 'smooth'? That could be a good thing, although in retrospect, smooth felt a little boring, a bit like running water. Did he mean smooth as in a lightly trickling stream, or smooth as in the Dead Sea? She hadn't ever met the man, or heard his voice when he'd said this, only remembered Ella's pen, the fingers. Amy wished she'd had someone else there, someone to interpret, someone besides Ella. But 'sophisticated.' Amy liked that word. Although 'sophisticated for a garden book' seemed like an insult. Some of Randall Pierce's better-selling hardbacks were garden books, travel books. She thought of the travel writers Paul Theroux and Bill

Bryson and wondered whether she could be like them. What if she was that good? Amy'd sensed that she was on to something when she'd started this project, had an eye for what made a garden unique, what made some gardeners, some people, so compelling to read about. It could just be that now was her time, that the editor had seen that in her. Randall Pierce might just be her ticket.

Her mind flipped again. But he and Ella wanted Amy to streamline the women, edit down the personalities behind her gardens, the very people whose endeavors, whose choices and vision, made the gardens what they were. That made Amy indignant.

She looked down at the traffic, peeling off to the right as the bus turned left onto Route 24. It wasn't a choice Ella had offered her so much as an ultimatum, something Amy was finding harder and harder to bear.

She picked up her phone to bitch.

Alice could be a sympathetic ear. Her sister understood personnel strategies, how to win an argument, but her sister didn't know publishers, and really, Amy realized, Alice didn't know Amy as a writer at all.

She dialed Sandy's number. Her friend and collaborator, Sandy understood the players, had been in on the project from the beginning. Best of all, Sandy loved a good bitch. But as the dial tone repeated against her ear, an awful possibility grew in Amy's mind: her friend might agree with Ella and Randall Pierce. Sandy, after all, had been the person on the road trip who had wanted to keep the politics out of the women's stories. When the recorded message came on, Amy hung up, saying nothing.

Of course, Amy thought, settling on the perfect person.

"What's up?"

"I've just come from Ella's office and my brain is exploding. She's had feedback from our editor. Got a minute?"

She could hear Zach put the phone down, plug her into his Bluetooth. "About one, I'm working. Tell me quickly: how'd it go? We still on the path?"

"Well . . ." Amy didn't know where to begin. "We are. He likes the collection. But there are some changes . . ."

"You know what?" Zach interrupted her. "Where are you?"

"On the bus from Boston."

"Come by here when you get back, would you? I've got to get this file off before noon, but I want to hear all the details. D'ya mind?"

It was annoying, probably something she shouldn't do, with Graham home alone all morning, but it was better than nothing. "Okay. Where's 'here'?"

He laughed. "My place. Eighteen Thatcher. Just over the bridge from you."

In all the months of working together, she'd never known where Zach lived. Amy had imagined an anonymous apartment somewhere, something like Jason's in New Haven, the kind that young, single men lived in. Driving down the quiet street in Padanaram, though, flanked by neatly groomed Capes and recently paved drives, Amy's mind began to spin. Did Zach still live with his parents, she wondered, acknowledging to herself that that would prove disappointing.

Number eighteen was painted on a large rock. It sat to the side of a dirt drive, the final stop of the street's dead end. She turned into the scrubby entrance, tall weed trees, overgrown brambles scraping the sides of her car. The Kia was parked in the small clearing, where the drive widened into a patch of packed earth and flattened yellowed grass. Behind it was the dwelling, a modest bungalow with a sloping front porch and a bright blue tarp roped over the rear section of the building's roof. If nothing else, this could be an adventure. She climbed the rotted steps and peered through the screen door to the one front room.

Zach was stationed at a wide semicircle of a desk, three large screens surrounding him. It looked like the command post for some starship fantasy, the broad surface tight with slim hardware and blinking lights, the space below snaking with cable.

"Knock, knock," she said through the mesh.

"Hey!" He looked up, holding up an index finger.

She waited as he clicked furiously, taking the chance to glance around. The room was the width of the house, bare-floored but for a riotous carpet across from Zach's desk. A futon slouched there, and a low coffee table, its lower shelf stuffed with books. Study and living room, all in twenty square feet. The economy impressed her.

"There!" Zach rolled off his chair and came to the door. "You made it!"

"You thought maybe I'd change my mind?" She smiled, self-conscious now as she entered his space.

"Not at all. I was just finishing up, thinking deep thoughts of lunch. You hungry?"

"Not wildly."

"Well, come back, I'm just going to make myself a sandwich. I want to hear everything."

He led them down a narrow central hallway, past a little bed-sized room on the left and what she guessed was the bathroom after it. The small kitchen was across the way, dull, uncluttered, an ancient electric stove. She stood in the doorframe while he whisked out some bread and peanut butter. "So he likes it so far, our publisher?"

"He said that we've got an eclectic collection. That we've got a good eye." Amy began.

"Alright!"

"But." Amy waited for the spreading to stop, for Zach to finish his task.

"Yeah?" Zach slapped the sandwich on a plate and grabbed two apples, passing one to Amy. "There's always a 'but'. What's his?"

"There's a lot,' Amy said. "I need to sit down, tell you all of it, so you can help me make sense of it."

Zach nodded. "Come on." He walked them back to the futon, claiming one corner. "Start with all the things he liked."

As she relaxed into his company, Amy recounted the comments that had made her feel so positive. She warmed in the telling, remembering the glitz of Ella's office, the glamour of Seaport's streets. Most of all, she rekindled the confidence she'd felt, knowing that it was her vision, her writing that had brought the project so far, and delighted that she was sitting here, in the company of this accomplished young photographer.

He licked a finger and picked up his apple. "This all sounds pretty good to me. What's the caveat?"

"He said to rewrite—shorten—the parts about the women. That they're a distraction."

Zach frowned. "I thought they were part of the point."

Amy's mouth dried, having to repeat the words. "He said I have a tendency to get caught up in the human mess."

"He used those words? 'Human mess'?"

Amy nodded, humiliated all over again. "That's what Ella told me. He wants us to lose the politics and think gardens."

"What a dick." Zach bit into his apple.

Amy watched him, his jaw moving slowly, and she waited, wanting more. "What do you think?" she asked at last. "What do you think I should do?"

Zach finished his bite. Then he pointed across the room to the three screens on his desk. "I just sent off a job I did for the Kalb Corporation. Interesting story: two Syrian brothers, came over just before the war heated up. One on a lottery visa, the other snuck in, undocumented. Married an American women, served in the military. The U.S. Army."

Amy waited patiently, frustration growing in her chest.

"They bought an old ice cream factory, used EB5 money, that's a kind of government grant, to fix it up, hired locals, other immigrants. Now they're running a thirty-seven-million-dollar business."

She stared at him. "What's your point?"

"The brothers wanted photographs for a revised website. They're changing their logo, their look. You'd think—I think—that the shots of them, of their people, the folks they hired, maybe shots of the factory, before and after, would be a lot more engaging, vivid. You know what they had me do?"

Amy sighed. "What?"

"Head shots. Of them in suits and ties. One rather grand one of the front of their building." He grimaced. "Not what I would have chosen." Zach's eyes danced. "But they paid me enough to fix the roof over the bathroom."

Amy's shoulders slumped. Why had she come here, she thought irritably. Even Zach didn't seem to understand.

"It's my project," she said, wanting to weep. "It's my writing."

"Those are my photographs."

She bowed her head, wondering how she could leave now.

"Maybe you just need a leaky roof," he said, grinning. "Sometimes a little poverty can go a long way to help focus the mind."

The smarmy comment hit her like a slap, and fat tears swam to the surface before she could stop them. "Fuck you!" is what she managed to say, stumbling to escape the suck of the futon.

But he was up as quickly, grabbing her before she reached the door.

"Hey," he said. "What?"

She tried to free herself, but he wrapped more tightly, encircling her. "Amy. I'm sorry. Tell me."

She clenched her mouth shut, her shoulders shaking now inside his hold. She could no more tell him what it was than she could fly to the moon. What? It was everything. Her own vanity and

239

pridefulness. Her lack of spine. Her women. She thought of Edith, at the small gathering on the island, of Mariann, building a garden in a swimming pool, Jada, fighting for her land, Gabriella. All that resilience. Was she supposed to whittle them down, after all they'd given her? Her brain spun back to Randall's suggestions, to Graham, dying in waves back at home. Heaving with sobs, she stood there, unable to move, caught in the arms of a confused young man, wondering what he'd done wrong.

She sniffed. Her nose had started to run.

Zach loosened his grip, letting her reach for a tissue in her bag.

Amy wiped her face, warm near his neck.

"Okay?" His hand cradled the back of her skull and she let him, resting her forehead on his shoulder.

"Oh my," she said, "Sorry about that."

She remained there as her breath subsided, feeling his chest against hers.

"It's okay." His fingers moved along her ribcage, his breath riffled her hair.

"Maybe you should stay for a bit."

*Stay?* Amy felt the word, like the tip of an arrow, piercing her sloppy fog of misery. *He wants me to stay?* The warmth of it, his easy calmness, was what kept her standing so close, for that moment, and then another. Stay? Of course she shouldn't stay. Already, she was probably late. At home, Graham would be looking at the clock, maybe trying to remember where she had gone, when she'd said she'd be back. And Haps, too, he'd be watching the door, wanting to be taken out for his walk. But it was as if she'd been slipped into a warm bath somehow, stripped of the weight of herself, and she wanted to rest there, floating in the heat.

She felt Zach inhale, his stomach pressing into her belly, and she arched her back, just slightly.

"Are you okay?" His voice was kind, respectful, as if acknowledging her options.

Amy felt like he was offering her a choice when really there was none. Like when you go out to dine with a friend after a month of dieting, and that friend, her eyes begging for forgiveness, orders a rich, warm chocolate dessert. And the waitress asks, "Two forks?" and you say nothing. Partly, you're thinking *Fuck you* to the friend, the waitress, when really, you know who's about to get fucked. *Choice? Really?*

Decades of marital loyalty reeled through Amy's mind, a silent movie of restraint: the occasional episodes of mild flirtation she'd pretended to ignore, the flickering signs of attraction from other men, once another woman she'd let pass unexplored. Much more than a month of dieting, Amy thought coldly. And the years of offering herself up to Graham, hungry for affection, bored with the repetition, and the nights when she'd lain waiting for him, awake in bed, sensing that he was with someone else, hoping he wasn't. She remembered the times she'd let her husband enter her, even when sure he'd been with another woman, and she remembered not daring to ask, for fear of never being filled again.

As conscious of herself as she'd ever been, Amy experienced the muscular tension, balancing on the precipice of betrayal. She was angry that that was the choice, resentful that she couldn't simply lie back, tired as she was of it all.

By way of response, Amy turned and planted her lips against Zach's chin, and when he hesitated, she repeated the kiss, over his jawline, finding his mouth.

Even then, she recalled later, it might not have led back into his bedroom, a whirlwind of clothes at the foot of his bed. It could have just been a flurry of kissing and stupid groping, like what she remembered from sock hops in junior high during the last slow dance in the middle of the crowded gymnasium floor, before the song ended and

241

they went back to their respective corners. But she and Zach hadn't stopped there; there'd been another decision, and another, each of which she'd made in the speed of events. And as every threshold was passed, the refrain in her mind—amidst the volcanic excitement of unpredictable touching, of shocking wetness—was a cool, fresh wave of relief, of gratitude, of why the fuck not?

# TWENTY-THREE

The shadows were already well across the yard when Amy pulled into the drive—just enough time to slip upstairs and grab a quick shower before starting dinner. When she stepped from her car, however, she saw Graham emerge from his. He'd been sitting there in the waning light, Haps next to him in the passenger seat. She fought for composure.

"Hi!" she said, too brightly.

"There you are. I was worried you'd forgotten our date."

Amy paused, her face a blank.

"Unless it was supposed to be Saturday and I got it wrong. Or maybe I've got the day wrong . . ." He hunched his shoulders, a helpless grin on his face.

He was wrong on both counts. They had planned to go out together, a kind of truce following the mediation, but the plan was for Sunday evening, and it was still Thursday. She searched for the right reply.

Haps had meanwhile found his way around the car, sniffing eagerly at Amy's skirt as Graham waited for an answer. She pushed the dog away, shielding herself with the green bag.

"You're right; I'm wrong," Amy said abruptly. "I'm so sorry. Things just . . . took longer." She tried an apologetic grimace. "Let me just freshen up, and I'll be ready to go in twenty minutes. Is that okay?"

More than anything, she wanted to clean up.

"What took longer?" he asked. "Your meeting with your agent?" He'd seen her racing off that morning to catch the eight o'clock bus.

She thought quickly. "Well, and then we needed to debrief. You know, discuss the recommendations."

Graham's face remained watchful as he listened.

"But the editor's still excited about the book!" Amy added, her face shining. She took Haps's muzzle in her hands, kissing him off her clothing. "Yay!" Then, not chancing further discussion, she turned toward the house. "Fifteen minutes!" she said, pulling at the dog's collar. "I'll tell you all about it."

Graham wanted to eat at their local restaurant, choosing a table by the window that gave the dual view of the water and the passersby. In the height of summer, the small ice cream shop next door attracted droves of pedestrians who wandered past toward the bridge late into the evening, busy with their cones. It made Amy uncomfortable. The little bistro was five short blocks from Zach's bungalow, and she kept imagining him passing by, imagined what he might do if he saw her there through the glass.

"So what's the verdict?" Graham asked. He looked as if he was less interested in the reply than in how Amy delivered it, testing the waters.

"Well, the publisher loves 'the voice,'" she told him carefully. "He wants some revision. I guess that's normal. And he gave me some suggestions of what other subjects to include." She held her palm up to the waiter, indicating they were not yet ready to order.

Graham didn't glance at the menu before him. "So you're moving ahead with it? Is that what the three of you all decided today?"

Amy shrank as the lie resurfaced. "Yes," she said.

"So that will mean more travel."

Amy nodded. "Not tomorrow. The rewrites will take me a few days. Then there's one garden he wants us to include—in Vermont. But that's one day only. And then, yes, one . . . trip."

"So, he's still committed."

"We're under contract."

Graham compressed his lips, as if considering her response. "Our closing is in under four weeks, Amy. We have to move before Labor Day."

"I know." She'd thought of little else. Count on Graham to mention it now.

"And this is something you think you can manage?" It was his lofty look, the one that so often made her feel small, unsure.

"I do." Amy spoke with feigned assurance.

"Even with packing, moving, settling into our new home? You can do all that as well as travel?"

"I can do it," Amy said. Then, with more acid, she added, "I'll have to."

She opened her menu, trying to hide there, amongst the entrees.

Once the food arrived, they spoke of other things. Graham described his final session with the clients in Bristol, his plans for completing the library wing. Amy distracted herself, listing the few pieces of furniture she wanted to move with them into the new condo, and she kept the conversation away from all her many reservations, the promised rewrites, the garden, her terror of leaving it. Graham replayed his latest conversation with Jason, about their son's job hunt, and they became Jason's parents again, united in that.

Amy began to feel strangely calm. She had spent the afternoon being intimate, sexual, foreign even to herself. The memory of it was like a finger held against her clitoris. Yet remarkably, the quick sponge bath earlier seemed to have wiped away more than just the smell of her deceit. Here she sat, easy and relaxed, in their familiar bistro with her partner of a lifetime, as naturally as if they had just spent the day together. She imagined spies lived with the same dexterity, flowing easily from one identity to the next, and she wondered what that made her.

Khayed and Betsy, their neighbors from down the street, passed by the window, and they stopped to sit with them at the little table for a while, nibbling down the stubs of their cones, joining Amy and Graham for coffee. They hadn't known about Graham's diagnosis. They didn't know that he and Amy were planning to move, that Graham had left his firm, that Amy was working on a book. She watched with wonder as her husband explained it all, earnest and articulate, speaking with apparent equanimity of his own diminished future, their radically changed lives.

"Thank God for this wife of mine," Graham said, pinning Amy to her seat with his penetrating gaze.

Betsy was soppy and sad, appalled that they'd be leaving such a house, convinced no one would preserve the glorious garden. "Oh, they'll maintain it," Graham insisted, "It's part of the sale agreement." He nodded at Amy, like he'd thought of everything.

"Not the way Amy did." Betsy cast pitying looks at them both that made Amy squirm.

But Khayed, big chested and burly, placed his paws on Amy's and Graham's shoulders. "You two are an inspiration," he said, his voice radiating warmth. And Amy sensed that Khayed was right, that she and Graham did appear something of an inspiration. To many people, they always had.

Only later, on the way home, did Graham remember to tell her. "Sandy phoned," he said quietly before turning off the car. "This afternoon. While you all were meeting."

He put on a pajama top that night, something he never did. And when Amy slid in next to him, Graham turned away, reaching for his book.

Long after he'd doused his light, Amy lay there by his side, awake and anxious, wondering what he knew. His long body facing away from her, she studied its outline in the hazy darkness, the curl of his shoulder, the hillock where his hip rose up and down again, the descending mound of him along his bent knees and relaxed feet. Somewhere tucked in there was his flaccid penis. Revolted suddenly, Amy shuddered, flooded with affection and empathy, both. As a kind of amends, she promised herself that Graham would never learn of how euphoric she'd been in another man's bed, how much younger she'd felt, nimble and frolicsome, laughing as Zach's tongue, as firm and resilient as the rest of him, had lapped at her, how her crotch had risen for more. A spasm of nerve memory shot through her groin, and Amy cupped her palm over it, encasing the warmth. Holding herself there, she drifted off into sleep.

Early the next morning, she brought her phone with her when she took Haps for his walk. Once out of earshot, she placed the call. "I promise this won't get to be a habit."

"No problem." Zach seemed unsurprised at the call. "How're you today?"

"I'm okay." Amy struggled, embarrassed with her question. "It's just . . . I wondered if you'd spoken to Sandy. You know, after I left."

"I haven't." Then he chuckled. "And if you're worried I will, well, don't. I don't see the need."

It seemed so simple for him; Amy was both relieved and slightly hurt. "Good. Me neither," she said.

"I was a port in a storm. And I know that storms pass." He spoke matter-of-factly, without any self-pity, sounding like the nice guy he was.

"Well," Amy said, "a really lovely port." She glanced down at Haps, tugging at her to speed up. "I guess I'd better go. Lots of work ahead."

"Indeed. Good luck."

"Bye," she said and pocketed her phone.

She longed to walk by his place again, just to see it once more, see where she'd been. But Haps kept her to their route, and she let the idea pass, following along.

There was still Sandy's call to return, but Amy decided to do that later. She wasn't steady enough to face her friend, the shock of betrayal too fresh in her mind.

Re-entering the house, pouring out food for the dog, Amy pondered the weight of all she was facing. The real burden, the real loss, was Graham's. She knew that. He was the one whose life was really on the line, and to the extent that she could commiserate, she thought she did. But the work, the onus of this transition was a different thing, and most of it was squarely on her. It was a punishing agenda. She filled Haps's dish with water, spilling some as she placed it on the floor. But why not? Surely, this was something she deserved, leaving her family as she had, after that awful mediation, to dance about at an island wedding, tantalizing herself with a friend and colleague—a colleague's lover, no less! And the infidelity of yesterday—the image of Zach's bare thigh, sticky with sex, lurched in her chest. What compassionate wife does that? She was horrified. Mystified. Amy calculated that she'd probably earned her punishment. Only in her case, she'd waited until after the ruling to commit the crime. She filled the kettle, pulling out a bowl for her breakfast. Now she had to get on with serving her time.

What no one had calculated were the hours and days it would take for her to manage the move. Matt's agreement hadn't provided for that. Amy had to sort through, select from, and dispense with decades of accumulated stuff, crammed into attic and basement, four bedrooms and two lounges, a shed and a large, furnished patio, not to mention Graham's cavernous, frightening, spilling-over study. The kitchen alone was a major project. She glanced around her, guesstimating the cartons it would require to empty the long stretch of cupboards. The new dwelling, a two-and-a-half-bedroom townhouse, with its galley kitchen and tiny back porch, would hold maybe an eighth of their possessions. She scooped coffee into the pot, preparing Graham's morning brew.

Only Amy understood what else she had on her plate. The family had already planned her mother's memorial service, scheduled for the Monday of Labour Day weekend, and the notices had been sent out months ago. Although there wasn't a lot more for Amy to do, there were the flowers for her to think about and last-minute conversations to have with the minister and church ladies over what refreshments would be served. Now, of course, she had the rewrites to do, and an additional garden to research and visit in upstate Vermont. Then her team would be flying to three more gardens this month. The days ahead almost made her faint.

Amy was making herself a schedule in her head, determined to accomplish it all, when Alice phoned.

"If you're calling to say they've just added more hours to the day, I'll give you my firstborn." Amy laughed, a new way of coping.

"I have," Alice quipped back. "Unfortunately, the new hours only come while you're asleep."

"Shit."

"And I don't want your firstborn. Jason's too high-end for me."

"Then what?"

Since Amy had told her about Graham, Alice had tapped into a deep well of utter compassion, showing the good side of older sisterhood: she was on Amy's side. Now, the two could joke about everything.

"I'm thinking that when I come to Providence for Mom's service, I might come early," she said, "to help you with your new place. You know, find the right blinds. Whatever."

Amy's face wrinkled with gratitude. "You're kidding."

"I'm not. Four nights over the holiday weekend is really all I can manage. But I'm yours, if you can use me."

"Oh, Alice!" Amy wanted to weep. "Yes! I'd love that. You really mean it?"

"Of course," Alice said. "And maybe we could do the memory walk together through the folks' old house and neighborhood. Once you and Graham are settled in. I'd like that."

"You're a saint." Amy couldn't believe she was saying this to her sister.

They penciled it in, and Amy hung up, gazing once again at the calendar. Twenty-nine days, four now, with some help. She could do this.

She brought Graham his coffee in bed, her second tea in the other hand.

He looked up warily as she entered the room.

"Hey," she said, determined to be cheerful. "Thought you might like this."

"Thanks." He reached for his mug. "Are you coming back to bed?" There was a vague hopefulness to his voice.

"No." She indicated with her head. "I'm off to my study, to start in on the rewrites. Here's what I've decided though, just so you know."

He watched her warily, the mug held tight by his chest.

"I'll spend four hours a morning on the writing, and the rest of the day I'm going to start working on the move. Set up the movers, maybe hire some people to help me pack up the kitchen, whatever books we want to keep. I'm also going to ask a friend from the paper to help me post some things on eBay, and line up a local charity to come review what we don't want to keep." He looked dazed. "And if you want to help out, you can finish organizing your study, maybe putting what you want to bring on one side of the room, what you want tossed on the other. That sound okay?"

"So you're not going anywhere today." It wasn't a question.

"I'm not. I'm going to be right here, all day."

"Until we move." His eyes were dark, watchful.

That stopped her. There would be two more road trips before September; she'd told him that already.

"If it works out, I may do a quick trip," she hedged. Then she held up her finger quickly. "But I promise you, we will be out of here with our bed made up in the new place by Labor Day Weekend. Promise."

He sighed, turning back to his book.

After a draining ninety minutes, Amy put the rewrites to one side. She hadn't landed on an approach yet that would suit Randall Pierce and do justice to her gardeners, so she decided to let that percolate. Instead, she pulled up the file of gardens still to see, refreshing her mind with what lay ahead.

For the August trip, there was the colossus of a playground garden near the former McDonald's World Headquarters in Oak Bluffs, Illinois. Established by the widow of a C-level exec, the garden mixed child-friendly constructions – bridges and tree houses, tunnels and rope swings, all set in a fairyland site. Odd and unique, it had caught Amy's eye, if only because it sat in the former neighborhood of Chicago's mafioso families. The irony made her smile. Then there was Charlayne Bruford, the daughter of a Texas lumber mill family and owner and manager of an expansive place in Love, Texas. There, out in the rolling hills of short leaf pine, on a rise overlooking her family's sawmill operations, Charlayne had created a winding shade garden, miles of dappled walkway, mostly warm and verdant throughout the 263 growing days every year. Then they'd scoop back to Charleston to see the sculpture garden. And whatever Shelburne Farm offered. That had to be in there too.

In September, once the move had happened, once the memorial service was over, once she'd closed on her parents' home, there would be just three gardens left to see. One was just outside of Boulder, Colorado. Established by two activist sisters alongside the Twin Lakes Open Space in an area called Gunbarrel, the short-seasoned garden celebrated the protection of wetlands, jogging trails and green spaces. She had liked it for the name alone, but the photo of the twin sisters tickled her too. Then there was the one in Bozeman, Montana, a memorial rose garden built by a high school teacher to honor her first student to perish in a war, developed over the years for all the fallen veterans she had educated into the military. The blossoms lasted from early spring to early autumn. There was a story there, too. Finally, there was also the extravagant holding in the hills of San Francisco. Another stunning garden, another motivated woman. Photographs of hunched, overheated Mexicans toiling amongst the bright, well-watered foliage made Amy uncomfortable, though, and she debated in her mind how to approach this one, in light of the editor's cautionary approach to reality. Maybe Ella and Randall would let her drop that one, now that Vermont had been added to the list.

Just envisioning the gardens, thinking about meeting the women in person, made Amy's mind dance.

A soft knock sounded at her door. She checked the time on her screen. Shortly after one. It was probably Graham, calling her out. She stretched her arms overhead, stifling a yawn. "Coming!" she said loudly.

But it was Sandy's head that poked through, not her husband's.

"Lucky you!"

# TWENTY-FOUR

I t startled her, seeing Sandy standing at her door. Blood rose to
her cheeks, as if caught in the act.

"Hello stranger," she managed.

"Hey," Sandy said. She stepped into the room. "Look at you."

Amy shrugged, lifting her palms. "It's where I hide." She thought
to bolt, but Sandy was blocking the way.

"I guess so."

"I was just about to take a break," Amy said. "Do you want to
come down with me? Grab lunch?" The parallel to her visit with
Zach raced through her mind.

Sandy frowned, shaking her head. Then she sat on the edge of the
guest bed, folding her hands in her lap. "Why didn't you tell me?"
she asked at last, her face almost compassionate, serious.

Amy couldn't breathe for the pounding in her throat. She thought
of Edgar Allen Poe, the heartbeat sounding through the wall. Her
only instinct was to lie.

"Tell you what?" she said. *Make sure*, she thought. *Make her say it*.

"I thought we were friends." Sandy's hair was getting longer,
losing its spikes. But she'd put on makeup this morning, and the
outlines of her eyes were vivid and bold.

Amy stared back, refusing to blink. "We are," she ventured.
Except nowhere—not in any definitions she'd ever known—did

friendship equate with fucking someone's guy. Amy felt the heat spreading toward her ears.

"Did you think I couldn't keep a secret? Wouldn't understand?" Sandy's gaze softened under a furrowed brow.

Amy had no idea where this was going.

"Graham told me," Sandy said.

Amy's heart stopped.

"About the Alzheimer's. Selling the house. All that you've been going through."

Amy almost blurted her relief. "Oh," she said, biting her jaw tight.

"How long have you known?" Sandy asked.

Hurt lived somewhere in the question, so Amy tried to answer accordingly. "The day after my birthday party, the party you threw for me." She waited for Sandy to absorb it. "But Graham asked me not to say anything. Not to the kids, my sister, not even you."

"Wow." Sandy's face registered the information.

"Mmm," Amy said. "And he'd known for months before that. He didn't tell me either." That should be some consolation to her friend, surely. That the women had been in the same boat, both kept in the dark.

"And all this time? While we were driving through Tennessee, working our way down the Keys? You were carrying around this information about Graham?"

"Yeah. But he was doing okay. That made it easier."

"Weren't you dying to tell someone?" Sandy's face wrinkled with incredulity.

Amy thought about it. "Uh huh," she acknowledged. "But Graham was trying to keep his work going, not let his clients find out. He was managing it all right, and that meant I should." As she spoke, Amy realized that this was only part of the truth. In fact, she had been glad to forget Graham's problem, remembered sitting happily in the hot tub, willfully oblivious to what was going on back at home.

Sandy leaned back, her hands behind her on the mattress. "You really are a good wife."

The irony of Sandy's comment roared up from inside, and Amy had to smother the laugh. "Is that what I am?"

"Yes! I think so." Sandy was grinning back, as if reappraising her old friend.

"You—the expert on good wives?" Amy was teasing.

Sandy chuckled at herself. "Okay. Maybe not an expert. But I know what I see. And if I were ever a wife . . ."

"Which you hope never to be," Amy reminded her.

"Which I pray on my knees every night never to be . . ." Sandy's head bowed with emphasis. "I hope that I would do what you're doing."

Amy thought of Graham, putting on his pajamas, withdrawing from her. "Thanks," she said, permitting Sandy her naivete.

The sound of something heavy scraping across the floor shrieked through the house, followed by a burst of profanity. Amy's chest seized up.

"So . . . this is going to be hard," Sandy said. "Do you kind of . . . know what to expect? I mean, obviously you're moving. You seem to have some plans in place." She was fishing, Amy thought sadly, wondering what the world wonders about living with dementia, losing a partner to madness. "Are you ready?" her friend asked.

Amy closed her laptop, pushed her chair back from the table. Downstairs, Graham was now in the kitchen, opening and closing the cupboard doors. He'd be wanting some lunch. "Not especially," she said, giving Sandy at least that amount of truth. Then she pointed to her computer. "Although, I was working on our next trip, thinking about the next gardens we'll be visiting, the gardeners we're going to meet? And when I'm doing that, I'm pretty happy. Like Abe Lincoln. You know, happy as I make up my mind to be?"

Sandy was watching her, obviously unconvinced. "Don't think it was Abe who said that."

"Well, whoever did." Amy wanted to get Sandy off the wife refrain and focus instead on the new prospects for their book. "Edith Roosevelt talked about that. The day she got married. Made me furious at the time, but she's got a point. She said we all have to find our own way to happiness."

"Zach said it was an odd wedding."

"Really?" Amy pretended to think back. "He looked like he was enjoying himself."

Sandy shrugged. "He said I didn't miss much."

Amy chose to leave it be. "It was fine," she said, dismissing the comment. "Anyway, Edith was right. When I work at it, it's not too bad. I even get the feeling that as long as I'm out there, meeting these people, focusing on their gardens, I'll never not be happy, in spite of what's happening with Graham. Gabriella—in Marathon Key? She has a life pretty much free of resentment and anger. Can you imagine? Because she's got her plants, is nourishing something." Amy let the logic flow. "So, if I keep my attention there, keep writing, find some soil to stick my fingers in . . ." The reality of moving from the garden outside stopped her there.

"Well, dirt wouldn't do it for me, that's for sure." Sandy's gaze was penetrating and gloomy. "I don't know how I would cope. I really don't."

No. Sandy was sticking with morose. *Okay,* Amy thought, *have it your way.* She cocked her thumb at the noise in the kitchen. "Of course, sometimes I think about what's going on, how much worse it's going to get, and I'd like to shoot myself. Just jump on a train and get the hell out of dodge." Amy smiled, seeing the shock in Sandy's eyes. "Sometimes," she confided, almost cruelly, "I think of my hillside in Sri Lanka, our little house all to myself, and I make a plan." She squinted her eyes, as if trying to blink away the thought.

"Yeah. Well . . ." As expected, Sandy had no response.

"Yeah."

"You won't do that." Sandy said it as if testing to make sure.

Amy shrugged her shoulders high, back down again, soothing out the tautness in her back. She grimaced, eyeing the woman on the bed. "Remind me again: why not?"

Sandy was ready for this one. "Because Graham's your husband," she said evenly. "Because he's stood by you for all these years. I mean, isn't that the deal you signed up for?" She paused. "Maybe because you owe him?"

*Wow*, Amy thought, shocked into silence.

"Because if it hadn't been for him, you'd probably never have had time to poodle around in your garden, wouldn't have had the luxury to contemplate the joys of Mother Nature, might never have started to write."

She could smell Sandy's jealousy, was horrified by it.

"But mostly because he needs you now." Sandy's face had gone stern.

"Amy!" The shout echoed in the stairway. "You guys going to eat?"

# TWENTY-FIVE

I t was getting stuffy in the guestroom and Amy's skin prickled with the heat. Only pollen and warm air came through the two windows, and the fan she'd hefted into place did a poor job of stirring it around. She leaned back in her chair, gazing at the screen. In the last couple of days, she'd labored to revise the narratives about Edith Roosevelt, Mariann Kingsley, and Gabriella Diaz. It made her uneasy, deleting the details—the interrupted marriages, the deceased child, holidays with the powerful brothers—what the publisher referred to as the "mess." It was a delicate balance, making the profiles tidy enough to satisfy the publisher and still evocative enough to capture the richness of these women's lives. Amy liked the stories less now. She worried they no longer rang with the gardeners' resilience, the central thing she most wanted to communicate about women who grow things. Reluctantly, she emailed them off to Ella.

Rewriting the Jada Reed section, however, was proving impossible. Without mentioning the struggle to maintain ownership of her land, Jada's story was no story at all. Because hers wasn't simply a tale of individual commitment. This was a social story, one of collective resistance, a story of racism. To say less than that would be a disservice to Jada and to the truth. But to use the "r" word? Good God. It was the ultimate third rail. Talk about political.

Amy aimed her armpits at the fan, one at a time, praying for inspiration.

If the writing had bogged down, her afternoons had not. In the two days since Sandy's visit, Amy'd been ferociously productive. That first afternoon Sandy had hung around, as if needing to reassure Graham that he was still smart and attractive, modeling what a loving wife should have done. It was obnoxious, Amy thought, for someone who had never particularly cared for the man, but while Sandy cooed and smarmed, Amy had removed every wall hanging in the house, later escorting Graham back through, together choosing only two pieces from each room. By eight that evening, she'd bubble-wrapped and taped every frame. She lined up the ones to keep against the windowed wall in the den, the ones to dispense with packed behind the couch in the living room.

The next afternoon Amy had spent on the phone, choosing the movers and selecting a charity that was willing to remove everything she and Graham didn't want. She'd contacted her friend at the newspaper and scheduled a walk-through with her, giving the woman carte blanche to sell whatever rare items and large pieces of furniture she could on eBay, giving Amy sixty percent. This afternoon, Amy was going to focus on the closets, putting aside only the clothes that had been worn in the last year. The restriction was harsh but realistic. Their new world order couldn't accommodate ancient sweatshirts that might someday come in handy.

She looked back at the screen. Only the description of the Reed farm and garden store had survived the cuts. Jada's face and voice hovered overhead. Amy was stymied: how to mention the woman's complexion? Whether to capitalize the word Black.

Her phone brought a welcome distraction.

"I'm guessing you've planned a yard sale." Betsy sounded energized.

Amy thought quickly. "I haven't, really . . ."

"Well, you should," Betsy insisted. "Particularly as I've got four folding banquet tables in our garage, and I'd be happy to help."

Amy chuckled inside. Sometimes good news arrived in pushy packages. "I've never had one," Amy said, feeling stupid. Truthfully, she didn't like the thought, having never been intrigued by other people's junk. But the opportunity to share the workload with such a bossy person felt like a cool breeze. The house was buried in stuff.

"Let me initiate you," Betsy said. "You'll love it."

"When?" Amy shrunk at the prospect of scheduling one more activity in an already short month.

"This coming Saturday."

"Yikes!"

"Not to worry. I'll put out the signs, haul over the tables, and you'll be counting the money before you know what's hit you." With a last flurry of instructions, Betsy left her alone again, promising to be there Friday afternoon with pen and labels, fifty dollars' worth of singles.

Dazed, Amy took another look at the half-empty page. In their stories, she hadn't thought to include the fact that Edith and Mariann were White. Of course not, she chided herself: these women were the norm, their race assumed. Now, trying to wrap her arms around the Tennessee scenario, she didn't know how to introduce skin color for the first time. Could she do so just for Jada's story, without it being awkward? And if so, how was she to slip it in there, discreetly, as it were, without references to an actual color? Then she remembered the photographs, Zach's contribution to the book, his wonderful shot of Edith's pale, softened jawline, the one of Jada's polished cheeks. The pictures would do the heavy lifting here, worth much more than a thousand words. Relieved, Amy went back to the keyboard.

But now Zach was stuck in her mind, and the words still didn't come.

That evening, they took their dinner to the patio, pleased to be outside. Having bagged so many outmoded dresses, worn sweaters, and faded pairs of shorts, Amy was sick of all their belongings, ready to dispense with decades worth of clutter and memories. Graham had poked through afterwards, grabbing back his favorites. Now he was wearing his "Free Nelson Mandela" tee-shirt, and—Amy had to admit it—he looked younger for a change.

The day had cooled to tolerable in the spreading shade, and they were supping easily on fresh gazpacho. At intervals they dipped crusts of sourdough in oil flecked with basil from the garden. Graham remembered their rooftop, the one in Baltimore. "Did you grow basil up there? Or thyme?"

"Both," she said, thinking back. She lit up at the memory. "And chives and mint."

"That was a nice garden."

"It was," she agreed. "Nice on a hot night." Amy recalled the scene, sitting in their lawn chairs, the sky turning dark as city lights flicked on around them, making it hard to see each other's faces.

"You can do that again," Graham said. "There'll be some room on our new porch."

Flashing on the balcony awaiting them in Providence, Amy recoiled at the suggestion. It was maybe eight by fifteen, about large enough for a patio table and two chairs, maybe a planter if you were careful where you stepped. Remembering her first impression of the place, Amy didn't expect to be out there much. With no shade to speak of, the view was of an over-manicured strip of hostas by the edge of their parking area, the rear of a neighboring yard filled with three desultory rose bushes, two Adirondack chairs. The new balcony would never feel like a garden, not after what Amy had built in Padanaram. Glancing around her, she couldn't bear to think of all she was losing, of all she'd built over the years. It was heartless of Graham, trying to make the tiny space in Providence sound like a fair trade.

"It'll be fine." Amy sponged up more oil with her bread, looking for a way to change the subject.

"I know this is hard on you," he persisted. "I just don't know what else to do. How else to prepare."

She chewed thoughtfully. "We probably would have moved eventually." It was the best she could do.

"I never thought that. I thought we'd be here forever." Graham's gaze rested on the trio of burning bushes, just beginning to turn. "When did those go in?" he asked.

She followed his eyes. "Years ago. Jason's high school graduation, in fact. That year." She'd made endless preparations for the celebratory cook-out, the grandparents all alive then, Catherine showing up with a boyfriend, Jason's preppy classmates breezing in and out again, off to the next backyard.

"I'd forgotten," Graham said. His voice became husky. "Like I forget titles of movies, the name of the town where we built the first house. Beginning with K."

"Kandy," she told him, surprised even that could slip.

"Mmm," he said. "Ask me tomorrow, I won't know it." He frowned, fingering his wine glass, taking another sip.

Just through the hedge, out on the road, they could hear a neighbor passing by, walking his dog. Amy and Graham listened quietly, heard the dog urinating against the streetlight. Heard them amble on.

"That's what terrifies me, you know. Losing all that. I mean, what are we—what is a person, if not his memories? All the years, all he's accomplished in his life—who he's known, where he's been?" He frowned down at his chest, pulling the hem of his shirt. "I mean, look

262

at this. What's an otherwise ordinary sixty-year-old doing wearing this? It has to make a difference, Amy. What this is. Who I was . . ." His tone became beseeching, needy. "That's why just the possibility of having to live with people who can't help me remember my own life horrifies me. What would be the point? You know? What?"

Amy sat silent. She, for sure, didn't have the answer.

"That's why I don't want to be put away. You get that don't you?" His eyes were dark and hard and Amy had to struggle not to look away.

"Of course," she said.

That next morning, Ella had all three of them on a conference call, and the atmosphere was buzzing.

"The publisher loves what he's seen!"

"Very cool!" Zach said.

"Great!" Sandy echoed.

Amy's heart swelled. This had been her win, she knew. The rewrites so far had obviously convinced Randall that her writing could be trusted. She was nimble and she was a player. Inside, even without any praise, she radiated a muted pride.

"Now, though, you've got to move quickly." Typical Ella, she could never soak in the applause, but was jumping ahead to the next order of business. "All the copy has to be in by September 30th. I know you guys know that. But I'm thinking you should get all the remaining visits in by the end of August, to give you a full month for doing some final pruning."

Zach whistled.

"Yeah," Ella added. "We want to make sure that when we deliver, the publisher accepts the draft without requesting many more rewrites. The second payment comes with acceptance, you know, not just delivery."

"It's money," Zach said. "We haven't forgotten."

"Holy shit!" Sandy said. "But that's like . . ."

"A lot of flying," Ella said. "And some very clever scheduling."

"No problem," Zach insisted. "We all get our check earlier, and it'll give us September off."

It hit Amy like a bomb. "From Vermont to Chicago to . . ." Amy had to spell it out, to be sure.

"—to Texas, Montana . . . You got it. One helluva trip. All before September. Yes. So, Amy, do you want to start making the calls?" When Ella asked if you wanted to do something, it was never a question.

"Sure," Amy said slowly, thinking of the plans she'd already made, the three gardeners she'd saved for September, the additional airlines and rental cars. This really *might* kill her. Carefully, she thought out loud. "But it might make more sense to do Vermont as a stand-alone. And Chicago. Then maybe bundle the others in a big circle." Her mind was spinning, racing ahead.

"A huge circle," Sandy emphasized.

"I'll let you three worry about the logistics," Ella said. "What we need to agree is that you'll pull it off. Randall is extraordinarily motivated right now, and there's no wiggle room. Got it?"

"Yup," Zach agreed.

"I'm for it," Sandy said. Then, sounding dubious, she spoke just to Amy. "Can you handle this, Amy? With everything else?" There was an ominous overlay to the question, and Amy recoiled. Unless Sandy had told her, Ella had no clue about Graham. Zach knew; Amy had told him that afternoon in his house. Sandy's comment was almost a taunt, referring to Graham now, almost as if Amy's professionalism was being questioned. That, or her loyalty as a wife.

"Will that be a problem?" Ella asked. "You should say something now if it is."

Amy bristled in defense. "I can do it," she said simply.

"You sure?" Ella's voice had changed, making Amy nervous. "Because if this is more than you can handle, Amy . . ."

"I got Randall the rewrites, didn't I?"

"Not yet. Not all of them."

"I'm just finishing the Tennessee story. Otherwise, they're all—"

"Maybe you should drop that one." Ella's tone was cold.

Amy gulped. "What?!"

"If it's causing problems, maybe you should leave it. It's not our favorite chapter in the book, and I'm sure Randall could live with one fewer chapter. In a pinch."

Amy could feel the gallop of anger charging through her. *Our* favorite? Who was the 'we' here: her agent and publisher? Ella and Sandy? Amy's response was clipped. "I'm doing it, Ella. I can do it."

Silence hung in the air. Amy watched Ella's face, thought she heard Sandy sigh.

"Good then," Ella said at last.

It was a backbreaking agenda, so many details to get wrong. But as she hung up the phone, Amy buzzed with resolve. What had it all been for—all that learned time-management, her years of managing a household, keeping other people's lives afloat—if it hadn't been practice for such a time as this? Maybe all those selfless acts of being responsible were only just the basic finger exercises of helping herself, putting her own interests first. It was August 2nd. The copy needed to be sent to Ella and Randall by August 31st. She was moving in a month. Rather than crush her, the challenge made Amy alive with determination.

She opened her laptop. Using the same two paragraphs of introduction and request, she emailed each of the additional gardeners, apprising them of her intended visit. She emphasized the urgency of the schedule, trying to impress them with the quality of the publishing house, the imminence of the publication date. The three missives shot out into cyberspace.

Amy couldn't remember ever having been so tired. The intervening days had remained hot, even the night temperatures sticking above seventy, and while overcast skies at least prevented the worst of the heat, the humidity kept everything close. Her arms and legs ached with it. The little yard sale had grown into a monstrous diversion, something she should have said no to from the beginning. Even with Betsy's ferocious efforts, the last twenty-four hours had been non-stop shuffling of stuff, affixing labels, determining prices. Starting early that morning, an entire banquet table had been buried in paperbacks, glossy hardbacks, textbooks and gardening magazines, a second in loose china, endless baskets, metal trays, a gravy boat and tea set. They'd piled up old tennis rackets and ancient skis, Christmas lights and boxes of unopened ceramic tiles, bedding and towels, a lumber jacket, a Lazy Susan. Table lamps, an iron, a bread machine, a lobster pot, a hand-painted dollhouse. Amy sat in her lawn chair, limp with the frenzy, gazing glassy-eyed at the couple still arguing over the child's rocker.

Graham had long since escaped back into the house, the trauma of watching his possessions walk down the drive and disappear into strangers' cars being more than he could stomach. She should have anticipated this, Amy realized, given Graham's already anxious state, but mid-stream, with sales flying about her, she hadn't managed to stop and follow him indoors. Betsy, bless her, was once again at the cashier's perch, counting out two dollars in change to a determined young wife. The bread machine had found a new home.

At four, they'd agreed, the sale would end, and the men from Second Chance were in the truck, just inside the drive, waiting to swoop in and, clear up. Amy had long since stopped contemplating the unsold items, stopped vexing over it all. How people could not treasure the dollhouse she'd put so much love into and kept in such good condition Amy couldn't fathom. That they'd had the nerve to offer such an insulting amount was beyond her. Like Graham, she was also in a mild state of shock, intrigued by what some people were willing to purchase and mesmerized by the speed with which things disappeared.

Betsy was holding her own against an antiques dealer. He'd arrived at six that morning, hoping to make off with the entire tea set for twenty-five dollars before the sale even began. Betsy had shooed him off, scoffing at the offer, and the man was back, like an impatient vulture, offering twenty.

"It's fifty now," she heard Betsy say, and the man took it, grumbling at the deal.

All of it was beyond her, Amy realized. Even Jason and Catherine hadn't shown such motivation when they'd looked over their parents' possessions—items that they might have taken, by right. Seeing strangers so engaged told Amy more than she wanted to know about needy acquisitiveness and petty greed. She stood from her lawn chair, yelling across the lawn. "We done?"

Khayed was by the far table, looking at the remaining books. He checked his watch and nodded. "It's four!"

Betsy heard the call, raising both hands. "Hallelujah!" she shouted back, beckoning the men from the truck.

"Come on," Betsy steered Amy away from the scene, leading her toward the house. "You don't want to watch this." She handed the wad of bills she'd been holding over to Khayed for safe keeping and gave Amy a sticky embrace. "We did it, kid."

Amy smelled the heat of her, the strange perfume. "You did," she said back. "Thank you so much." Then, wanting to sit again, she indicated with her head. "Time for a beer?"

"Absolutely," Khayed agreed.

They trooped into the kitchen, flopping gratefully around the table while Haps bustled at their knees. Amy pulled the cans from the fridge door. "Honey?" she yelled. "Want to join us?"

Within seconds, Graham rounded the corner, lugging a small footlocker. "Did you forget this?" he asked, lifting it up.

Amy and Betsy glanced at each other, both ready to cry. Khayed laughed. "I'll give you three bucks for it." He held up his hand. "Just leave it right there." Graham complied, taking a seat at the table, glad for the company.

As they each sank into their beer, Khayed remembered his pockets. He rose again, and like a dramatic magician brought four packets of bills from his clothing, laying each grandly on the table between them. "Shall we calculate the proceeds?" His eyes danced.

It was a filthy job. Amy counted out her pile into bundles of ten, crisscrossing each group on top of the first, ironing the bills flat with the side of her hand. Betsy, she noticed, organized hers so that all the presidents faced the same way, and Khayed's stacks were grouped by dollar amount, the fives in one pile, the tens in another. Graham simply counted. Finished his count and started again. They were into their second beer by the time the tally was in: $1,803. Not bad for a day's work; nothing at all for a lifetime of small purchases.

"So, tomorrow, you sleep!" Betsy said, leaning back in her chair. "You've earned it."

"Tomorrow, she goes to Vermont," Graham corrected.

"Work. We've got a tight deadline," Amy explained quickly, wishing she didn't feel the need. "But it's just a drive up, stay one night, and drive back. Pretty short."

"Long drive," Betsy said.

"We carpool," Amy clarified.

Khayed noticed Amy's discomfort. "Well, it's cooler up there. All those mountains."

But Graham couldn't let it go. "Then Tuesday, they're off to Chicago. Not so cool there."

Everyone could hear the judgment in his tone, and Amy's face started to burn. She defended herself quickly. "Once this month is over, that'll be it, though. We just need to get through August—the

268

last trip and then it all goes into publication. And moving. That's the hard part." She reached for the bills, pulling them toward herself.

"It doesn't have to be this hard. You could prioritize." Graham spoke directly to Amy now, ignoring his neighbors. She ducked her head, feeling the hit. She wanted to throw the money in his face, storm out, but she held back. She stood to take a paper bag from a drawer.

"I stink," she said into the awkward silence. "I'm going to bag this and head for the shower." She shook her head, smiling. "I can't thank you both enough for all you did today." She rolled the top of the bag and patted its contents. "Maybe a thank-you dinner when I get back?"

She noticed Betsy's wary look in Graham's direction, but Khayed was gracious. "Of course," he said, pointing at the bag. "Bring your loot."

Later that evening, Amy snuck off to the garden with her phone.

"It's another favor," she said. "But it would really help."

"What's that?" Khayed's manner was as it always was, affable and easy.

"Would you mind just popping in tomorrow sometime? While I'm away?"

"On Graham?"

"Yeah. Not to do anything," she said hastily. "Just to . . . see that he's there."

There was a pause at the other end, and Amy worried she'd overstepped. "And if you can't . . ."

"Nope. I can," he said. She heard him thinking. "And Tuesday too?" His voice was more guarded this time, as if seeing a pattern.

Amy swallowed. "That'd be great, Khayed. Thanks."

# TWENTY-SIX

The Kia was quieter this time, heading up to Vermont. Zach had opened the roof, and the wind whistled between them, the strands of radio noise splintering off behind. Watching the two from the back seat, Amy wondered whether Zach and Sandy had been talking about her, whether that was the cause of the quiet. She was quite sure Zach would keep his word, and seeing him in person again, Amy had noted his professional composure. Amy was both safe and sorry. Maybe Zach *had* been simply a port in a storm. She caught moments of his face in the rear-view mirror, earnest and focused. No, he and Sandy probably hadn't discussed her on that score.

But Amy's success with the publisher had effectively signed them all up for a strenuous couple of weeks. When much of the world was vacationing somewhere, grabbing their final fortnight before Labor Day yanked everyone back into harness, these three were belting up the hot highway for a work assignment, with other assignments looming just ahead. *Maybe that was it*, Amy mused. *Maybe it was the pressure.*

And then there was their actual departure. That had been more than odd. Before taking off, Sandy had spent a good twenty minutes with Graham. She'd gotten out of the car and come into the kitchen, even though Amy was packed and ready to go. Sandy had stood

270

there while Graham munched on his bagel, looking for things to chatter on about, his final project, how the packing was going. It was as if she wanted Graham to know that *she* knew, *Sandy* understood how difficult their travel schedule was for him, even if Amy didn't. As if Amy wasn't showing the appropriate concern. And only when Zach honked a second time from the car did Sandy pull herself away, leaving a lingering look of empathy in her wake as Amy kissed her husband goodbye.

Amy shifted in her seat, her mind churning, hair whipping at her face. She wasn't well prepared for this trip, hadn't had time to learn much about Gillian Curran, except to arrange for a 3:00 p.m. interview and a walk-through of the garden. It wasn't the location Randall had suggested. Randall hadn't known that the restoration at the Shelburne Farms gardens was firmly in the hands of a man. But Gillian, the woman who was acting as a consultant to the conservation project did have a garden of her own, only miles from the farm and Amy'd decided that hers would do. The photos, in any case, looked promising.

Over lunch, Amy filled her colleagues in on what to expect.

"Think sensory overload," Amy said. "It's not a massive place, from what I can tell, but the colors are vibrant—heady, bright, really dazzling, especially for August."

"Good." Zach smiled between bites of his grilled cheese. "I'm for that."

They had stopped at a rest stop outside of Concord, New Hampshire, and the relief of clean toilets and instant food had made them all a bit chattier.

"And who's the woman?" Sandy asked. "Seventh generation Vanderbilt?"

"Not at all," Amy said. "She a professional landscape conservator. No relation to anyone. But she's working at the farm, and when I was given her name, I took a chance. She sounds knowledgeable, and really eager to show off her personal style."

"And you think she's right for the book?"

It was a snide kind of remark, almost hunting for friction, and Amy was quick to shut it down. "Once your sketches and Zach's photos are attached? Absolutely." Sandy wasn't going to make anything easy, it seemed, so Amy stuck with optimism and good cheer. "Anyway," she added, trying not to lose confidence, "She sounds passionate. I like a woman who's passionate."

"Me too," Zach said.

Gillian Curran looked like a conservator: lean and toned, with a thick braid of dirty-blonde hair. In her leather clogs, wide straw hat, an apron of heavy duck cloth, Gillian appeared as if she handled wooden tools and precision equipment with equal ease. In the woman's deliberate, fast-paced stride, Amy recognized the person she'd heard over the phone.

"Welcome to Sylvan," Gillian said, wiping her hands on the soiled apron. She introduced herself to the visitors, avoiding a dirty handshake. "I was worried that we might not have enough time to do this!" Pointing upward, she acknowledged some fat, gray flannel clouds assembling on the horizon.

"We're pretty fast," Amy assured her. "And we'll stay as long as you let us."

"We're also waterproof," Sandy added, accommodating.

"Can I start with you, then?" Zach asked. "I'd like to get some shots of you before you're drenched."

"Of course," Gillian said, wiping her hands again. "Although I look about as fetching, wet or dry."

She was a handsome woman with easy humility, and Amy found everything about their Vermont subject natural and attractive. Zach set his case on the hood of the Kia, assembling his camera and lens.

"It reminds me of a pop-up store," Sandy said, looking across the garden. "As if you airlifted this plot and just plopped it here overnight."

Amy could see Sandy's point. They'd driven about eight miles from the nearest town center, through what must one day have been old farms, patches of woodland, passing a small gas station, a Dunkin' Donuts. Several miles further on was a hairdresser, a lawn-mower store and a small day-care center, fenced in by large plastic Crayola crayon posts. When the GPS notified them that their destination was in eight hundred feet on the left, suddenly the garden had appeared, bright against the tarmac road, the thickly wooded area behind. Directly on the road was a modest storefront, an engraved wooden sign announcing *Sylvan Pottery*, room for several cars to park. But behind and beyond the store stood Sylvan Garden, Gillian Curran's outrageous and vivid half acre.

Zach positioned Gillian underneath a wide archway, the ostensible entrance to the site, dripping with orange trumpet flower.

"It kind of was a pop-up store," Gillian said, trying not to watch the camera. "When I moved in, this was a used car lot, although they mostly sold snowmobiles, and I was in a hurry."

"But . . ." Sandy sought the polite way to ask it. "Why here?"

"Oh . . ." Gillian grinned. "My partner. She bought this place." Gillian pointed to the storefront. "So she could sell her pottery and have her studio in one place. And then I moved in. And about a month later, the car lot went belly up and wanted a fast sale."

"It's gorgeous." Amy couldn't find a better word.

Zach waved Gillian on, and the foursome stepped through the arch. "And completely nuts," Gillian added. "I travel a lot for work, sometimes weeks at a time, yet somehow I managed to build one of the more labor-intensive gardens one could hope to find." She crouched, pulling a couple of volunteer daisies from the shingled path. "My current gig is local, thank heavens, so you'd think I'd have time to relax, slow down a bit. But I guess that's not how it works."

They ambled together along the path with a fulsome pagoda dogwood, a magnolia tree and several fat-headed Annabelle hydrangeas creating the sense of movement, as if they were traversing room to room. What struck Amy was the intensity of it all. Scarlet crocosmia, deep-orange hot pokers, towering woolly-stemmed Verbascum bearing soft yellow flowers. There were cherry-red spears of lupines and bright yellow evening primrose everywhere. Only the sea holly, its stems as steel blue as its spiny leaves, cut through the heat of the display. Invasives such as Queen Anne's Lace and willow herb nestled closely with a stately group of delphiniums. It felt like a sea of well-timed explosions.

"You use a lot of annuals," Amy said, impressed as they passed by some sunflowers taller than her.

"I use thugs," Gillian said. "Early on, I wanted instant fill and lots of color, just to kind of claim my space." She pulled some gardening scissors from her apron and snipped the stem of a shriveled rudbeckia, sticking the seedhead in another pocket. "All my money went on hauling out the pavement and buying the bigger bushes and trees, and all my time went on encouraging monsters like these to make themselves at home." She indicated the clumps of evening primrose, a gang of hollyhocks. "Now I have to watch them like a hawk. In a week, they take over."

Forgetting the time, they roved, even as the sky turned dark overhead. Amy continued the conversation, learning more about a conservator's life, this conservator's history. At one point, Zach was balanced behind some speckled Peruvian Lilies, trying for a longer shot of the garden and the road; later, he was doing closeups of the hellebores and phlox. Sandy had sketched just one wide swath of the garden, using the app on her cell phone to identify some rare form of fireweed, filling in the details of the complex bedding. Amy longed to linger, soak in the magic of the place. Seeing the ingenious use of wildflowers, the rich combinations of fiery blossoms, she did what she always did, seeing someone else's handiwork. She thought of her own garden, the several spots that could be improved. It had been ages, she realized with a start, since she'd taken the time to focus on her beds at home. In all the mayhem of deadlines, she'd missed the relief of tinkering there. Maybe she should introduce some of Gillian's aggressive giants back home, some black hollyhocks near the pinkening sedum, maybe an orange hot poker next to the anemone. But then the futility of it all stopped her short. There wasn't time to coddle such newcomers into place, not before the clock stopped. The impending loss nearly choked her. Shaking the sadness from her brain, she turned it into a friendly compliment. "Makes me want to try this at home."

"That's the idea," Gillian said. "And copying from others is exactly what I've done. That's the fun of it!"

The rain started as isolated drops, as if a child were drawing them, one at a time, with a fat magic marker. Amy noticed Zach capturing it, the blazing peaks of garden against the navy sky, and herself, Sandy, and Gillian hovered out there, unwilling to surrender to the elements. Within minutes, though, the heavens opened, and they all darted for the entrance. Zach reached the car just in time to close in the roof.

"I'd ask you in," Gillian said, rain dripping from her hat, "but I don't live here anymore. We no longer live together." She wrinkled her nose, as if embarrassed. "But I think you've got all you need, yes?"

It took them a moment to register.

"Yeah," Zach said, "I've got plenty!"

"I'm all set," Sandy said, scrambling into the Kia.

Amy felt glued there, unprepared for the forced retreat. "You mean you have to travel here—to keep the garden up?"

Zach dove into the driver's seat, his camera close to his chest.

Gillian raised her palms, catching the rain. "Until I start another," she said, almost glowing in the wetness.

"Let's go!" Sandy barked from the car.

Amy was beginning to get soaked through, still, she couldn't resist. "And then you'll just let this garden go." It was a question.

For a wet moment, the two women stood there together, locked in understanding. Gillian glanced behind her, casting her eyes over the beautiful flowers, glistening and bent under the downpour. Then she turned back to Amy. "I think probably," she said, wiping her nose with the back of a hand. "But not before bagging a helluva lot of seeds." Laughing, she backed toward her car. "I'm a pocket-your-goodies kind of a girl. Force of habit."

Amy nodded. "Well, I'm impressed."

"Come on, Amy!"

That was it then. Amy suddenly felt the cold against her skin. She held up a hand in goodbye. "Thanks again, Gillian."

"You're welcome. It was nice." Gillian swept the excess drops off her jacket and climbed into her car. She rolled down her window with one final comment. "Another motto of mine: 'Grow where you've landed.'" She chuckled. "It makes for a very useful plan B!" Then the window rose again, and Gillian was a blur, washed away by the rain.

They could have made it back that night, even with the storm. But they were wet, and the motel room was nearby, with a KFC too close to resist. Over the greasy repast, they compared notes. There was an energy to the project again, a shared sense that they were creating something special, that they were on the right path. All three were satisfied with the visit, impressed with the dramatic display along the nondescript country road. Sandy thought Sylvan Gardens was one of her favorites, due to the complexity of the design, and Zach almost agreed, excited by the shots he'd captured. Only Amy worried about the future of the garden, wondering aloud when Gillian would move on, start again somewhere new.

"When she finds a better gig," Sandy guessed, callously.

"When it's right," Zach said to Amy. "Like you'll do." It was the first thing he'd said all day that suggested intimacy, and she caught his eye, grateful.

When they eventually retired for the night, Amy found it harder this time, going into the room on her own, parting with the couple in the hall outside. And the space was cold, overly air-conditioned, smelling something of wet dog. She had to muster all her will to phone Graham, to say goodnight.

"Weirdest thing," Graham told her. "Khayed called to invite me to dinner."

Amy swallowed. She hadn't meant for Khayed to put himself out that much. "Did you go?" she asked, praying it had worked out.

"No. I said I might, but then the time got away from me."

Amy bit back her disappointment.

"Anyway, I'm making progress on my study. Wait till you see."

Amy didn't want to see. Didn't, in that moment, want to go back at all. She had in her mind the vibrant garden by the pottery shop, the haze of the Green Mountains behind. "Can't wait," she said. "I'll see you tomorrow."

The turnaround was both bearable and productive. In the forty-eight hours she had at home, Amy managed to write up a strong draft of the Vermont chapter, bag up three closets worth of items for Goodwill, and give Haps an August tick-bath. She even squeezed in a long beach walk with Graham, determined that he not experience the frenzy she was feeling. When rattled, Graham got testy and argumentative, and Amy didn't have the time to fit that in before flying to Chicago. The night before leaving, she phoned Khayed again.

"I really just meant for you to pop in for a second," she said. "Not to put you out."

"Yeah. He didn't want to come here," Khayed agreed. "I'll just stop by tomorrow, sometime after work."

"Thanks again," Amy said, feeling like the burden she'd become.

Chicago proved even easier than Vermont. They met at the airport, rented a car at O'Hare and arrived in Oak Bluffs by early afternoon. Amy had expected something on the commercial side, what with the site being the former headquarters of McDonald's. The place had been billed as a child-friendly garden playground, and Amy had imagined beds of fleshy gerbera daisies, boxed in amongst red slides, bright yellow jungle gyms. But the campus was easy-going, the structures more nuanced. Statues of Peter Rabbit, Winnie the Pooh, Paddington Bear, Jack, Kack, Lack, and the rest, all peeked from behind short hedges. The figures were accessible, easy to climb. And the garden beds were resilient, soft with grasses and puffs of tall phlox, streams of daylilies. There were frog ponds and gentle water-falls, shady arbors of wisteria and grape vine, everything to make a visit relaxing and cool for sweaty parents, open and accessible for their rambunctious kids.

The woman responsible for it all was clearly corporate, but in the way of being driven and sure of herself, nothing worse. With a single-minded dedication to children's playfulness, Helen Ramsgate was also very funny, rich with anecdotes and not afraid to acknowledge all that still needed doing. "Princess Truly, Peppa Pig, Clifford—all on the agenda," she said. "'Captain Underpants', though? Shoot me now. Or if we must, we put him in a patch of poison ivy."

They stayed past closing, Zach shooting the enticing shadows by the statue of the Cheshire Cat. And later, when they were starving, they shared two deep dish pizzas, the best nod they could give to the windy city in such a short visit. On the airplane back, Sandy and Amy were seated next to each other.

Sandy made a point of checking in. "So, how're you doing?" she asked, putting down her book.

"I'm okay." They had passed through a deep pile of clouds and the sky above was bright and clear. The wing of the plane shimmered outside their window.

"Really?"

"Really," Amy said, but Sandy's gaze kept her pinned. "Better than, in fact. All I've got left to finish is the attic and the shed. And the attic's mostly stuff to chuck."

Sandy clicked her tongue. "I'm impressed." She shifted in her seat. "And how's Graham?"

It irritated Amy that Sandy homed in on Graham. There was so much else going on, so much else that Amy was juggling. "He's fine," she said, turning away. Below them was a quilt of downy white, and Amy imagined herself barefoot on it, trying to walk as if on a feathered trampoline. Of course there were things, little ones, that had been piling up. The misplaced shoes, the lapses in speech. He'd left the car running in the driveway the other day, going indoors and forgetting it. But these weren't things Amy was going to mention, not to Sandy. She shifted the subject back. "I'm struggling with the shed, though. I've got a lot of tools I may not need . . ."

"Yeah," Sandy said unhelpfully. "I imagine you do."

When she got home, Amy flopped down on the couch, too tired to think. Even the ringing phone couldn't make her lift her head from the cushion. When it rang again, however, she picked up. It was Khayed, and she knew she owed him the courtesy.

"Now it's my turn to apologize," he said.

"Why?" Amy asked, happy to hear from him. "Graham said you popped in. I think you're magic." She didn't say what was coming next, that she'd love it if he would help again, at least for some of the days she'd be away. While she tried to find the words to ask, Khayed cleared his throat.

"He's not well, Amy."

The easy bonhomie was missing, and Khayed's seriousness stopped her.

"Well, I know," she said.

"I think he's worse than you know."

Amy fought a trickle of annoyance. "Tell me then," she said. "What is it I don't know?"

"When I got there last night, the dog—"

"Haps."

"Haps was out on the street."

Amy stumbled. "I guess I knew . . ."

"And when I got to the door, Graham had been cooking."

Amy braced herself for what was coming. "Was the kitchen a mess?"

"The frying pan was on one burner, cold as a stone. The flame was on in the other burner, on high. He could have burned the place down, Amy."

She sighed, newly terrorized. "Oh, Khayed, I'm sorry. Sorry to put you through that."

He hmphed gently. "I'm fine!' he said. "But I think you'll need more than the occasional visitor. It's really past that now."

# TWENTY-SEVEN

It was frightening how many people responded to Amy's posts, and how quickly. A dozen people emailed that first day, and over the next several, even more trickled in. By Friday afternoon Amy had a good handful of qualified candidates to screen, some experienced home health aides, a couple of housewives seeking mothers' hours, one graduate student, and two Marias from Haiti.

It scared her, how determined she was to bring strangers into the home, but there was no alternative now, and even less time to worry about it. When she'd phoned the kids, both had proven utterly unhelpful. Jason wanted to argue her need to go at all. "What about writing makes you need to leave home all of a sudden?" His voice had dripped with censure, as if she'd planned a trip to the moon.

"I need to see the gardens, Jason, interview the women who created them. It's what the book is about."

"And pictures won't cut it? You can't talk on the phone?"

Amy bristled at having to explain herself. "I'm the point person; I'm bringing a team. It's not just me who has to fly out to these places—other people's professional success is invested in this project. It's important to all of us." But even as she rattled on, her voice low, she was unable to persuade him or get any encouragement at all.

"I don't think you get it," he grumbled before hanging up. "That, or you just don't want to."

Catherine wasn't critical, simply tied up. "Hire some people," she said. "You've got to work, you need daycare. It's what people do. Anyway," she added, "Graham will be pissed whatever you do, so just bite the bullet." At least before hanging up, Catherine had wished Amy luck and a productive trip.

In her frenzied logic, Amy tried to keep the sanctuary of September clear in her mind. All she needed was three people to help her out. If she could find these three, hire them, then she could barrel through for several more weeks, complete this last cross-country trip, finish clearing the house, manage the move. Then there would be a chance to breathe. Come September, once they were in their new home, with her mother's service behind her, maybe then Amy would find time to breathe. Maybe even start another book and relax for a minute. A kind of harvest time.

It hadn't been an easy conversation with her husband. In having to prepare him for what she was doing, why she was interviewing unknowns to stay in the house for ten days straight, Amy had had to say out loud what Khayed had told her.

"So, he was your spy?" Graham was peeling a mango and stopped midstream, the long shiny coil hanging from his knife.

"Not at all," Amy lied. "He just . . . wanted me to know."

Graham watched the juice drip across his thumb. "That I'm incompetent." He looked up, his face fierce. "That's rich, coming from Khayed." Graham had always felt an insufferable superiority over his neighbor. Khayed, with all his courage in making it out of the camps of Beirut, creating a new life in the States, had settled affably for a dull job in insurance. In Graham's hierarchy of needs, this settling for so little was a kind of crime.

Amy kept her breath shallow, despite the racing heartbeat. "That you're forgetful. We know that."

282

Graham finished with his fruit, running his hands under the tap. "And presumably you've asked the kids."

In another life, asking his children for help wasn't something Graham would have ever done, even if he believed help was needed. It had always been Graham's position that Jason and Catherine had lives and professions to be getting on with. Staying home and looking after things were Amy's responsibility. Now, however, Graham was seeking allies.

"They're both tied up this month," Amy said. "It's not a lot of days, but they're the wrong days for them." She watched as Graham spooned some yogurt over his fruit and returned the container to the refrigerator. She waited for his next objection.

"Do they both think I need daycare?" It was a sly question, one Amy chose to sidestep.

"We all knew it might come up. We discussed it. When Matt was here. You were there." Amy felt herself getting edgy, having to remind Graham what he already knew.

"But you're convinced we have to do this now, sure you have to make a three-thousand-mile journey. Now. Two weeks before we move." The tone was as thick as the yogurt, and Amy tightened in response.

"I'm under contract. I've got to." Amy knew Graham knew this too. She followed the spoon, watched his jawline, and waited for the bob of his Adam's apple. It occurred to her then, all the weeks and years Graham himself had been the one jetting off, leaving the house for days at a time, never once asking himself how it might impact those left behind. She stifled the outrage.

"Ten days, Graham. That's all. And then that'll be it."

He gave her a wry look, the lines around his eyes deepening. "You believe that? You think you'll ever stop wanting more?"

It stopped her, this characterization. As if her writing, her interests, her research excursions, were somehow acts of wild self-indulgence, something aberrant. As if she were taking more than her due. But then memories of Zach tumbled into her thoughts, his legs stepping into the steam bath, bathing suit plastered to his frame. She saw the three of them, that balmy evening in Key West, chickens clucking at their feet. The rush of it caught her up short. Amy wanted to scream back, concede that of *course* she would travel again. *Of course* she would because the thought of being stuck at home forever was something she dreaded with a passion. But in that moment, she needed Graham's permission just to proceed. In searching for the right words, she paused for too long.

Graham's eyes washed over her, dismissive. "Knock yourself out."

In the end, she arranged for six people to meet, first with her, then, if Amy liked them, with Graham. There were five women and one man. He was the outlier, but Amy was trying to be open-minded.

By noon on Saturday, she'd sat with three of the women. Claire was a nondescript mother of four. "Grown and gone," Claire had told her, flinging her wrist with happy dismissal. Claire had spent the last two years caring for her mother until cancer "freed them both." Claire liked seniors, she assured Amy, and, having learned to tolerate the old lady's irritating habits—ones that get worse the closer they get to death, she'd intoned—she was sure she could deal with anyone. Amy had shuddered as she saw Claire out, horrified that anyone would equate Graham with a senior, troubled by what Graham had in store.

The second woman earned a longer, more hopeful interaction. Liselle was in her thirties and in an earlier life had even worked on and off as a CNA. Now, having returned to grad school for an MFA (perfect! Amy thought), Liselle had been attending classes during the day and waitressing four nights a week. The hours were grueling, she admitted, and she would be glad for a night gig that involved sleeping over.

"I'm expecting there will be some light responsibilities. Cleaning up the supper dishes, that kind of thing," Amy explained. "Graham isn't inept, but he's never been particularly prone to housework."

"Oh, I know what you mean," Liselle said. "I've got a father."

"And he's still engaged intellectually. My husband is an accomplished architect. Might well want to talk design, given your interests."

"Cool."

That was Liselle. She was smart and attractive and might have made a wonderful companion. Still, Amy had misgivings, inwardly offended at Liselle's use of the word "gig"—not exactly a term Amy would have chosen for looking after her husband of thirty years.

The third, Hawa, was a retired LPN from Sierra Leone with the most impressive hair weave Amy'd ever seen up close. Attractive and direct, Hawa's presence made Amy forget mid-interview to ask all the questions written in front of her, lost in the intrigue of this woman's story, her worldly sensibilities and beautiful skin.

"I can see why you need help," Hawa had said. "And I can help—both your husband and you." That was the line that touched Amy and won her over.

The initial screenings behind her, Amy was bleary-eyed.

"How's it going?" Graham's head popped around the door frame, checking on the progress.

"Lots of people want to do this."

"Any sane ones?"

"Two out of three so far. I'll bring back the best for you to meet."

"I saw a nice-looking young one. Tall? Orange scarf?" His eyes glimmered, warming to the possibilities.

That was Liselle. Clearly, she would be back.

By Tuesday, Graham and Amy had made their picks. Hawa would be the anchor woman, taking the day shift, overseeing meal prep, keeping the place tidy. She would take both weekends off. A lovely guy named Bertrand, a widower from Providence, cello teacher and member of the Rhode Island string ensemble was the perfect choice for night watchman. Bertrand was to arrive around seven each evening, heat up the dinner Hawa had left, do whatever needed doing to prepare Graham for the night, and otherwise be around. He opted for the guest bedroom, and, like Hawa, would take off at the weekend. And Liselle accepted the weekend slot. It freed her from two of her restaurant nights, gave her a quiet space to study and, if Graham left her alone, no doubt plenty of time to sleep. A great gig, as it turned out.

Liselle, Hawa, and Bertrand all understood that the job at the house was temporary. They also all hoped there would be more work, once Amy and Graham moved to Providence. Amy expected there might.

As far as Graham was concerned, he'd ignore them all.

# TWENTY-EIGHT

"I've never felt so guilty," she admitted to her sister. The night before take-off, Amy was pulling clothes from her closet, laying them on the bed next to her suitcase. "All Graham does is mumble under his breath and sigh."

"Oh God, tell me about it. My kids perfected that. They'd smell the babysitter walking up the path and it was instant grief: '*Not again!*'" Alice replicated the whingeing, gave a sympathetic chortle. "As if all I ever did was work!"

Amy wanted to say that that *was* all her sister had even done, but she refrained. Alice was her new ally now, and Alice's choices had begun to appear different to her. Amy took a pale summer sweater from a hanger and set it to one side. "Well, I'm feeling guilty because it really is an awful time to be going away. Every room is a jumble of half-finished projects, there are cartons everywhere. And I'm worried it's too disruptive for Graham. All this mayhem, virtual strangers coming into the house." She flipped through more items on hangers. "Hell, I can hardly think straight myself: it's just crazy-making!"

Alice's voice was soothing, firm. "It'll be over. Just be grateful you can escape for a few days, that you can leave him in good hands."

"You know what makes it worse?"

"What?"

Amy sobbed a half-laugh. "What makes it worse is that I really enjoy these trips. I love this work!" She considered the blue dress again. "And there's no excuse, really. It's not even like I'm earning serious money. Not like you had to."

"Don't fool yourself: I loved what I did, still do. It was the complaining I could've done without." Alice chuckled, a low, gravelly vibration. "But all working women with families get it—heavy, heavy guilt—and it sucks."

"Yeah." Amy realized it as she said it. "Although, this guilt stuff is new for me. I was never a working mom, not really." While women around her were juggling day care and trying to advance professionally, packing their children off with a Granola bar for breakfast, Amy was waiting with the neighborhood kids for the school bus. She was there with a needed Band-Aid and time to talk. Looking after things and people was what she'd done for a living.

Alice was quiet, reflective. "No, you're right. You were that rare breed, the happy housewife. I could never quite understand it, but it seemed to work for you."

"Mmm." Amy wondered at the portrayal, interested in how she had changed.

"Well, you'll figure it out." Amy could hear another phone ringing on Alice's desk. "Anyway. I'm planning on meeting you in Providence on Sunday the 1st. Right?"

"Right."

"Meanwhile, you take care." Alice's voice was a tonic.

"Thanks, you too."

"Oh, and Amy?"

"Yeah?"

"Have a wonderful time!" Alice nearly shouted it. Then more softly she added, "And I won't tell a soul."

Amy laughed. Excited again, she put down the phone and finished filling her suitcase.

She was tired. She knew that. But she was on a roll, and Amy figured there was just enough time to box the rest of Graham's library before calling it a day. Seventeen cartons of books were taped and stacked against his study wall, ready for the moving van. Maybe there were just five or six cartons to go, and another room would be finished, another room she could tick off the list.

By now, the whole house ached with strangeness. Several rooms were completely empty. Now, in Catherine's and Jason's bedrooms, rays of sunshine shot uninterrupted across the squared expanse from floor to wall early in the morning, the curtain-less windows stared, bright-eyed and astonished. Closet doors stood agape, yawning with vacancy. Their bathroom gleamed, a blank slate of pristine ivory. In the den, without its furnishings, the ceiling's cypress beams drew the eye upward. There were cornices and moldings she hadn't noticed in years, bare bamboo floors that seemed to stretch longer and wider down hallways and up steps. The attic was as it had been when Jason was a toddler, a plane of endless flooring atop the entire footprint of the house, where only two chimneys interrupted a child's vast racetrack.

It was a beautiful space, no less so as Amy worked to denude it. The high windowsill over the front stairs, the elongated fireplace surround in the living room, the window seat in the den. Even without their familiar objects, the structure of the house was something she had loved. That was Graham's great gift, that he could create such an edifice, and Amy allowed herself moments to cherish it, even in the rush to depart.

But the ghosts she sensed flitting by her as she emptied the house were not all friendly ones. The walls didn't just echo with joyous shouts and murmurs of love. Sighs of damage and hurt, disappointment and loneliness also waited behind doors. The living room alone whispered plenty. There was that rainy day years back when she and Jason had spent hours together constructing a Blanket fort over upturned chairs and tables. The whole room had been filled with their masterpiece, its uneven tents of quilts and sheets, draped atop each other, secured with clothespins and rubber bands. The only way to enter the room was on your knees through a toweled door, and the light inside was diffuse and cozy. They brought their hotdogs and potato chips inside to eat, under the curl of the toppled couch. But Graham returned home that day with a future client and was unamused. "Take it down," he told Jason. "You have an attic for this kind of thing."

The living room also echoed with the December afternoon she'd planned for decorating the tree. It was Jason's first year of boarding school, and Amy was eager to have him back in the family home. She'd brought the decorations up from the basement. Needles and thread, bowls of cooked popcorn and cranberries sat ready. She made mulled cider and sugar cookies, prepared the strings of Christmas lights in advance, tightening or replacing the bulbs that didn't light. Everything was ready for when Graham and Jason returned, to bring in the season together. But they didn't come back as planned. They stayed out, ate out. "Boys' night," Graham explained. And Amy decorated the tree herself, ate the whole bowl of popcorn.

Amy shook the memories from her mind, hardened herself to their complaint. It was time to leave all that behind.

In their bedroom, only summer clothing hung loose in the closet. No photographs remained on their dressers; the paintings were gone from the walls. Amy noticed a scatter rug by her bedside table. That needed to be rolled. Another item she'd overlooked, another thing that needed doing now. Or not. The day before their move, August 30th, the crew from GreenDrop would arrive to claim everything not boxed, packed, or nailed in place. That her oversights might prove valuable to some charitable cause filled Amy with a resigned acceptance.

She descended the stairs, her steps reverberating against the bare wood. Once this last job was finished, she would return her thoughts to tomorrow's trip and catch her breath. The air was still warm in the house, the day's heat clinging stickily to every surface. Amy steadied herself for the last slog of the day and opened the door to Graham's study.

He was on his knees in the middle of the space, shoulders hunched over an open carton. Books were scattered about, concentric rings of them, rippling outward. Other open cartons dotted the floor, like volcanic islands in a broad sea. Books were everywhere. And the sturdy wall of sealed boxes, the one that Amy had built through hours of work, three deep and six wide, lay in ruins, like a seawall after a storm.

"What are you doing?" Amy's voice was strangled in her throat.

"I can't find the Lall book," he said, slamming another hardcover onto the floor. He dug back into the carton, scrutinizing the next in the box. "Where the hell did you put it?!"

"What Lall book? What are you talking about?"

"Lall," he said. "Vikram Lall." Graham pulled out another two books, stretching across to spread a clear spot on the floor, and dumped them on it.

He was like a wrecking ball gone rogue. She kept her volume low, like a patient mother, hoping that would work. "Please stop, Graham."

He waved an angry hand in her direction, grabbing another bright tome from the carton. "Help me look or go away."

"Could you just stop for a minute?"

The firmness in her voice made him glance up, but he cut across her before she could say more. "I'm busy. Can't you see that?" His look was one of a baffled authority, perplexed by insubordination. "I've got work to do, and I can't do it when you've hidden everything out of sight." Finished with that carton, he stood to retrieve another.

291

"Stop it!" Amy shouted. "I just packed all those. I spent a fucking day packing all of those! Just stop!"

He shot her an irritated look, like he might at a barking dog, lifted a carton, and began peeling at the tape.

She lunged toward him, reaching to pull the carton away, but as he turned, his elbow jutted upward, catching her below the jaw. Her teeth clamped together, gripping her tongue. Amy reared back, pain radiating through her head. Her mouth tasted of copper. "You bas—" she tried, but blood dripped from her mouth, and she had to swallow it back, holding a cupped palm to her chin. Careful of the books, she stumbled from the room.

*We're going to kill each other!* she thought franticly, the bile surging up her gut, more blood spilling down her chin. *I hate him! I hate that man!* She rushed to the kitchen sink, dropping her head over the drain as the mantra played over and over in her mind.

Haps was now at her side, bumping her gently.

"Go away." The words bubbled from her, slippery in blood. But the dog stood there, tense and soft. She could feel his ribs by her leg.

"Go away!" She shoved Haps with her knee, now angry at him, too. He backed off, retreating to his corner. Through her veil of hair, she saw the dog making his two desultory circles before settling onto his mat. At the sight of it, Amy began to weep.

She heaved, her shoulders collapsing with every sob. Tears spilled from her eyes and slime ran from her nose. Blood continued to fill her mouth. The waterworks seemed endless, as if sourced from an underground sea. It was back now, that familiar sense of hopelessness, the terror of undirected rage, and Amy felt the shroud of despair envelop her, hold her in its grip.

A pink curl of water circled the drain as she stood over the kitchen sink. Hot tears still stung her face as Amy struggled to regain composure. It had been an accident; she knew that. But he was also unstoppable; she knew that too. And the steady undoing of all her hard work in the other room would run its pace, until he tired of his search, or found his book, or whatever. But then there would be another project, another endeavor of hers that Graham had the power to obliterate. The futility of it all made her weak. She rested her arms on the sink's edge, head limp.

The realization that chilled her was that it wasn't just the sick Graham that had caused such chaos. That's what shook her. This was also the essential Graham, the one he had always been. The man who did what he chose to do in spite of the world about him, whatever her efforts. She hacked up a lozenge of phlegm, spat it into the drain.

In twelve hours she was supposed to be headed for the airport, her detailed itinerary typed and ready, her favorite clothes packed to go. Hawa would arrive just before. It was the woman's first day in charge. Amy sighed at the prospect, the unmanageability of it all. How would Hawa cope with all of Graham's undoing? Would she be able to prevent him from opening more boxes, upending all the work Amy had so far accomplished? Would Amy be returning to a total nightmare in ten days, with no time to recover before moving day? Amy splashed some water on her face, letting it drip from her chin.

The toll of creating this book was becoming more than she could handle, and Amy wondered whether she was losing her mind in the process. What was it all for, her wild forays into the world of magnificent gardens, of other women's lives, when she had this to return to? When her own responsibilities were so pressing, why should she tease herself with notions of another life, one that might have been?

Amy cupped a handful of water from the faucet and sucked it in, sloshing it around her mouth. She spat again.

"You okay?" Behind her, Graham stood in the doorway.

Amy nodded.

"I'm sorry," he told her back. "It was an accident,"

"I know." Amy turned off the water, wiping her face with her sleeve. She glanced at her reflection in the dark window, her cheeks and forehead shiny under the light.

"I found the book," he said, holding it up.

Amy turned to face him. "Good."

Outside, she heard the cry of a cat in heat, shrieking its needs across the yard.

"It's hard, having you come and go all the time, Amy. Look what's happening to us." He spoke as if her mottled face and his missing book were the proof.

Amy saw them both in that moment as if from a great height, Graham imploring, Amy the one pulling away. Their places had changed sometime in the past months, and Amy felt the sharp irony of it. How finally, Amy was becoming independent of the man, standing up for herself.

"Now isn't a good time," he said.

There it was again, Graham's understated power of veto.

Rocking slightly, she sucked at the thickened flesh in her mouth, testing its tip between her lips. Numb with hurt, she tried to think things through. Zach was picking her up in the morning. She'd been looking forward to that. Now, though, she probably looked a sight, her tongue too sore to speak. She'd rather not show up than show up like this. But she had to. She'd made a commitment to her colleagues. Amy thought of Sandy and Ella prodding her during the last conference call, their voices sweet, taunting: *Can you handle this? Will that be a problem?* She bristled inside. Angry at them both. And at the publisher. Asserting his right to insist on his rewrites, his orientation to her book. Fuck all three of them.

Like a slow clap after the lights fade, an inevitable conclusion surfaced. Maybe Sandy and Ella were right. Maybe she couldn't handle this trip. Her husband was ill, for God's sake; there was a house to pack. In fact, maybe Amy wasn't needed on this trip at all. Zach and

Sandy were the essential ones. They needed to witness the gardens in their final show of glory before season's end. They needed to take the photographs, sketch the designs. All Amy had to do was speak to the gardeners, and Jason was right on that score: that could be done over the phone. After all, how important was it that she actually spend time with these women? Where had that imperative come from?

Amy shrank inside, imagining the trip without her. Without her as the third wheel, Sandy and Zach could have nights on their own, just the two of them. Breakfasts in bed even. They might prefer not having Amy there, delaying progress with her extensive interviews, constantly arguing the politics of the book over dinner. Sandy had no interest. Zach, with all his insight, had already accepted that some things get lost in the shuffle. Maybe the book could be as effective as Randall saw it—a glossy coffee table piece—commercially viable without her unique perspective at all. Amy gulped down her hurt. Panic rose in her chest.

For months now, Amy had convinced herself of the centrality of this work, that her unique take on this odd set of gardeners had mattered. Out there on the road, meeting face-to-face with these women, she'd discovered lives worth knowing and stories well worth writing. She'd become sure that—if only she found the right words—the resilience of these women could be revealed through an exploration of their gardens, a project that on the scale of things counted for something. Was worth it. But maybe that was simply wishful thinking, a rationale for jaunting about the countryside, ignoring her obligations back home. And if that was true, maybe it was also true that Amy herself wasn't the inspired writer she'd hoped she was. Maybe she would never find the right words, could never. Maybe she was just that "little column" writer, with a little gift for a few short inches of newsprint, the housewife that writes about flowers. Nothing more. Maybe she'd been fooling herself, an excuse, perhaps to escape her own terrible insignificance.

She went to the study to make her calls, wary of being overheard. As she dialed Sandy, the pounding in her head threatened to drown out the conversation.

It took Sandy a moment to register.

"I said I'm going to have to bow out," Amy repeated. "You and Zach will have to do this trip on your own."

"You're fucking kidding!"

"No, I . . ." Amy stuttered over her defense. "I can't leave Graham right now. I'm needed here."

Sandy huffed, almost a bark. "And you wait til the night before to tell anyone?!"

There was no good answer for that.

"What about the new chapters?" Sandy's anger was quick, as if it had been lying in wait. "How the hell are we supposed to complete this thing without any words? Or are we supposed to write it too?"

"I'll still write it. I'm going to call the gardeners, interview them over the phone." Amy's voice sounded surer than she felt.

"You're something else, Amy."

"I'm sorry."

"No . . ." Sandy wasn't offering forgiveness, not at this late date. "I'm sorry. I'm sorry I got into this with you. You're such a self-centered wuss!"

Amy bridled at the word. "I thought you were the one telling me I should stay home and look after my husband!"

"But now you've got people lined up for that. And now we need you to run this stupid trip. You're just so self-absorbed, Amy. Like the world shouldn't put too much pressure on you." Sandy let that sink in. "I'll call Zach," she said at last, before hanging up. "You don't need to."

Bertrand and Liselle were thrown by the change of plans. Even when Amy promised them their expected compensation, those calls were short, awkward. Only Hawa had anything comforting to say when Amy called to cancel their arrangement.

"It was a lot you were trying to pull off. I'm not completely surprised," she said.

"You're kind to say so." Amy was almost overwhelmed with the kindness, thirsty for it.

"Well, I've worked in lots of homes. Some are like yours. It takes a while for everyone to adjust. No one likes bringing in outsiders, paying for professional help. The family feels guilty, a little annoyed at the cost. The clients feel cornered, as if their rights have been taken away."

Amy visualized the lovely face, the tapered fingers, and sank into the woman's understanding. "That sounds like us. I'm very guilty, and my husband is very angry." It was pointless, though, confiding all this to a stranger, and Amy cut herself off. "Anyway, I'll pay you for this next week, but that will be it for now."

"Good. Thank you. And please think of me again when you're finally ready. If I'm available, I'd be happy to work with you."

"I'm glad."

"Meanwhile, you take care, Mrs. James." And Hawa, too, was gone.

Graham was seated in the living room when she returned downstairs. The television was on and he seemed either fully absorbed or utterly lost. He looked up as she entered.

"I can't go tomorrow." She told him this with no affect, not actually looking for a response. "There's too much to do here, and I can't go looking like this."

There was blame in the statement, but his eyes lit up; his face came alive. "After all that?"

"Yup," she said. She was angry again but determined to be calm.

"Well . . ." He nodded, as if she'd finally come to her senses. "That's probably best. Don't you think?"

Amy sighed. "Yup." She turned again, leaving him to his program.

When she opened the door onto the patio, the cooler air wafted around her. She made her way to the far end of the yard, by the birches, and sat there on the small bench, the moss soft underfoot. It was a clear, quiet night and a scattering of bright stars pricked through the darkness. She could hear the low clang of the bell buoy far out in the harbor and smell the rank odor of low tide.

Haps was the first to join her. He trundled from the house, padding his way to her side. Amy reached out to stroke his head, and the dog sat dutifully by her feet, facing out like a sentry.

They remained still like that, her fingers on his soft fur. A car passed by, and something small rustled by the hedge.

Graham's shadow stretched toward her from the lit door. He approached, not coming too close. "You'll have to call those caretakers," he said, "before they show up tomorrow."

"I did already."

"Oh," he said. "Good. You've got it all sorted."

*That, too*, Amy thought, wishing it would end.

# TWENTY-NINE

Writing the new chapters from home was odd, like having sex with a condom—it wasn't the same. She fell into a pattern, though, over the next ten days, phoning each gardener in the evening and writing every morning. From the road, Zach had begun emailing her his favorite photographs of each site and gardener, giving Amy at least the sense of who and what she was dealing with. So Amy churned out the final chapters, doing her best if feeling like a fraud.

She had just the last garden to write up, the stunning site on the rise in San Francisco's Pacific Heights District, with a clear view of the Golden Gate Bridge. Ironically, this was the garden Amy had worried about earlier, the one with the Mexican workers, apparently doing all the work. But the woman herself, at least over the phone, was engaging and talkative, only too ready to discuss her own role in the history of the place, and Amy's perspective had changed. A television researcher-turned-editor, Holly Maddow had moved to the City of Fog from LA to live with her husband, one of the more successful realtors in the Bay area. Holly's original passion— besides her husband, she'd chuckled amiably—had simply been the view of the bridge. However, once taken with the resilience of the tiny succulents he'd positioned on every bookshelf and windowsill, Holly had developed a new passion: growing her own, giant-sized specimens in the yard outside. Through years of trial and experimentation, she'd built a maze of exotic coastal wonders, spiral aloe plants and whimsical, leggy aeoniums, brilliantly flowering protea, all skirted by feathery fern and sheltered by mid-sized palms and delicate Japanese maples.

The gardener's enthusiasm was enticing, and Zach's photographs made Amy's fingers itch just to touch. One shot he sent, however, suggested a curious element to Holly's chapter. Seated on an upturned bucket somewhere in the dense understory of the prized garden was a burly, dark-skinned worker, his thick arms crossed over his chest. His worn, straw hat balanced on a knee. Standing behind was Amy's gardener, Holly Maddow, leaning over this man, her arms wrapped around him, their smiling faces cheek-to-cheek.

"Who's that?" Amy asked, wanting more than his name.

"My husband," Holly said. The smile in her voice radiated from three thousand miles away.

"The realtor?!" Amy couldn't hide her surprise.

"Hah! Oh, no, the realtor left years ago," Holly laughed. "He's found himself another two wives since me. No, that man in the picture is the one I'd been eyeing ever since he began working for us, when I was still a dutiful married wife. I spent maybe seven seasons watching Mateo bending over my plants, digging up new beds. Shirtless."

Amy was delighted. "I guess good things come to those who wait."

"Apparently," Holly agreed.

The third week of August, just four days before the move, Amy completed her final chapter and emailed it off. She was relieved to be done and pleased enough with the results. If Ella and Randall had problems with the San Francisco chapter, if they managed to find "the mess" in this account, they were just being difficult. Holly Maddow's garden—Holly and Mateo's garden—that was a love story.

Now that the draft was off her to-do list, however, Amy's life felt suddenly reduced to nothing. Nothing but clearing, packing, more downsizing. Like Cinderella, tasked with a home that seemed to get larger and more cluttered with each passing hour, Amy's brain became jumbled with every kind of uncategorizable detail: the kids' old crabbing net in the back hall, a discovered dozen mason jars in the basement, a bag of cut fabric squares for a long-intended quilt—things she'd saved, might need again, hated to part with.

Worst was her collection of tools in the shed, ones she hadn't had the heart to sell in the yard sale. But now, as she approached the deadline, she admitted to herself she'd have no need for these in their new location.

In a moment of desperation, she put in a call to Betsy, wanting her neighbor's strident advice.

"Call in the gardening club," Betsy recommended. "Those folks know the value of each tool. And you'll know everything they take will be going to a good home."

"And anything they leave?" Amy asked, too tired and despondent to imagine the best.

"Fuck it. Anything they leave, you leave behind. If the new owner is true to his word, the old bastard is going to need some gardening equipment."

Betsy was right. Seven of her compatriots showed up over the following day, each taking something, some plenty. Amy's favorite Japanese soil knife and weeding sickle, her pickaxe and ratchet loppers, the half-moon garden hoe and folding saw. Her wheelbarrow and knee pads, garden rakes, three tub trugs, and both edgers. Even her spades and pruning shears, items Amy knew her fellow gardeners must already possess, these too went in the process. If anything, her friends understood what Amy was going through and were eager to assist her as she cleared the decks. However, they all hesitated at taking a ceramic planter. Amy had built a wonderful collection of these, mint green and indigo, barn red and charcoal, ones she'd put out every spring and filled with bright annuals, dripping vines, blasts of new foliage. *You'll want to keep these*, they insisted, thinking Amy and Graham would have at least a back porch, a step by their front door where her beautiful pots could act as a stand-in for the garden they used to inhabit. But Amy sent those off too, imploring her friends to think of her next spring, to do the planters justice. Then she sank further into a determined stoicism.

If this transition was about acceptance, about doing the right thing, she would do it all the way.

# THIRTY

"I like those." Amy watched as the long curtains went up. The blocks of pale yellow and cobalt added some depth to the soft blue-gray of the walls.

"Lucky," Alice said. She positioned the wrought iron curtain rail evenly onto the brackets over her head, the tabbed drapes hanging heavy on each end. Having arrived on moving day afternoon, a clear late September miracle of warm sun and blue, blue sky, Alice had taken over the settling in. She'd spent hours marking where to position the rails, screwing the supports into place, and she seemed determined to have the job over and done with.

Amy went back to the cupboard where she placed the last of her glassware into the newly washed interior. It was a relief having her sister there with her. Already, the beds upstairs were assembled and made, and the curtains were almost up. New rolls of toilet paper and fresh towels had been placed in the bathrooms, and the electric kettle was unpacked and ready for service. The awful departure from Padanaram was a thing of the past.

It had been awful. Not organizationally, so much. The movers had arrived earlier than expected and set to work with almost orchestral precision. Mummified in quilt, major pieces of furniture flowed like lava from the house; no walls were scratched. Haps stayed out from underfoot and nothing was dropped, no one had to swear.

Only once did Graham lose it, yelling at one of the men for the way he'd handled a lamp, nestling it too tightly into the truck apparently. Amy had only overheard that encounter. But by midmorning, her husband had been seated behind the wheel in the Volvo. Khayed, his wingman, had arrived to accompany Graham on the drive north. Having offered to see Graham to the new place in Providence, Khayed had extracted the promise of a beer, lunch and a paid bus ride back home. And Amy had been left at the house, alone for a spell, doing a last check of the rooms.

The family ghosts had departed like rats from a ship, and the walls were silent again, just plaster and brick.

But outside, in the garden, the earth heaved with protest. Ivy climbed angrily up trees and over fencing, armies of leaves chased madly across the lawn. Tall grasses tumbled in slimy layers onto perennials below, and a merciless squirrel dug deep black holes in the turf. Her favorites, the iris and peony, the ground phlox and wisteria, shouted like prisoners in a sinking barge. *Save us! Bring us too!* And her red-twigged dogwood flashed angry arms as Amy walked by. *Who are you without us?* they all seemed to say, the foxglove and anemone, amsonia and lavender—a chorus of complaint filling the air. *Who indeed?* she wondered, mystified, soaking in her final goodbye.

She was barely breathing by the time she climbed into her car. Haps was jumpy in the backseat, but Amy kept her eyes from the rear-view mirrors as she drove from the property, too terrified to turn around.

She located Haps's dishes in the carton marked "K3" and poured him some fresh food and water. It was strange having the kitchen, dining area, and living room part of one open space, all on one level. But she told herself that the ease of it all, being able to potter about by the stove while her sister carried on by the couch, that was convenient.

An unfamiliar noise buzzed at them from the front hall, and Graham's voice bellowed from upstairs. "Food's here!" Haps barked, still jittery from the upheaval.

Amy looked about for her purse amidst the clutter of pots, dishes, and packing paper covering the counters. "Coming!" she shouted, responding to the door before locating her wallet. A slender man stood outside, two large brown paper bags clutched in his fists.

"James?"

"Yes. Please come in." She smiled apologetically, waving her hand. "I just need to find my money."

The man hesitated, leery of the sizable dog's eager smile. To Amy's relief, Alice swept forward with some large bills and told him to keep the change. The uneasy visitor disappeared as quickly as he'd arrived. It was like childhood, Amy thought, when her older sister was there at every turn, taking care of the household, and all Amy had to do was show up. She felt the comfort of being the younger one and wished Alice could remain for a while, during the nesting, while she became accustomed to this new reality.

At Alice's suggestion, they'd left the extension leaf hidden inside the dining room table, right-sizing it for the smaller space. She had spread a freshly ironed tablecloth over it, a vase of fresh flowers at its center. Now, Alice laid some cutlery and plates at each place and set out three glasses and a pitcher of ice water, and Amy tore sections of paper towel off the roll, folding them into napkin size and tucking them under the forks. It was like playing house.

Graham arrived in time to rip open the first bag.

Alice pointed, explaining. "I got three of the Pad Thai, one chicken satay, two green papaya salads, and three rice. No one should go hungry." She retrieved extra plates to slip under the white cardboard buckets as Graham unloaded them from the bags.

"Did you get peanut sauce?" he asked, seating himself at the table's head.

"Extra." She reached across him for one of the plastic tubs. "You always take too much."

"Really?" He appeared surprised.

"Like you've forgotten," Alice teased.

All three settled into place, passing the dishes from one to another. The spicy steam rose around them and for a moment the table was quiet, but for the scraping of spoons against cardboard, the clicking of forks on china. Alice was the first to break the silence.

"This is nice," she said, nodding at her two companions, their strange new environment. "Pour me some water, Graham, and I'll make a toast."

"Must you?" he asked, grinning. But he obliged, handing her the filled glass, pouring glasses for his wife and himself. "To a successful move?" Graham raised his eyebrows in Alice's direction.

"That," Alice said, dismissing him. "But a real toast to my favorite younger sister, for pulling it off. I am amazed that you could manage it all: your travels, the book, the move. I don't know when I've been so proud." Alice beamed at Amy, her lips pressed. Amy hadn't told Alice about the canceled road trip. She ducked her head, pretending to be gracious.

"Hear, hear!" Graham raised his glass and drank thirstily. "And to your favorite brother-in-law . . . ?" He waited for Alice to say something about him.

Alice almost smiled, her face pensive. "Okay, yeah. And here's to my favorite brother-in-law." She pushed her glass toward his, and her voice dropped a decibel. "Who had the good sense to shift gears when he did, and the good graces to embrace misfortune with courage and style. To Graham."

Amy could see Graham's jaw muscles tighten, and she jumped in, eager to repair the damage.

"To family," she said simply. "Who make it all possible."

Later that evening, Graham took Haps for a walk, and Amy finally shared with Alice all that the move had cost her.

"I didn't have a choice, really. I had to let the trip go."

Alice was surprised. "But why?! You had it all lined up. You were excited about that trip. Hell, I was excited for you!"

Amy settled for a simple explanation. She didn't describe the fight with Graham. "When it came down to it, I realized I was trying too hard. Already the book was going in a direction I didn't like. And I just couldn't make it work, couldn't convince everyone involved that it had to be a certain way." Her mouth curled down, and she admitted the worst of it. "I didn't really try. I'm just not sure I'm that good a writer." She'd begun to choke up, the frustration inviting self-pity.

"But this is something you wanted." Alice's insistence didn't help.

"Of course I wanted it!" Amy exploded. "But you try doing your best work with Graham around! I can't think straight! I couldn't. And it was never going to change. It isn't." Amy swiped tears from her eyes, angry at the world, at Alice. "Anyway, you can't always have everything you want."

"Of course you can't," Alice agreed, trying to soothe. "But you should at least know what it is you want. Be honest with yourself."

Amy was tearing through the taped cartons with a steak knife and noticed the blade shaking in her hand. "What I have to do is accept. I'm the only one he's got," she said, "And sometimes you just have to do what's right." She noticed the sadness in her sister's eyes, sensed the judgment and compassion. "Anyway, I'm tired. You must be too. We should get some sleep, eh?"

At that moment, Graham walked back into the space, interrupting their standoff. Amy went to him, kissing her husband on the cheek. It was what her mother used to call a Public Display of Affection.

# THIRTY-ONE

L
uckily for everyone, her mother had left instructions: what kind of service, what minister, her chosen readings, favorite music. Even the organist had been given a heads up, over a year ago, when Julia had first begun to fail. And the good ladies of the parish had a routine for receptions. All Amy and Alice needed to do was follow the dots.

Amy arrived early on her own to put out the flowers. She had grouped bright, white lilies and pillows of blue hydrangea, simple dabs of daisies, and ribbons of dark ivy into two simple arrangements. They fit nicely at the altar, giving just a touch of life to the deep, high-ceilinged sanctuary, bright with its tall, clear glass windows. This was her parents' church, and Amy wished Julia could be there to see it again, dressed just for her.

Amy was raw again with the shock of Julia's death, as if all the trips to the doctor, the cannisters of oxygen, and the warning signs had not been real for her, not as true as the solid presence of a mother who always was.

Graham's confusion from the move was augmented by Julia's service and his wife's resurrected grief. More than ever, he was distracted and argumentative. So Amy assigned Jason to stick by his father for the day, to make sure Graham ate some breakfast that morning, remembered his tie. Jason would be driving Graham over

308

shortly, and Amy promised to herself that she wouldn't dwell too much on her husband's issues. She would give herself the luxury of celebrating Julia this one last day.

Standing alone by the communion table, Amy tried to summon some reserve of strength. She wasn't a religious person, had always been unmoved by the myths of the Bible. God was just hyperbole, a term of wishful thinking, as close to spiritual as Amy could come was appreciating a rainfall or standing in awe by the ocean. Still, she longed for something to fill the hole inside, the space her mother had left. Her bones felt too light to carry such a weight. Through the high windows she noticed a tiny airplane cross silently overhead, its jet stream powdery in the deep autumn sky. Some leave and some are left, she thought to herself, sick with abandonment. Even more than wanting to go somewhere, Amy prayed for the desire to stay put. More accurately, she wanted to want it.

Catherine slipped into the sanctuary carrying the programs. She'd designed and printed some tasteful ones, featuring a joyous headshot of Julia, taken that summer by the harbor. It looked as if the woman in the picture was still enjoying life, taking it all in her stride, much as she'd always done. Soon, the others arrived, Jason and Graham, Alice, her children and their partners, cousins and second cousins, some from their father's side. The minister led the family back to a waiting room where they whispered their shared condolences, caught up, acknowledged how long it had been. A few of those around Graham noticed the changes in him. Amy caught pinched smiles as he struggled for words, forgot names he'd known for decades. But there were also easier interactions as they all waited there, the family nicknames surfacing, the familiar anecdotes repeated, and it was almost fun seeing her people again. Amy began to relax into the warmth of it all. Julia would have called it wonderful.

Walking back into the church to the organ's first chords of music, Amy noticed how full the place was. Ancient, familiar faces, shrunken people from her childhood, formerly good-looking boys who'd left the neighborhood before she had, gone off to college. She saw Khayed and Betsy in a row near the middle. Edith Roosevelt and Joao seated with Zach toward the back. Sandy, Ella and Sam sat by an aisle, chatting quietly together. Folks who'd never met her mother, friends who had showed up just for her. It struck Amy, the goodness of such people, and she glowed with gratitude.

Alice's son was reading a Robert Frost poem from the pulpit when the floorboards started to vibrate. Amy only sensed it at first, then tried to ignore it, keeping her eyes glued to her nephew up ahead, but the tremors were palpable, and after some painful moments, she couldn't help but look down. Over to her right, Graham's knee had started to bounce. He was seated one person over, Jason between them, and she tried to nudge her son gently, hoping he'd do something to stop the distraction. By now the whole pew was trembling. Even Alice, seated on Amy's left, looked away from the speaker, across to the bobbing leg. It was maddening, Graham's long, flannel thigh jouncing raucously, Jason's willful ignorance. Compelled by embarrassment, Amy leaned across her son's lap and placed a firm hand on the knee. As quickly as it had started, it stopped. Graham shot Amy a knowing look, pulled his other ankle atop the offending leg, and slumped down in the pew, sighing loudly.

During the reception, Amy got lost in one conversation after another. There were funny stories, of course, interesting anecdotes, several former students needing to imagine their own importance in the span of Julia's many years of teaching. Julia's brother-in-law, her husband's only living sibling, was hard to hear with his raspy voice. Holding gamely to his stout cane, he told Amy how their family had celebrated Julia's inclusion into the clan. "We'd never laughed at Thanksgivings before, not like that, not until she married into the family," he said. Then he patted Amy's hand, his fingers like a worn leather glove. "We all loved your mother," he said, sad, Amy guessed, to be the last of that generation standing.

Between these exchanges, Amy looked up, trying to track Graham in the crowd. She saw him with Alice early on, tall and handsome next to her elegant sister. There had been times in the early years when Amy had been jealous of the two of them, as if they were better suited to each other, both able and attractive, teasing each other in that intelligent way they both had. Now, she wondered if Alice hadn't dodged a bullet. Later, Graham was with his children and their cousins, laughing at something, glad to be the center of attention.

Edith and Joao were brief with their greeting, confident that their presence was enough. Joao just said he was sorry for her loss, and Edith told Amy to call her, when she was ready. When they walked off, Ella and Sam stepped toward her.

Sam engulfed Amy in a comfortable embrace. "It'll get better," he told her, "You'll find your way." Over Sam's shoulder, she saw Graham wandering aimlessly across the floor.

Ella's hug was more tentative, awkward. She made a point of telling Amy about the book's progress. Only the chapter about the memorial rose garden would need to be altered in any significant way, she insisted, to remove any mention of the growing number of war dead. And the Tennessee chapter would be dropped completely.

Sam tried to interrupt. He looked embarrassed by his niece's shop talk, inappropriate at a funeral.

"But it's looking good," Ella added hastily. "And I think you'll be pleased. As it happens, the shorter chapters work well. You've captured a great selection of women and locations, Amy, and that's what stands out."

Amy wanted Ella to stop. "I'm glad," she said curtly. Then, remembering the drama she'd caused by bailing from the trip, she added guiltily, "I was sorry, you know . . ."

"Don't mention it," Ella said. "It's turned out for the best. It's still your book."

Amy didn't agree. It felt like the book had galloped off without her. She thanked Ella and Sam for showing up and turned to greet the next person.

More names than she could remember came, introduced themselves, and went.

A man from her mother's covenant group at church, a man just her age, took the time to bring Amy a cup of coffee.

"You looked parched, standing here talking all this time." He was a pleasant-looking man, unassuming in his corduroy jacket. He wore a necktie with children's handprints on it, one that UNICEF had made popular about a decade earlier. A decent sort of person.

Amy thanked him. Her throat was dry, something she hadn't noticed until the liquid hit her mouth.

"Julia told us all about you, about your gardening." The man had obviously come over simply to make her feel good, and Amy appreciated the effort. "Each week or so, we'd read your column." He gave her a bountiful smile. "She said you were also writing a terrific book."

It struck her how close she was to tears, but Amy managed to keep it light. "I wish she could have seen it published," she said. "Then she would have had some proof."

The man seemed uneasy with Amy's comment, the hint of self-denigration. He responded earnestly, as if his message hadn't been heard. "She was very proud of you. She didn't need proof."

"I know. I know she was," Amy had to assure him. "Thank you," she added before he too turned to go, relinquishing his space to the next person in line.

It was Amy's oldest cousin. Married to a gold-plated name dropper, Alissa could one-up a person just waiting for a stall in the public toilet. Give her an entire Thanksgiving meal to let loose, the woman could outrun a champion before the gravy was cold. Amy shuddered as Alissa moved in to embrace her.

"This was a truly lovely service, Amy. Julia would have been pleased." Alissa smelled of Diorissimo, a perfume produced in Amy's teens. The hint of lily of the valley reminded her of more vulnerable days.

"It's so nice seeing you looking so well," Alissa said. "You and Graham." Alissa hit her target perfectly. "It's just so unfortunate how things worked out."

A discordant note went off in Amy's brain, unsure where this was going.

"Mmm." Amy frowned, hoping that would do. She wouldn't discuss Graham's condition, not with Alissa.

"Graham told me that the two of you gave up that stunning place of yours so a new young family could move into your old house." Alissa's face radiated with empathy.

The lie snaked its way around them, leaving Amy short of air. So that's what Alissa thought, what Graham had told her. He'd converted their move to Providence into an act of charity, of selflessness? Amy's stomach curdled.

By the far banquet table, Graham was helping himself to a small plate of something, touching each item, as if checking the count. From a distance, the man appeared so fine, so attractive. Obviously, up close, too, at least with people like Alissa, her husband could still impress. Dishonesty was a feature of the dementia, she knew, but one Amy hated. Calling out his confusion was rude, something she had learned to avoid—confronting his outright lies, though? Amy longed to crush Alissa's illusions.

"It's so sad, the timing of everything," Alissa continued. "Such a loss."

Amy couldn't be sure whether the woman was referring to the house or Julia. She guessed the former. "It's a big loss," she said, her muscles tightening in her face.

Alissa put her fingertips on Amy's wrist, the polished nails, the gold bracelet glimmering. "I'm just so pleased Graham is back at RISD, though. Teaching, at least, is a consolation."

The horror was getting worse, and Amy jerked her hand away, pretending to scratch her head, fluff her bangs. "It's incredible, isn't it?" Amy flashed an open-mouthed grin, backing away apologetically. "I'm so sorry, but I need to speak to . . . someone before they go. Good to see you, Alissa." She almost ran from the woman, flustered and furious.

It felt as if there was no escape from her husband's illness, the long reach of his dementia. Even from the other side of the room—Amy saw Graham talking with some college-aged woman, his long fingers elucidating some interesting point—just by opening his mouth, he had the capacity to disrupt, to poison. Amy tried to control the tremors in her chest, catching the minister's eye three people over, exchanging a forced smile.

One by one, her allies began to leave. Catherine was the first of the family to depart, heading for the airport. Amy saw Jason kiss his sister goodbye in the far end of the hall. Alice then left, driving north with her son's family. By the time the coffee urns were empty and the church ladies had begun clearing the platters from the banquet tables, Amy was spent.

Judith Jeffers was the last to approach, while Andy stood some steps behind. Judith folded Amy into an embrace. "I just wanted to say goodbye before we left, Ame. We'll see you again, I know, but, you know . . . I wanted to wish you luck."

"Thanks, Judith." They probably wouldn't see much of Judith and Andy now, but Amy'd run out of words.

"I also wanted to tell you . . . something your mom told me, years ago."

"Ah?" Amy noticed Graham was seated now, staring at them from across the room.

"Yeah. It was that summer when Andy and Graham were sailing almost every day? You remember? Julia'd been at your house, and I'd arrived to pick Andy up, I guess. I don't know."

Amy didn't remember, truly didn't care, but listened patiently. She stared back at Graham, felt a frown forming on her face.

"Well, I ended up having a cup of tea with your mother. She was such a gracious lady, wasn't she?"

"She was," said Amy.

"Anyway, for some reason—I don't remember why or how—I think Andy and I'd been going through one of our can-we-keep-this-marriage-going periods, which we did pretty frequently for a while there."

Amy did remember that.

"Anyway, your mother was so sweet. She said, 'Well, not all marriages are like Amy and Graham's.'"

"She said that?" Amy was surprised. "What did she mean?"

"She meant not all marriages have such a willing partner, the one that will do anything to make the thing work."

"Hmm." Amy felt cool. It wasn't clear to her why Judith had chosen to share the anecdote now, but she put an arm around her old friend's shoulders, pulling her close.

"We need to go." Graham was there suddenly, hands in his pockets.

Amy looked up. "Give me a minute, Graham."

"No, I need to get out of here." He flashed Judith a scowl.

"That's okay," Judith said, backing off. "It's been a long day." She gave Graham a lingering, soulful look and nodded quickly to Amy. "Take care, you guys." Judith took Andy's arm and led him away.

"I'm not ready to go yet, Graham," Amy said. "Just *wait* a moment, would you?" She had noticed Zach idling nearby, waiting to speak with her. His posture suggested conspiracy, and Amy longed to talk with him. She left Graham standing on his own and beamed Zach a grateful smile.

"I've been talking with Jada Reed," Zach said.

It wasn't what she'd expected, and Amy tensed, hearing the name, "Oh. My." Then she remembered the dropped chapter. "God. Was she pissed about the book?"

"Not really. Not at all, in fact. Jada's probably learned not to expect much from strangers."

Amy grimaced, feeling the jab.

"But I told her that you and I *would* deliver. I told her, 'You don't know Amy James like I do - that she's a surprisingly able and reliable lady'". Zach took Amy's hand in his and gave it a gentle tug, emphasizing the point.

Seeing the respect in his eyes, Amy felt her ribcage swell. "Aww, that's nice of you, Zach," she said, almost tearing up. "Thank you."

"Anyway," he said, releasing her hand, "Jada wants some PR. I've already shown her the photographs. So she's counting on us."

"Yikes." Amy blew out. "I guess that's good news."

Graham interrupted their huddle, putting his hand on Amy's back. "More plans, guys?"

Amy jumped. "No. Nope."

But Zach was cool. "Hey, Graham. How's it going?" he said, his eyes still on Amy. "I told Jada you were working on an article."

"You're writing something else?" Graham's hand inched round Amy's waist.

Amy shook her head. "It's nothing for you to worry about Graham."

"Good. Let's go then." Graham pulled at his wife.

"Stop it, Graham. Please don't do that." Glancing about her, Amy sought some sign of her son. "Jason!" Amy shouted across the room, releasing herself from Graham's grip. "Could you come here a moment?"

"I said now," Graham insisted, this time grabbing his wife's hand. "I want to go home!"

Zach raised a palm. "Hey, it's cool," he said, edging back. Before turning to go, though, he shot a last wink at Amy. "Sooner the better."

Jason rose, approaching slowly.

"Could you take your dad home now?" Amy asked. "He wants to go home."

Jason looked from one parent to another.

"Can't *you*?" Jason tried.

"One day," she hissed under her breath. "One day is all I asked for." Around them helpful church ladies still bustled about. Zach was heading for the door.

"Okay," Jason said. "I'll do it." His look was one of resentment. "You ready then?" He shrugged a shoulder at Graham.

Graham sniffed and raised his chin, looking down at Amy as if he'd won. "Will you be coming shortly?"

The superiority in his voice, the relentless self-centeredness of the man struck Amy afresh. "No," she said finally. "No, I won't."

# THIRTY-TWO

Amy let herself in by the kitchen door. The outdoor sensor had picked her up, casting her long silhouette across the room. Instinctively, she tiptoed, as if out of respect, to the vacant space. It didn't feel ghostly, passing through into her mother's living room. Rather, Amy was prepared for Julia to reappear, emerge at any moment from the bathroom, dragging her plastic leash behind, her oxygen on wheels. Still, being there in the dark downstairs was disconcerting, and Amy took some moments to quell the turmoil inside. It wasn't breaking and entering; the closing wasn't scheduled for another week, and she still had possession of the key. Amy walked to the window overlooking the backyard. The impatiens she had planted there in May were puffs of bloom now, turtle-shaped mounds of gray, barely visible in the dark. Julia's wrought-iron chairs were gone, the little table as well, and the lawn looked smaller without them. Only bushes and grass, impersonal and forgotten.

For a third time, Amy's phone beeped. In the last several hours, Jason had gone from phoning to texting. She hoped he'd soon give up, although she wasn't so brave as to shut the thing off. Grimly excited by his perseverance Amy was determined not to pick up. All she'd asked for was just the one day, and he couldn't even manage that. Let him experience being relied upon, she thought viciously, making her heart race. She was scared of Jason's anger.

The hum of the old refrigerator kicked in, startling her, and Amy backed away from the window. There hadn't been a plan. She'd brought no clothing, there wasn't a bed to sleep on. A part of her wished she'd eaten more at the church. Now she would relish one of her mother's whiskey sours, a small bowl of goldfish, something to nibble while they talked. Amy looked to the space where her mother used to sit, noticed the small black hole on the wall behind, where a framed print had hung. Everything seemed so nearly there, so recent, then, like her mother, gone overnight. She took it all in, letting the memory of voices drift back.

Across the long room, through the door to the foyer, Amy noticed the lone writing table standing out of place by the front door. In the empty hall, the piece looked spindly, insubstantial, its fluted legs and mounted brass feet like the limbs of a colt too frail to carry weight. It had been Julia's upstairs desk. Amy imagined Victorian ladies in long crinolines, seated, delicate and pensive, fountain pens in hand.

Crossing to it, she ran her fingers across the surface. She'd always loved this table, its inlaid mahogany, rounded corners, and tooled leather top. Her plan had been to move it home to her writing space. Now it stood like an immigrant, waiting to be delivered to an uncertain future. Amy fingered the brass handles of the two drawers, pulling the left one open. The slide was easy, the drawer loose with age. A person could fit several pens, a bottle of ink, and clean stationery in one side, she mused, unanswered letters in the other, as if there were such things anymore. Amy told herself no, the table had been bought, don't even go there. She opened the other drawer, just to feel it slide.

There were two framed photos inside, ones that Julia must have kept on the desk at one time, meant to bring with her. One was of Amy's father, taken decades earlier. It was a faded black-and-white shot, showing a tall, young man, resplendent in his satin-lined hood, the long academic gown, three velvet stripes prominent on his wide sleeves. Amy recognized the picture, the worn frame. The person didn't resemble the father she remembered. Only the expression was the same: thoughtful, serious.

The other photograph was newly framed, a colored picture of a middle-aged woman. Amy pulled out her phone to illuminate the faces, surprised to see her mother and sister emerge. Alice's arm draped Julia's shoulder, Julia's fingers peeked out at Alice's waist. They were smiling. It was a more recent picture, taken by some roadside café, pub maybe, the countryside green, generic, unrecognizable. Holding the photograph in her hand, scrutinizing the two faces in the harsh beam of her phone, Amy felt a hurt climbing up her throat, the tingling of it in her nostrils. Where had she been, she wondered, while Julia and Alice were taking this picture. When had this happened?

It seemed suddenly a dangerous choice, having come here. The day had left her emotions raw, and Amy sensed she was too fragile to cope with any more. She returned the picture to the drawer and went to sit on the front stairs, her back against the banister. It was becoming a pattern, taking off like she had. This wasn't the first time she'd bolted—attending Edith's wedding, spending the afternoon with Zach. Amy had imagined that by canceling her trip, she had finally put aside those selfish whims, that by moving to Providence, she'd come to accept her place by Graham's side. But another day of frustration, another row, and here she was, once again, dashing for the door. She worried it would never stop; she'd never surrender as she should.

Slumped there in the shadows, alone in this house, Amy had not even the consolation of freedom, the security of being loved. No photograph of her sat hidden in her mother's desk.

Amy rested an elbow on the tread of the stairs and lowered her face into it.

Her phone shuddered before the ring sounded, echoing off the empty hall. Amy jumped to attention. Jason must be furious now, no longer satisfied with the unanswered texts, he was back to phoning. She glanced at the screen, her heart pounding at the insistent noise, too terrified to answer. But as her thumb hovered over the red reject button, she read Alice's name, center screen. Would Jason have phoned Alice? Tentatively, Amy pressed the green.

"Hello?"

"Hey. Is this too late?" Alice was whispering, as if that would help.

"No. I'm awake." Amy, too, kept her voice low. Hers was the only sound in the house.

"I just thought I'd say goodnight," Alice said. "Before I turn in." She sounded tired but happy. "That was a nice service. I think Mom would've liked today."

"Yeah. She would have." Amy felt self-conscious now, sitting in Julia's home in the darkness, and she let the silence take hold.

"Are you okay?" Alice asked.

"Mmmhmm." Amy didn't want to cry, was too weary for much else. In the gap, she thought of the photograph and leapt to that. "I found a picture of you and Mom. Some café somewhere. Fairly recent. Where was that taken?"

Alice chuckled. "Oh. That's Provence."

"As in France?"

"Yeah, uh huh."

"You were together in France?!" Amy sat up, the stair hard on her backside.

"Yeah. I took her there. The year that Dad died. We went for a week. It was nice."

"I never knew about that. Was it a secret?" Amy felt foolish, asking.

"Nope. No secret."

"And where was I?"

"I think you were at home. I think Graham had a thing, you know. I don't remember, honestly. But Mom needed cheering up. So I took her."

"That was really generous of you!"

"It was a nice trip."

"I never knew."

Alice laughed. "You aren't the only good daughter, you know. She had two of us."

The statement came as face slap, albeit a gentle one. Amy huffed an acknowledgement. "Huh. I thought I was. The good one. All this time, I really thought I was."

"I know." Alice said it with affection. "I know you thought that." She allowed the acceptance to settle. "Don't we just surprise ourselves?"

Abruptly, Amy admitted something else. "I'm not at home, Alice. I'm at Mom's."

She heard the pause at the other end, a long stillness.

"Are you okay?" Alice asked. Louder now, more alert.

"No. Not really," Amy said. "I just couldn't go back with Graham. Not to that house. Not to him. Not after the church. I really can't." Amy waited for some reaction, some guidance, but got none.

"Where are you going to sleep? You need to get some sleep, Ame." The older sister in her surfaced.

"I'm tired enough, I could curl up anywhere." Amy scanned the wooden floors, almost believing it.

"Go upstairs to my old room. At least there's carpeting." After Alice had left for college, Julia had installed a thick, soft Berber on Alice's bedroom floor, turning it into a sewing room for herself. "In the morning, things will seem clearer."

Amy dropped her head, and tears filled her eyes. "Do you think I'm bad?" she asked her sister.

A rumble of humor came over the line. "Oh, wow. That's not a question you should ever ask someone else." Alice's chuckle petered out. "And I'm not even sure it's a thing, 'bad.'"

"No?" The notion struck Amy as original.

"Ask yourself if you're the person you want to be. That's probably the question to ask."

# THIRTY-THREE

The drive back took no time, and Amy was at the condo before she was ready. Jason's car was parked in her place in the lot, the other assigned spaces filled. Amy pulled into a guest spot, good for only an hour. Before getting out, she pulled the visor down and checked herself in its mirror. The skin under her eyes was puffy and loose, and she appeared pallid in the harsh angle of the morning light. She pinched her cheeks, ran her fingers through her bangs. It was the best she could do. She longed to brush her teeth, instead slid a Listerine strip onto her tongue.

Crossing the parking area, she glanced up at their balcony, looking for signs of life. The curtains were open, but the door to the balcony was closed, and no lights were visible inside. It remained an undesirable location, she thought to herself, the crush of matching facades, the false village of vinyl windows and fiber cement siding. She wondered again how she had managed to find herself here and why. A shape crossed the window in an adjacent unit. The locals were beginning to rise. Amy scooted around the building, toward the front. It was early to be arriving home, and she didn't fancy being seen in yesterday's dress, approaching on her own.

At the top of the front steps, Amy craned her head side to side, hearing the cartilage creak. She inhaled deeply and blew out to the count of five. It was time.

The door swung open with her hand on the knob.

"Oh," she said, falling forward.

"Fuck." Jason stood back, avoiding the collision. He gave his mother a swift flicker of recognition, a fleeting head-to-toe of content before passing without a word.

Amy let him escape, silent hostility trailing in his wake. There was little point in appealing to civility now, not after a night of avoiding his calls.

She stepped through the entrance, bracing herself for the next encounter. Within seconds, Haps rounded the sharp turn in the hall, bobbing with welcome. In her anxiety, she'd forgotten all about him. "Hey, bud," she cooed. "Hey." Haps's tail switched energetically, his smile showing the black of his gums. Haps, at least, was direct with his emotions: feed him, take him for walks, give the occasional bath and brush, and he loved you. It was that simple. Gratefully, she crouched to kiss his snout, press her cheek to his silky jaw. Returning was already more difficult than she had imagined, and Amy soaked what warmth she could from the touch of him. Around her, the condo was quiet, her favorite Bukhara red runner underfoot, their oval mirror on the wall. Home now. Finally, she stood, calling Graham's name. Getting no response, she walked down the short hall to the big room.

Graham was seated at the dining room table, nursing a coffee. Like her, he looked as if he hadn't slept, his face soft with patches of blue and gray. She wondered suddenly what he had been thinking, where he'd imagined she'd stayed all night, and Amy felt a quick surge of loyalty, eager to appease his fears.

He cut her off with a frivolous sneer. "Did you sleep in that dress?"

Amy flattened her palm against the creases. "I did, yeah."

"Looks it." His eyebrow danced. "See Jason?"

Amy tried to match his casualness. "We bumped into each other."

"The kid can't start his day without Starbucks. Did you know that?"

Amy shook her head.

"We went wrong somewhere," he said, as if that were the issue between them. Graham's eyes scanned her face, looking for clues. "So, I guess we have to go through the ritual for times like this, is that the plan? You apologize, I accept. We pretend like nothing has happened?"

Amy shifted her weight onto her other foot, moving further into the room. She put her bag on the kitchen bar. "We don't have to do that."

"Or maybe you're thinking that I apologize, and you say, 'That's okay, hon,' and then we forget about it." Graham fingered the handle of his coffee mug. His foot began to bounce.

Amy had practiced a script for this moment. She had had the words ready: I want to start another project, I need a larger space in which to write. She glanced across the counter, considered distracting herself with the kettle, maybe a toasted bagel. But when she looked back and saw him sitting there, the intense way he was watching her, the script failed her. Other words came from nowhere. "I'm not who I want to be, Graham."

His eyebrow jounced. "Shit, Amy, who the fuck is?!" His laughter was open-mouthed, and he let it fill the room, noisy and aggressive. "Anyway," he continued, more softly this time, "I'd be surprised if you were. You're still mourning your mother."

She felt herself tremble inside, weakened by the reminder. "I feel like I've lost everything, moving here."

His mouth twisted to one side. "So what else? What is it that you had that you think you've lost?" he asked. "Besides a pretty remarkable house, that is. But to be fair, we both lost that."

"And my garden! That was pretty remarkable too, Graham. But you sold everything!"

"That's right. And you picked this place," Graham rebounded. "We could have moved somewhere else. You chose Providence." This wasn't the argument she wanted, had little to do with all she needed to say.

"Everything I loved! My writing?!" She felt her words whirl around, flailing at the walls, incensed that they even needed saying. "There's no space here for me to think!"

Graham was cool, his tone like lead. "You could write if that's what you really want. Find a little garden somewhere. I'm not stopping you, Amy."

"God!" she exploded. She spun on her heel, rigid with frustration. The tiny kitchen enclosed her in a curl of counterspace, an unwashed dish beckoned from the sink. She swung back to him, eyes burning. "How do you not know what I've been going through, Graham? All this time, how have you managed to care so little about my needs?"

He faced her squarely, adjusting his posture. "Sit down, would you?" He pointed to a stool by the counter. "Why don't you sit down? You tell me."

It took her a moment, her brain racing. Finally, she pulled out a stool and let herself sit. She tugged at her hem, pulling it over her knees. "I feel like all I'm allowed to think about, all I'm expected to do is . . . cater."

"To me?"

"Of course to you!"

"Here we go . . ."

"Everything's always about what's best for you!"

He grimaced, as if trying to be patient. "We moved here to prepare for my memory loss, Amy. Do you think that might have something to do with it?"

It was a leading question, a lawyer's sarcasm, and she shook it off. "It's always been about you. That's all that's ever been expected of me. That I take care of everything, everyone. As if that should be my life."

"I never thought that," he said calmly. "That's your conceit. That you've been so necessary. That's been your hideout."

"You're saying I'm not needed?!"

"Now, yes. Absolutely. I've been diagnosed with dementia. Of course you're needed now."

"But all those other years? You didn't expect me to take care of everything, while you went off and pursued your interests? Followed every damn dream you ever had."

"You mean built my career? Brought in the income that kept us all afloat?"

"That . . ."

"And did I ever say you shouldn't do the same? You think I spent my time hoping you'd just sit around the house, amounting to nothing?"

A familiar shame, hot and liquid, gushed into her. Like a bucket about to spill over, her many sacrifices and missed opportunities slopped to the surface: the cinnamon farm in Sri Lanka, her undergraduate degree in Maryland, the last canceled trip for her book. "I couldn't. I tried . . ."

He let his head drop back, as if seeking solace from the ceiling. When he looked back at her, his tone was resigned. "I think sometimes you just look for reasons to be miserable, Amy. You hold onto it with both fists."

It was meant to hurt, and it did. As if a dam had burst somewhere inside, the reserve of kindness she'd always held for the man suddenly drained from her, leaving her empty and dry.

"I hate being here with you," she said evenly, her fist grazing her lip. Just having said it terrified her.

He leaned back in the chair, stretched his legs in front of him. "Wow, that's impressive. You 'hate' it here now." His pursed his mouth as if appraising her words. "I don't know, I may be losing my mind, but it sounds like, in your inept little way, you're trying to say that you want to be on your own for a while. Is that it?"

The question struck Amy like a blow, and the air lodged in her chest. Maybe that was what she was saying, and Graham had seen it first.

"Like a separation?" His calmness made it sound so reasonable.

He was handing her a shortcut, an easier out than she'd ever imagined, and the option frightened her suddenly, had come too quickly. Inside, her brain shrieked with insistence: *Take it! Take it!* She reached for the bar to steady herself. Haps brushed up against her leg, his soft body cautioning her.

"That's right," she said.

Graham crossed his arms over his chest, dropping his head.

The cowlick at the crown of his skull sent a curl flopping forward and Amy almost reached over to touch it. Every bone and muscle in her ached to retract her words, soften them somehow, but she bit back the impulse. Nails tight in her palms, she held herself, watching his lowered face, his breath lifting his shoulders and releasing them again.

Composed, he looked up, the hatred gone from his eyes. His tone was eerily academic. "I think you're probably grieving, Amy. Maybe overtired. If I had to put a wager on it, I'd bet you'll be back. But if it'll make you happy . . ." He showed her his palms. "You should do it. Pack up today and go." Then lightly, he clicked his tongue. "Here, Haps," he said, reaching out his palm. "C'mere, boy." The dog trotted over to him.

The maneuver worked and Amy reacted as expected. "I'm not saying I'm leaving today. Obviously, there are things we have to work out."

"Like what?"

"Things like who's going to keep an eye on the place, make sure you're all set. That you're safe here."

He laughed aloud.

"I'm worried about you," she insisted. "I need to know that you're going to be alright."

He cocked his head, gave her a sideways look. "Well, I can't help you there. When you walk out, you pretty much relinquish the right to worry. That's the tricky part. I become no longer any of your business." His long fingers clutched and stroked at Haps's head, one ear then the other. He seemed so good at this, as if he'd been prepared, known what was coming all along.

The cool dismissal burned into her, making her insistent. "I can set up some people. I want to help."

Graham raised an index finger. "Stop." A shallow whine came from the dog. "I want you to pack a suitcase and be gone before Jason comes back. I don't want him to see this." There was no misunderstanding Graham's meaning.

It was as if the recess bell had rung, the class was free to go. Amy hesitated momentarily, overwhelmed by the choice. Then, excited, she slipped from the stool. As she grabbed her bag, Graham asked one last question. "Where are you staying?"

She almost didn't say, wanting to keep her secrets close, but in the recklessness, she relented, telling him the truth. "My mother's."

He chuckled, as if amused. "Of course. The girl has options now." He spoke to the dog. "Lucky Amy."

# THIRTY-FOUR

For several hours, Amy drove around Providence, waiting for the buzz to die down. The panic of packing, the items she'd left behind, spun about in her like gnats. She struggled to keep to the road, respond to traffic signals, avoid people in the crosswalks.

Twenty minutes doesn't suffice for thinking clearly and she hadn't. Like being forced to evacuate with the roar of a forest fire fast approaching, she'd grabbed a suitcase and shoulder bag, taking just what she'd seen: her phone charger and laptop. Her prescription meds and bag of toiletries. She'd taken the electric toothbrush but left him the Crest, packed a small, zippered bag of makeup and took the hand lotion, her favorite brush. From her dresser top, she'd scooped up her tray of earrings, forgetting the necklaces in the top drawer below. Socks and panties, tights and three bras, an armful of tops, two pairs of trousers. Whatever was clean, folded in the drawers she'd selected, cramming it all in: her jeans. Some sweaters. The nightgown from beneath her pillow. Only when she'd seen Jason's car through the bedroom window had she quit, giving up on the rest, racing from the unit, skirting the bushes at the far side of the building.

She decided to give it some time before returning to Julia's house. Give them time to chase her down there, if that's what Jason or Graham decided to do. Give them time to see that she'd been lying: that it wasn't where she was staying after all.

Passing by Brown's central campus, Amy drove cautiously, wary of careless students, absorbed with their cell phones, each other, sometimes both. Just a month earlier, these same youngsters had returned to the city, filling the narrow streets with laundry carts of belongings, hangered clothing, table lamps and mini fridges, and Amy remembered her disdain, her impatience with such abundance. Who needs so many possessions? she recalled thinking at the time, watching the young packrats from her queue of immobilized vehicles. But Amy flashed back on her own slippers, still lined up neatly beneath her bed, her favorite fleece, the raincoat in the guestroom closet, and pined for her things.

In North Providence she stopped at a drive-through and sat in the parking lot with a black coffee, nibbling on a cruller. Almost calm at last, she dialed Matt's number. He picked up on the first ring.

"I can't do it, Matt. I'm sorry."

The line went dead for a moment, as if they'd been disconnected. "Where are you?" he asked at last.

"I'm in Providence. I've left Graham at the condo. Jason's there with him."

"I know." Of course. Matt always knew. "Do you want to talk about it?" he asked.

She didn't. Even with Matt, the one adult who more than anyone in her life had seen and understood what this marriage to Graham had been about. Amy brushed some crumbs from her lap. "Graham and I interviewed some good caretakers. There are three he really liked. I'll send you their information."

Matt sighed. "So this is what it's come down to, Amy? After all these years, you're giving him back?"

It was.

"I'm sorry," she repeated. Not knowing what else to say, Amy rang off.

# THIRTY-FIVE

It was early days yet and she took them just one at a time.

The earliest ones were mostly filled with activities, a to-do list of discrete tasks: doing a final walk-through of her mother's house, opening a new bank account. Amy had to find a temporary place to stay, and she had to keep herself fed, remembering to charge her phone, do laundry. The sticker on her car became due, and she had the oil changed. She rocked from one action to the next, wondering when the bubble would burst, when she'd give up the work of it, crawl back to Graham, beg to be let in.

And when the cottage came up, even as she signed a lease, scoured the inside of the old cooker, even then she held her breath, knowing it might not last, the horror of having walked out, the terror of staying gone was that strong.

Except for her calls to Alice, Amy hardly spoke. She had nothing for Ella, nothing to discuss with an agent, and little interest in seeing Sandy. She wasn't ready to phone Sam at the paper, with no columns she wanted to write, and now, with the sale of Julia's house, little immediate financial pressure to do so. Hopefully they'd meet for coffee, but later.

Zach, Amy would reserve only for such a time when—if, really—she managed to complete the article he'd suggested. Zach wasn't an option for anything else—or shouldn't be, she cautioned herself.

There were times when she longed to talk with him again, but she was too unsure of herself, too steeped in her own escape, worried still about her own motives.

One evening, she looked up flights to Colombo, shuddering at the cost. But that option too, glorious in its possibilities, seemed overwhelming to her, and Amy put it on the growing "maybe later" list.

For three weeks, no one else in her family called. Not Jason or Matt. Nothing from her husband. It frightened her, as if a conspiracy was afoot, that some legal plan might be operating around her, tying her up in some tight mesh that would one day lock her in. Or out. And it offended her that no one had a question, not even one, about how things should work at the house. But she, too, refused to pick up the phone, more afraid to learn that these people whom she had loved so hard for so long no longer loved her. It was as if she had disappeared, and while the silence was a godsend of sorts, giving her hours and days of freedom, it bellowed through her consciousness, a drumbeat of emotional debt.

Catherine did finally reach out. Some days after Amy moved into the cottage, her late afternoon's quiet was interrupted by a rare but insistent ringing. Apprehensively, Amy took the call. "Hey, stranger," she said.

There was a blip of silence at the other end. "Not sure I'm the one who's estranged," Catherine said.

"No," Amy corrected quickly. "I just meant hi. It's good to hear your voice." She meant it.

"So," Catherine continued, "how are you? Where are you?"

Amy wanted to lie. Instead, she told her. "On West Island. Not far."

"Okay." Catherine paused. "So, you've found your own place? You've really left?"

It seemed to Amy an odd question. "I guess I have, yeah."

"Like . . . permanently?"

Amy didn't respond.

"Wow." The word vibrated with judgment.

Amy waited for more but got nothing. "I know it's . . ." She'd been about to say "awful" or "selfish" but opted instead for "difficult." "I know it's difficult," she said.

"You think?!" Catherine's voice flashed. "Jason and Matt have been running around like madmen, trying to get things organized. Dina and Charles were there for over a week . . ."

A heave of nausea rose in Amy's throat at the reminder of how much resentment must be spinning about, directed at her.

"And Dad's gone nuts."

Amy choked back her response, deep and instant, thinking of Graham, lost—probably enraged—in the midst of family mayhem.

"*More* nuts," Catherine clarified. "He doesn't have a clue where you went."

"He knows!" Amy cut her short. "I told him." But as the words echoed back to her, Amy knew that defense was pointless. "Yeah," she conceded, "I'm sure he's shocked. After all these years."

"After all these years of getting his way?" Scorn rippled down the line. "Helluva time to find your backbone, Amy."

There was no response for that. Amy settled into a kitchen chair, preparing for a lecture.

"You might have spoken up earlier. I mean, the poor guy stayed impossible because you let him. Now he's unbearable and confused and completely alone."

Catherine's charge struck a nerve, but Amy didn't swallow it whole. *Maybe* is what she thought. Maybe she was responsible for Graham's behavior all these years, but it was long past time to go there. She reached for the vase on the kitchen table, turning it so the large sunflower was facing her. "Have you seen him?" she asked.

"Nope. Not yet." Catherine added defensively, "But I will."

*Thought not*, Amy said to herself.

It maddened her, listening to her stepdaughter's hopeful silence. Catherine was calling, Amy knew, wanting what she'd always wanted, what they'd all wanted—for Amy to fix things, make everything right. She fingered the flower's buttery petals, breathing out fear. Then carefully, with neither anger nor promises, she found the words. "Good," she told her stepdaughter. "That's kind of you."

Occasionally when she walked by the outer beach, fondling seashells she'd picked out as gems from the wet sand, she imagined Graham, his wonderful curls, his deep, sad eyes, and guilt rolled over, like a mammoth wave. The image of him wandering somewhere, Haps as lost by his side, sucked at her like a mighty undertow, and all she wanted to do was run to him, care again, be the person she knew how to be.

She felt less good at so much else.

Often, she heard her husband's refrain of contempt. While sweeping the floor, slicing up a ripe tomato. *You could write if that's what you really want. Find a little garden somewhere.* And she steadied herself, shored up her energy to face that challenge. Because that was what she wanted. Looking in the mirror over the bathroom sink, its mottled edges framing her face, she watched her own eyes and tried not to wince, tried to find the courage in the woman looking back. She thought of Edith on the windswept hillside of Cuttyhunk, and Jada, in the deep, rich farmland of Tennessee. She invoked their resilience, inhaled their gardens, imagined them on their own, building, having hope.

Afternoons some days, many days, approaching the hour she used to think about Graham's dinner, or concern herself with Jason's homework, she clutched at the nothingness, craving the purpose of doing something for someone else. She felt her hands around the car keys, propelling her as far as the car door, and she fantasized of returning, reassuring him that she was back, that his memories were safe. One day, though, she opened her laptop instead, and wrote through it. Starting the first sentences about Reed Farm, she wrote until the craving passed.

She wanted to believe that at some point in time she'd be able to visit her husband. She conjured up a vision of herself, building a perennial bed by the car park, something Graham could see from his balcony. She saw him standing at the railing, waving down at her in her clogs, her hair in a bandana, a trowel in her hand. There were sturdy cone flowers everywhere, some black-eyed susans and tall white phlox, and Graham shouted down, "I love it!" And she shouted back, "I know you do!" Then Hawa, or Bertrand, or maybe Liselle, joined Graham on the balcony and when he was tired of watching her garden, they ushered him back in for his dinner.

If she waited too long, he might not recognize her. Amy knew that too.

One morning, a couple of weeks later, when she woke, her first thought wasn't of him at all. She'd had a dream and it lingered with her in the early gray of dawn, the ephemeral characters still chattering, still running past her as she surfaced in the small loft, the clock ticking loudly by her bed. The extra comforter she had added for warmth the night before was pillowed over her and she was wrapped and cozy, safely on her own. Her first thought was how nice this was, to lie in the stillness, listening for the birds outside. Today, she thought, she would plant some bulbs.

THE END

# ACKNOWLEDGMENTS

Many people have helped me get to here.

My former colleague at IEc, Cynthia Manson first suggested we partner in taking the NANOWRIMO challenge over a decade ago, when she learned we were both moonlighting writers. She has remained my writing buddy - even during times of incredible personal odds - ever since.

Henrietta Lazaridis, teacher at Grub Street's Novel Generator class and a dozen classmates, Deborah Mead, Andrew Tonelli, Scott Sonnenberg, Neshat Khan, Amy Houton, Lori Likis, Deborah Bennett, Rob Medley, Robin Schneider Haug, Elizabeth Kahrs, Robin Facer and Christine Murphy, lived with this novel for nine months as I wrote and ditched, helping me discover more about myself and the story. Of that class, Robin, Christine and Elizabeth beta-read the first completed manuscript with thoughtful, critical and encouraging feedback.

Joann Green Breuer, Susan Turnbull, Carleen Larsson and Joan Hancock also read different iterations, each with her own take on this novel's look at being a good wife.

My two sisters, Lisa Phelps and Judith Felton obliged me with their thoughts too, both touching and affirmative.

Henrietta Lazaridis sent me back to the drawing board when I asked for further assistance, providing a sharp-eyed editorial letter and a file, dense with comments, the dope slap I needed to begin again.

Offering her home in Maine as a writing retreat, Robin Facer invited Christine Murphy, Audrey Burgess and me one long weekend, where we wrote each day, floated on the lake for respite and shared our favorite passages late into the night. A shot of heaven.

Ellie Sawatzky, my editor at Friesen Press, found me a better title and much more.

Upstairs neighbors also worked miracles. Mercy Bell built me a website and Chad Milner took a picture of me that I put on it, giving me a place to showcase my writing.

And John Forcucci, Story Board artist, now meeting with Cindy and me each morning in our early Teams session, created the cover, giving the novel the look it needed to face the world.

My thanks to all of these smart and generous folk.

My most heartfelt thanks to my husband, José Soares, a contemplative sailor and a man of few words. Cocooned with me in our pod of two during the long months of the lockdown, walking together every day, around Columbia Point or through Franklin Park or sailing in the Boston Harbor islands, José gives me a quiet, steady support and the space I need in which to imagine.

# ABOUT THE AUTHOR

**KATE PHELPS** was born and raised in New England. A graduate of Brown University (where she was awarded an Arnold Fellowship to study political theatre abroad), her first writing was for the stage. She became a playwright in England where she lived for fifteen years, producing six plays on the fringe and repertory theatre. After returning to the States, she earned a Master's in Dispute Resolution from UMASS Boston, and began a dual career in human resources and professional mediation, later becoming a part-time writing tutor at Roxbury Community College. A lifelong writer and gardener, Kate lives with her husband in Roxbury, Massachusetts.

Printed in the USA
CPSIA information can be obtained
at www.ICGtesting.com
CBHW031213150524
8601CB00009B/283